NOMAD

THE NEW EARTH SERIES

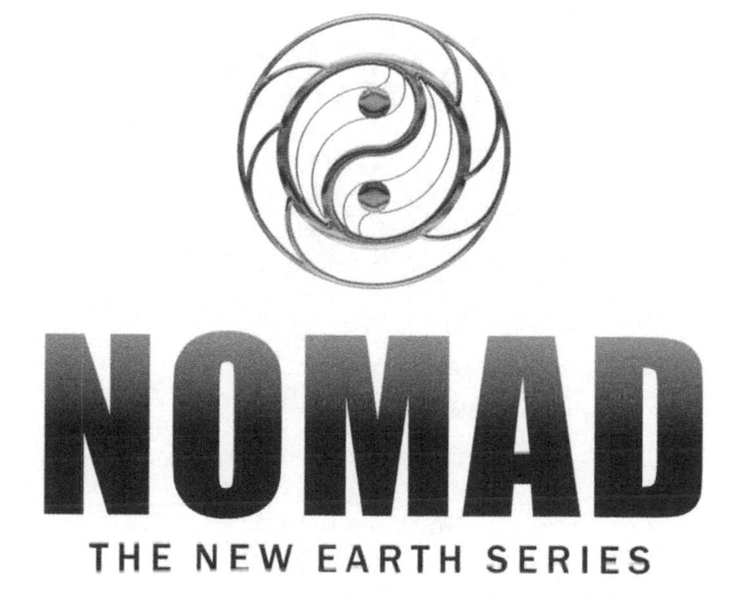

MATTHEW MATHER

NOMAD

Matthew Mather ULC
www.matthewmather.com

ISBN: 978-1-987942-04-0
Cover image by Damonza.com

NOTE FROM THE AUTHOR

FOR THEIR GENEROUS HELP
developing the science and story behind Nomad,
I would like to thank the generosity of

Dr. Ramin Skibba
Center for Space Sciences at UC San Diego

Dr. Kevin Rauch
University of Maryland Astrophysics

Dr. Seth Shostak
Director of SETI

Dr. James Gillies
Research Fellow at CERN

SPECIAL FEATURE

You can enjoy this purely as an exciting story, but Nomad is unique in being perhaps the only fictional novel that comes with its own detailed physics-based simulation—all the events described in the book are based on real-world science. At the end of the book, I have a video you can watch where I run and explain the simulation, describing what happens. You can even run it yourself, if you're so inclined, and feel like destroying the solar system in your own ways.

For free Advance Reading Copies of my next book and more, join my community at
MatthewMather.com

Find me on Facebook and YouTube
search for
Author Matthew Mather

OTHER BOOKS BY MATTHEW MATHER

Standalone Titles
Darknet
CyberStorm
Polar Vortex

The Atopia Series
Atopia Chronicles
Dystopia Chronicles
Utopia Chronicles

The New Earth Series
Nomad
Sanctuary
Resistance
Destiny

The Delta Devlin Series
The Dreaming Tree
Meet Your Maker
Out of Time

THE NEW EARTH SERIES

SURVIVOR TESTIMONY

#GR12;

Event +49hrs;
Subject Name: Dario Holder;
Reported location: Central Florida peninsula;

What do I see? *(multiple coughing sounds in background, ed. note)*

I'm staring out the window of a wrecked home on Sugarloaf Mountain, the highest point in Florida…but Sugarloaf Island would be a better name, and Florida is gone. Just gone, like we've been transported into some other *(static for several seconds)*…waves sweeping over…*(crying in background)* I see black water, endless dark skies, no day or night…gray snow is falling, a dirty blanket of it a foot deep between…or at least it looks like snow. Only three of us left alive here, myself and two children, we have nothing to eat, no fresh water…freezing…send help…for love of God, please…

Transmission ended in high ionization static.

Freq. 7350 kHz/LSB. Subject not reacquired.

DAY ONE
October 6th

1

Rome, Italy

"BIG ENOUGH TO *what*?"

"Destroy the entire solar system," repeated Dr. Müller, a sixty-something, pot-bellied man with thick spectacles below a tangle of gray hair. "And the Earth with it."

Ben Rollins stared at him in dumbfounded silence and rubbed his bleary eyes. "That's what I thought you said." He wiped his hands down his face to pinch the bridge of his nose between his forefingers, squeezing his eyes shut. Opening them, he brought his hands away from his face together, as if in prayer, and exhaled slowly.

"Are you serious? Is this a joke?"

"No joke. We need you, Ben." Dr. Müller pointed at a chair.

Ben stared around the wood-paneled conference room he'd been unceremoniously dragged into at three in the morning. Familiar faces, many looking even more haggard than he felt, nodded at him. Ben did a quick inventory: five people he recognized as fellow astronomers, all of them exoplanet hunters like himself. He didn't know the other dozen dark-suited shadows hanging near the edges of the room.

Taking a deep breath, Ben focused on Dr. Müller—his clothes rumpled, two-day-old stubble on his chin—behind the podium at the front of the room. What the hell was he doing here? And what did he say? *We need you?* Ben hadn't seen, or even heard, from Müller in twenty years. He slumped into the seat, his mind still off-kilter.

"In 2015 we discovered that 70,000 years ago, Scholz's star passed through our solar system," Dr. Müller said, continuing his presentation. "We now know that other stars transit our solar neighborhood every few tens of million years, some close enough to disrupt the orbits of the planets."

He paused to take a drink from a glass of water on the podium, his hand visibly shaking. "New data from NASA has uncovered that our solar system has been falling toward a massive object we previously mistook for dark matter in the nearby arm of the Milky Way. However, the anomaly is much closer than that."

"What kind of mass?" someone asked.

"Perhaps tens of times larger than our Sun."

"Have you been able to image it?"

Dr. Müller shook his head. "Thus far we are only detecting it through gravitational effects."

"And how far? What path is it on?" Ben asked.

"That's why I've asked you here." Dr. Müller began pacing again. "I need to get access to your data; need you to assemble your teams."

"But you must be certain enough to drag us out in the middle of the night," Ben persisted. "What's your best guess?"

Dr. Müller stopped to grip the podium and stared down at the plush red carpeting. "Our best *guess*..." He paused to emphasize the word, looking up to lock eyes with Ben. "...is that Nomad—"

"Nomad?"

"That's what we're calling it—whatever *it* is. It's heading directly toward us at extremely high speed." He enunciated each word clearly to make sure nothing was misunderstood. "We estimate it is now less than twenty billion kilometers away. At most, we have a year, perhaps only months until the anomaly reaches us."

Ben stared into Dr. Müller's eyes, and a tingling of dread shivered from his scalp to his fingertips. He'd expected some answer, perhaps on the order of centuries and light years.

But not in kilometers.

And not in months.

2

Chianti, Italy

"A THOUSAND YEARS of family weapons," Jessica Rollins whispered in awe. "That's not something you see every day."

In a red velvet-lined display case in front of her, an array of ancient weapons glittered; daggers mounted side by side, and below them, a collection of swords. The smell of old wood and damp stone lingered beneath the pine-fresh scent of polished cabinets.

"Yes," replied Nico, the tour guide, "this *castello* has been the seat of the Ruspoli family for eleven centuries of unbroken succession."

Crossbows filled the next display case—*ballista* said the inscription—with strings and winching mechanisms intact, some of them intricately carved, some worn and workman-like. Several dated to the twelfth century, and below the weapons, inside the case, sat piles of crossbow bolts. Unused ammunition. A collection of pikes, the long spears infantry used to carry into battle, rested against the display cases.

"Today we will be visiting the armory museum and family crypts below," Nico continued. "But this is still a home." He pointed to the window. "The red brick buildings on the other side of the courtyard are the residences of the Ruspolis when they come out of Florence in the summer."

"Over a thousand years," Jessica said in a low voice to her mother, Celeste, standing beside her. She took a sip of white wine from the almost-empty glass in her hand.

"Puts other royals to shame," Celeste whispered back. "Even the Hapsburgs managed only what, six hundred years?"

Jessica paused to admire her mother's olive skin bronzed from years doing geological fieldwork, her blond hair proudly streaked with gray—still a beauty even in her mid-fifties. No wonder their tour guide

Nico kept staring at her.

Catching her own reflection in a window, Jessica had to admit that she'd gotten her good looks from her mom. Almost a mirror image of photographs she'd seen from when her mom and dad got married. Jess hoped she'd look so good in middle age, but a part of her doubted she'd even live that long. Just making it to twenty-six was an accomplishment.

"A fortification has stood on this mountaintop, at the western edge of the Chianti region, for time beyond history." Nico smiled at an elderly couple, the only other people in their small tour group. "The original foundations are built atop ruins that date back thousands of years. The wine cellars are built in three-thousand-year-old Etruscan caves that burrow deep into the mountain below us."

In front of Jessica, one particular dagger caught her attention—bejeweled with rubies and sapphires, its glitter hypnotic. "It's beautiful," she whispered under her breath.

Nico, the tour guide, heard her and smiled. "Ah, the Medici dagger. A gift to the Baroness Ruspoli by the Medici family in 1434 following the Ciompi revolts in Florence, for their support in defeating the Albizzi family." He paused, allowing the group to have a closer look. "In the next room," Nico continued in a loud voice, walking around the corner, "we move up through the centuries…"

Jessica stopped to look out the window. Rolling mountains stretched into the blue distance. Dense green forests covered the landscape, of course with groves of olive trees and iconic cypress standing at attention, but also oak, juniper, and thickets of fir trees amid the bursting lines of grape vines. Nothing like the dusty roads and baked orange hills most people imagined of Tuscany. More like the mountains of the Catskills in upstate New York where she grew up, where her family had their own cottage, or did have, far back in time. Jessica pushed a memory from her mind, of a face disappearing into a black hole ringed in white.

Celeste stood behind Jessica. "So when can I meet Ricardo?" she asked. "Is he coming out to meet us? Is this the big secret?"

Her mother had flown in from JFK and landed the previous morning at Fiumicino, Rome's main airport. Jessica had said she had a special surprise.

Jessica took a deep breath. "No, you're not going to meet Ricardo. That's over." She couldn't tell her mother the real reason she dragged her out here. Not yet.

"Over?"

"Over. I broke up with him."

"You're a wandering nomad, you know that, Jess?" Her mother's lips pressed tightly together. "When are you going to settle down?"

"Settle?" Jess clucked. "Mom, please…I'm happy. I like my life."

Celeste winced, crinkling her nose. "I'm sorry. I didn't mean to say that."

Jess exhaled, silently counting to five. Maybe this was a mistake. "It's okay," she muttered, turning from the window. She followed the tour guide into the next room, finding row upon row of muskets, revolvers, and a whole range of everything in between.

Celeste came up behind Jess and caught the look in her eye. "Your favorite," her mother whispered, "guns."

Jess contained herself this time, trying to ignore the passive aggressive tone. "I'm done with all that," she whispered back, but they both knew it wasn't true.

"The Ruspoli family were experts in weapons, building many of these themselves," Nico explained, seeing all four of his tour group had made it into the room. "From the Dark Ages, through the Renaissance and up to the late 19th century, the Ruspolis operated their own gun smithy. Renowned the world over for their precision weapons, they were major suppliers of the Genoese crossbowmen that signaled the end of armed aristocratic knights in the Middle Ages."

Celeste pursed her lips and changed topics. "So what did you want to talk to me about at brunch?"

Jess sighed. It had taken three glasses of prosecco at brunch for her to bring up her problem, but she was interrupted by the announcement of the start of the crypt tour. Jess gulped down the remainder of her fourth glass of wine and put it down on a shelf near the entrance. She was drunk, just as she'd hoped she would be. Pulling her mother away from the other people in the tour group, she said under her breath, "I'm in trouble."

Celeste knitted her eyebrows together. "What kind of trouble?"

"The kind that involves me going to jail."

3

Rome, Italy

BEN SETTLED INTO his chair, putting his espresso down on the café table. Behind him a buzzing growl erupted, and he turned to see a scooter loaded with two riders, one of them clutching a brown bag of groceries, roaring toward him. He flinched backward, the mirror of the scooter flying just inches from his face.

A close call. A near miss. But he was none the worse for it, except for a jolt of adrenaline to go with his caffeine.

Shifting his seat closer to the wall, Ben watched the scooter disappear down the cobbled street in a haze of blue exhaust. In the stifling air, a fetid aroma wafted from garbage piled near the corner. The collectors were on strike. Unseasonably hot weather for Italy in early October. Looking up, he admired the French-shuttered windows lining each story of the tiny alley up to three stories above him, cables and wires stretched like jungle vines from one side to the other with a thin blue strip of sky beyond that. A flock of birds fluttered across the rooftops.

If there were ever a day for alcohol at breakfast, today was that day, but Ben kept to coffee. The meeting the night before had been short, with Dr. Müller giving precious little information except that he needed Ben to help assemble a trusted group.

Ben hadn't seen Müller in years before last night, not since Müller was his thesis advisor at Harvard. Ben heard the old man had gone into the private sector; either that or retired. Apparently not.

Dr. Müller wanted Ben's data; that's why he needed him. Ben both loved and hated being in charge of the exoplanet group at the Harvard-Smithsonian Center for Astrophysics. Sometimes there was excitement, like when he co-discovered one of the first planets orbiting another star in 1992. But ten more planetary discoveries took ten more years of drudgery after that.

In the last decade, though, the floodgates had opened with the development of new telescopes and sensing systems. Now the list of exoplanets—planets that orbited stars other than our Sun—stretched into the many thousands, with dozens of them similar in size and orbit to Earth. What they were looking for now wasn't a planet, but a lot of the data they'd collected could be used for what Dr. Müller needed.

Ben still had a headache.

The night before had been a celebration of sorts. This year was a big event for the International Astronomical Union, one hundred years since its inception. Five thousand astronomers and physicists from all over the world assembled here in Rome, back at the place it all started—in Italy four hundred years ago when Galileo turned his telescope skyward and championed the idea that the Sun, not the Earth, was the center of the solar system.

"So this is where you're hiding," said someone behind Ben.

Turning, he discovered the smiling face of Roger—the graduate student attending the IAU meeting with him—looking down at him with a quirky grin. Dr. Müller had made it clear that only a small group of senior people was to be included at this point, so Ben couldn't say anything to Roger yet. He did his best to smile.

"What, the Grand Hotel isn't grand enough for you to enjoy your coffee there?" Roger said, laughing. "You look terrible. Too much *vino* last night?"

"Maybe." Ben shrugged limply. "You know what it's like when us old boys get together."

"Sure." Roger sat opposite Ben, his hands wide apart on the table. A white-aproned waiter wheeled out of the café entrance and Roger mouthed, "Espresso," while pointing at Ben's empty cup and saucer.

Ben held up a finger, requesting his third. The waiter nodded and turned back.

"Are you going to the seminars this morning?" Roger asked, pointing at the IAU meeting schedule open on the table between them.

Ben stared at the thin strip of blue sky between the rooftops overhead. Was destruction really coming? With dozens of countries with active space programs, hundreds of spacecraft and telescopes peering into space, how could it be possible to miss something like this? Did this thing suddenly appear from nowhere? It seemed impossible, but Dr. Müller promised more answers at the meeting later this morning.

Even after thirty years as a professional astrophysicist, Ben was amazed at the detail of the universe that humans had managed to construct, all by staring up into the sky and by peering through tiny devices. A collection of fantastical objects—dwarfs, red giants, black holes, dark nebulae—sounded more like fantasy than reality. But it seemed the fantasy was about to deliver a cold dose of reality.

"Earth to Ben. Are you going to the seminars this morning or not?"

Ben caught himself staring up, lost in thought. Rubbing the back of his neck with one hand, he turned and met Roger's quizzical smile with an awkward grin.

"Sorry, coming back to Rome brings up a lot of memories. I honeymooned here." He folded his arms. "And to answer your question, no, an emergency meeting was called last night."

"An *emergency* meeting? At the Union?" Roger snorted. "What, they want to turn Pluto back into a planet?"

The waiter appeared as if by magic and hovered over the table. He delivered their two espressos before vanishing again.

Ben picked up his cup and took a sip, resisting a strong urge to spill the beans. "Something big must be up."

"What is it?"

"I don't know." Ben did his best to look mystified. "They invited all the senior exo-hunters, that's all I know."

"And they didn't invite me?" A frown flitted across Roger's face, but his smile returned and widened. He picked up his espresso. "Must be above my pay grade."

"Must be," Ben agreed grimly. This was above everyone's pay grade. He finished off this third espresso, savoring the richness, and tapped his cell phone screen. Swearing under his breath, Ben stood and patted Roger on the shoulder. "And I'm late. Can you pay?" His brain was still recovering from an excess of wine and lack of sleep, all of that wrapped in a tight fist of anxiety.

Roger nodded and picked up the program schedule. "Sure, it's your expense budget."

"Thanks." Ben squeezed Roger's shoulder and strode off down the alleyway, turning the corner to the Grand Hotel.

A uniformed attendant nodded at him, saying, "*Buon giorno, Professore Rollins*," and stepped back to pull open a large glass-and-brass door.

Air-conditioned coolness swept over Ben as he walked onto the thick carpet of the hotel's entranceway. Glittering chandeliers hung beneath gilt frescoes. Hurrying up the expansive main staircase, past a menacing lion marble statue, Ben stared at an image of God painted on the ceiling. The Creator hurled bolts of fire down at mankind from the heavens.

Someone grabbed Ben by the shoulder, almost spinning him around. "Identification please."

A large man in a dark suit held him gently but firmly in place. Ben produced his IAU all-access conference pass. The man nodded and held up some kind of scanner, and Ben tried to wave his pass in front of it.

The man grabbed his hand. "Sorry, I need a DNA scan, Dr. Rollins," he said as he pressed Ben's thumb against the device.

"Hey!" Ben tried to pull away, but the man held him firm until the machine pinged.

"Apologies, but I have orders." The big man stared impassively at Ben. "Please step inside, sir."

Ben saw complaining would be wasted, and the man was polite if firm. Shaking his head, Ben pushed through the doors to the main ballroom. Even more elaborate crystal chandeliers hung under dazzling sky-blue frescoes. Desks arranged in neat rows lined each side of the room. Ben decided to stand at the back.

Dr. Müller had already started his presentation. The lights dimmed and a projector displayed the blue-and-white NASA logo next to the bright red block letters of JPL—the famous Jet Propulsion Laboratories. The group of five astronomers from the previous evening had expanded to thirty. Many, Ben realized on a quick sweep, recommended by him.

"…everyone has heard of the Pioneer Anomaly?" Dr. Müller asked from the front of the room.

Everyone in the room nodded at Dr. Müller's question, murmuring their familiarity. When the Pioneer spacecraft—the first probes launched into the outer solar system—reached the edges of interstellar space in the 1980s, they accelerated at rates that couldn't be explained by the sun's gravity alone. After two decades of guesswork, the commonly accepted solution was a slight acceleration from their internal heat radiating into the ultra-vacuum around them, but still many people weren't convinced.

"As you know," continued Dr. Müller on-stage, "we lost communications with Pioneer 10 at a distance of 12 billion km in 2003. We observed similar anomalies with the Voyager 1 and 2 spacecraft as they left the solar system and ventured into interstellar space, which we attributed to the same causes."

Ben nodded along with everyone else. Common knowledge. Every space probe launched into the outer reaches experienced some form of the same thing, and so did some comets observed at great distances.

Dr. Müller stopped to clear his throat. He picked up a glass of water at the podium, pausing to take a drink. The image on the screen behind him changed from the NASA and JPL logos to a graphic detailing the spiraling paths of Pioneer 10 and 11, and Voyager 1 and 2 on their journeys out of the solar system.

He took a deep breath and put the glass down. "Several months ago, from a distance of over 20 billion km—five times the distance to the orbit of Neptune, our outermost planet—we began receiving unusual acceleration signals from Voyager 1…"

Ben had read about this in online journals, along with speculation about problems with radioisotope electrical systems, or gremlins in the ground communications.

"…but what has not been made public, yet," Dr. Müller continued, "is a sudden spike in these signals four weeks ago. We initially attributed this to some kind of on-board system failure, but soon afterward, we had a similar spike in readings from Voyager 2."

Dr. Müller adjusted his glasses.

"We know now that this was no anomaly in sensor reading. The Voyager spacecraft are, in fact, working perfectly." He coughed. "I know you are all familiar with the accepted solutions, but today I am going to explain how we have all been wrong." He pulled off his glasses, rubbed his eyes with the back of his hand before looking around the room. "How we have all been terribly wrong."

A murmur rose from the crowd in the room.

"What we now know is that a massive and previously unknown object is on its way toward us at extremely high speed."

"Wouldn't we have detected this in our radial velocity searches?" asked a voice from the left side of the room.

Ben squinted. Who was that? A young man wearing a knitted cap pulled halfway back on his head, a scarf carelessly hung around his neck, silver earrings dangling—he looked too stylish to be an astrophysicist.

It took Ben a second to realize he was looking at Ufuk Erdogmus. He'd only ever seen him on TV before. After earning a fortune of hundreds of millions on Internet start-ups in his twenties, he turned that into tens of billions by founding the world's first private space-launch company and an electric car company, and by developing human life-extension technology. Not bad for a forty-year-old.

Erdogmus was best known, however, for launching Mars First, a one-way, privately funded mission to send humans to Mars. The Apollo program took less than a decade from John Kennedy's famous speech to landing men on the moon, and five years ago Erdogmus had boasted that he could do better. And he made good on his promise—just three years after he announced it, the Mars First mission was launched two months ago. Eight humans, in hibernation sleep, were now aboard a one-way, three-year, long-trajectory flight path to Mars. The one-way part of the mission description was controversial, to say the least, but hundreds of people had volunteered for a chance to be the first to walk on Mars.

Ben had thought the project was madness; a suicide mission dreamed up as a promotional stunt for Erdogmus's empire. But on reflection, he realized that *real* explorers of the past usually *were* on what amounted to suicide missions. We just didn't have the risk appetite anymore—maybe Ufuk was right in what he was doing.

All that aside, what was Ufuk Erdogmus doing in this room right now? Then Ben remembered reading that he was doing the keynote speech for the IAU meeting. And regardless, Ufuk's question was exactly the right question to ask; the reason why the exoplanet people had been called into this meeting.

The search for planets around other stars used several techniques, one of them called "radial velocity," which detected the "wobble" in a distant star based on the change of its speed toward or away from us. Radial velocity measurements were extremely precise—Ben could record differences in speed down to meters per second, about how fast someone walked, when measuring a star trillions of kilometers away moving at hundreds of kilometers a second. And it could certainly measure whether the Earth, and the solar system with it, was falling toward some nearby object.

Dr. Müller turned and smiled. "The answer, Mr. Erdogmus, is that we *have* measured the presence of this object in our radial velocity searches. We just didn't know it. This independent verification is why I have called all of you here today. I've gone through NASA's own data and analyzed our 'fudge factors'—and time after time, the signal is there, staring at us in the face. An acceleration factor that we had previously attributed to dark matter in the nearby spiral arm of the Milky Way."

Fear jangled again in Ben's fingertips. He was hearing the full explanation for the first time, and he hadn't been entirely convinced the night before.

When measuring radial velocity to search for an exoplanet, only the wobble was of interest, not the constant effects. You subtracted the Earth's rotation, the movement of an orbiting observatory, the motion of the Earth around the sun, the motion of the Sun around the galactic core—everything pushed and pulled apart by gravity—and after that, even allowed for the heating or cooling of the device itself, down to the tiniest of imperfections in the system. Each observation team had a long list of "fudge factors" they used for their own systems.

The question Dr. Müller now posed: was there an overlooked

factor they all shared?

If so, what exactly *was* it?

4

Chianti, Italy

JESS STARED AT HER mother.

"Jail?" Celeste winced. "Again?" Her shoulders dropped but hitched back up quickly, her lips pressing together as she took a long look at her daughter. "Is that why you rushed me all the way out here?"

"No, the *reason* we're here is to have a girls' trip," Jess half-lied, taking a step back. "And to find this long-lost cousin of yours."

Her mother had received a Facebook message from an Italian relative a few weeks ago, asking her to come and visit. Totally unexpected. As far as her mother knew, none of their family still lived in Italy after moving to America generations ago. But this wasn't the real reason. The surprise was going to be reconnecting Celeste with her estranged husband, Jess's father. But that wasn't something Jess was going to reveal, not yet, because if she did her mother was just as likely to get straight back on a flight to JFK.

Celeste broke eye contact and tilted her chin downward, shaking her head. "Okay, so what are you in trouble with?"

"I need money."

"For what?"

"A lawyer."

"For *what*?"

Jess gritted her teeth. "It's complicated. This guy I was dating, Ricardo—"

"The one you just dumped?"

Shifting her weight from one foot to the other, Jess said, "I need to hire a lawyer. The police are looking for me."

"So what did you do?" Celeste asked once more.

Jess closed her eyes. "Ricardo and I got into a fight, and he hit me, so I decided it was enough. I grabbed my things and took off. I sold my car to get cash, but it was registered under his name. He got mad and called the police. He said I stole it, but I didn't."

It was a stupid fight that had spiraled out of control. She'd lived in Rome with Ricardo for the past three months. It wasn't serious. Or at least, it hadn't been. Now it was. To be honest, she hit him first, and much harder. Shame burned Jess's cheeks. More proof of her own inability to act responsibly. Her anger always brimmed just under the surface; too often it darted out to taste the air, and disappeared just as quickly.

"Someone hit *you*?" Her mother didn't seem so much concerned with her daughter getting hit, as amazed the offending party wasn't in the hospital. "And they want to arrest you for that?"

"No." Jess shook her head. "But I've been working here illegally, and Ricardo can be a real asshole. I don't want to get stuck—"

"Everyone," Nico said loudly from the front of the room, "I'd like your attention please."

Jess looked away from her mother's eyes, glancing at the tour guide before feeling a presence behind her. The door to the room must have opened while they were talking, and someone had stepped in behind them. Moving forward, Jess turned and mumbled an apology, but stopped and blinked twice.

A man stared at her, a deep scar creasing his forehead under a mop of black hair. The man smiled, fixing Jess with penetrating brown eyes. *Where had she seen him before?* In the parking lot on the way in, she remembered. She had almost run into him. Tattoos didn't impress Jess, but scars were another matter. The temperature in the room seemed to rise. "*Scusi*," she mumbled in Italian, getting out of the way.

"No, I apologize," said tall-dark-and-scarred. He smiled awkwardly, nodding at the floor.

Looking down, Jess found a pair of small eyes staring up at her. A boy held the man's hand. Jess took another step to the side to let the two of them pass.

"Today we have a very special honor," Nico continued from the front. "We have the Baron Giovanni Ruspoli and little Hector joining us. This is their castle—their home—we are visiting."

Baron Ruspoli stepped forward between Jess and Celeste, smiling.

He turned and offered his hand to Celeste. "Giovanni Ruspoli," he said, nodding as Celeste took his hand.

"Celestina Tosetti," Celeste replied.

Jess thought she detected the faintest of shadows pass across the Baron's smile, but it vanished in an instant. She glanced at the boy, Hector, holding the Baron's hand. Not more than four years old, he stared back at Jess with wide brown eyes under a mass of black hair. She stared back at him, feeling her pulse skip a beat, an image of children chasing each other through a snow-covered field flitting through her mind.

"A pleasure," the Baron replied to Celeste. He turned to Jess.

"Oh, sorry," Jess said after a moment, tearing her eyes away from the little boy. The Baron's hand hovered empty in the air between them. She took it. "Jess—"

The Baron bowed and kissed her hand.

"—ica." Jess finished her name in barely more than a whisper, the Baron's lips leaving her hand. If the temperature in the room seemed to rise before, now someone had turned on a burner. Her face flushed.

"A pleasure," repeated the Baron. He looked down. "And this is Hector."

"*Buon Giorno*," little Hector said to Celeste and Jess.

"*Buon Giorno*," Jess and Celeste both chimed back.

They all stared at each other for a moment.

The Baron leaned over and said softly, "*Vieni*, Hector, let's greet our other guests." He straightened up and smiled at Celeste. "I am trying to teach him English," he explained, then turned and walked to the front of the room, holding his hand out to the other tourists. Hector trailed Giovanni, his eyes still glued to Jess.

"I think he likes your hair," whispered Celeste to her daughter.

"Who?" Jess was still flustered. "The Baron?"

Celeste laughed. "No, Hector." She reached to hold her daughter's hand. "I think Baron Giovanni was interested in more than your hair."

"Mom!" Jess's cheeks burned.

"He kissed your hand, not mine, and the way he stared at you?" Celeste smiled at her daughter. "A *barone.*" She pronounced the word in Italian, *baro-nay*. "Now how much money do you need for this lawyer business you've—"

The door behind them swung open again. A grizzled face lined with deep creases poked its way in; above the furrowed brow, fly-away white hair sprouted in clumps from a deeply tanned scalp. The old man pulled a pipe out from between his teeth with stumpy fingers on a hand like a meat hook. "*Barone*," the old man growled, "*Polizia all'ingresso*."

The Baron turned from chatting with the tour guests. "*Polizia*?" he asked the old man. "*Qualcosa con... controversia*?"

The old man shook his head. "*Non la controversia*." He turned his eyes from the Baron to glance at Jess. "*Qualcos'altro*," he grunted, frowning at Jess before closing the door.

Even with Jess's limited Italian, she understood: *Police. At the entrance.* The other part she didn't understand—something about a controversy? That part didn't seem to have anything to do with her, but from the old man's body language, it was clear these police were here for her. How did they find her so fast?

Swearing under her breath, Jess remembered leaving an itinerary for this trip pinned to Ricardo's fridge. "Mom, can we go?"

The third floor of the museum was one large hall, sixty feet long, separated into three twenty-foot square rooms connected by a wide hallway down one side with large windows facing the courtyard. Jess and Celeste stood by the door to the main entrance, next to the windows, with the tour guide and the other couple standing on the other side of the room. Down the hallway from Jess and Celeste, at the opposite end, was another exit that led onto a balcony.

Jess glanced over her left shoulder, through one of the large lead-glass windows. Two police officers, in short-sleeve blue shirts with red-striped pants and peaked hats emblazoned with a gold feather, stood at the closed iron gates of the castle. "I need to get out of here," she whispered, flicking her chin at the back entrance down the hallway.

Celeste saw the panic in her daughter's eyes and gripped her hand tighter.

"Excuse me." The Baron stood in front of them again.

Jess thought he was going to grab hold of her, drag her outside for the police—that somehow the old man had communicated something to him—but he eased himself between Jess and Celeste and opened the door behind them. He stopped and turned. "Could you watch Hector for a moment?" he asked Jess and Celeste. "Please? Nico is here, in all cases."

Panic rising, Jess looked down. The boy stared up at her. Why was the Baron asking them to look after his son? Why was a *Baron* even talking to them at *all*?

"Of course," Celeste replied. She took Hector's hand. The Baron disappeared out the door.

Celeste and Jess both craned their necks to look out the window across the gravel courtyard. The Baron had already made his way down the two flights of exterior stairs. The old man stood by the gate, staring at the police. They gesticulated, seemingly to convince the old man to open the gates, but he stared at them coolly and puffed his pipe.

Jess looked from the window at her mother, now holding little Hector's hand. Hector tried to reach up to Jess as well, but she shrugged him off. "I'm going out the back," Jess said over the top of Hector to her mother, "I'll call you later."

Celeste grimaced. "Jessica, we can talk to them, you don't always need to run away."

But Jess had already turned to stride off, glancing left through the windows as she passed them, leaving her mother's admonishing words behind. The Baron was talking to the police now. He glanced up at the museum. Jess looked back at her mother, still holding Hector's hand, watching in disbelief as Jess fled.

Jess reached the back door, and without hesitation she grabbed and tried to turn the handle. It was jammed. With both hands she gripped the door handle, and after two tugs it turned. She stepped outside onto a small deck leading down a rocky slope into a grove of fir trees lining that side of the castle.

Stepping onto the slope, her left leg wobbled, alcohol and adrenaline competing to confuse her senses. Shouting erupted behind her. Jess glanced back at the entrance to see the Baron flicking his hands at the police. Stumbling forward, she lost her balance on the loose soil. Jess gasped as she pitched sideways, sending her tumbling down the rocky embankment. She automatically tucked into a forward roll, spotting a rock on the edge of the steepening incline she could swing her foot onto to stop her momentum.

Spinning, she perfectly timed jamming her right foot against the rock to bring herself upright, but halfway through the maneuver the rock skidded away, sending her tumbling out of control. Putting her hand out, she tried to stop her fall, but her arm twisted backward and her head slammed into the ground. Her world exploded in a flash of pain.

5

Rome, Italy

"QUIET!" DR. MÜLLER yelled from the front of the room, trying to regain some control of his presentation. "Please, let me finish."

"Are you drawing this conclusion *only* from the Voyager data?" asked a voice from the back of the room.

It was a good question. Several incredible discoveries had turned out to be of less-than-spectacular origin. One that came to Ben's mind was faster-than-light neutrinos that ended up being nothing more than measurement error.

"No, it is not," replied Dr. Müller. "You just haven't been able to see the forest for the trees, so to speak. Please, let me finish."

The noise in the room died down.

"For hundreds of years, our entire solar system has been falling toward this massive dark object. A part of the observed effect in the Pioneer Anomaly is due to thermal radiation, but a part is not due to the spacecraft itself, but tidal effects."

"Tidal effects?" someone asked.

"Yes, tidal effects," Dr. Müller said. "But tidal effects across the entire solar system." Nodding, he crossed and uncrossed his arms before pointing at the graphic detailing the paths of the Voyager and Pioneer spacecraft into interstellar space. "Because the planets are bound closely to the sun, as a whole we experience more or less the same gravity of the object approaching us. Everything in the solar system is falling toward it at the same rate."

He pointed outward, away from the cluster of planetary orbits at Voyager 1. "But here, at almost five times the distance to Neptune, the Voyager spacecraft are experiencing a slightly different gravity from this object. To begin with, the difference was small, within the limits of what we attributed to the Pioneer Anomaly, but with this object drawing closer, the effect is growing."

Dr. Müller nodded, and a new graphic appeared on the screen behind him. This one was an image of the paths of Voyager and Pioneer, but instead of a view from the north polar axis of the solar system—looking down—it viewed the orbits of the planets side-on. "As you can see, the Pioneer spacecraft both exited in the plane of the solar system, but Voyager 1 and 2 both left at fairly high angles." He illuminated a laser pointer that traced their paths, at angles of about thirty degrees upward, for Voyager 1, and downward, for Voyager 2, from the plane of the planetary orbits.

"Several months ago, the slight acceleration experienced by Voyager 1 changed from being an acceptable error to being some kind of system malfunction. Voyager 1 is over a billion kilometers farther out than Voyager 2, but within weeks the same thing began happening to it as well." He moved his laser pointer to the image of Voyager 2. "At that point, both of the probes accelerated toward each other, and now they've reversed course and begun slowing down. We have one other probe out there, the New Horizons spacecraft that flew by Pluto, and we are getting measurements from it that are consistent with our Nomad hypothesis."

"What trajectory?" someone asked from the front. "Is it going to enter the solar system?"

"As I went over last night with Dr. Rollins..." Müller pointed at Ben, by inference making him complicit in knowing about this beforehand. "...that is exactly what we need your help with. By going through all of your collected radial velocity data, with the assumption that the solar system is falling toward some nearby massive object, we should be able to determine its path. Or better still, whether this is somehow an error."

Or a hoax, Ben thought grimly. It still seemed impossible.

"We are also in the process of conducting a new round of measurements of planets against background star fields," Dr. Müller added. "An object this massive, this close, should be perturbing their orbits."

And should have been perturbing them for a very long time already, Ben thought. Dr. Müller had a solid reputation as a careful researcher and was a respected member of the community, but this had too many loose ends.

"You said Voyager 1 was affected, and then Voyager 2 a few weeks later," said another voice in the crowd. "They're more than a billion kilometers apart. How fast do you think this thing is moving?"

Looking up from the podium he hung onto like a life raft, Dr. Müller grimaced. "At hundreds of kilometers a second. Perhaps thousands."

"That's not possible," someone said from the front row.

Even the fastest hyper-velocity stars inside our own galaxy moved at only twelve hundred kilometers a second. Ben had made the same objection the night before.

Dr. Müller held his hands out. "We don't have the answers right now; that's why we need your help."

"What is it?" Ufuk Erdogmus asked. "Have you been able to image it?"

The list of options was slim. Up to five solar masses, it might be a non rotating neutron or quark star, but this would be no more than fifteen kilometers across. At twenty billion kilometers distant, it was probably impossible to see. Could it be a black hole? Or perhaps something more exotic, perhaps an encounter with dark matter? They should have detected something—if not in visible light, then in x-ray or infrared or some other spectra.

Then again, thought Ben, astronomers were usually only staring at very specific parts of the sky. Very few projects ever tried to look at wide swaths of the sky. Some that did, like the Sloan and Catalina sky surveys, detected thousands of unknown objects that nobody had had a chance to look at yet. It was a subject he dabbled in, ever since he had participated in the Red Shift survey in the 80s. He had his own collection of anomalous objects he researched as a hobby.

Dr. Müller shook his head. "No, we haven't been able to detect anything except the gravitational signature. Whatever Nomad is, right now it is almost directly behind the sun." Which made Earth-based telescopes and orbiting platforms almost useless for trying to look at it, he didn't have to explain.

"Until we get some confirmation," Dr. Müller added, "secrecy is of the utmost importance. We don't want to create panic."

Ben's stomach fluttered. "Wait, you said it was coming from the direction of the sun. What *exact* direction?"

"We've sent information packets to all of your emails, including our best guess at the right ascension and declination—but in general terms, from the direction of Gliese 445." Müller locked eyes with Ben.

Ben returned his gaze, the fluttering in his stomach rising into his throat.

Gliese 445.

Thirty years earlier…

December 5th, 1989
Harvard Campus, Boston, Massachusetts

"WHAT THE HELL is that?" Bernie jabbed a finger at his computer screen.

Paul, his research partner, had his attention focused on a small TV jammed into a corner of a shared office at the Harvard-Smithsonian Center for Astrophysics. He stared at a grainy image of people on top of a wall, hacking off chunks of concrete with crowbars and pick-axes. "That's the Berlin Wall coming down!" Paul replied. "The end of the Cold War. Amazing, huh?"

"Not that. This!" Bernie pointed at his glowing green display again. "A bright flash at Gliese 445."

After combing through twelve-years' worth of data collection from the first all-sky optical survey, the Red Shift project, Bernie had never seen anything like it. "Gliese 445 is a red dwarf in the Camelopardalis constellation, usually not visible to the naked eye." He grabbed a sheaf of papers and shuffled through them. "But it just had a massive wide-spectrum flash. Too fast for a nova, but not regular like a pulsar, either." He squinted and checked other data. "And it doesn't have the signature of an M-dwarf."

Paul sighed, his eyes still glued to the TV. "There are a million things we can't identify. Just make a note and move on." Outside it was darkening, the lights coming on between the red brick buildings of the Harvard campus.

"Sure, you're right." Just the same, Bernie pushed a floppy disk into the drive of the IBM/400 minicomputer and saved the data. He could look at it later. Maybe he'd get Dr. Müller to take a look at it sometime.

6

Chianti, Italy

AN IMAGE DANCED in front of Jess's eyes, a black hole ringed in brilliant white, framing a small boy's face. Two children played in a white field of snow, laughing. The image faded, but the boy's face remained. Jess blinked, fully opening her eyes, and the boy smiled.

"*Zio*," the boy said, turning away, "*zio, sveglia*."

Blinking again, Jess turned from the boy and looked around her at rough-hewn rock walls adorned with finely detailed hanging tapestries. Twenty feet overhead, large wooden beams supported a ceiling of terracotta tiles, and a huge dark wood chandelier hung down from there, almost to head height. Sitting upright, she found herself surrounded by a sea of brightly colored pillows. A man sat on the foot of the bed, by her left leg, while two other men stood at a distance in the corner of the room. The small boy retreated and pulled on the man's arm.

The man at the foot of her bed looked familiar, his long black hair pulled back in a ponytail over broad shoulders and his face square-jawed with a scar above his left eye. "*Signora*, how are you…?" Leaning forward, he touched her leg.

"Don't touch me!" Jess yelled, recoiling and pulling her left leg away from him. "Get away from me." She pushed pillows to cover her leg. She still wore her jeans and sneakers, with her hoodie on top.

The man withdrew in haste. "I am sorry, I didn't mean—"

"Jessica, are you okay? You were out for a few minutes, gave us a scare." Her mother's voice echoed from a hallway, and an instant later Celeste appeared through the bedroom door, rushing to Jess's side. "This is Baron Ruspoli. You remember, from the museum tour?"

*That's righ*t, the castle museum tour. Her mind was still foggy, a dull ache behind her eyes, with the metallic tang of blood in her pasty mouth. A breeze from open windows pulled freshness into the musty room. Jess closed her eyes, drawing her body together. *The tour. The police.* She opened her eyes in panic, trying to focus on the two men in the corner of the room.

"Please, call me Giovanni." The Baron stood but hovered over her, the boy clinging to his side.

The boy. *Hector*, Jess remembered. The Baron's son.

Jess craned her neck to one side to look out of the half-open door to the room leading into the hallway. No one else out there. She looked back at the two men in the corner of the room. They didn't look like police. "Mom, are—"

"Everything is fine, Jessica." Celeste sat beside her. "Calm down. You took a nasty spill."

"I'm sorry, I didn't mean to make you uncomfortable," added Baron Giovanni, taking a step back.

"Where are we?" she asked her mother. This wasn't their room. They were supposed to stay one night here, in a small cottage at the side of the castle; part of the whirlwind "castles in Chianti" mini-tour Jess had organized.

"I hope you don't mind, but I moved you into our private quarters," Giovanni said. "This is a room in the main tower of the castle. The doctor is on his way." Giovanni slipped his hands into his pockets and took another step back while clearing his throat. "Your mother said it would be all right."

So I'm in a castle tower. It sounded like a prison. Jess pushed her arms down to sit higher, and pain shot through her head. Reaching one hand up, she felt a goose egg on the side of her head. Tender.

"Nico and Leone saved you," Celeste said, her voice low and soothing, motioning to the two men standing behind Baron Giovanni.

One of the men, the younger one, waved a tiny salute. It was Nico, their tour guide from earlier. Where the Baron had rugged good looks, Nico had more of a boyish charm—tousled brown hair pulled back to one side, a carefully groomed beard of two-day-old stubble on a slender, smiling face that radiated warmth. Jess smiled back.

The other person was the old man who had poked his head into the museum, the one with white fly-away hair over the deeply tanned scalp. He'd announced the police at the gate. The pipe still in his mouth, he narrowed his eyes and nodded at Jess.

"You would have fallen right off the ledge, twenty feet at least." Celeste added, "They might have saved your life."

How was she so careless? Jess cursed at herself. The alcohol did it, added to her nerves at seeing the police. "Thank you, Nico and Leone," she mumbled.

Her head throbbed, but it wasn't just the fall. A midday hangover from four glasses of sparkling wine at brunch contributed, she was sure. "Thank you," Jess repeated, "but we can't stay."

She had to find a phone and call the lawyer. Looking out the nearest window, she scanned the courtyard for any sign of police.

Giovanni caught her looking outside. "That's L'Olio," he said, thinking she was looking at the tree in the middle of the courtyard, "our matriarch, the old olive tree. Had you visited her yet?"

It was mentioned in the castle tour brochure. Jess shook her head, but took a closer look—the tree's roots dug their way into the ground like old arthritic fingers, gnarled and misshapen, an equally tortured knot of branches spreading out above the roots in a half-dead tangle.

"Over three thousand years old, our L'Olio," Giovanni added. "She was here when the Etruscans dug their caves into the hills below us."

"It's beautiful," Jess lied. Old. Twisted. The tree looked in pain, hanging on to a bitter end. She'd never be like that. She would never hang on past her time.

"You didn't finish the tour?" Giovanni looked at Jess, then Celeste. "Then I insist. Please make use of these rooms, and I will take you on a proper tour of the castle myself." He smiled and nodded. "When you are feeling better, of course."

Jess smiled thinly. "We can't—"

"I do have a confession." Giovanni smiled awkwardly.

This completely threw Jess off. She blinked. "A confession?"

"When I arrived, we passed in the courtyard, do you remember?"

Jess did. The deep scar above his eye. It wasn't a face she would forget. Jess nodded.

"I recognized you. Sorry if I stared. Jessica Rollins, yes? I'm a fan of extreme sports, and I've seen your YouTube videos, your ascent and mid-climb BASE jump from El Capitan. It was the reason I joined the tour group, to say hello to you."

Flustered, Jess didn't know what to say. "Well, I—"

"It would be an honor if you'd allow me to show you and your mother around the castle myself. Please."

Jess was about to say no again, but Celeste interjected. "We'd love to. That is very generous." She glanced at Jess, frowned, then returned to smiling at the Baron.

Giovanni's smile broadened. "Perfect, then it's settled. I'll go out and see when the doctor will arrive." Nodding curtly, he excused himself and exited the room, trailing Hector, who kept staring and smiling at Jess.

Nico stepped forward from the back of the room, extending one hand to Celeste. She took his hand, and he bowed and kissed it. Her mother blushed. "A pleasure, Madame Tosetti, a real pleasure." Straightening up, he took a step toward Jess, but she edged away. "And Jessica, I look forward to seeing more of you as well," he said, leaving Jess her distance.

"You two, you could be brother and sister," growled a voice from behind Nico. It was the old man, holding his pipe in one hand, glowering at Nico and Jess.

Celeste reached to hold Jess's hand. She smiled at the old man Leone. "Our family was from the valley below here, many generations ago." She glanced at Nico. "Are you from here?"

"No," Nico replied. "I am from Napoli. I came here looking for work, years ago, and Giovanni's father took me in."

Leone grunted and narrowed his eyes. "I have work that needs attending." He nodded. "Madame Tosetti, Jessica."

"Thank you again, Leone," Celeste said to the old man as he disappeared out the doorway, just as another man came in, suitcases under both arms.

"Old Leone is just a little grumpy," explained Nico, turning to the doorway. "Ah, and this is Enzo," he added, introducing the small man that deposited their luggage just inside the entrance.

"*Buon Giorno,*" Enzo said, his voice bright. "Anything you need, you come to me."

Enzo had a thin, angular face with a goatee and a large mole on his left cheek. A brown pork-pie hat covered his head, which Jess imagined was balding. Sitting forward, she pulled her left foot under her right leg. She felt like an invalid. "Thank you very much, but I'm tired…"

"Of course." Nico bowed. "How rude of us. Come, Enzo, let's leave our guests."

"Yes, yes, I just have a few more bags to bring in. Is that all right?"

"Of course," Celeste replied.

Enzo and Nico both smiled at Celeste and Jess, and then left the room, leaving the door ajar.

"Are the police here?" Jess asked her mother in an urgent whisper.

"No, and in fact, the Baron refused to let them in the castle. He had a huge argument with them at the gate just before the excitement of saving you from almost killing yourself."

"I wasn't trying to kill myself—"

"It's just a figure of speech." Celeste turned to her daughter. "Giovanni is a very nice man. Why don't we relax, take our time? We don't need to be in Rome for a few days, do we? For this surprise of yours?"

Her father's conference ended in three days. That was when Jess planned on trying to get them together. "No, we're not in a hurry."

"Good, then we can stay a few days," Celeste said cheerfully. "I like it here, and I think you could use a day off your feet." Her mother winced, looking at her left leg. "Sorry, you know what I mean."

"A warning," said a voice from the hallway. It was the Baron, his face hanging in the doorway.

Jess flinched. Were the police back? "Wh…what?" she stuttered.

"The doctor will be here in two minutes, just giving you a warning."

Enzo watched Baron Ruspoli hanging in the doorway ahead of

him, fawning over this new American girl and her mother. He could see the way the Baron looked at this young woman, Jessica. This little dove with her broken wing. "Here are the rest of the bags," Enzo called out as he barged past the Baron, dropping what he carried onto the floor.

He smiled at the Baron, then at Jessica. He had to admit, she was beautiful—long blond hair, slender, but with fire in her eyes. There were so many things he'd like to do to her himself. Hold her, protect her, show her *his* love…

But he had to smile, to pretend.

He couldn't let anyone know what he was thinking, who he was. And he couldn't go back to jail, couldn't go back to those men. Not after the last time. Never again.

"Is that all, Baron?" Enzo asked.

The Baron put a hand on Enzo's shoulder. "Yes, thank you. And please, whatever Jessica and Celeste need, you make sure you give it to them."

Enzo turned to smile at the women. "Yes, of course. Whatever they need."

Looking at the Baron, Enzo smiled at him as well. Soon the Baron would be getting what he needed as well. Soon the pig would pay for his crimes.

SURVIVOR TESTIMONY

#JR6;

Event +55hrs;
Name: Sergio Solano;
Reported location: Salt Lake City, Utah;

We took off from the Seattle area just after half past three. All airspace was officially closed, but by then the water had already dropped ten feet in the Tacoma Narrows. We still had six or seven hours, that's what they said. Enough time for me to get my son and fly back the three hours to Dallas in my Cessna Citation jet. But it wasn't. Not enough time. Forty-five minutes into the flight, I'd climbed to thirty-three thousand feet, scanning the airspace for any oncoming aircraft as all ATC were down; clear blue skies, no pressure fronts along the whole route. Perfect day.

That's when it happened. Bands of white light appeared in the deep blue sky, rippling, and a second later all the electronics went blank. Just like that. Everything gone. No GPS, no digital displays. My old Citation works off manual hydraulics, thank God, so I switched to dead reckoning and the six-pack of analog controls. Then straight ahead, a black smudge appeared. It seemed to engulf the entire horizon. Never seen anything like it. It stretched up, high into the sky, higher than any thunderhead I'd ever seen. Those usually flatten out at the tropopause, at the edge of the stratosphere, thirty or even forty thousand feet. But this was a black wall, shooting into the sky, way beyond that.

I changed course away from it and was picking up my altitude when a shock wave hit us. Damn near tore the plane apart, dropped us to twenty thousand before I regained control. By the time I looked back, the wall had mushroomed out at over a hundred thousand feet, an inky black pool spreading across the sky… I put us down in Salt Lake after the second shock wave ripped into us. The black cloud enveloped us by the time we secured the jet on the empty runway.

That was two days ago. Now there's three feet of it in the streets, a suffocating sludge coating everything… I don't know how long we'll be able…

> Transmission ended high ionization static. Freq. 9660 kHz.
> Subject not reacquired.

DAY TWO
October 7th

7

Chianti, Italy

JESS AWOKE TO birds chirping in juniper trees outside the open windows of her room. In the huge bed, set high from the floor with a sash draped along the headboard and with tapestries flowing over the stone walls—fairy tale princesses came to mind. Would she let her hair down? Let the prince climb up and save her? The idle daydreaming screeched to a halt almost before it started. She was the last person on Earth who needed saving.

And fairy tales were just that.

She'd spent the balance of the day before in bed, enjoying the doting attention of her mother. Maybe that's why she dropped off to sleep early. She had awakened earlier than she usually did, but Jess got up and showered. After toweling off, she didn't feel like leaving her sanctuary, so she deposited herself back in the luxurious bed and pulled her pajamas back on. For a while she just lay there and listened to the chirping birds, but she eventually opened her laptop, answered some emails and started a game of online chess.

Jess pondered the long-lost relative Facebook-messaging her mother. Jess had nothing to do with the message, but it had given her the perfect excuse to convince her mother to come to Italy. A cover for Jess's real motive of getting her in the same country as Jess's father. Now she just needed to connect her mother and father in Rome. They had honeymooned here, and as infantile as it sounded, Jess wanted to get them to meet and spend time together here in Italy with her as a family. For once.

She'd tried pinging her dad that morning, but he wasn't available, and didn't return any of her calls. Unusual, but then Jess didn't take it the wrong way when people didn't answer their phones right away.

She liked to have her own space too.

A knock at the door.

"Yes?"

"It's me." Her mother didn't wait for a reply. She opened the door, asking, "You spending today in bed as well?" Closing the door behind herself, she dropped a cup of coffee next to Jess and draped herself across the foot of Jess's bed. "Giovanni already took me on a tour of the castle, but we didn't want to wake you."

"Thanks."

Her mother frowned. "Do I detect sarcasm?"

"No, really, I mean thanks for letting me be." She pushed her laptop forward and picked up the cup of coffee to take a sip.

Her mother glanced at the laptop screen. "Are you still playing chess with your father?"

"Sometimes, but not today." Jess put the coffee down and pulled her legs to the side of the bed. She noticed her mother watching her. "Mom, could you give me a minute?"

Celeste smiled. "I'm your mother, sweetheart."

Jess sighed. "Fine." She swung her legs off the side of the bed, pulling off the covers, and her right foot dropped to the ground. Her left leg, however, ended in an angry red stump just below the knee.

Her mother tried not to stare. "Does it hurt?"

"See, that's why I asked for some privacy," Jess groaned. "And no, it doesn't hurt." But it did. In the fall yesterday, she'd twisted her stump painfully.

Leaning over, she picked up her prosthetic from the floor next to the bed, angled her lower leg upward, and pulled the socket into place. It was a custom fit, with a new suction valve that kept it on securely. A smooth stainless steel rod connected the flesh-colored socket to her new foot. She'd just gotten it a few months before—a multiple-axis stored-energy one in lifelike plastic. Better than her old leg, she liked to joke.

Six years now, and she could hardly remember the difference. Six years ago she'd lost her leg. It was the last time that her parents had come together, that day when she'd been shipped back to the US, damaged and broken. They'd been like a real family again, for a short time at least. But she didn't have another leg to spare. This time she hoped they could do it without her needing to lose a limb.

After attaching her leg, she pulled on a pair of jeans and stylish gold flats, then a red short-sleeved blouse. Searching through her luggage, she found her makeup kit and walked into the bathroom, clicking the light on.

Her mother watched her, smiling. "Makeup? *You're* putting on makeup?"

Jess rolled her eyes but grinned. "Give me a break, huh?"

Knocking on the heavy wooden door, Jess said, "Mr. Ruspoli, ah, I mean, Baron Giovanni?" The door was open just a crack, and she heard paper shuffling. "Sorry, Nico told me to just come up."

The shuffling stopped. "Jessica, yes, please, come in! And please, call me Giovanni."

Jess swung open the door, expecting a dim medieval interior with suits of armor and swords on the walls, but instead she found a bright open space. Giovanni was sitting behind a computer monitor at a large L-shaped desk in the corner of the room. Bookcases lined the wall to her left, behind the open door, filled with a jumble of books and odds and ends.

The wall to her right had an enormous flat screen television covering most of it, but was otherwise lined with shelves of electronic gear to both sides. The other two walls were floor-to-ceiling windows looking out over the tops of the castle walls to the rolling vineyards and hills beyond. Pictures hung on the walls between the bookcases; one of them, Jess noticed, showed the Baron sailing on rough waves, sea foam spraying around him. Another picture was of him atop a mountain, distant peaks stretching into the distance, and beside that a large print of him in full arctic gear, smiling in front of a frozen wasteland.

"How are you feeling today?" Giovanni asked, turning to face her. He'd been staring at the computer screen. Littered across the floor were large cardboard boxes, stacked up, with backpacks scattered between in clumps. A set of scuba tanks sat in the corner. "Please excuse the mess, I've just moved back. Please, come, sit." He indicated a chair next to his desk.

Jess picked her way through the boxes. "I'm the one that should be apologizing. And I'm feeling great, thank you. How are you?" She sat.

"Good, good." He glanced back at the computer monitor. "I'm just trying to understand the family business, so much to do." His voice faded. Shaking his head, he looked back at Jess and smiled.

"Giovanni, thank you for…" Jess started to say, but then stopped. She hated apologizing. In her world, either you did something or you didn't. If you did it, then you meant it, and there was no need to apologize. If you didn't mean it, then don't do it. It was that simple. But in this case… "Thank you for keeping the police out, yesterday, I can't tell you how embarrassed I am."

"Nonsense, the police have no business here. This is my sovereign ground. My family has defended this place for a thousand years. Two little police officers are nothing."

She couldn't tell if he was being funny or not. Was this *really* his sovereign ground? Like his own country? "Still, they were here because of me."

"I know."

"It's just, this guy I was—"

"No need to explain." Giovanni clicked off his computer. "So, how about that personal tour of the castle?"

Was this guy for real? Some kind of Italian machismo? Fending off the police, rescuing the damsel in distress? Jess felt a prickling of resentment under her gratitude, but said nothing.

"Are you ready?" Giovanni stood and came around his desk.

Jess took a deep breath and smiled, consciously smoothing down the hackles in her mind. "Sure, that would be great."

Giovanni took Jess on a whirlwind exploration of the castle, explaining when each wall and tower had been built, what battles had been fought and won. They stopped in at the kitchens first, where he explained they only had evening staff for three nights a week, usually for the guests. He mostly cooked his own food.

Then he took her on a quick march around the periphery of the outer walls, through the olive groves, pointing out the vineyards that stretched down the sides of the mountain. Olive oil was still an important family business, he said, as well as the wine that the estate produced. From there they went down below, into the catacombs of the wine cellars, ancient Etruscan caves carved out thousands of years ago. For three thousand years, he said, the caves had withstood every earthquake and disaster Mother Nature threw at them.

They ended the tour at the southwest corner, the highest point where the top of the castle walls met the peak of the mountain. They climbed up through one of the tunnels to a ledge, then up a ladder to the top. A cable stretched across the small valley to the next property, a much smaller *castello* on the side of a hill opposite, so that a small cable car could be ferried across. Below, the town of Saline nestled in the foothills. The view to the west was breathtaking, the flat plains of Tuscany stretching into the distance, the Mediterranean visible as a blue line on the horizon forty miles away.

"Is that your property as well?" Jess asked, squinting down the length of the cable that strung across the valley, looking at the smaller *castello* on the opposite side.

"No," Giovanni replied, then corrected himself. "Well, yes, it is, but much more recent. We've only owned it for a hundred years." He grinned. "A new addition. We built the cable car to connect them."

"A new addition?" Jess held one hand over her eyes to shield the sun, taking a closer look at the structure on the other side of the gorge. "What, you bought it?"

The grin evaporated from Giovanni's face. "Not exactly, it was…" He looked away, exhaling, then looked back at Jess. "It was a rival family, but they left."

Jess glanced at him, noticed a strange look in his eyes. "Like a feud?"

"Yes, like that."

"Huh." Jess shook her head, not sure what to say. She shifted her gaze down the cliff wall under the cable car shack where they'd come from. It was thirty feet of sheer rock, with a large grassy ledge at least twenty feet across, then a drop of a few hundred feet beyond that. "Great for rock climbing," she observed.

"Jessica, I do have another confession."

She was still staring down the rock wall, her mind constructing possible routes for climbing up it. "What's that?"

"Yesterday, at the museum, I overheard you telling your mother that your boyfriend hit you, that you needed money."

Lifting her head up from looking down the cliff face, Jess shielded her eyes again from the setting sun. "Is that why you're being so nice to me?"

"Partly." Giovanni nodded.

"And the other part?"

Giovanni looked uncomfortable. "The videos of you on YouTube, the famous American girl, BASE jumping, sky diving and rock climbing, the…" His voice faltered.

"What, the cripple?" Jess finished the sentence for him. Her cheeks flushed, and she struggled to keep her temper from flaring. He was being nice. He didn't mean anything.

"Sorry, I don't know—"

"It's okay. Disabled, that would be the right word. But I'm not a cripple. I don't need any special treatment."

Shaking his head, Giovanni agreed, "No, you are no cripple. I was so surprised when I saw you here. You are magnificent, beautiful." He winced. "Sorry, my English is a little rusty, perhaps not the right words?"

Jess laughed, her flash of temper burning into one of embarrassment. "No, those are nice words."

Giovanni's smile returned. "I was wondering if you might do me a favor."

Squinting into the sun, Jess took a long look at him. "What did you have in mind?"

"If you might give my little Hector a rock climbing lesson,

perhaps?"

She looked down the rock face. "What, now?"

Giovanni looked down. "Yes. I have all the equipment. We could set a top rope, no?"

She looked down at the rock face. "Sure, we could do that. One thing though."

The Baron looked at her. "Anything."

"If we're going to be friends, call me Jess, okay?"

Giovanni stored his climbing equipment just inside the doorway of a tunnel carved into the side of the rock face, on the twenty-foot-wide ledge of grass below the cable car station. While he went to fetch Hector and Nico, Jess set up two ropes from a metal gantry sticking out from the top of the cliff face, and having enough cord, she also rigged a rope swing from the cable car platform to let someone drop from there to the grassy ledge thirty feet below.

She'd just finished when Giovanni returned with Nico and Hector. Only five years old, Hector scampered around the low rocks like a monkey, smiling a big grin at Jess as he jumped around. He was fearless, and earned large return grins from Jess.

She attached the two topes to Giovanni and Hector in their climbing harnesses. Jess and Nico strapped into harnesses and attached themselves to the other ends of the ropes, taking up the slack as Hector and Giovanni climbed, with Jess calling out suggestions and encouragement.

"So what brought you to Ruspoli Castle?" Nico asked Jess. With Giovanni and Hector twenty feet overhead, Jess and Nico stood shoulder to shoulder, carefully taking in the excess rope as the two ascended.

Jess glanced at Nico, then returned to watching Hector, taking up the slack with the braking mechanism attached to her. "Funny story. My mom got a Facebook message from a long-lost relative a few weeks ago, said he still lived here and wanted to meet us."

Nico jammed his brake into place and looked at Jess. "What? Who? Did you meet him?"

"No, not yet." Jess frowned at Nico. What had gotten him so excited? "He hasn't responded since we've arrived. Why?"

Nico stared at Jess for a long second, then looked up at Giovanni and released the brake. "Just curious. So your family is from here?"

"My mom's side, but from years ago. We didn't think anyone from our family still lived here. So we came to investigate."

"You came all the way from America just for that?" Nico nodded. "Family must be very important to you."

Jess let her head sag to one side. "Well, it wasn't *just* for that." She pulled in two more feet of rope into the brake as Hector climbed. "And I don't know anything about the old family. My mom says her dad refused to talk about it."

"You know nothing?" Nico turned to look at Jess.

"Nothing at all." Jess wagged her head, shrugging. "And you, do you have family here?"

Nico's jaw muscles rippled, but he smiled. "No, I have no family."

"You're from Naples, though. Isn't that what you said earlier?"

"That's right."

"And Giovanni's father hired you to work here."

Nico nodded. "Seven years ago he took me in. He was like a father to me, and I did my best to look after him when he got sick, even when Giovanni left." He let out a long sigh. "Ah, I forget myself. I really should not talk of the Baron's family."

Where was Giovanni's father now? In Florence, Jess guessed, but she didn't want to pry, so she switched topics. "The police who were here this morning, did Giovanni really just shoo them away?"

"Yes."

"He can do that?"

Nico grinned at Jess. "This is not America. The Ruspolis, well…I wouldn't worry, not while you are his guest."

"And Leone mentioned something about a *controversia*, what was that about?" Jess whispered.

Glancing to his right, toward the cable car and the *castello* on the opposite side of the gorge, Nico replied, "I don't know." He shrugged and jerked the cord tight, earning a muffled complaint from Giovanni thirty feet overhead. “Of that, I have no idea.”

8

Rome, Italy

BEN PULLED BACK the curtains of his hotel room window and peeked out. Brilliant sunshine streamed in from a perfect blue sky. The traffic growled, and people shuffled by in the street, some shopping, some sipping coffees in the café.

A beautiful day for predicting the end of the world.

"Well, have a look in the back!" Ben shouted into his cell phone. Mrs. Brown, their seventy-eight-year-old administrative assistant, was going deaf. She refused to retire, and there was no way Ben would fire her. She'd been a part of his life longer than he could even remember now. "Yes, I know what time it is. I'm very sorry."

Almost ten at night in Boston. He'd dragged her out of bed to search his office, to dig through the mountains of papers and boxes he'd accumulated in his thirty years at Harvard-Smithsonian. He needed data, *really* old data. Spools of tape he'd collected that dated back to the 1970s, before he'd even started at Harvard as a student, along with magnetic tapes; floppy disks from the 80s; CDs from the 90s. Ben was a pack rat, his office the epitome of the disorganized professor, but he knew what he needed was in there.

Ben let go of the curtain, casting the hotel room back into darkness. "Mrs. Brown, I know this is difficult, but please keep searching. This is an emergency." He rubbed one temple to try to ease back a throbbing headache. The fate of the world might rest in the eyesight of Mrs. Brown, twice over a great-grandmother. "I'll stay on the line while you look."

Pushing *mute* on his phone, he turned to Roger, his grad student, sitting cross-legged on the room's double bed. Although the Grand Hotel was fancy, the rooms were tiny. Ben had installed himself at the sliver of a working desk near the window, so the only other place to work was on the bed.

"Did you get the new data downloads?" Ben asked.

"Just getting them now," Roger replied. A nest of papers surrounded him, his face staring into his laptop screen. "The wireless in this hotel sucks. Even if I get it downloaded, it's going to take time to unpack and normalize."

It was one thing to say you had the data, but another to decode it. Never mind trying to figure out how to read the magnetic tapes or floppy disks he had Mrs. Brown hunting for. Just trying to make sense of the compression algorithms and file formats of ten years ago was proving more difficult than Ben had imagined. He would bet the other teams were having the same problems. Making sure apples were apples wasn't easy, especially over the Grand Hotel's feeble wireless connection, four thousand miles from the office.

"Just make it happen. This is important." Ben clicked off the *mute* on his phone. "Yes, that's right," he yelled. "The one marked 'Red Shift 1977', that's the one." Mrs. Brown might be old, but she was a wizard at picking through Ben's messes. "And you have a list of the others? Good." He clicked *mute* on his phone again.

"Want to tell me what this is all about, Bernie?" Roger asked from the bed.

Bernie. Ben's old college nickname. His students liked to use it to rile him up. "I can't tell you. I need to see if you find it for yourself," Ben said.

It was a valid point, one Roger would understand. A problem with searching through huge amounts of data was that, eventually, you could see almost anything you wanted. If he told Roger what he was looking for, he'd probably find it. That was Ben's main misgiving with Dr. Müller's hypothesis. So Ben was having Roger comb through their radial velocity searches of stars to look at the subtractive factors, see if any of them were changing significantly over time. It was a big undertaking, looking in all directions at the celestial sphere to see how the solar system was moving, and not just a snapshot, but over time.

"Okay, boss, but you owe me," Roger said, his face bathed in the glow from his laptop screen.

Ben smiled. "Next conference in Hawaii."

Roger's face brightened. "Deal."

"Oh, and could you email Susan and ask her if she could check the Red Shift, Sloan, Catalina surveys for any changes in variability of stars in vicinity of Gliese 445?"

Roger frowned, his face still glued to the laptop screen. "*Changes* in variability?"

Time domain astronomy—seeing changes in objects over time—was still in its infancy. "Yes, not regular variability, but any significant changes over the past decade."

"Sure." Roger raised his eyebrows, clearly not confident that it would be possible. "Anything for a trip to Hawaii."

Ben pressed his ear back to the phone, clicking *mute* back off. "Yes!" he shouted into the phone. "Overnight the boxes to the hotel, under my name. Thank you, Mrs. Brown."

Taking a deep breath, he hung up and looked at Roger. "I've got to go upstairs."

Ben walked down the carpeted hallway outside his room and took the elevator to the top floor. He was having Roger search through the data, but Ben already had a good idea of what he'd find. He'd checked a few data points himself, in the direction suggested by Dr. Müller, and could see a growing acceleration factor. It was one that they'd fudged over as a mass of dark matter in the nearby spiral arm of the galaxy, just as Dr. Müller had described.

When the elevator door pinged at the top floor and the door opened, two large security men greeted him and repeated the biometric routine. Ben was used to it now. Fourth time today. They weren't meeting in the ballroom anymore.

"Dr. Müller's room?" Ben asked.

One of the gorillas pointed down the hallway. "Last door at the end."

Most of the other teams had already moved up here, but Ben

wanted to keep a little distance. He wasn't sure who was paying for all this security. Walking to the end of the hallway, he opened the door, revealing an opulent suite with marble floors and period-piece 19th-Century furniture, the chairs and couches filled with people slouched over, staring into laptop screens. A wall of whiteboards, filled with sketches and numbers, obscured the windows looking out over Rome. The air was thick with cigarette smoke.

"Ah, Dr. Rollins," Dr. Müller said, turning from one of the whiteboards. "Good. We were waiting for the Harvard-Smithsonian's opinion."

Ben strode forward into the middle of the room. "It's not official, but yes, from my preliminary assessment, it is possible that a large mass is moving toward the solar system."

Dr. Müller pursed his lips and nodded. "Five of the six teams have reported the same thing." He motioned at the whiteboards.

"Might be confirmation bias," Ben pointed out. "We need more time."

"I agree, but you must see that there is something there?"

"Yes, I think something is there," Ben agreed. "But how far, how fast, I don't know. What else are we doing?" Something of this magnitude needed proof beyond a doubt.

"The European Space Agency, NASA and the Russians, Japanese and Chinese have begun re-aligning their orbiting and ground-based observatories to look in the direction of Nomad. But if it's there, it's coming from almost exactly behind the sun. Our best hope is the Gaia observatory. It's the only space-based observatory not immediately near Earth."

Ben nodded. Gaia's Lagrange 2 location was a point about 1.5 million kilometers away from Earth, in a direction away from the sun. The Gaia observatory was the most sophisticated exoplanet-hunting tool they had. If anything could spot this thing, Gaia was their best hope.

"What was Ufuk Erdogmus doing at the meeting? I thought you only wanted astronomers."

Dr. Müller slipped his hands into his pockets and lifted his chin. "Why? Did he talk to you?"

"No. Why would he?"

"I don't know." Dr. Müller rocked back on his heels. "Erdogmus wasn't expected, but it's hard to stop a man such as this, yes?" He licked his lips. "And the man has eight frozen human popsicles halfway from here to Mars. He offered to wake some of them up, to try and use the Mars First ship-board instrumentation to look at Nomad's location."

"Wouldn't that be a death sentence? That ship isn't designed for years of life support en-route, is it?"

"It's already a suicide mission, no?" Müller stroked his chin with his right hand, and Ben noticed a signet ring.

The ring looked like it had a yin-yang symbol on it. In the twenty-odd years since Ben had seen him last, Müller hadn't changed much—a few extra pounds, a little less hair, a little more wrinkled and gray—but the signet ring was new. Ben didn't remember him being Taoist, or even religious in any way. Müller pulled his hand away and slid it back into his pocket.

"In any case, we declined his help as ridiculous," Dr. Müller said. "It's a foregone conclusion that something is there. We're already seeing a shift in Neptune's orbit."

And Neptune was the closest planet right now.

Any hope Ben had of this being an elaborate hoax or miscalculation was evaporating. It would be hard to argue with something as straightforward as measuring a planet against the background star field. The cigarette smoke in the air burned his throat, his eyes teared, and the temperature in the room seemed to rise.

"Are you going to make an announcement?" Ben asked. But where would people go? There was no way to escape the *planet.*

"Of course," Dr. Müller agreed. "Not yet, though. It will take days, weeks, for us to decipher the data properly and figure out the path of Nomad, what its mass is, and how it might affect us."

Weeks? By then it might be too late. But too late for what? What were the options? "I think we should bring in a larger community of scientists, at least."

Dr. Müller held up his hands. "We don't want to be alarmist. We don't even know if it will come close to the inner solar system yet.

This thing is, what, twenty billion kilometers away?"

Ben looked Dr. Müller in the eye. "I need to get back to my data."

Ben was still lost in his thoughts when he slipped his keycard into the hotel room door. Before he could open it, it swung back by itself. Not really by itself—Roger stood in front of him, his face ashen.

"Gliese 445?" Roger said slowly. "Variability? Microlensing, is that what you're looking for?"

Ben pushed his way inside and closed the door. "What did you find?"

Roger pushed the papers on the bed aside and sat down. "Something big is heading this way, isn't it?"

There was no point in trying to lie. "Yes," Ben replied simply.

"What do you know?"

"Not too much yet," Ben answered honestly. "But I have a feeling it's not going to be good when we do find out."

"Do you want me to keep looking through the data?"

Ben nodded. "And I need to make another phone call."

9

Chianti, Italy

CELESTE AND JESS walked along a gravel path through the gardens outside the west walls of the castle, underneath huge oak trees, with a view down the mountain to the twinkling lights of the village far below.

"You look nice," Jess said, admiring her mother's calf-length black dress and heels with envy. Rarely, if ever, would Jess wear anything but jeans in casual company, and she always wore flats or sneakers. High heels didn't work well with a prosthetic foot. In sports, she'd wear shorts or Spandex pants, but only when she was mostly alone. She wouldn't admit it, but it was probably the reason she enjoyed hiding on cliff faces and mountaintops.

"Thank you." Celeste looked at her daughter. "And you're stunning, Jessica." She smiled. "You seemed to have a nice time with Giovanni and Hector this afternoon."

"He's a nice kid."

Giovanni had invited them to dinner in the main dining room of the castle. Stopping in front of a huge open doorway at the corner of the interior walls, Jess asked her mother, "Is this the dining room?"

They were given directions, but the room seemed empty. Pushing the door open, she peered inside. No, not empty. In the far corner people sat at a table, light spilling onto them from an open kitchen where she saw a chef in a white hat. Giovanni saw her and waved them over.

Jess turned to Celeste and shrugged. "I guess it's just us for dinner." She opened the door and walked in—a huge room, with at least forty tables all set in white linen and shining tableware. Twenty-foot high arched windows lined the walls, with even higher cathedral ceilings. Lit tea candles burned in the centers of all the empty tables.

"Sorry," apologized Giovanni as they approached, standing to greet them. "This dining hall was built in a different era. We still use it to host weddings from time to time. I wanted it to feel, well, lived in." He hung back, seeming awkward, but stepped forward to kiss Celeste on both cheeks.

He turned to Jess, leaned in, and she felt his warmth and the stubble of his cheeks on hers as he kissed both sides. "The hall is beautiful," she said. "And please, stop apologizing."

At the table, Nico and Hector both stood. Nico kissed Celeste and Jess on both cheeks, while Hector stood at attention.

"Good evening, Madame Tosetti," Hector said when they all looked at him. "And Mistress Jessica, you look lovely."

Jess rolled her eyes and looked at Giovanni. "You taught him that."

Giovanni shrugged and smiled. They all laughed politely.

"Please, sit." Giovanni pulled back a chair for Jess, while Nico did the same for Celeste. "I hope you don't mind, but I took the liberty of ordering a set course from the chef. I hope there are no vegetarians?"

Celeste and Jess shook their heads.

"Good."

A waiter swooped in and arranged napkins in their laps. Another appeared with a heaping plate of antipasto to place in the middle of the table, poured glasses of wine for everyone, then described the elements of the antipasto plate.

"So are those all pictures of you, Giovanni? All the mountaintops?" Celeste asked after the waiter finished his explanations.

"Yes, those are of me," Giovanni admitted, almost sheepishly. "My father put them up all around the house. The family wealth afforded me a certain"—he paused to carefully choose his words—"lifestyle. I have been on many expeditions. Of course in the Alps, but also the Himalaya."

"Jess is an outdoor nut as well." Celeste grinned at Giovanni and then Jess while picking up her glass of wine.

"Your father?" Jess asked, ignoring her mother. "So there are two

Barons? You're very young to be a Baron, aren't you?" In the afternoon, she hadn't pushed Nico, sensing his discomfort, but she was curious. "Sorry, I'm not familiar with royalty conventions."

Giovanni smiled sadly. "My father died recently, after a protracted illness. My mother, she died when I was young."

Jess's smile slid from her face. "I'm sorry. My condolences."

"Thank you." Giovanni took a sip from his wine. "I was on an expedition in Antarctica. It took me a long time to return," Giovanni added. "Nico was here, however, caring for him." He smiled at Nico, who nodded and smiled a tight-lipped smile in return.

"And what about little Hector?" Jess asked, looking at her mother, then at Giovanni. "Does Mrs. Ruspoli take care of him while you're away? He calls you 'Zio'...is that short for Giovanni?"

Giovanni put down his glass of wine before laughing. "No, *zio* is 'uncle' in Italian. He is only visiting. I'm not married."

Jess had to purposely avoid her mother's eyes at that revelation.

"Little Hector's mother and father are on holiday in Zambia, on safari," Giovanni continued. "Hector is staying with me for two weeks, a small adventure for the both of us." He paused to smile at Jess. "Family is the most important thing in life, no?"

"I guess." Jess picked a piece of bread and tore it in half.

"No, you don't think so?"

"I don't want a family, not of my own, if that's what you mean." Jess stuffed the bread into her mouth. "I think what's important in life is to be free, be independent, to explore." She swallowed the bread. "Like you. If I had your money, I'd do what you're doing."

Everyone at the table stared at her, and Jess felt her cheeks burn. "I mean, I love my mom and dad." She glanced at Celeste, only now realizing that she'd been speaking with her mouth full. "But most people I know, they're in a relationship because they can't stand being alone. It's a form of co-dependency. I want to be an individual, not half of some compromise."

In past relationships, Jess had tried to be the doting girlfriend, had tried to put on the mantle of the wife role. But she couldn't stand waiting on someone else, waiting for them to come home. She had no idea how someone could love a person like that. How someone could love *her* like that.

"I have to disagree," Giovanni countered gently. "I don't think a person can become a true individual being alone. We only become unique and authentic by entering a community of two, by sharing our lives. Community, family, that is what is important."

"If family is so important, why were you off trekking Antarctica while your dad was sick?" Jess shot back before she could stop herself. She didn't like the feeling of being lectured.

"Jessica!" her mother exclaimed.

It took Jess a moment to regain her temper. "I didn't mean—"

"No, no, it's a fair question." Giovanni took a deep breath. "Family is everything, but sometimes, family can be… complicated."

"I'm sure there was nothing you could have done." Jess tried to backtrack.

Giovanni forced a smile. "But, what a terrible host I am. Let's change topics. Your father?" He looked at Celeste. "Is there a Mr. Tosetti?"

"Tosetti was my maiden name," Celeste replied. "We're separated."

"But not divorced," Jess added, looking at her mother and raising her eyebrows. "He's an astronomer, works at Harvard."

"An astronomer?" Giovanni's eyes lit up. He looked at Jess. "Then there is something very special I would like to show you. After dinner perhaps?"

Jess hadn't meant to be so sharp-tongued. A bad habit, but mentioning her father's profession had a calming effect. "Yes; I'd like that."

The rest of dinner went smoothly. Giovanni was the perfect host, and the food and wine were spectacular. Afterward, Nico offered to take Celeste for a walk through the gardens, while a nanny ushered Hector off to bed just before the final round of *grappa* was served. Which left Giovanni and Jess alone.

"It's amazing."

Jess stood on a stepladder, admiring the mirror of a large reflecting telescope in the castle's observatory. It was similar in design to the one her father had taught her to use, back at their cottage in the Catskills. Jess had seen the dome-shaped roof on one of the castle turrets, but she hadn't thought anything of it. Giovanni had just clicked on a set of motors that winched back the covering, revealing a beautiful Tuscan night sky; a carpet of stars thrown across the inky blackness above.

"It's, what, a meter across?"

"One point one," Giovanni said. "My grandfather's hobby, his passion, was astronomy. In the tradition of Galileo, yes? He lived not far from here."

"Amazing, and it's in such excellent condition." She stepped down. "Can I give it a try?"

"Of course, be my guest," Giovanni said, inviting her to the controls.

Jess did a quick calculation in her head. Early October. That meant Venus should be near Pisces. Looking up, she started by finding the Great Square, just like her father taught her as a child. There, in the south, four bright stars glittered. Three of them formed the edge of Pegasus, and she traced the outline in her mind. Just beside it was Pisces, and Venus should be just at its left tip at this time of year. Unscrewing the stops on the telescope's gimbals, she swung it around, first eyeballing the approximate direction, and then looking into the viewfinder.

She found the tail of Pisces, and after slowly adjusting she found the bright yellow dot of Venus. Carefully, she focused. "Beautiful," she whispered. Leaning away from the telescope, she turned to Giovanni.

"Yes, beautiful," he said softly, but he was watching her, not the night sky. She felt him reach to hold her hand, and he leaned in to kiss her.

Jess recoiled. "Whoa, hold on. I said we could be *friends*."

Giovanni let go of her, backed up two steps. His face fell. "*Scusi*, I didn't mean to—"

"And, I told you to *stop* apologizing."

They stared at each other. The stars glittered above.

She sighed. "If you're going to do something, just do it."

He stood back, the look on his face perplexed. A warm Tuscan breeze blew between them, and Jess felt the walls inside her crumble. Just a little. She took a step toward him.

The door to the observatory swung open and bright light spilled in from the stairwell. Enzo's head appeared through the crack in the door, his brown pork-pie hat casting a saucer-like shadow across the stone floor. For a second, Jess could have sworn she saw a flash of something in his eyes.

Giovanni frowned at Enzo. "*Che cos'è?*"

"Many apologies." Enzo grimaced. "But there's a phone call for Ms. Jessica."

"Who is it?" Jess asked.

"*Te padre*, your father."

"My dad?"

Enzo nodded, offering a phone. "*Sì*, Dr. Ben Rollins. This is your father, yes?"

Jess stepped across the platform and took the phone. It was a strange time to return her call. "Dad, what's up? Are you okay?" She listened for a few seconds. "What? You want me to do what? Wait, slow down. You're still at the Astronomical Union meeting, right?"

"Is everything all right?" Giovanni asked.

Jess listened to her father for thirty seconds, holding her hand up at Giovanni and Enzo. Then, setting down the receiver, she looked at both of them. "I'm sorry, but I've got to go." She pushed past Enzo and hopped down the stairs as quickly as she could.

SURVIVOR TESTIMONY

#GR14;

Event +62hrs;
Name: Aubrey Leaming;
Reported location: England, undetermined

My name's Leaming, engineer onboard the RNLB Jolly Roger out of Gravesend station, just south of London. Suppose I'm captain now. We lost Valentine, first mate Ballie Booker too. Horrible. Did save eight civvies, got 'em secured down in the survivor room, for what that's worth.

When they ordered the evacuation of the city, we knew it was madness, but then the whole thing was madness, wasn't it? Where d'they expect people go? So me and the boys decided to hoof it into Tower station, see if we could pick up a few. I mean, we had the Jolly Roger, the steel-carbon Severn-class lifeboat of the RNLI, bastard can take anything...anyway, we race up the Thames as it empties out. Twenty feet of water gone in an hour. We make it as far as Canary Wharf before our keel hits mud.

We know it's coming, but people are standing there on the walls, just staring. Captain Valentine, God bless him, gets up there, convinces a few to trudge through the muck and we secure them, like I said. But then...we thought it was a cloud, mate. It was Ballie who realized what it was. A wave, man, maybe a thousand foot high. Ballie screamed at me to get inside, strap in while he battened down the hatches. The first sheet of water hit us like we'd been fired out of a cannon, cracked the superstructure and half the starboard windows on impact, but she held, our Jolly Roger, she did. Old Ballie never strapped in...we were tossed around like a cork in a blender, puke and blood everywhere. For best part of an hour we were submerged before popping to the surface and the Roger righted itself. Unbelievable, mate, absolute madness.

I was the only one still conscious, so I set the bilge pumps and went to check our position, radio for help. But the electronics was down, the VHF antennae sheared off. Just this shortwave, and thank God for that. So I went topside, took the sextant and charts. Didn't know what to expect, but certainly not bloody blue skies. As if nothing had happened. Like we'd been transported into another world. I got latitude of 52.4 degrees north. Can't measure longitude in daylight, but we started in London and were swept along, and that wave came from the south, near enough. So I was over Leicester. Or Birmingham. But nothing, just churning blue. No land visible at all and I was supposed to be in the middle of bloody England…

Transmission ended signoff. Freq. 2182 kHz/USB.

Subject reacquired pgs 16,24.

DAY THREE

October 8th

10

Chianti, Italy

JESS FOUND HER mother waiting for her at one of the stone tables in the garden outside the western wall of the castle. A cloudless, aquamarine sky hung over spectacular views down the valley and into the plains sloping to the Mediterranean. On this side of the walls stretched manicured lawns crisscrossed by gravel paths and trimmed hedges, shaded by huge, ancient oaks. Hector was playing soccer next to the reception building with Raffael and Lucca, teenage brothers who performed odd jobs around the castle. Enzo was playing with them as well.

"Someone slept in," Celeste said in a singsong voice as Jess approached, the leftovers of a breakfast of cheese and cured meats spread on a plate before her. "Want some?" Celeste asked, holding up a cup and carafe of coffee.

Nodding, Jess slid onto the stone bench opposite her mother. She hadn't slept in. She hadn't even slept. All night she'd been on the phone with her father, going over the information he had. About Nomad. About the unknown anomaly approaching. This morning she'd hidden in her room, needing to be alone, needing to think.

"Did you have a nice evening with Giovanni?" Celeste asked, filling the coffee cup and handing it to Jess. "You seemed to hit it off. I saw the two of you up in the observatory when I was walking down here with Nico."

Taking the coffee, Jess took a sip. She stared down the valley, at the village of Saline far below, at the networks of roads and towns in the plains beyond that. Soon, in a matter of months, all of this could be gone. Just like that, as if it had never been here. Nothing seemed real, as if a plastic sheet had been pulled over reality, insulating her from it.

"This place is magical," Celeste said, following Jess's eyes looking down the valley. She reached across the table to hold Jess's hand. "You were right to drag me out here. It does feel like home. And what a silver lining!" She laughed. "The police, your fight with your ex…if it hadn't happened, Giovanni wouldn't have invited us to be his guests. He came by this morning, said we should stay the week, invited us to go horseback riding through the vineyards. We can stop for lunch down—"

"We have to go," Jess said in a dead voice, still staring down the valley at the village. She hadn't seen her mother this happy in years, and it broke her heart to ruin it. But she had to. And, in a funny way, she might get what she wanted: get her mother and father together.

"What?" Celeste squeezed Jess's hand. "Don't be silly. And can you imagine? Giovanni's grandfather was an astronomer, just like your dad—"

Jess pulled away from staring at the village and put her coffee down, turning to look her mother in the eye. How could she even start to explain this? "We—have—to—*go*," she repeated.

The carefree smile on Celeste's face slid away into concern, her brows furrowing together. "What happened? Something with Giovanni?"

"No." Jess shook her head. "He was lovely, a perfect gentleman."

"Then what? Jess, you can't always be running—"

"I talked to dad last night. He's in Rome."

"In Rome?" The furrow between Celeste's eyes deepened, and she leaned toward Jess. "Why is he in Rome?"

"He's at the Astronomical Union meeting."

"The Astronomical Union…" Celeste whispered. Her frown dissipated, and she cocked her head to one side and grinned. "What are you up to, missy?"

Jess pressed her lips together. "Look, I wasn't being entirely honest. I wanted some one-on-one time with you, but when you got that Facebook message from the long lost Italian relative—"

"Who we haven't heard from since," Celeste reminded her.

"I know, look, it seemed like a perfect opportunity to get you and dad back together, you know, here in Italy, where you spent your honeymoon. I thought, I don't know, maybe…"

The edges of Celeste's smile trembled, her eyes tearing as she stared at her daughter. "Oh, baby, that's what all this was about?"

"It was, but something's happened."

Celeste dropped her gaze, laughing. "Something is always just happening with you, isn't it?"

"This is serious."

"Is it something else to do with Ricardo? I'm sure that Giovanni could help—"

"Mom! STOP!"

Celeste blinked twice, letting go of Jess's hand. "What?"

Jess took a deep breath. "Dad's at this meeting, and they discovered something coming from deep space. It's heading toward the Earth. He needs us to leave with him, get back to the States and go to the cabin in the Catskills—"

"From space?" Celeste shook her head, and then pursed her lips. "The cabin, but I thought he sold that years ago?"

"So did I."

"What's coming from space?"

"They don't know, but it's not good."

Jess knew her mother, knew she wasn't one to panic. She didn't have to sugarcoat. Her mother had spent most of her life in the field as a geologist, exploring remote backcountry. Leaning across the table, Jess explained what her father told her the night before, and the look of disbelief on her mother's face slowly turned to one of shock.

"Are they *sure*?" Celeste asked as Jess finished. "Shouldn't we tell people?"

"Dad said not to, that they don't know all the details yet." As she said this, a soccer ball bounced off her right leg. Hector came running over, and Jess leaned down to retrieve the ball and give it to him.

"*Prego*, Miss Jessica," Hector said as he took the ball, smiling at her before turning to run back to Raffael and Lucca and Enzo.

"Nobody?" Celeste stared at Jess, then looked in the direction of Hector.

Jess followed her eyes. "You're right." Enzo caught her eye and waved. She smiled, tight lipped, and waved back. Something about that guy was creepy. Nico was just coming out of the reception building behind them, leading another tour group. He waved, and she waved back.

"Nico," Jess called out. "Do you know where Baron Ruspoli is?"

"Just out for five minutes," Nico replied. "Down to the town."

"Can you get him to meet me up in the observatory when he gets back?"

The view from the observatory tower was even more amazing during the day than it had been at night. Jess had an unobstructed 360-degree view of the surrounding countryside. Giovanni had left a note under her door in the morning, giving her access. She'd just finished rolling back the observatory's roof covering when she heard footsteps coming up the stairs.

"Jessica?" echoed Giovanni's voice through the half-open doorway. "Jess?" He appeared and stood on the landing, concern worrying his eyes. "Enzo said you wanted to see me? Are you all right? Is your father good?"

"He's fine. Everyone's fine." At least for now. She let out a long sigh and looked at the plains again, imagining them flooding, the oceans rushing over them.

"Are…we okay?" Giovanni asked. He took a tentative step forward. "I told your mother we could go horseback riding."

Men. Jess shook her head. They always think that it's something they did, that it's something to do with them. And then they try and fix it without even understanding. This wasn't something someone could fix. Nobody could fix this. She looked toward the horizon.

Giovanni took another step toward her. "What's wrong? What happened?"

How could she bring this up without sounding ridiculous? "My father, he's an astronomer."

"Yes?"

"They found something, in space, that's heading toward the

Earth."

"What?" Giovanni took a second to process. "An asteroid? Is there danger?"

"Not an asteroid, something else. They don't know what yet." Jess looked away, up at the sky. Not a cloud. Perfect. "Nowhere will be safe."

"Do they think it might hit us?"

"I doubt it. At least, that would be one in a million, whatever it is."

"Then there's really little danger?" He cocked his head to one side.

"You don't understand." Squinting, she shielded her eyes and looked at the sun. "This thing has fifty, maybe a hundred times the mass of our Sun, and is coming from right behind it. It seems to be heading straight into the solar system."

"A hundred times the size of…" Giovanni's jaw dropped open. "Will it destroy the sun?"

"A hundred times the mass, not the size. Nomad is probably very compact, not more than thirty kilometers across if it's compressed matter, but it's traveling at more than a thousand kilometers a second. Even if it hits the sun, it'll be like a bullet going through a ball of foam. It wouldn't damage it, not much, but its gravity will drag the sun away from us, eject all of the planets into deep space. Including Earth."

"My God." Giovanni sat down on a bench beside the telescope. "I didn't hear anything on the news, the radio…"

"Nobody knows yet. And I wasn't supposed to tell you."

Giovanni stared at her. A gust of wind blew through the treetops, washing over the observatory turret. Jess shivered.

"So, this is true?" he asked finally. "This is not some game…?"

"No game." Jess shook her head. "I'd stay away from the big cities, move everything you can here. Get all your family and loved ones together."

"Can't they stop this thing? I don't know, fire nuclear weapons at it? Push it away?"

"It'd be like a mote of dust in the path of a charging elephant."

Giovanni rocked back and forth. "I see."

"My dad says he has evidence of seeing this thing, decades ago."

"So they can see it?" Giovanni stopped rocking and steepled his hands together, elbows on his knees, and rested his chin on them. "What is it?"

"That's the thing." Jess pursed her lips. "They can't see anything there. So far they haven't been able to detect anything directly, but something of this mass, coming undetected, there're only a few options—or its some strange form of dark matter, something we don't understand. It seems like it appeared from nowhere."

"Dark matter?"

"Ninety percent of the universe's matter is invisible, what they call dark matter."

"How do they know it's there if they can't see it?"

"Same way they know this thing is there. Gravitational influence. Like an invisible bowling ball thrown onto the plastic sheet of space-time." Jess dragged a hand through her hair.

"I see."

But Jess could see he didn't, and that he didn't entirely believe her. Not everyone had a father who was an astrophysicist. "I'm sorry, but I don't have time to give a physics lesson right now. I need to get to the airport. All I can tell you is—this thing is coming. Trust me."

Giovanni stared at Jess. She saw something behind his eyes. Distrust? A calculation? Something hidden. Something he wasn't telling her, but she didn't have the patience. Or the time.

"And how long do we have?" he asked finally.

"If it's heading into the solar system, which we don't know for certain yet"—she wagged one finger back and forth to make the point—"it will be a few months. My dad said they'll make an announcement in three days when they know. Celeste and I are going to meet him at a hotel next to the airport this afternoon, to take a flight back to the States tomorrow."

Giovanni rolled forward onto his feet. "I will have Nico drive you—"

Jess opened her mouth to object, but Giovanni held up one hand. "—I insist. And please, stay in touch with an email or text. Update me if you hear anything more."

"Of course." She stared at Giovanni, then looked away, her

shoulders slumping. "I need to go."

"Of course."

Jess smiled weakly and turned for the staircase. Getting to the top of it, she found Enzo staring up at her, his pork pie hat cocked back at an angle.

"Your mother wants to see you," Enzo said, hovering.

This guy *really* creeped her out. "Thank you." She jumped down the stairs, pushing past him. At least it would be the last time she'd have to see him.

SURVIVOR TESTIMONY
#GR4;

Event +47hrs;
Survivor name: Daly James;
Reported location: Alice Springs, Australia

What the hell happened, mate? Christ, you're the first person I've spoken to in weeks.

Okay, okay, I'll start. I was on my walkabout, mate, spring every year I piss off into the outback. A month by myself, you know, keeps the head straight. Anyway, two weeks out of Alice Springs and I'm taking a nap when a stampede of wallabies going like batshit tears into my tent. Never seen anything like it. Maybe ten in the morning, and when I've finished yelling at the bastards I look up. Blue skies, but these snakes of white light are coiling around the sun, all around it. Had to rub my eyes, thought I was losing it, too much grog the night before, yeah? I decide that's enough and pack up, start heading back.

About mid-afternoon, these rivers of light in the sky are almost touching the ground, the fear of God rising up in me, and it shakes. The ground I mean. Knocked me clear off my feet, had to be ten minutes before I could stand, it shook that long. When it stopped, I damn near started running. But big cracks opened in the ground, everywhere, like chopped up with a mountain-sized meat cleaver, the ground shaking again. So I got back into Alice Springs, and the place is a ghost town. Nobody here. And the skies, they're getting dark. Not clouds, mind you, but just dark, like God pulling the shades. Temperature's dropped twenty degrees in a day. Found this shortwave in the postal station, so I turned it on, and there you are, mate. Now can you tell me what the hell is going on? *(laughs nervously)* Is this it, mate? Armageddon? Where is everyone? What happened?

pgs 112-114 for complete transcript. Freq. 7652 kHz./LSB/USB

DAY FOUR

October 9th

11

Fiumicino Airport, Italy

"THEY ANNOUNCED THE boarding gate," Celeste said to Jess, nudging her shoulder.

Jess nodded and looked up at the departures board: *New York 10:00 AA1465 - Go to Gate C23*. She looked back at her phone.

The man sitting beside them looked up at the board as well, then folded his newspaper and stood, smiling at Celeste and Jess. He walked off. A young woman in heels and a short skirt immediately took his place. The food court waiting area of the International Terminal of Fiumicino Airport was packed with people buzzing around. In front of them was an empty Gucci store, its sales staff standing at attention next to the entrance. The recycled air smelled of carpets and coffee, the same as airport terminals the world over.

Celeste put her latte down and unzipped her suitcase. "Call him again." She stuffed her Economist magazine into her carry-on.

"I just did, he's not answering." Jess dialed her father's number again anyway. She'd arrived with Celeste at the airport the evening before and stayed at the Hilton next door. One ring, then two. It went to voice mail. She jerked the phone away from her ear, hung up and threw it into her purse.

Jess's father, Ben, was supposed to meet them at the Hilton last night, but he called to say he would arrive in the morning. Then he sent a text and email saying he'd meet them in the International Terminal food court. Now he wasn't answering his calls or messages.

"Maybe he's at the gate," Celeste suggested, standing to knock the crumbs of her croissant breakfast off her blouse and jeans.

A man pushing a baby stroller eyed Jess and Celeste. He wanted their seats. Jess shrugged aggressively at him, *what?*

Celeste saw it and smiled at the man. "Yes, we're leaving." She turned to her daughter. "Come on, let's go."

Shaking her head, Jess stood and grabbed her carry-on. "Fine."

She ran a hand through her hair and rubbed the back of her neck. She'd left most of her things at a friend's house in Rome, said she would call when she knew where she was headed. This didn't surprise anyone. After nearly a year in Italy, all she was leaving with was this one small carry-on. And that didn't surprise her, either.

"*Grazie, grazie,*" said the man with the stroller, angling in behind them to get the seats.

Celeste pointed down a hallway to their right, past the Gucci store, to the "C" concourse. "This way."

Jess's phone buzzed in her hand. She looked at it right away, thinking it was her father, but it was a message from Giovanni: "If you stay in Italy for any reason, feel free to come back." Even in her deepening frustration, she managed a small grin.

"I'm sure Ben's on his way," Celeste said as they walked down the concourse, passing gate C1. "Your father and I may have—"

Jess's phone rang. She checked the screen. "It's him." She pushed the *answer* button. "Dad, where are you?"

Ben Rollins cringed. He knew his daughter wasn't going to like this. "I'm on the next flight, right behind you. I'm sorry honey, but normalizing the data is taking longer than we thought. We need certainty before we make an announcement."

He put one hand over the receiver. "How much time, Roger? What do you think, another hour?"

Sitting in the growing nest of papers on Ben's hotel bed, Roger nodded. "Maybe two, tops. You can be out of here by noon."

Ben took his hand off the receiver. "Sweetheart, I'm leaving in an hour, two maximum.

"But you said that last night," Jess complained on the other end.

"I know I did, but I promise. I'll be right behind you." He pulled up a list of flights on his laptop screen. "There's a direct flight on United at 3 p.m. I can catch. I'm booking it now."

No response.

"Jessica, honey, please, promise me you're getting on that plane."

"Okay," came the quiet reply.

"Good. Listen, if I want to finish this, I need to go. Love you, and give your mother a kiss for me."

Another pause. "Love you, too."

Ben took a deep breath and hung up.

"By the way, your boxes arrived." Roger pointed in the corner of the room. "Just got here."

Ben looked at them. Mrs. Brown might be an old horse, but she was reliable. "Roger, we need to get this done—"

The door to his room opened. He hadn't given anyone else a key. "We don't need any room service…"

But it wasn't a maid. It was one of the sunglass-wearing security goons from the top floor. "Dr. Ben Rollins, I need you to come with me."

"What?" Ben slapped his laptop closed. "I'm not going anywhere, I need to finish—"

"This is not a request," the big man said in a flat voice, his accent vaguely Swiss. Another man appeared behind him.

Jess stared at the phone in her hand. She hadn't put up much of a fight, but then there was no winning an argument with her father. Not when he set his mind to something.

"What did he say?" Celeste asked.

They'd arrived at C23, and the waiting area was jammed. An American Airlines Boeing 777 sat hunched on the tarmac in front of the gate.

"He's not coming."

"At all?" Celeste frowned.

"On the next flight," Jess corrected. "He said he'd be on the

United flight at 3 p.m." She put her phone back in her pocket and looked up at the ceiling. Black signs with orange letters indicated directions, "*Trasiti* - Transfers," said one, and next to it, "*Uscita* - Way Out - *Roma*." She stared at the sign. *Roma*. Rome. Way out.

A three-chime tone played over the public address system. "American Airlines flight 1465 now pre-boarding," announced the flight steward at the check-in desk. "Families and anyone needing assistance can now—"

"That gives us a little more girl time, no?" Celeste said with a smile. "Come on, we can watch a romantic movie, have a few glasses of wine. It'll be fun."

"Yeah, sure."

Jess closed her eyes. She opened them to see a young family pressing through the crowd, the mother and father loaded down with bags; the father held his little girl's hand, the mother held her tiny son in one arm. The two children batted at each other, the girl smacking the little boy with an inflatable dolphin. The boy erupted into tears.

"Susanna," scolded the mother, "if you can't play nice, there's going to be quiet time."

Jess watched them disappear past the check-in and down the gangway. Again the image of two children playing in a field of snow flitted through her mind. The tears seemed to come by themselves, running down Jess's face. She gritted her teeth, tried to hold it back, but she couldn't. She sobbed, bending over, stepping to the row of seats behind her and sitting. People around her backed away.

"Baby, what's wrong?" Celeste knelt beside her. "Are you hurt?"

"It's my fault," Jess gasped between sobs. "Everything is my fault."

"What's your fault? Do you mean what happened with Ricardo?"

"No." Jess clenched her jaw. Tears streamed down her cheeks. "You and Dad splitting up, all of it."

"Oh, sweetheart, come here." Celeste put an arm around her daughter. "You were a child, it's not your fault. It was an accident. You can't blame yourself."

Jess nodded, but she knew it wasn't true. She'd never been honest, had never been able to admit what she did, even to herself, certainly not to her mother and father. Closing her eyes, the image of the small boy's face disappearing into the black hole, ringed in brilliant white, floated into her mind. She opened her eyes. "I want us to be a family again."

The three-chime tone played again. "Now boarding all rows," said the airline steward over the public address.

"Baby, it's okay. We *are* a family. There's a reason your father and I never divorced. We just needed space."

"He's not coming." Jess breathed deep and regained control of herself. "You know how he is. When he gets a thing stuck in his head."

"He'll come," Celeste insisted, but then hung her head and nodded. "But maybe you're right. Why don't we go and get him, then? You just talked to him. He's at the hotel, right?"

Jess nodded.

"An hour in a taxi and we'll be back in Rome. Then we can all go together at 3 p.m. Is that what you want? You decide."

Wiping her tears away, Jess nodded. "Yeah, I'd like that."

Celeste stood. "I'll cancel our reservation." She pointed at the check-in desk, an attendant standing and talking to passengers. "We have no checked luggage. I can just cancel this flight, and we'll go meet your father."

Taking a deep breath, Jess pushed her long blond hair back from her eyes. She felt ridiculous. With the back of one hand she dried her cheeks. "Yes, let's cancel it."

Nodding, Celeste strode off purposefully toward the check-in desk. Jess rubbed the tears from her eyes. In what seemed a minute later her mother returned. "Done. Why don't you give Ben a call, tell him we're coming?"

The crowd of people around them faced toward the gate, waiting to board, but some of the people had turned. The noise in the concourse hushed, then people started talking loudly, a wave of noise rising up from the lower gates. More people in front of Jess turned around. She had her phone out, was about to dial her father, when she looked up to see what was going on.

People pointed at the television monitors lining the center of the concourse. Standing, Jess turned to see what was going on. In bold letters on the screen behind: "Massive Object on Collision Course for Earth." A BBC news anchor filled half of the screen above the headline. The people crowded around Jess shushed each other to be quiet.

"We are joined now by the head of the Swiss Astronomical Society," the anchor said. "Dr. Menzinger, what can you tell us?"

In the other half of the split screen, a diminutive man, balding with wire frame glasses, chewed on his lip. "Exactly what I've already said. A massive object, many times the size of our sun, is heading directly into the solar system. The government has been hiding it."

"The government?" asked the news anchor. "Which government?"

"Any of them," Dr. Menzinger replied, still mashing his lip. "All of them."

"This is an incredible claim. Can you back it up?"

Dr. Menzinger laughed. "Go and look yourself. Any amateur can point their telescope into the skies tonight and look at the position of Uranus or Neptune. Are they where they're supposed to be? The gravity of this object—they're calling it Nomad—is already pulling the planets away."

A third box opened on the screen with a blond-haired, tanned man in his mid-thirties. The news anchor introduced him: "This is Professor Hallaway with the Siding Spring Observatory in Australia."

People around Jess had their phones out. They tapped on their screens. Dozens of conversations erupted, breaking the near silence that had descended on the concourse moments before.

"G'day," said the blond man on the TV screen, nodding.

The news anchor nodded in greeting. "Professor Hallaway, can you confirm what Dr. Menzinger is saying?"

The blond Professor Hallaway took a deep breath before responding: "I can't confirm what he's saying, but we are seeing a disturbance in the orbit of Uranus. Something is happening."

"You see!" Dr. Menzinger shouted on-screen. His video box was grainy, and faded out and then back in. "You don't need to trust me, go and look for yourselves."

The anchor turned his attention back to Dr. Menzinger. "So what are you saying?"

"I'm saying that the planet Earth has, at most, months before utter destruction."

Around Jess, shouting started, people yelling into their phones to be heard above the rising background noise.

"Call Ben."

"What?" Jess pulled her eyes from Dr. Menzinger ranting about black holes and Roche limits tearing the planet to shreds.

"Call your father," Celeste repeated.

Jess's phone was in her hand, her father's number on it. She'd been distracted in the middle of calling him. She pushed the *call* button and held it to her ear. Busy signal. She tried again. Busy signal. She looked around at the people around her, all of them on their phones.

"The cell networks are jammed," Jess whispered in horror.

People mobbed the airline desks. There was no way they'd get seats on the 3 p.m. flight. She doubted they'd be getting on *any* flight.

Not anymore.

12

Rome, Italy

"WHAT DO YOU mean, he's not registered here?" Jess demanded.

The little man behind the huge marble reception desk checked his computer again. His pencil-thin mustache twitched, and he smoothed his slick hair back with one hand before looking up. "We have no record of a Ben Rollins staying at the hotel."

Jess clenched her fists. "But I met him here, four days ago. Check again. Doctor *Ben-Ja-Min"*—she enunciated each syllable of his full name—"Rollins." She pointed at workers disassembling a booth on the other side of the lobby, an *International Astronomical Union* poster on the wall behind it. "He was here for the meeting."

Stray bits of papers and packaging littered the deep carpeting of the Grand Hotel's lobby. Men carrying crates flowed in a steady stream out a service entrance to one side, sky-blue frescoes of angels hanging above.

"I'm very sorry, *signora*, but we have no record of a Dr. Benjamin Rollins staying with us."

Jess leaned over the desk to try and look at his computer screen. "Do you even know how to use that goddamn—"

"Sorry, it's been a long day," Celeste apologized. She hauled Jess back.

It had taken three hours to get from the airport into Rome, normally less than an hour's trip. Chaos erupted after the news reports, and they waited in the taxi line for two hours. They tried calling and texting Ben on the way, leaving messages for him. Sometimes a call managed to go through on the mobile network, but so far, no return messages. Not since Jess had talked to her father in the airport.

Jess's phone buzzed. Her heart skipped a beat, hoping it was her father, but it wasn't. Still, she smiled. Giovanni texted her: *You still here? Saw the story on the news.* She texted back: *Yes, in Rome now.*

"Do you have a room available for the evening?" Celeste asked.

The mustache quivered again as the little man winced. "Very sorry, but we are fully booked."

"Is there somewhere nearby you could recommend"—Celeste inspected the brass nameplate pinned to his suit—"Vittorio?"

Vittorio's lips mashed together as if he tasted something sour. He pulled a sheet of paper out from behind the counter. "These hotels are close, but I'm afraid they are *all*"—he paused to add weight to the word—"full, *penso.*" He nodded in the direction of the doors. People filled the streets outside. "Many people are coming."

"My friend Angela lives a few blocks away," Jess said to her mother. At least she had made *one* friend in her months here. Grunting, she exhaled to let her frustration out. "Did Dad go to the airport?" she muttered under her breath, glancing at her phone's screen. Almost one o'clock. Maybe her father left to make the 3 p.m. flight?

"He'll see we aren't there." Celeste leaned on the reception desk and turned to face Jess. "Don't worry. We'll find him."

"Can I get the wifi code?" Jess asked Vittorio, flashing him her best smile. She needed to check her email.

"Yes." Vittorio's mustache quivered in a forced smile. He produced a slip of paper with the wifi code. "But it's very slow."

Jess took the paper. "Thank you." She opened her phone and texted a message to her friend Angela: *I'm back in Rome - can I stay at your place?* No way they were getting out of Rome again, not today. They might need a place for the night. If the text didn't work, she could try webmail to reach Angela, and see if her dad had emailed her, too.

"*Scusi*, did you say, Doctor *Rollins*?" asked a uniformed attendant behind Celeste. "You are looking for him?"

Celeste turned to him. "Yes, Dr. Rollins."

"I saw him, this morning. He left about ten o'clock, three hours ago."

"Are you sure?"

The attendant stepped back to open the door for two guests arriving from outside. "*Sì*," he said as the guests passed inside. "Dr. Rollins, the famous TV *persona*. Very nice man. He left this morning, with his friend, the one with the *occhiali*...the eye glasses."

"He must mean Roger," Celeste said to Jess. "His research assistant. Did you meet him?"

Jess nodded. She'd done more than meet him. "But why would he just leave without telling us?" She opened her laptop on the reception counter.

"Maybe he had no choice." The attendant took a step toward them and lowered his voice. "Dr. Rollins was, how do you say...*escorted* from the building by two large men. They left in black limousines, *molti*, all together."

"Why would you say he had no choice?" Celeste asked in a hushed voice.

The attendant looked left and right. "*Non lo so*. I just work."

"Thank you," Celeste whispered to the attendant. "Thank you, very much."

"*Prego*." The attendant smiled and stepped back to open the door for other guests.

"What, was he kidnapped?" Jess asked her mother.

Celeste looked as mystified as Jess felt. "I don't know."

The web took forever to load on Jess's laptop. Finally, her browser popped to life. *Cosmic Hoax?* read the top story on her MSN homepage. She scanned the list of articles headlining everything from apocalyptic disaster to conspiracy theories. One image popped out, of riot police lined up behind the flaming burnt out shell of a car: *Riots sparked in Los Angeles blamed on cover-up...*

"My God." Celeste held one hand to her mouth.

Jess glanced out the front doors of the hotel, at the crowds in the street outside. Her cell phone pinged. A message from Angela: *Sure, come over, but I leave in half an hour. Hurry.*

Jess checked her webmail. No messages. Her phone buzzed again. A text from Giovanni again: *Are you okay? Where are you staying?*

Smiling, Jess texted him back that they were fine, and included Angela's address—just in case her father managed to get in touch with

Giovanni. He knew they'd stayed at the castle.

"Come on, let's go." She flipped her laptop closed, stuffed it into her backpack and put it on. "Angela's home, it's a ten minute walk. Let's get somewhere safe."

"Great." Celeste grabbed the handle of her rolling carry-on and followed Jess to the entrance. The attendant opened the doors ahead of them, smiling and bowing. "Thank you again," said Celeste.

An assault of sirens and shouting greeted them outside, cars honking and people yelling. A crush of people walked the street, swamping cars that crept along between them. A policeman on a horse clip-clopped past. A dozen more police wearing white helmets and day-glow yellow vests amassed on the next corner. The Grand Hotel was on a side street next to the Tiber River in the heart of Rome, just a block from the *Via dell Conciliazione*, the wide boulevard that cut from the *Castel Sant'Angelo* all the way to St. Peter's Square at the basilica in the middle of the Vatican.

Celeste stopped and stared at the crowd, then up at dark clouds threatening rain overhead.

"Come on." Jess grabbed her hand. "We need to hurry. We'll cross the bridge over the Tiber. Angela's place is next to *Piazza Navona*. We need to hurry."

Jess followed the flow of the crowd, past the knot of nervous-looking police on the corner, onto the *Via dell Conciliazione.* Looking right, the dome of St. Peter's loomed over the masses. "Hold on a sec," she said to Celeste.

Next to the UniCredit Banca on the corner was a concrete pylon lamppost, and Jess pushed through the crowd, grabbed onto the ledge of the pylon and hoisted herself up. She looked down the boulevard. A sea of people flooded all the way along it, fed by tributaries of smaller alleyways, all ending in a jammed crowd of tens of thousands inside St. Peter's Square. Maybe even hundreds of thousands. She jumped down.

"The Pope announced a speech tomorrow," said an ancient woman sitting on a bench next to the lamppost. She wore a brown suit jacket with matching skirt and a wide-brimmed hat. A strand of fat pearls sat around her neck. "The Day of the Lord arrives, Judgment

Day, that's what they're saying."

"Is that right?"

The old lady worked her arthritic fingers together, purple veins showing through her papery skin. "Oh, no, this is all a game," she laughed. "War of the Worlds all over again, when Orson fooled us. He's at it again, the clever deceiver."

Someone crashed into Jess, almost knocking her over.

"Are you okay?" Celeste grabbed Jess's arm from behind her.

"Yeah, I'm fine." Jess regained her balance and looked back, but the old lady was gone. Disappeared. What was that about? She shook it off.

"Come on, this way." Jess grabbed Celeste's hand and pulled her against the flow of the crowd, back toward the center of Rome across the bridge, under Italian pine trees forming an archway of umbrellas against the dark skies.

On the other side of the Tiber River, the crowds thinned, and Jess led her mother through a maze of alleyways. She stopped halfway down an empty cobbled street, at a huge door, ten feet high in weathered wood. Jess inspected a row of brass buttons and pressed one. "This is it."

The door buzzed a second later, and Jess pushed against it, heaving it open. Celeste followed. Inside stretched a white marble hallway, dusty, half-illuminated by a flickering fluorescent tube twenty feet above. It ended in a set of stairs next to the tiny black metal cage of the elevator, a discarded baby stroller lying beside it. "Up the stairs, third floor," Jess said. "Don't bother with the elevator, the thing's a death trap."

They tramped up, the noise of their footfalls echoing off the walls. It felt abandoned, empty, a strange transition from the bursting crowds just blocks away. Two entrances led off each landing, the doors studded sheets of metal with three or four locks each. "An old building," Jess said. "They like to be safe."

On the third landing was an open door. Jess went straight in. "Angela, sorry about what happened with Ricardo," she said right away.

A thirty-something woman in shorts and tank top, with long blond dreadlocks, was stuffing a pile of clothes into a suitcase on a dining table. "Don't worry, he's an asshole." A news channel played silently on a TV in the corner.

"Mom, this is Angela, Ricardo's sister," Jess said as Celeste rounded the corner into the apartment.

Celeste took a sharp intake of breath and crinkled her nose. "Ah, I see. Um, pleased to meet you."

"Don't worry," Angela reassured her, "like I said, Ricky's an ass." She closed her suitcase and faced Jess. "So you want the keys? I'm going south to my family's place. Rome is going *pazzo*. Crazy." She looked at Celeste. "Maybe you should come? Into the countryside?"

Jess threw her backpack onto the couch. "Think Ricardo would like that?"

"Screw him. He'd handle it." Angela hoisted her suitcase off the table onto the floor. "You sure?"

"Yeah, I'm sure. I need to wait for my dad. He's in Rome somewhere."

Angela tossed Jess the keys. "Okay. You can have the place while I'm gone. But you'll be waiting a long time for your dad."

Jess caught the keys and narrowed her eyes, frowning. "What? Why?"

Angela strode toward the door and Celeste stood aside. "Because he's in Germany."

"Germany? What do you mean? Did he call you?" Jess didn't know her father even knew Ricardo, never mind his sister, but then her father was resourceful.

Stopping at the door, Angela shook her head and pointed behind Jess. "No, he didn't call me, but maybe you should call *him*."

Jess turned to see what Angela pointed at, and found herself staring at her father's face. On the TV. Below his face, in block red letters: *Dr. Ben Rollins, European Space Operations, Darmstadt. Germany.*

13

Darmstadt, Germany

BEN HATED HELICOPTERS. Coming in low and fast, they skimmed the treetops, the town of Darmstadt just visible in the distance. Darmstadt was famous for two things: the heavy element #110, Darmstadium, was named after it, and in 1912 chemists at Merck first synthesized the drug Ecstasy here. Actually, it was famous for three things, Ben thought as the pilot banked sharp right at almost ninety degrees, giving him a view straight down onto the glittering solar-paneled roof of ESOC—Darmstadt was also home to the European Space Operations Command.

The undulating carpet of green forest gave way to a compound of buildings bordered by a train yard on one side, and an intersection of the *autobahn* highways on the other. A huge white radar dish towered above the trees; a giant mushroom nestled above other smaller dishes and antennae. Snow-capped mountains shimmered on the horizon.

His lunch almost came back up as the helicopter executed another swinging turn to bring it to a stop, hovering in mid-air. Ben burped. Herded into a cavalcade of black limos outside the Grand Hotel in Rome, they had sped off to a small airstrip where they'd been whisked to Frankfurt airport on a ten-seater Learjet—the last few hours were a blur. This helicopter was the final leg of their sprint to Darmstadt, and Ben still had no idea why.

"You okay?" Roger asked as the helicopter sank below the tree line. "You don't look so good."

The landing skids settled onto the ground, shaking them, as the whine of the engine and rotors came down a notch. "I am now," Ben groaned.

Out the window he saw Dr. Müller waving at him with one hand while shielding his eyes from the rotor blast of leaves and dust with the other. He ran toward the helicopter, two guards in black fatigues trailing him. The copilot turned around to open Ben's door, the engine still whining, the rotors still spinning.

"Ben," Dr. Müller yelled over the noise, "glad you could make it." He extended his hand to shake.

Unstrapping his harness, Ben shouted back, "You didn't give me much choice." Ignoring Müller's offered hand, he jumped down onto the grass. Roger stepped out behind him, turning to collect their bags.

"Sorry for rushing you in like this, but we need your help," Dr. Müller explained, leading Ben away from the helicopter, pointing toward a set of blue glass doors in the side of the ESOC building.

The whine of the engines ratcheted back up several decibels. "With what?" Ben asked, leaning into Müller's ear.

Behind them the helicopter roared, and Ben glanced back to see it leap into the sky, kicking up a new cloud of dust and dirt. Loaded down with their bags, Roger followed. One of the guards in black ballistic vests opened the door ahead of them, and Müller let Ben enter first.

"With media," Dr. Müller said as they walked inside. "While you've been traveling, a lot has happened. This idiot Dr. Menzinger of the Swiss Institute has been on all the news networks ranting about Armageddon. Chaos erupted in some cities." He held out a hand and stopped Ben. "You're as close to a celebrity astronomer as we have."

Five years ago, Ben did a series of hugely popular PBS specials that were syndicated internationally. Off to one side of the entranceway, beside a set of escalators fronted by security guards and x-ray scanners, Ben saw a mob of cameras and microphones. "I'm not going to lie to them," he replied in a hushed voice.

"Not lie, of course not." Müller held him in place and leaned close. "But we don't know what's happening, do we? Just tell them that."

Ben grabbed Müller's arm and pulled him close. "But we might have known. Does this have anything to do with *that* research paper?" He didn't need to say which one.

Müller stared at Ben, his face blank. "We don't even know if *that* had anything to do with *this*. But it is one of the reasons I got you in early."

Ben looked at the reporters and cameramen. By the way they pointed and swiveled their cameras around, some of them already recognized him. "I'd prefer to stay off the record, if that's all right."

Müller looked Ben in the eye. "There are riots in LA and Sao Paulo. Don't lie, just tell a *calmer* version of the truth."

Roger dropped their bags onto the polished marble floor behind Müller and Ben. "Where to, boss?"

Ben looked at his watch. Jessica and Celeste should be landing at JFK in under two hours. Back in Rome, the security guards chaperoning Ben and Roger had taken away their laptops and cell phones, said that they'd get them back on the other end. "I want my cell phone back, and outside network access for emails. And Roger and I need a flight to JFK, tomorrow night at the latest. I need to get to my family."

"Done." Dr. Müller nodded. "Just talk to the media, and I'll have your cell phones returned and get you set up on the ESOC network. And I'll book you on flights to the US tomorrow, on the condition that we finish looking at all of your data before you leave."

Ben looked back at Roger, who shrugged. Ben didn't want to get involved like this, but then he needed to get to Celeste and Jessica. "Okay, but I'm not lying to anyone. I'm going to tell the truth."

"Good." Dr. Müller removed his hand from Ben. "A *calming truth*, yes?" Without waiting for a reply, he turned to the media. "Ladies and gentlemen, I am pleased to introduce Dr. Ben Rollins, a key part of our team and head of the Harvard-Smithsonian Center for Astrophysics."

Ben gritted his teeth. He wasn't head of the Center for Astrophysics, just the exoplanet department, but he let it slide and followed Dr. Müller toward the pack of media.

"Dr. Rollins," asked a woman at the front row, holding a microphone out. Her cameraman swung around to focus on Ben. "Is it true that a planet-swallowing black hole is heading for Earth?"

"We don't know what…" Ben started but then caught Dr. Müller frowning at him from the corner of his eye. Ben coughed. "Excuse me. No, we don't know that; in fact, so far we know very little…"

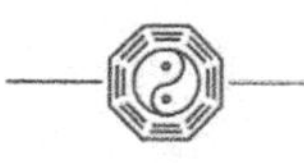

"That was a good show, Bernie." Roger smiled and nudged Ben in the ribs with his elbow. "You still got it, old man."

"Thanks." Ben rolled his eyes. They still didn't have their cell phones or laptops back. Security protocols, Müller had apologized, but they'd have them soon. Ben wasn't so sure.

Ben and Roger crowded onto a platform at the back of a voluminous room with six large screens hanging across the twenty-foot-high wall at the opposite end. Three semi-circular rows of workstations lined the lower level of the room, each piled with flat-screen displays and keyboards and telephones amid a tangle of wiring. The spaceflight operations command center smelled of coffee and sweat and crackled with hushed tension.

"We're on," said a woman in the front row of workstations. The wall-screens blinked to life.

A hundred and fifty million kilometers away at LG2, the Gaia space observatory re-aligned itself from staring into the Orion Nebula to focus its instruments on their best guess of Nomad's position.

"Yes, you did a good job, Ben," Dr. Müller agreed, standing shoulder-to-shoulder beside them in the packed room.

Ben exhaled slowly as they all waited for the images to come on-line. "Maybe too good."

How easy it was to slip into technical double-speak. *No, we're not sure what's happening. Yes, of course we would say if we knew.* There was truth in Ben's denials, however. Some of the data coming in gave Nomad's size a hundred times smaller than other estimates, so either Nomad was a hundred times the mass of the sun, or about the same size, or traveling at thousands of kilometers a second, or just hundreds. The Gaia observatory should resolve the issue.

Jessica and Celeste's plane was landing in an hour. "Where's my phone?" Ben demanded for the tenth time.

"Half an hour, maximum," Müller whispered back.

Ben glanced at the CNN and MSNBC reporters, everyone's eyes glued to the screens. Ben convinced Müller to let them in.

Transparency builds trust, he'd said.

"We have images," the woman from the front yelled out.

A star field popped onto the first screen. An automated computer software tool highlighted each of the specks of light, one by one, in blue for known objects. A few popped up in red, eliciting excited whispers, but each time a human astronomer checked the item off into blue. Nothing that looked like Nomad was in the first frame. The other screens filled with new star field images.

Again and again, the wall screens filled with images at higher and higher magnifications. Nothing. The same result. There was nothing in the images that shouldn't be there.

Nothing but empty, black space where Nomad should be.

Nothing at all.

14

Rome, Italy

"WE DON'T REALLY *know what's going on,"* Jess's father, Ben, said on the TV screen. *"We don't even really know if anything is there yet."*

Jess stuck her bottom lip out. "That's not what he said to me."

She arranged pillows around her on Angela's couch. Her friend's apartment was one long room with a kitchen area and dining table at one end, and a white L-shaped couch and flat screen television at the other. Four windows, looking down onto the alleyway below, lined the wall behind the television, and over the couch hung a large original artwork—an impressionist's version of Phoenix rising done in yellow oil over white canvas. A small hallway between the living and dining area led into the bedroom and bathroom.

"Maybe the situation changed," Celeste said from the kitchen area. She opened the refrigerator door. "Maybe that's why he went to Germany."

Jess flipped through channels: BBC, CNN, and MSNBC in English, then through the Italian channels. Sitcoms and soaps on many stations, but half covered the "event," and more than half of those featured hysterical ranting.

"Doesn't explain why he hasn't called us yet." Jess flipped back to BBC to catch the end of her father talking.

Celeste closed the refrigerator then opened the cupboards beside it. "Your friend doesn't cook much."

"She mostly uses this as a vacation rental," Jess explained. "We'll go downstairs to the market in a second." A *Breaking News* headline appeared on the TV. "Something's happening, come here!"

"We go live to the European Space Operations Center, where images from the Gaia orbiting observatory are now coming in," the BBC anchor said. Images

filled the screen behind him, of star fields. A box opened on-screen with a reporter's face. *"So far, researchers at ESOC have reported finding nothing at all in the vicinity of the supposed Nomad object…"*

"You see?" Celeste walked over to Jess and put a hand on her shoulder. "Maybe it's a false alarm."

The commentators on-screen began arguing the same thing, one of them describing other ways to explain the reported discrepancy in Neptune's orbit.

"Just because they can't see it doesn't mean anything." Jess logged her laptop into Angela's wireless, and checked her email again. Still nothing. She looked out the window. Getting dark. "Come on, if we're going to hole up here, we need some food."

Closing her laptop, Jess grabbed the keys and her phone, and they left the apartment. Outside, the alleyway was eerily calm, the warm night air pungent from garbage piled at the corner. The small market across the street—where Jess remembered going to buy wine on more than one ocassion at Angela's—was closed. A bigger supermarket was a few blocks away, so they walked toward it, the street opening up onto the *Piazza Navona*, one of Rome's most famous squares.

"Wow." Jess and her mother stopped at the edge of the *piazza*.

She wasn't sure what to expect. They entered the square from the center of the west side, in front of a large fountain topped with an Egyptian obelisk. Crowds filled the cafes and restaurants lining the *piazza*, candlelight glittering, tableware and plates clinking between the murmurs of conversation echoing off the five-story buildings lining the square. People walked by in groups, some pushing baby strollers. As if nothing unusual was happening.

And nothing had happened.

Not yet.

"Over there." Jess pointed at a lit sign in an alley on the other side of the square, *Desparo*. "That's the store." It looked open.

They crossed the square, past the fountain's splashing and bubbling water. Street vendors tried to sell them plastic replicas of the fountain's obelisk, glow-in-the-dark Pantheons, and wind-up helicopters with LED lights that winked and flashed as they spun into the sky. Squealing children chased the helicopters across the cobblestones. A sense of unreality flooded Jess; she felt like she floated across the square.

Reaching the store ahead of Jess, Celeste grabbed a basket by the entrance. "What do you feel like getting…?"

"Whatever we can." Jess pointed at the shelves inside. Empty.

The man at the checkout, balding and wearing a black apron, shrugged.

But not quite empty, Jess discovered as she walked inside. The refrigerated and freezer aisles were still half-full, and cans of tinned vegetables remained at the backs of shelves.

"We'll make do." Celeste filled her basket. "Look, here's some pasta, sun-dried tomatoes…"

"Cash only, yes?" said the black-aproned checkout man behind them.

Jess turned. "Why? I've used credit cards here before—"

"The boss told me, cash only." The man shrugged. "And the cash machine"—he pointed at an ATM at the corner of the shop—"it's empty."

Jess's faced flushed. What stupid kind of…"How the hell are we supposed to—"

"I've got some money," Celeste said quietly, holding Jess's arm. "It's okay."

"Idiots," Jess muttered under her breath. She returned to scavenging the shelves.

They paid, the checkout man withering under Jess's glare, and walked back across the *piazza*.

As they passed a restaurant terrace filled with people, a man got up, swearing, and fell over, crashing into the table next to him. Clams and pasta flew into the air, followed by the shattering of glass and plates. Instead of apologizing, the man got up and swore at people whose table he wrecked. The man he shouted at stood and punched him square in the mouth.

Jess watched two waiters join the patio brawl. She grabbed her mother's hand and urged her on. "Come on, let's move."

Some patrons scattered, screaming, but others watched and laughed. Jess looked closer at the faces of people she passed, at the strain in their eyes, the white knuckles of the woman pushing a baby stroller next to her. A man sitting on the fountain wobbled, drunk past his senses. Barely past eight p.m., but half of the restaurants now looked closed. Beneath the veneer of normality, a quiet desperation filled the eyes of people she passed.

She checked her phone. Still no messages. Dammit. Why hadn't her father called yet? She quickened her step, pushing out irrational thoughts. *Why had she cancelled the flight?* They'd be in New York by now. Hurrying down their alleyway on the other side of the square, she fumbled with the keys and then opened the huge metal front door of Angela's apartment building.

"Slow down, Jess," Celeste said as she followed Jess inside. They climbed the stairs. "Are you okay?"

"I'm fine."

The overhead light was out on their landing. Almost pitch black in front of their door. Jess swore under her breath and pulled her phone out to use its light to find the keyhole. Pushing the door open, she let her mother in first and stepped in behind her, reaching to turn the light switch on. She tried to shut the door.

It wouldn't close.

Clicking the interior lights on, Jess grabbed the door handle to open and shut it again, wondering what was wrong, when she saw a foot jammed in the bottom of the door. What the…?

The door flew back into her. She wobbled on her prosthetic leg, almost falling. Her mother grabbed her. Two men in long coats and hoodies filled the open door, the sour tang of alcohol wafting in ahead of them.

"The apartment's not for rent," Jess said, thinking maybe they were looking for somewhere to stay. People sometimes came knocking. The place was listed on a few websites.

But they didn't look like tourists.

Her martial arts training kicked in automatically. She stood, using one arm to push her mother behind her, placing her good leg back and prosthetic forward in a fighting stance.

"We no want to stay," the taller of the two men said in broken English. He smiled a mouthful of yellow teeth and pulled down his hood, revealing greasy black hair. Something came from his pocket. It snicked open. A cruel blade glittered.

"Take...take whatever you want," Celeste stuttered from behind Jess.

The tall man laughed and nodded at the man behind him, who stepped into the apartment, unfolding a large carryall. In it he tossed Jess's backpack and laptop from the couch, and Celeste's carryon from in front of the TV. He disappeared into the bedroom.

"What do you want?" Jess stood defiant as the tall man advanced on them.

At least twice her body weight, and strong, judging from the size of his shoulders. Still, she could drop him; duck down and one shot into his groin, then an uppercut into the throat. She eyed the glittering blade, gritted her teeth.

"Jess, don't..." her mother whispered.

"No trouble." The tall man held his knife wide. "Okay?"

Her skin crawling, Jess tensed. The tall man came close and used his free hand to pat her down. He took her cell phone, keys, purse, then did the same to Celeste. He backed up.

Thuds from the bedroom as the smaller man rifled through it, then he went into the kitchen area, piling things in his arms. He did a quick sweep, and not finding much, returned to deposit what he had into the carryall. He zipped the bag up and shouldered it.

The tall man backed up two more paces, the smaller man exiting the apartment behind him. "See? No trouble." He turned to leave.

Their cell phones, their wallets, her laptop—they took everything. They'd be stranded. Red flashed before Jess's eyes, and without thinking she jumped forward three steps and grabbed the man's hand holding the knife, twisting the wrist at a savage angle. The knife fell from his hand, clattered to the ground. The man dropped to his knees and cried out.

Jess swung around him, jamming the door shut, twisting his arm further.

Something snapped.

The man screamed.

"Mom! Lock the door!" Jess yelled as she twisted further.

Roaring, the man grabbed Jess with his other hand and tossed her against the wall. She cracked her head, the impact knocking the wind out of her. He was too strong. There was no way she could control him. He threw her back on the couch, while the smaller man shoved his way back in through the door, a knife now in his hand.

The tall man advanced on Jess. She kicked at him, and he grabbed her leg and pulled.

Jess felt a suctioning *pop*, and her prosthetic leg came free. The man stumbled back, shocked, looking at the leg in his hand. He waved it in the air, looked back at Jess, and then smiled. Tucking her leg under one arm, he stooped to collect his knife with his good hand. "Now we have everything, yes?"

"No!" Jess screamed. "Give me my leg back!"

The man laughed and pushed his partner out the door ahead of him.

Jess jumped up from the couch and hopped to the door on one leg. "No, please," she pleaded. "You don't need that."

The men disappeared down the stairs, and Jess jumped after them, using her hand to steady herself on the walls. She screamed, begged them to give it back. Celeste followed behind Jess, imploring her to stop.

Reaching the bottom floor, Jess hopped to the front door, exiting just in time to see the men getting into a car. "Stop!" she yelled. "Someone, help!"

She blinked and looked at the man driving the car. Pork pie hat, and was that a mole on his cheek?

Enzo?

The car pulled off.

Celeste ran behind Jess, steadied her as she balanced on one leg. It had started to rain, making the cobblestones slick. "Are you okay? Did they hurt you?"

"Why did he take my leg?" Jess cried, tears coming, mixing with the rain running down her face. Who would do something like that?

Behind them, the apartment door swung shut. Realizing too late, Celeste let go of Jess and jumped to try and catch it, but it banged closed. She tried to open it, but it was locked.

"It doesn't matter." Jess shivered in the rain, balancing unsteadily. "The door upstairs locks by itself, too." A putrid river flowed from the pile of garbage to the drain by the one foot she stood on. They had no money, no phones, and no shelter.

Her mother came back to help her, and Jess put one arm around Celeste's shoulder.

She looked down, bile in the back of her throat.

They stole my leg.

15

Darmstadt, Germany

BEN ROLLINS STARED at the six wall-mounted displays in the ESOC control room, image after image of star fields appearing and then disappearing. Nothing. Absolutely nothing where Nomad should be. After three hours, the room had nearly emptied out. Ben sat beside Roger and Dr. Müller, in the front row of chairs on the raised viewing platform behind the operations teams. A skeleton team of media remained on the chance something might appear.

But it didn't.

And neither did Ben's laptop or cell phone.

"If it's a black hole, wouldn't we see gravitational lensing?" Dr. Müller mused.

In theory, a black hole's gravity should bend light passing close, like a cosmic bead of water lensing starlight around it. The black hole itself would be invisible, but there would be a telltale shift of starlight if it were there.

"Yes and no," Ben replied. "A black hole of ten solar masses has a Schwarzschild radius of thirty kilometers." The Schwarzschild radius was the famed "event horizon" of a black hole, where the escape velocity exceeded the speed of light. Beyond that boundary, all of our physics and knowledge became useless, so this boundary became the commonly accepted "size."

"From twenty billion kilometers," Roger added, "too small to see."

Dr. Müller looked at Ben. "So it's smaller than we thought. We should update the media."

Ben gritted his teeth, his patience far since worn out. "If you want another word out of me..." Jess and Celeste had been on the ground in New York for two hours already. They must have seen his face on

TV by now and know that he wasn't on the airplane behind them.

Dr. Müller nodded. "Let me check again." He stood. "Sorry, the network security team was overwhelmed today."

Ben clenched his jaw and watched Dr. Müller wind his way out of the room.

"He does have a point." Roger nudged Ben, pointed at the star fields on the screen. "Something that big, even at this distance, with Gaia's instruments we should be seeing microlensing. That's what you asked me to look for around Gliese 445, right?"

Ben nodded. Microlensing meant a tiny shift of intensity in the light coming from a star. A small black hole—small relative to the millions-of-solar-mass ones at the centers of galaxies—wouldn't be big enough create a fish-eye kind of lensing. It would only shift some of the light away from the observer, making a star it passed in front of appear to twinkle. Teams around the world were processing Gaia's images, looking for this signature, but it was maddening work. Every star had some small variability.

The door to the control room opened. Dr. Müller's face appeared. He motioned for Ben to come to the door. "I have your equipment."

Ben looked at Roger and shook his head. "Finally." They stood and walked to the door, exited into the hallway.

"Here you go. There are instructions for logging into our imaging network" Dr. Müller gave them a folded sheet of paper along with their laptops and cell phones. He pointed down the hall. "I've reserved room 304 for your use." He looked at Ben and pursed his lips. "Your emails and calls will be monitored. It's the best I can do."

"Great." Ben grabbed his stuff and stalked off without looking back. He opened the door to room 304. Not more than twelve-foot square—two cubicles with workstations, and a gray couch next to the entrance with a flat screen TV on the wall beside it.

Ben turned on the TV and tuned it to CNN, while Roger opened his laptop to log into ESOC.

"You getting the feed?" Ben asked.

Roger held up one finger, waiting for the connection, then nodded. The newest images from Gaia loaded up, and bright pinpoints of starlight spread across his screen. They were linked into the satellite data feed from Gaia, as well as a dozen other ground-based and orbiting observatories connected to Darmstadt.

"Perfect." Ben sat at the workstation to Roger's right and opened his own laptop.

Roger looked over his shoulder at the news feed on CNN. "The riots stopped in LA. Maybe you helped. Maybe Müller knows what he's doing." He pointed at a headline scrolling across the TV's display.

Ben glanced at it, then returned to logging into the ESOC wireless network. "Doubt it. People are in shock, acting emotionally. Random outbursts. To be expected."

"Expected? You think this was expected?" Roger cocked his head and stared at Ben.

"Not Nomad, that's not what I mean." Ben typed in the password taped to his laptop. "I mean, through the magic of modern media, we've just told seven billion people that they have months left to live. Like we've told everyone on the planet they have terminal cancer. Classic seven stages of grief, starting with shock and emotional acting out."

Roger grabbed the remote and turned up the volume. An "expert" was in the middle of explaining how the whole thing was a hoax. "What about denial?"

"That's in the first phase as well." Ben waited for the network to accept a connection. He opened his phone and turned it on. "Still nothing?" He flicked his chin at the Gaia image on Roger's laptop.

"Nothing." Roger shook his head. "Don't you think they should have found something by now?"

Ben leaned back in his chair and stretched. "I don't know. I mean the thing is, just like we humans somehow imagine we're separate from our environment, we also imagine that the solar system is separate from the interstellar environment, but it's not."

He pointed at the star field on Roger's laptop. "Sedna, our tenth planetoid beyond Pluto, was captured when our solar system collided with another star system a billion years ago. Thirty-five million years ago, the Earth's orbit changed, triggering a massive ice age and asteroid impacts that formed the Chesapeake Bay. I'd bet it was caused by another star passing through our solar system, just like Scholz's star grazing us only seventy thousand years ago. ”

“Four million years ago, a star three times the size of the sun passed a half parsec from it.” Roger had obviously done some homework. “And a million years from now, a K7 dwarf will skim us at less than a tenth parsec.”

“Exactly,” Ben said. “We’re intimately connected to other stars around us in interstellar space. How many extinction-level events have there been in Earth’s history?”

Roger scrunched his face and smiled. It was one of his favorite topics. “Five big ones that wiped out more than half the life on Earth, plus dozens of smaller ones. Two hundred and fifty million years ago, the Permian extinction took out over ninety percent of life worldwide. It was tens of millions of years before the planet was inhabited by more than protozoa.”

“Caused by what?”

An almost rhetorical question, but Roger played along. “Asteroids, comets, and volcanoes...”

“But the real answer is, we don’t know. What about a star exploding, a supernova, within a few dozen light years?”

“That would do it,” Roger agreed. “Irradiate the Earth and kill nearly everything.”

“With no warning.”

“Nope. Can’t outrun the speed of light.”

Ben pointed at a new image on Roger’s screen. “In our galaxy there are billions of stars, bright points we can see, but there are hundreds of millions of neutron stars, collapsed remnants of stars, that float around between them and are almost invisible. That’s what we know, but it’s what we don’t know that I’m worried about.”

“And that is?”

“Dark matter. Ninety percent of the material that makes up our universe, that makes up our *own* galaxy, is made of something we can’t see. All those stars”—Ben stabbed a finger at the screen—“there’s ten times more stuff floating between them that we can’t see, but we know it’s there by its gravitational signature, by the way the galaxies hold together. Exactly the same way we know Nomad is there, that *something* is coming. We detect the effects of its gravity, but we can’t see anything."

"So what are you saying?"

"That we *don't* know. Who knows what wiped out life on Earth before? Maybe we're about to have a cosmic encounter with something we don't understand." Ben hung his head. "I've always had the feeling we think we're wizards."

"You mean astronomers?" Roger's face twitched into an expression halfway between a grimace and a grin. "Like we gaze into our crystal balls? It's called *scrying*, I think."

"Right. We stare at patterns of light, and imagine that we can divine the history of the universe, even predict the future. It's pride, pure hubris. Five big extinction-level events, but maybe this one won't just destroy life. Maybe it'll actually destroy the planet."

Roger turned his laptop off. "Do you think it'll hit us?"

"Doesn't need to. We can't see it, but whatever it is, it has a massive gravitational field. The Earth is like a giant water balloon, the solid crust beneath our feet just the thin, stretched plastic surface. If this thing comes close enough, past the Roche limit, the Earth will burst from the tidal forces."

"No matter what, it'll fling the Earth into interstellar space," Roger added quietly. "The atmosphere would freeze solid in a few weeks."

"Let's not get ahead of ourselves." The connection symbol on Ben's laptop winked on. He logged into his email. "We don't know what it is; we have only a general sense of its path. Maybe it'll miss the solar system. Maybe it will disappear."

"Maybe." But Roger didn't sound convinced.

Ben scanned his inbox, flooded with media requests and colleagues requesting calls. But…there, an email from Jess, and not just one but a dozen. He opened the first one. "Oh, no…"

Roger blinked. "What?"

Ben read one email and then another. "Jess and Celeste didn't get on that flight. They came to find me. *Damn* it."

"Where are they?"

"I have an address. Go get Dr. Müller. I need him to arrange a pick-up in Rome. Arrange a military transport."

"Okay." Roger snapped out of his daydream, stood, but stopped and turned. “One thing, Ben. You said this was predictable, the shock and emotion. That this was the first step of grief.”

“And?” Ben chewed on his thumbnail. Why didn’t Jess take that flight? On the TV, an image of the candlelight vigil in the rain at St. Peters’s Square at the Vatican. Over a million people.

“What’s the next step?”

“That’s what I’m afraid of.” Ben looked Roger in the eye. “The next stage is anger.”

16

Rome, Italy

"ANGELA POLIDORO," JESS yelled into the intercom. "*Amici di* Angela."

"*No, appartamento trecento,*" crackled the reply. "No Angela."

"Please, buzz us in," Jess pleaded. "We're stuck outside."

They hung up.

Jess cursed in frustration. It was dark out. Rain hammered onto the cobblestones in a downpour. A river flowed down the middle of the alley, plastic bottles and papers from the garbage piles clogging a drain in the middle. They buzzed all the apartments. Nobody would let them in. Jess tried to explain, but they spoke no English, and her Italian wasn't good enough to charm her way past their suspicions.

"Sit down for a second," Celeste urged. She found wooden packing crates around the corner and arranged them, upended, under a small awning next to the apartment entrance. It offered some shelter.

Shivering, Jess took Celeste's offered hand and hopped over to sit. They huddled together. Jess wore only a thin tank top and jeans. Celeste offered her soaked sweater, but Jess refused, told her to keep it.

"We can't stay here, we'll freeze to death." Jess's teeth chattered. Clenching her jaw to stop it, she wrapped her arms tight around herself. It had to be past ten. No shops were open. Reaching down, she rubbed the stump of her leg. Not used to being exposed, the cold and wet made it ache.

Celeste put an arm around her daughter and laughed. "You wanted some bonding time…"

Jess gritted her teeth, but despite herself, laughed as well. "Not quite what I had in mind."

"I know. Come on, let's think."

That was just like her mother. Jess wanted to kick and scream, find someone to take her frustration out on, but Celeste was more cerebral. She said Jess was hot-headed like her grandfather, Giancarlo. "We need to get in touch with Dad, that's what we need to do."

"No, what we need to do is take care of you," Celeste said, her voice low and soothing. "Get you some crutches, maybe a replacement."

Jess pulled away. She hated feeling like a cripple. She didn't need anyone's help.

"Baby, come on." Celeste gently pulled her back. "I'm your mother."

Jess relaxed her shoulders and leaned back into Celeste. She was right. Without her prosthetic, without even crutches, she was a liability. The humiliation. Worse, she couldn't protect her mother; not even herself. "There's a hospital just across the river," she sighed. "Maybe we can get a taxi there. I'm sure we could stay the night."

Celeste smiled and squeezed Jess harder. "See, that wasn't so hard, was it?"

"No." Jess flashed a tiny smile and wiped her soaked, long blond hair from her eyes.

"And where could we get a taxi?"

"Three blocks on the other side of the Piazza, there's a main road." Jess straightened up. "And there's a pay phone at the bottom of the square."

"We can call the police."

If they got to a police station, maybe they could call Darmstadt. "And we could get to the American Embassy." It wasn't far, half an hour walk from where they sat. Jess went there to renew her passport a few weeks ago.

A block away to her left, another group of people huddled. Homeless. Surrounded by piles of shopping bags and blankets. What Jess would give for one of those blankets. Glancing right, a shape came out of the dark rain, two people walking.

"Hello?" Celeste stood. "Please, can you help us?" She took two steps toward the people, stepped out into the pouring rain.

It was a man and a woman, tight together under an umbrella.

"We have an emergency." Celeste reached toward the man.

He shied away, exclaimed, "Ehi! *Non mi tocchi!*" his body language screaming, *Get away*. They hurried off and disappeared back into the fog of the rain.

Jess stood, balancing with one hand against the wall. "Mom, don't beg. Come on, let's go." One of the homeless people, a young woman, came closer and stared at them. Jess stared back at the woman, then looked away.

Celeste came to support Jess, and they slowly made their way through the downpour to the *piazza*. Water streamed into Jess's eyes, and she strained to remain stable on the slick cobblestones. All the shops were shuttered; all the restaurants closed. Not another soul around. They walked across the square to the other side, past the fountain, and continued two more blocks to *Via Rinascimento* where they stood in the sheeting rain and waited. No taxis. No police. A car appeared and Celeste almost threw herself in front of it, but it honked and swerved, then sped off in a spray of water.

The rain hammered down. Leaning against a stone wall, Jess shivered violently. She couldn't stop her teeth chattering now. Her leg ached. A cold fire burned in her thigh. "Let…let's try the phone box," she stuttered. They'd been out in the rain for maybe two hours already, and Jess felt her core temperature dropping, her fingers going numb.

Celeste stood at the edge of the road, her hands in tight fists, her arms shaking. Water poured down her face. "Okay, let's try it."

"Excuse me?"

Jess glanced to her left. Someone stood under an umbrella, huge raindrops exploding like staccato gunfire off it.

"You need help, yes?"

The person stepped next to Jess. It was a young woman, slender, shorter than Jess. Smooth skin with freckled cheeks, her eyes so blue they seemed to pierce the darkness.

"I have somewhere warm," the woman said. "I am Massarra, come. Come with me."

"Yes…yes," Celeste stammered, coming to hold Jess. "Please."

"This way." Massarra turned and disappeared into the rain.

Jess and Celeste followed. Jess hobbled and leaned onto her mother. "Do you think this is a good idea?" she whispered to her mother.

"We don't have much choice. We need to get out of this, get warm somehow. Maybe I can go and try the phone."

"Don't leave me alone." Jess said this without thinking. "I mean, that's fine, but don't go—"

"Don't worry." Celeste squeezed Jess.

They followed Massarra back across the empty *piazza*, back down Angela's street. Water flowed in torrents around their feet as they struggled. Jess was about to ask where they were going when Massarra pointed at a gap between the buildings, barely two feet wide. She peered down it through the rain. A light glimmered at the end.

"It's okay, it's safe," Massarra assured her, and she turned sideways and shimmied her way through the gap.

Celeste and Jess stood shaking in the rain. "What do you think?" Celeste asked.

Jess didn't answer, but hopped forward. Anything to get out of this rain. She pushed herself between the buildings and edged forward. Empty beer cans and discarded food containers littered the gap, a waterfall pouring from the tops of the buildings onto her. The light at the end glimmered brighter. A fire. The gap widened into an interior courtyard between the buildings, and, finally, no rain. Looking up, awnings stretched between the walls, interlacing one over the other for four stories. Rainwater gushed from drainpipes. Reaching the end of the gap, she hopped forward, steadying herself with one arm against the wall.

Three old men sat around a low concrete urn containing a bright fire. They looked at Jess and nodded before returning to staring into the fire.

Massarra came to Jess with a blanket. "I saw you in the street." And she had crutches. "One of my uncles had this from an old accident." She offered Jess both.

"Thank you," Celeste said from behind Jess, taking the blanket and wrapping it around her daughter.

"Come, sit." Massarra indicated a wooden bench to the side of the fire. She smiled at Jess. "These are my uncles. Two of them speak English, just so you know." She said something in what sounded like Arabic, and all three of them nodded.

Jess convulsed in a fit of shivering, her leg almost buckling. She held back. Four of them, and just her and Celeste. She doubted anyone would even hear them scream from the alleyway. Even if the streets weren't deserted. Even if the rain wasn't pounding, drowning everything out.

"Come on," Celeste whispered into her ear. "They look nice."

They didn't look nice. The three old men sat like goblins, hunched over, their beards hanging between their knees. The closest turned and looked at Jess, one eye seeing, the other an opaque silver pool reflecting the firelight. She shuddered again, this time only half from the cold.

But the fire's warmth beckoned.

Leaning on Celeste, she muttered, "Thank you," to Massarra and stumbled to sit on the bench. Celeste sat beside her. Jess put the crutches down but kept them close, in case she needed to stand quickly. Or fend off one of the goblins. Shivering, she held her hands to the fire, beautiful life-giving warmth spreading into her fingertips.

"Most of our luggage was stolen." Massarra brought Celeste a blanket she took from a backpack next to the fire. "My uncles and I were traveling home. Tomorrow we get money, drive north."

"Really?" Celeste took the blanket and wrapped it around herself and Jess, pulling her closer on the bench. "That's what happened to us, too."

"I suspected," Massarra said as she sat opposite them. "I heard you asking for help." She pointed out the gap between the buildings. "The world is going crazy today."

Jess stopped shivering. "Yes."

"You heard, then? About Nomad?" Massarra asked.

"Yes."

"And you believe it? There was a man on television today that said they didn't know yet. The one with a graying goatee, black rimmed glasses…did you see him?"

Jess leaned toward the fire, watched the flames dance. She had to mean her father. Jess nodded, clenching her fists. Where was he? "He's lying," she grunted. Celeste clutched her under the blanket, frowned at her.

"Lying? Why would you say that?"

Jess pushed her mother away, ever so slightly. "Because they had to know, for a long time." And that was true. When she spoke to her father two nights before, he said he had evidence of Nomad over thirty years ago. Data he recorded when he was a grad student. Mysterious flashes in the night sky.

One of the old men, the one with the silver eye, asked, "So, they've been hiding it?"

It wasn't true her father had exactly *hidden* it. He'd theorized about it in a research paper—rejected by his peers as far-fetched speculation. But why had he abandoned Jess and Celeste? Why hadn't he called? "Yes, that man on television is a liar."

Her mother's nails dug into Jess's arm under the blanket. "Let's not jump to conclusions."

The old men exchanged glances, muttering in a guttural language Jess didn't understand. Silver-eye looked at Jess again. "And now the world is unprepared to meet God."

Jess clenched her fists. "Nobody is ever prepared to meet God."

Silver-eye erupted into a phlegmy laugh. "Not true. You only fear God if you haven't made your peace, haven't placed death at the center of life."

Thawed out, blood pumped through Jess's veins again. "Now that sounds cheerful."

"The only thing that burns in hell is the part of you that won't let go of life." Silver-eye worked his mouth around into a rotten-toothed grimace. "Hell is no punishment, but a process of freeing the soul. If you are frightened of dying, you'll see devils tearing your life away when death comes. But, if you've made peace, then you'll see angels freeing you when death comes."

Rubbing her hands together, Jess stared at Silver-eye. "I appreciate you letting us sit here, but I don't want to talk. Is that okay?" It creeped her out. *He* creeped her out.

"Sorry, my uncles, this is affecting them," Massarra apologized.

Silver-eye looked at the other two old men and shook his head. He looked back at Jess, held her gaze. "As you wish. But you might want to think, what is it that holds you here? What demons tear at your soul, keeping you from freedom?"

Jess stared at the man's silver eye, a puddle of light, a boy's face disappearing into it. Clenching her fists, she turned away and huddled under the blankets with her mother.

#GR17;

Event +68hrs;
Survivor name: Eveline Goff;
Reported location: Nuuk, Greenland;

Ah, where to start, my God…I was part of a University of Cambridge expedition, studying the aquifers under the Greenland ice sheets. Makes the bedrock slippery. That was the idea, you know? We spent a month trekking across the high glaciers, installing cameras and sensors, and were on our way back when the buzz about Nomad hit. We got into Nuuk, but all flights were canceled. No way of getting to Reykjavik, but maybe that was a good thing… *(long pause)* Sorry. Right. On the day.

About 4 p.m., the ocean swelled right up over Nuuk's sea walls, and it just kept coming, flooded half of the city, but slowly, like a foot an hour. Everyone just got out of the way, hoping this was the worst of it. By 9 p.m., the sea started to pull out, but much faster, and the Northern Lights intensified. They aren't unusual. But these, they flared. By midnight it was almost as bright as daylight, and that's when we felt the first tremor. I was inside, glued to my monitoring station readouts, not believing my eyes. The ground shook continuously, and the glaciers, they weren't moving at feet per year, they started moving at feet *per second,* sliding down off the highlands.

That's when Piers came and grabbed me, rushed me into the helicopter, a terrible roar filling the air. Barely got off the ground when Nuuk was razed, ice boulders the size of skyscrapers sweeping the city into the half-empty bay. We kept aloft until we were almost out of fuel, maybe four hours, circling over ice shelves sliding into the oceans. Hundreds of miles of it from what I saw on the sensors before they went dark. We found a patch of high ground to land on, but there are still tremors, and the skies are black with ash clouds that came with the easterly winds. The temperature is dropping fast; we have no food, no gas. Four of us stranded in the dark. Do you have any idea how much water…

Transmission ended ionization static. Freq. 4135 kHz/NSB.
Subject not reacquired.

DAY FIVE

October 10th

17

Rome, Italy

PITTER-PATTER, PITTER-PATTER.

Jess opened her eyes. In front of her, in the middle of a crabgrass-infested courtyard, smoke curled from charred embers in a low concrete urn. Windowless, red brick walls surrounded her on all four sides. She looked up. Waxy light filtered down from a gray sky. Water dripped from awnings above her, onto the slick flagstones and puddles by her foot. She tried to move, but her bones ached. Her arms were stiff. A throbbing pressure banged behind her eyes.

"Mom?" she whispered, stretching her neck forward.

She shook herself awake.

Adrenaline sharpened her senses.

"Mom?!" Jess cried out. The three old men, the goblins around the fire—where were they? She threw off her nest of blankets. What did they do to her? She didn't remember falling asleep. Was she drugged?

"I'm here." Celeste appeared from the gap between the buildings. She held out a Styrofoam cup.

"What happened? Where is…"

"Massarra? She left early this morning. You were asleep against the wall, so I didn't want to disturb you."

Jess groaned and stretched. The morning air was cool, but warming up, and at least it wasn't raining. She took the coffee, smelled it, and took a sip. She felt its warmth slide down her throat. "Oh, that's good." She looked at the cup. "Did you get some money?"

"A nice man at the cafe across the street, I explained what happened. He gave me some coffee and loaned me ten Euros. Said he could call the police."

Jess relaxed, letting a small grin creep across her face and took another sip. Her mother could still charm anyone. She stiffened. *The police.* Her grin disappeared. "And did you?"

"Not yet. I wanted to talk to you first." Celeste sat on a box in front of Jess and crinkled her nose in an awkward smile.

"Maybe we just go to the American embassy?" Jess suggested. After last night, she didn't want to risk spending tonight in an Italian jail.

"The hospital first?" Celeste leaned forward to put a hand on Jess's knee. "Get you sorted out?"

Jess tried to imagine waiting to fit a prosthetic leg in an Italian hospital. "No, let's get in touch with Dad, or at least, try, and then head to the embassy. I've got crutches. We'll fix my leg when we get back to the States."

Celeste frowned. "You sure?"

"Going to the hospital will just waste time." Voices echoed from the street, the growl of a scooter rising and falling as it passed. The city was alive again. It was time to get moving. The night before felt like a dream, a nightmare, and Jess didn't dwell on the past. "There's an Internet café three blocks from here, on the other side of *Piazza Navona* toward the Trevi fountain. We can make calls from there, even get money wired, and it's on the way to the embassy."

"Are you sure?" Celeste repeated. She leaned forward and knelt in front of Jess, put her hands on each side of Jess's waist and held her. "Those men assaulted you, stole everything we had. I think we should talk to the police."

Jess laughed. "If you remember, *I'm* the one who assaulted *them*. They mugged us, but I don't think they wanted to hurt us." She poured more coffee down her throat, felt her joints loosening.

"Jess, they took your leg…"

"I know. I shouldn't have attacked him. That was stupid."

"It *was* stupid, but brave." Celeste squeezed Jess. "And he bashed your head against the wall. Are you sure you're okay?"

A jackhammer pounded between Jess's temples. "I'm fine." She squeezed her eyes shut and exhaled. "I mean, I'll *be* fine. I need some water."

"You mean you didn't get enough last night?" Celeste laughed.

"You're crazy, you know that? They could have killed you."

Jess grabbed the crutches and stood, giving the empty coffee cup to her mother. "They weren't going to kill anyone. They were bullies, that's all." She piled the sodden blankets on the bench. So Massarra had left her the blankets? That was awfully nice of her. "Hope I busted that guy's arm."

Shaking her head, Celeste stood as well. "I think you might have."

Swinging forward on the crutches, Jess moved into the gap between the buildings, then hopped along it. People crowded the alleyway on the other side, and all the cafés were open. She glanced at Angela's apartment, half a block down, and shook her head. At the corner was a military Humvee. A young man in Italian military dress stood by it. The fear and uncertainty of the night before melted into the reassuring presence of other people.

"Come on, slowpoke, let's go," Jess chided her mother as she swung forward on the crutches.

They walked back across the *piazza*, crowded again with tourists and street vendors, and past the street they'd waited at the night before. Everything looked so different in the light of day. Alive. Gray skies hung low over the *piazza*, the air humid and still threatening rain. They hurried past a line of stalls vending Papal calendars, artists selling sketches of the Vatican and posters of the Colosseum.

"It's here." Jess stopped under an "Internet" sign. A couple sat with a map of Rome spread out on a table outside, with another table empty beside them. Jess held the crutches in one hand while she hopped up the stairs. Inside, she nodded at the man behind the cash register as she sat down at a computer station.

She logged in, then started up her webmail. An email from her father popped up right away.

"Look," Jess exclaimed as her mother sat down beside her, "it's Dad."

In the email, her father apologized profusely, said they rushed him out of the hotel, that they needed to use him for media to calm people down. He added that they took his laptop and cell phone temporarily, as a security precaution, but that he had them now. Jess nodded. That made sense. She was just happy that they finally got in touch with him.

"He said to stay at the apartment." Jess turned to Celeste. "An Italian military attaché was supposed to pick us up, to take us on a private flight to Darmstadt to meet him."

"I guess we weren't there to meet them." Celeste offered a plastic cup of water to Jess. "Come on, drink this."

Jess took it and gulped the water down. *Military attaché.* The Humvee parked on the corner. That had to be for them. She typed a quick email back to her father, saying that they got locked out of the apartment, but they were fine.

"Should we go back to the apartment?" Celeste asked. "Or up to the Embassy? We'll need our passports, won't we?"

"Not to travel to Germany."

Jess's email pinged. A return answer from her father. Get back to the apartment, he said, there's a military transport, a Humvee, you can't miss it. He added that the driver was instructed not to leave for *any* reason, not until he collected Jess and Celeste. Ben attached his Italian phone number, an emergency number for Darmstadt, and the contact information for the driver picking them up. Jess and Celeste read it together.

"I guess we go back to the apartment?" Jess looked at her mother, then winced. Pain shot between her eyes, the pounding headache getting worse.

"Sure, but let me chat with your Dad." Celeste nodded at a Western Union money wiring sign over the counter. "I'm going to get him to send us some money, just to be safe. I asked the owner, he said it takes only a few minutes to wire cash from a credit card."

"Maybe we should call him?" Jess saw someone talking on an Internet phone next to the man at the register.

"I'll call him." Celeste rubbed Jess's shoulder. "Why don't you sit down outside? I think the sun is coming out. Drink some more water, relax. I'll take care of this."

Jess took a deep breath. "Okay. Perfect." She stood, placed her crutches under her arms and swung forward to the entrance.

Her clothes were just about dry, still slightly damp, and she could smell herself. Never a good sign. What she would give for a hot shower.

"*Cafe, madame*?" asked the man behind the cash register.

"Yes, please. And some water." Jess held the crutches in her left hand, gripping the stair's railing. "And do you have anything to eat?"

"Croissant?"

Jess smiled. "Perfect."

She hopped down the stairs and squinted in the brightening light outside. The couple was still there, staring at their map, and she sat at the table next to them. The sun poked momentarily through the heavy clouds overhead. Closing her eyes, Jess took a deep breath and relaxed into her chair. She'd almost forgotten about Nomad, but that was a problem for later, for when they met her father. And he would know better than anyone.

Everything was going to be fine.

She opened her eyes and looked at the couple beside her again. Holding hands. Leaning into each other. She thought of Giovanni, of her tour around the castle. She wondered what he was doing.

A bright light flashed, a searing white that reflected off the windows and lit the sky. Jess blinked. Did someone just take a picture of her, pop a flash an inch from her face? The ground rumbled, glasses rattling on the table next to her, then a whomping concussion blew Jess backward, slamming her head against the concrete, a roar rising to overload her senses. A super-heated blast of air tore through the street, shattering windows, burning into Jess's flesh.

18

Darmstadt, Germany

"STILL NOTHING?" ROGER asked. He sat on the gray couch of their improvised office, bouncing a plastic model of the Philae comet-lander spacecraft off the wall.

A whole collection of European Space Agency spacecraft models were arranged on the shelf next to his workstation. He kept one eye on his plastic model, the other on images of star fields from the Gaia observatory flipping through on his laptop screen.

But Roger wasn't asking about the Nomad image search.

Ben held his phone to his ear. Four rings, then five…"*You know what to do*," came Jess's singsong voice on her answering message. "Dammit." He hung up.

The driver sent to pick up Jess and Celeste at the apartment had called and said that nobody was there. The driver buzzed all the other apartments in the building, but nobody knew anything. He'd waited downstairs, in the alleyway with his Humvee, but no sign of them. The police complained about the truck blocking the alley, so the driver had been forced to move and park on a wider street five minutes away to wait.

Ben checked his email again. Relief washed through him.

There, in his inbox, was an email from Jess. "Thank God," he muttered.

Roger sat up on the couch, putting down his Philae lander. "What?"

Ben read Jess's message. "The girls got locked out last night." He typed a quick response, telling them to get back to the apartment. "They're just around the corner from the apartment I sent the driver to." It was just in time—Dr. Müller was about to cancel the private jet he'd commandeered to get Jess and Celeste, after Ben twisted his arm. Literally.

"Good." Roger got up and returned to his laptop. "So they'll be here, in what, two hours?"

Ben nodded. "Something like that." In time for the 4 p.m. flight from Frankfurt to JFK. Ben had tickets for the four of them, Roger included. He turned his attention to Roger's screen, letting his mind return to Nomad. "Nothing unusual in the images yet?"

"Nope." Roger clicked some options on the visualization tools, clicking through different spectra. "If it was a black hole, shouldn't we be picking up microlensing by now? Or Hawking radiation?"

"When Steve"—Ben was on a first name familiar basis with the famous physicist—"proposed black holes as the invisible 90% 'dark matter' of the universe in 1974, I bet he never suspected the Earth would be the experimental guinea pig to test the idea. But a ten-solar-mass black hole would emit his Hawking radiation too weak to pick up at billions of kilometers."

"Nomad had to pass through the Oort cloud of comets and debris on its way into the solar system," Roger said, furrowing his brow. "Wouldn't any material it encountered be spun around it in a super-heated accretion disk? That should light up right across the spectra from x-ray to visible, right?"

Ben shrugged, *maybe*.

"If Nomad has been passing through the Oort cloud for hundreds of years," Roger continued, "there had to be something out there it would've hit. *Somebody* would have had to see *something*." He paused and raised his eyebrows. "Right?"

Ben sensed the leading question. "Maybe." If a black hole traveled through the Oort cloud, eventually it might suck in a comet or other object. Depending on the geometry of the event, it could create a brief accretion disk—a flash of light in the sky.

Roger narrowed his eyes. "What's in the bags, Ben? What did you get Mrs. Brown to courier to the hotel?" He flicked his chin at the backpack by the door, the white courier package delivered at the hotel just poking out through the open zipper.

"Old data."

Roger stared at Ben. "I read that paper." He raised his eyebrows. "That one you wrote in grad school."

Ben didn't need to ask which one. The way Roger looked at him, he knew. But it was never published. "How did you get it?"

"I'm trying to get my PhD. You don't think I did a little digging on the guy who's supposed to give it to me?"

"Mrs. Brown gave it to you."

Roger grinned and nodded. "I told her I wanted to know *everything* about your research. You proposed evidence of a black hole hiding in our solar system's Oort cloud using data from the Red Shift Survey."

"More idle speculation than anything else." Ben leaned back in his chair. "Just a grad student with too much time and imagination on his hands."

Ben hadn't told anyone else about the old data he had Mrs. Brown send him, but Roger was like family. Ben suspected Müller dragging him out to Darmstadt wasn't only based on Ben's media credentials. Müller was covering his ass.

"Müller was the one that convinced me not to publish, did you know that?" Ben asked.

Roger shook his head. "How could he have known?" He stared at Ben. "Wait a minute. Do you suspect…what? What are you thinking?"

"Nothing." Ben rubbed the back of his neck. Müller might be trying to cover his ass, but having Ben here was smart, too. It made sense. "Nothing. There's no way he could have known. I didn't even know. It was just a wild guess at the time."

Roger leaned in close to Ben. He pointed at the backpack and whispered, "So that's the old Red Shift Data? Gliese 445?"

Ben nodded slowly. "Not sure how we're going to read it. There's old magnetic drum tapes from the 70s, floppies from the 80s, CDs from the 90s…"

Roger let his breath whistle out. "And who knows what formats. How could you even decode it?"

"I don't know. But what's in there,"—he pointed at the backpack—"if that's evidence of Nomad, it'll pinpoint a starting trajectory, thirty years ago. Problem is, the data never fit theoretical models of a black hole accretion disk."

"But isn't all the data in that paper you tried to publish?"

"Not quite."

Roger stared at Ben. "Not quite?" He sat upright and pressed his lips together. "What do you mean, not quite?" He opened an email on his laptop screen, then began typing quickly.

A knock on the door.

"We're busy," Roger said loudly. He turned back to Ben and pointed at his laptop screen. "You gotta look at this."

A louder knock.

"I said, we're—" Roger started to say, but the door opened.

A face appeared, smooth and olive-skinned with piercing green eyes above a manicured two-day-stubble beard, a brown knitted-wool cap set askew atop a thick head of jet-black hair. "Dr. Rollins?" Ufuk Erdogmas said, peering around the door. "You are here?"

"Sorry, but this is a private room," Roger said, getting up and standing between the door and Ben.

"It's okay," Ben said. He got to his feet and stepped forward to open the door fully. It wasn't every day that a famous billionaire entrepreneur came knocking.

Ufuk frowned at Roger, and then turned to face Ben and smiled, reaching out to shake his hand. "Dr. Rollins, I can't tell you what a honor this is. I tried to find you at the IAU meeting. I've studied your work in Doppler spectroscopy. My name is—"

"I know who you are, Mr. Erdogmus." Ben took his hand. It felt dry and warm. A firm handshake. Ben's grandfather always said the mark of a good man was a firm handshake. "What can I do for you?"

"I need to speak to you. Urgently."

"Come in, then." Ben took a step back.

"Sorry, but this needs to be in private." Ufuk glanced at Roger, smiling thinly.

"I can go out," Roger said after an awkward pause.

"No, you stay here." The thin smile disappeared from Ufuk's face.

Ben frowned, glancing at Roger and then back at Ufuk. Did they know each other? "I'm sorry, but what is this about, Mr. Erdogmus? I appreciate what an important person you are, but right now…does this have something to do with the Mars First mission?"

Lines creased the smooth skin around Ufuk's eyes. He pressed his lips together. "Yes, you could say that."

"Mr. Erdogmus, can't this wait?" asked Roger, stepping forward again. "Right now isn't—"

Someone screamed in the hallway. Someone else swore loudly in German.

"What the hell…?" Ben took two steps around the door and looked down the hallway.

More loud voices. People ran toward the lounge, a crowd already massed there, staring at the television screens.

Ben turned and grabbed the remote from beside Roger and clicked on the TV above the couch. A grainy picture of an orange fireball roiled into an overcast sky—not just a fireball, but a mushroom cloud.

"These images are from webcams in the center of Rome," said the news anchor, his face ashen. *"We have reports of what appears to be a nuclear device detonated over the Vatican…"*

The blood drained from Ben's face, a ringing in his ears suppressing his senses. "Oh, my, God…" The apartment Jess was in was a mile from the Vatican. He staggered back, his hands numb, and slumped into the chair by his workstation.

In the hallway, cursing and crying.

"…perhaps hundreds of thousands dead," continued the news anchor, *"and ten times that many wounded. Over a million people were assembled around the Vatican today for a Papal address. Reports are that the Pope has been killed, a smoking crater and rubble all that remains of St. Paul's and the Sistine Chapel…"*

Ben turned to Ufuk. "I'm sorry, Mr. Erdogmus, but right now isn't a good time."

"Make sure you talk to me, it's very urgent. It's about sanctuary," Ufuk said as Ben pushed the billionaire out the door and closed it.

Roger stared slack-jawed at the TV screen, but then looked at his laptop again. "Ben, I know this is insane, but you've got to look at this…"

Ben fumbled with his phone and tried Jess's number again. Busy signal this time.

"They weren't at the apartment when the driver came, maybe they were out of the city," Roger said in a gentle voice. "But you gotta look at this," he repeated.

"...initial reports of a blast radius of two thousand feet, suggesting this was a small nuclear device..."

Two thousand feet. Ben walked from the Vatican to *Piazza Navona* a few days ago. *Piazza Navona* was what? At least a mile, Ben calculated in his head. Five thousand feet. And they weren't at the apartment. There was still a chance...

"Ben!" Roger shook his arm. "You *gotta* look at this."

"What?" Ben blinked. What could be more important than the destruction of Rome?

"The gravitational wave detectors at the LIGO facility have been set off."

"By a bomb over the Vatican?" Ben was stunned, his mind scrambled.

Roger shook his head. "Of course not. That wouldn't affect LIGO."

"LIGO?"

"The Laser Interferometer Gravitational Wave Observatory, the physics experiment joint venture between MIT and CalTech, remember? One end in Livingston, Louisiana, with the other two thousand miles away in Hanford, Washington. It was built to measure fluctuations in space-time—"

"The gravitational wave detector, of course I know what LIGO is." Ben's brain recovered from shock and clicked Roger's words into sense.

Roger paused before turning his laptop screen to Ben. "So then look at this."

Ben blinked and reminded himself to breathe. The room receded from his senses. He turned to look at Roger, then at the screen. LIGO. They spent hundreds of millions on the gravitational wave detector, but it hadn't spotted a thing. No gravitational waves. It was one of the last of Einstein's predictions remaining unproven. A few months ago, LIGO was taken offline and new sensors were put in to boost its sensitivity.

What Ben saw on the screen wasn't some marginal signal, though.

He zeroed his attention on the graphs and tables. LIGO was like a giant guitar string, stretched two thousand miles, waiting to be plucked by a perturbation in space-time, but it wasn't just vibrating—LIGO sang. LIGO screamed.

"When is this from?" Ben asked.

"The advanced sensors came online three days ago with readings almost off the charts. They figured it was an error and recalibrated, but…"

"It has to be Nomad," Ben whispered.

"Maybe, but then what is it…?"

A slim list of options.

While anything with mass produced a gravitational field, creating gravitational *waves* required events of almost unimaginable violence. His colleagues at the LIGO facility said they were waiting and hoping that something violent enough would occur close enough to Earth to be noticeable.

They may have gotten their wish. Nomad was ripping apart the very fabric of space and time around the planet now.

Ben pressed his hands together as if praying. "Make a list of what could cause this, and link it back to all the other data. I've got to talk to Dr. Müller."

"I'm on it." Roger said and swallowed.

Ben looked back at the TV, at the mushroom cloud rising over Rome. "My God…"

19

Rome, Italy

JESS CLAWED HERSELF upright. Her ears rang.

A hot wind blew through the alley, scorching her skin, the sickening stench of burnt hair and flesh in her nostrils. She blinked. Tears streamed from her eyes. The ground shook, reverberated through her bones. A deafening roar overloaded her senses. An earthquake? The searing wind slackened, then reversed course, sucking bits of papers along the street in the opposite direction. She blinked again. No, not an earthquake. A mushroom cloud roiled into the dark skies above her, fiery orange flames wrapped in fingers of billowing black smoke.

The reversed wind intensified, dust and debris dragged by it biting against Jess's exposed arms and neck. She strained to keep her eyes open, transfixed on the surreal billowing blackness that grew above; rising, crackling in red and orange, folding into itself as it climbed toward the cloud layers above. The wind howled around her, whistling through the alley.

"Jessica!"

She turned to look at the café entrance.

Her mother hung onto the railing. "Jessica!" Celeste screamed again.

"I'm here," Jess croaked, her throat sandpaper. She sat upright, stunned. The ground vibrated cyclically, a dying thunder echoing between the buildings.

Celeste staggered down the stairs and turned to the sky and stared. The mushroom cloud roiled ever higher. "My God…." Tearing her eyes away, she stumbled to Jess.

"Somebody, please help."

Jess rubbed her eyes and glanced to her left.

The couple at the table next to her were splayed on the ground, the woman leaning over the man. She looked at Jess with wild eyes. "He's bleeding," she whimpered.

Celeste scooped Jess into her arms, pulled her tank top up. "Baby, are you okay?" She inspected Jess's stomach, turned her to look at her back. She held Jess's head in her hands and looked into her eyes. "Jess?"

"I'm fine," Jess replied automatically.

But she wasn't sure.

Her ears rang, her body felt numb. She fought the feeling of *deja vu*. The day she lost her leg crowded her mind, images of blood and fire flashing into her senses.

She shook her head.

Stay in the now.

Stay here.

Focus.

Behind Celeste, the café manager stumbled out of the doorway and down the stairs. He turned and stared at the sky. The wind slackened, the air suddenly calm. Screams pierced the eerie silence, distant booms echoing. High above, the head of the mushroom cloud impacted the layer of rain clouds, a halo of clearing around it like a door opening to heaven. It punched a hole through the clouds, then sucked them upward after it.

"Someone call an ambulance!" the woman next to them screamed. She'd pulled the man into her arms, blood soaking the both of them.

"Go help her." Jess struggled out of her mother's embrace. "I'm fine, go help the lady."

"You sure?" Celeste stared into Jess's eyes.

Her ears still rang, but Jess felt her strength returning. She nodded. "Go, please."

From the doorway beside the café, a wood-paneled door opened. A man appeared holding an infant in his arms. Glancing left and right, he jumped into the street, then turned and looked up. His wife followed, holding the hand of a young boy. All along the street, doors opened and people streamed out and stared into the sky. Everyone began stumbling back, away from the explosion. They turned and ran.

Jess grabbed her crutches and struggled upright. Unsteadily, she stood, then swung over on her crutches to the woman cradling the man in her arms. Celeste crouched over the man, shielding him from the crowd. Jess leaned over to get a better look. The man's body convulsed, blood spurting from a shard of glass embedded in his neck. His fingers clawed at Celeste, his knuckles white. He gagged, blood spitting from his mouth.

His grip on Celeste's shirt slackened.

"What do I do?" Celeste turned to Jess, her face white. "Do you know what to do?"

The man's arms fell to his sides, his body twitching. Jess knew death throes. "There's nothing we can do," she whispered.

"We just got married," the woman cried, pulling her husband into her, rocking back and forth, a low keening wail rising from her trembling lips.

Another man crashed into the woman, fell onto the husband and tumbled past Jess. Slipping and sliding on the blood, the man stood, wiping blood from his hands. He glanced at Jess and Celeste, then at the dead man, but returned to staring at the sky. Shaking his head but not saying anything, he turned and ran. People streamed by, running, screaming, all of them looking up at the sky.

Jess pulled on her mother's arm. "We need to go."

The woman cradled her husband in her arms, rocking back and forth as the sea of people streamed past her. Celeste let go and stood, nodding. Taking one last look, she turned and walked with the flow, reaching to grab Jess.

But Jess stood still.

Her instincts told her to run. Away. To follow the herd. But the first rule of tactical decision making was to follow the plan—unless there was a good reason to deviate. Jess gripped her crutches, felt them dig into her armpits, and steeled herself against Celeste trying to pull her with the crowd. She stared up at the disappearing mushroom cloud, the rain clouds now coming together under it, a pillar of black smoke rising to meet them. Sometimes the right thing to do was the thing that felt wrong.

"Come on, we need to go," Celeste urged, her voice desperate.

"No," Jess said from between gritted teeth. She pulled away from her mother. "This way." She swung forward on her crutches, straight against the flow of the crowd.

"JESS! What are you doing?"

The military Humvee on the corner, the man in the military uniform. That had to be whom her father sent. He said he told the driver to return, and not to leave, not for *any* reason. She glanced up at the column of black smoke. She hoped that this didn't exceed *any reason* for an Italian military attaché.

"Dad sent someone to get us." Jess pressed through the crowd. "If he's still there, that's our best bet on getting out of here."

"We need to go to the American Embassy!" Celeste screamed. She followed Jess anyway.

"Are you kidding? No way we'll be getting in there now. And if we weren't getting out of here by ourselves before, now there's absolutely no way." Jess swung forward, swearing and screaming at people to watch where they were going, to get out of her way.

"Are you sure?" Celeste muscled her way beside Jess. She looked into the sky. "Was that a nuclear bomb? Should we be walking toward it?"

Jess shook her head. "It seemed too small for a nuclear blast, as big as it was." She had firsthand experience with conventional munitions, but the truth was, she wasn't sure. Small tactical nukes existed. "Five minutes this way, and we can see if the driver is still there. If not, then we can go your way."

A gamble.

They crossed the *Piazza Navona* again, pushing through the crowds choking the streets. The flood of clean-faced, scared-looking tourists clutching their children became interspersed with the staggering, ragged and bloodied. A woman, naked, her body burnt and flayed, ran past them screaming. By the time they reached the other side of the *piazza*, everyone was covered in soot, their clothing ripped to shreds over fresh scarlet wounds.

Black smoke billowed up Angela's street when they turned into the alley, dust and debris scattering into the *piazza*. Jess stopped to pull her tank top around her mouth. She squinted into the dust. She couldn't see past the sea of people flowing toward her, the alleyway fading into grayness. Gritting her teeth, she squinted and swung forward on her crutches, doing her best to ignore the wailing people passing her. A woman screamed, appeared out of the grayness holding a bloody mess in her arms. A tiny baby. She disappeared into the brown-gray mist.

Jess's eyes teared.

There.

On the corner.

A car pulled up and its driver jumped out and looked around, then waved at her.

"Mom!" Jess screamed, turning to find Celeste stumbling behind her. "He's here, the man Dad sent!"

Jess hopped forward, swung as fast as she could on the crutches. The outline of the car grew clearer. But that was no Humvee. She swung another few steps closer.

And that was no military attaché.

It wasn't even a man.

"Jessica!" yelled Massarra, the young woman who'd helped them the night before. "Come on, get in." She ran around the other side of his car, a small Hyundai, and opened the door.

Swinging the last two paces to the car, Jessica grabbed onto the door and stared at Massarra. "What are you doing here? Did my father send you?" This didn't make any sense. Jess glanced inside the car. One of Massarra's uncles nodded at her, urged her to get inside the car.

"I knew you were here," Massarra replied. "As I said, we were driving north. We need to hurry."

The billowing smoke thinned, and dark droplets inked the cobblestones. Jess looked up, the smoke clearing enough to see the clouds again, churning in the sky. Her hair blew back in a sudden wind, and a squall of raindrops fell across the car. Black streaks ran down the windshield. If that was an atomic blast, this rain could be toxic.

"Please, help me," a woman pleaded in front of Jess, half of her face gone, replaced by an angry red mass of blood and blackened flesh hanging under one eye.

Huge black drops fell from the sky, spattering off the cobblestones. Tactical decision making dictated following the plan, but it also meant being flexible when needed. The black rain pelted against the windshield, ran in dark rivulets down Jess's arms.

"Mom!" Jess yelled. "Get in!" She opened the back door for Celeste and waited for her mother to get in beside the uncle.

Jess jumped into the passenger seat and slammed the door shut.

20

Rome, Italy

"SORRY, BUT I cannot drive to Germany." Massarra's smile turned to a grimace. She shifted gears and accelerated onto the on-ramp of *Autostrade 90,* Rome's ring road. "We are driving home to Turkey. It's a twenty-hour drive, but it's the only way. I can drive you near to Florence, but I must go east from there." Her two other uncles had managed to get a flight, she explained. After getting the car, she decided to look for Jess and Celeste. She knew they needed help. Once you became involved in someone's life, she explained, there was an obligation to stay involved. At least, that was he way her world worked.

*Whomp-whimp…whomp-whimp…*the windshield wipers swished back and forth, slicking the rain away. Jess glanced to her right. Through the mist, a gray smudge over the center of Rome stretched into the clouds. Stopped cars lined the *Autostrade*, the passengers outside them hanging over the guardrails, everyone staring at what was left of the Eternal City.

Massarra's uncle sat stoically in the back seat beside Celeste. This one didn't speak English, Massarra explained, switching into Arabic from time to time to update him.

In their flight from the center of Rome, the crush of people—ragged and bloody walking corpses—had thinned after a few blocks. There was nothing they could do but get out, get away from the noxious black rain. At the first roundabout, they passed a knot of overwhelmed ambulances, and after a few more blocks, only the noise of sirens and police cars screaming past into the city gave any indication of the destruction behind them. They'd been caught in a heavy downpour, but the rain was almost finished. Just a spattering onto the windshield. The sun broke through the clouds.

Massarra turned off the wipers. "You said you had a friend you stayed with, in Chianti?" She glanced at Celeste in the back seat. "Giovanni? Perhaps I could drop you there?"

"It's not a *bad* idea." Celeste leaned forward. "Giovanni sent you a text, saying we could come back there, right?" she asked Jess. "If we needed help?"

Jess nodded. "But I haven't talked to him. And how did…?" She looked at Celeste, flicked her chin in Massarra's direction.

"You fell asleep, but Massarra and I talked for hours. I told her about where we stayed, about your father. If anyone has communication gear to reach Ben, I'd bet Giovanni has it. Short wave radios, all sorts of stuff in his office."

Jess nodded. It did make sense.

"And…" Celeste whispered, beckoning Jess to lean closer. "…We don't know what's happening. Maybe this is just a small part of something larger. We need to get somewhere safe."

Jess hadn't thought of that. Was this the first salvo in the start of a global war?

Images of New York burning flashed through her mind. They had the radio on, but they could only find Italian stations. None of them, not even Massarra, spoke Italian well enough to decipher what the radio announcers screamed about. They kept the radio on anyway. After stopping at a gas station on the way out of Rome, they managed to piece together that there hadn't been any other attacks. Not yet, anyway.

Massarra took the exit for *Autostrade* A1, the highway connecting Rome and Florence. The skies cleared, patches of blue showing through, and apartment blocks gave way to rolling hills.

"Giovanni's castle withstood a thousand years of everything the world threw at it," Celeste said to Jess in a low whisper. "Those Etruscan caves, I'll bet people hid in there from earthquakes, eruptions…"

Jess stared at a village nestled on a mountaintop in the distance. High up. Protected.

"Okay," Jess conceded, "let's go back to Giovanni's place."

Celeste squeezed her shoulder. "Good."

Even so, something about this felt wrong. The most important thing in any crisis was to collect information and find a safe place to regroup. Jess just lived through a horrific disaster, but that wasn't it. She couldn't put her finger on what it was, but something wasn't right.

Then again, they didn't have many options.

Massarra had probably saved their lives not once, but *twice* in the past twenty-four hours, and Castello Ruspoli was about as safe a place as she could imagine.

"Massarra, can you take us to the Castello?" Celeste asked, sitting back. "It's 45 minutes off the A1, to the west."

"Yes," Massarra replied. "But I can't stay. Do you know the way?"

"I know the way."

Jess settled into her seat and watched the countryside slide by. The drive from Rome to *Castello Ruspoli* wasn't far—not in North American terms, not even two hours. The change in scenery was dramatic; in twenty minutes they went from cityscape to the rolling, baked-earth hills of central Tuscany. Surreal. She watched a man in a tractor till his fields, as if that mattered anymore.

At *Bettole* they pulled off the main highway and wound their way through small towns. At open-air cafés, people stood in groups watching TVs, images of a wrecked Rome flashing as they passed. The setting sun lit high, thin clouds pink as Massarra pulled the car onto a dusty road with a sign for *Castello Ruspoli*. Climbing the zigzag road up the side of the hill, through the olive groves, at the top they followed a brick-walled alley to the main castle gates.

Massarra stopped the car at the entrance. It was closed. "This is it, yes?"

Staring out the windshield, Jess saw the first star of the night in the darkening sky—not a star, she realized, but Venus. But there were no lights in the castle. Strange.

"Yes, this is it." Jess stepped out of the car, arranged her crutches, and swung to the small wooden entrance beside the massive iron portico gates. "Hello?" she called out.

"Are you sure you won't stay the night?" Jess heard her mother ask Massarra.

“I will make sure you have somewhere to stay, but we need to go,” came Massarra’s quiet reply.

“It was nice to meet you again,” Celeste said to Massarra’s uncle as she got out.

Jess searched for a buzzer, a knocker. Nothing. She banged the door with her fist, as hard as she could. “Giovanni!” she yelled. “It’s Jess and Celeste.”

The place felt deserted.

Had something happened? Maybe Giovanni left for Florence. Massarra could drop them there, but the prospect of another city felt dangerous. And how or why would they look for Giovanni anyway? She liked being in the countryside. Open space. Calming her breathing, she listened. Crickets sang in the silence, their chirps echoing off the walls.

She turned to Massarra and Celeste. “I don’t think anyone is”—the door to the castle swung open—“here.”

Giovanni stood in the doorway, a holstered handgun on his hip. “Yes?” he asked, his brows knitted together in a scowl.

“Ah, sorry for not calling,” Jess mumbled. “But, we got stuck in Rome.” As her eyes adjusted to the darkness inside, she saw two thick-set men in bullet proof vests and dark clothing standing behind Giovanni. Between them stood Nico, who smiled warmly and waved.

But Giovanni didn’t smile. He stared hard at Jess. “And…?”

She hadn’t given much thought to how Giovanni might react when they showed up on his doorstep. He had invited them, after all. She imagined an impassioned reunion, tears over the horrors of Rome. It made sense that they might show up. She didn’t expect this cold, standoffish reaction. She felt self-conscious, exposed, the stump of her leg cold. “We were hoping we might be able to stay here. You invited us.”

Giovanni stared at her. Seconds ticked by. “And who is that?” He flicked his chin in the direction of Massarra.

“A friend,” Celeste answered. “She gave us a lift.”

“And you want to come in?” Giovanni asked. “Anything else?”

Were those bodyguards behind him? That made sense, but not the way Giovanni acted. Hadn’t he asked them to come here if they needed help? What game was he playing? Jess felt her hackles rising. "We need help. That's why we're here. We exchanged texts, you said to come back if we had problems."

"You need help?" Giovanni took a step back. "Then come in, by all means."

Nico stepped forward. "Jessica, I tried talking to him, but—"

"Silence!" Giovanni turned to glare at Nico. "No more talking." He smiled at Jess. "Please, come in."

The feeling of a surreal break from reality intensified. Jess swung forward on her crutches, through the door. Celeste followed. Except for the two bodyguards and Nico and Giovanni, the interior gravel courtyard was empty, the lights everywhere off.

"Did you see what happened in Rome?" Jess asked, taking two loping steps in before stopping.

That had to be it, why Giovanni was acting so strange. Maybe he'd lost friends or family. Jess cursed herself for being thoughtless. For her it was a terrifying shock, but for him, it must be like a New Yorker who lived in lower Manhattan after 9/11.

Jess tried to reach for Giovanni. "I'm so sorry—"

"What do you have to be sorry for?" Giovanni asked sharply, pulling away from her. He turned on his heel and crunched across the gravel, past the gnarled roots of the ancient olive tree. "This way." But he didn't lead them up the main stairs to the living quarters. He walked toward an open wooden door with metal bars just off the courtyard.

Jess followed him. Nico hung back behind the bodyguards, his head hanging low between his shoulders. She heard the car's engine start outside the walls, gravel crunching under its wheels, the sound fading.

"Do they know what happened yet?" Celeste asked from behind Jess.

Giovanni stopped at the door, indicating that Jess should enter ahead of him. "And who is '*they*'?"

Jess and Celeste glanced at each other. *What was going on?* Jess shrugged and turned back to Giovanni. "The media, the government, I don't know."

She swung forward through the open door into darkness. He

hadn't even asked what happened to her leg. Inside, she stopped and let her eyes adjust to the darkness. She expected to see a staircase, or perhaps a lobby to rooms on a lower level. These were the stables. Rough stone walls with floors covered in hay. No horses. The door swung shut behind her, a grinding *ka-chunk* signaling the lock closing.

"But as to what's going on," Giovanni continued, "that's something I would like you to answer."

Jess wobbled around on her crutches. "What are you doing?"

Giovanni pressed his face against the metal bars of the door's window, pointed a finger at Jess. "The question is, what are *you* doing?" He disappeared.

A muffled scream. "Let go of me!" Celeste yelled. Thrashing in the gravel.

Jess hobbled back to the door. "Mom?!"

Another scream, louder this time, and then a door slamming shut.

21

Darmstadt, Germany

"AN EVACUATION OF *Rome has been ordered...*" said the CNN news anchor.

Ben watched the TV screen in their office with dread. Still no word from the driver. Still no word from Jess or Celeste. He had yelled at Dr. Müller, vented his frustration and fear on him, but really, it wasn't his fault. After his public tantrum, Ben went and locked himself in a bathroom stall where he cried—and prayed.

When times were good, when he felt healthy and optimistic, there was no need for God. Brought up Protestant, Ben now thought of himself as an atheist. He saw no cracks in the fabric of existence that demanded a Creator.

Not until his existence cracked around him.

But there was no answering call to his prayers, no signs, no telephone calls or emails. It was just the universe, ticking over, oblivious to the wants of humans, even the billions now praying with Ben—and certainly oblivious to the individual needs of Benjamin Rollins.

And so what if a few hundred thousand people were killed? In months they'd all be dead anyway. What was coming, nothing could stop.

"My big question." Roger sat in his cubicle, bent over his laptop with scraps of paper littered around it. "If Nomad is a black hole, how did it get moving so fast?"

Ben stared at the TV, the image of blackened corpses laid out beside the Tiber. *Is one of them Jess? Celeste?* Something inside Ben told him, *no*. If something had happened to one of them, he'd know. Something inside of him would know. For a man of science, the sudden belief in a mystical connection seemed beyond argument.

"Not one black hole—but two." Ben forced part of his mind back. "Nomad is a binary pair of them."

It was the only explanation for the rising intensity of gravitational waves LIGO measured. Now that they suspected the readings weren't a glitch, Ben was trying to match the data to theoretical models. They'd sent a request for all of LIGO's data from the past three days. If Nomad was a binary pair, two black holes sweeping around each other in tight orbits, this information could confirm it.

They hadn't told Dr. Müller yet. The ESOC teams were focused on the Gaia observatory and new radial velocity measurements coming in from around the world. The LIGO connection could still be a red herring.

But if it wasn't, LIGO could pinpoint the incoming velocity of Nomad. So far they only had one data point: LIGO measurements from the end of the day before. In a few minutes, they should be getting all its readings from the past three days. Any changes in intensity should give a straightforward answer to the speed of Nomad. So far, the new radial velocity measurements only provided an order-of-magnitude of a thousand kilometers per second, on a route inside the orbit of Saturn.

Ben glanced back at the TV on the wall. Massive street demonstrations in Karachi and Baghdad.

"…officials in Washington pin the attack in Rome on the Islamic Caliphate terrorist organization. The Caliphate is denying involvement for the attack, but claiming this is the starting signal for a final jihad before the hand of God wipes the Earth clean…"

If the world was thrown into shock at the announcement of Nomad, now it was a mix of equal parts panic and anger. For some people it meant a finite amount of time to prove that they were right—one last chance for vengeance. The ultimate last words were about to be spoken.

"But over a thousand kilometers per second?" Roger furrowed his brows together. "Nothing should move that fast."

"Not true," Ben replied. "A billion light years away, whole galaxies are moving away from us at 20,000 kilometers a second."

"But that's on the other side of the visible universe. And other galaxies are moving *away.*"

In 1929, Edwin Hubble had famously discovered that all other galaxies moved away from us; that the universe was expanding. Except that *not* all galaxies moved away from us.

"Not our closest galaxy, Andromeda," Ben said. "It's moving toward us at over a hundred kilometers a second. In four billion years, it'll collide with the Milky Way." He smiled wryly. "But that's a problem for another day."

"Sure, Andromeda's moving toward us at a hundred kilometers a second," Roger agreed. "And our solar system is moving around our galactic core at two hundred kilometers a second, but thousands of kilometers a second? Even in the detonation of a star, the expanding material has to push against something to accelerate it. With black holes, there's nothing to push against—even a supernova wouldn't give it that much kick."

Ben shook his head. "This wasn't pushed, and I don't think Nomad was ever a part of our universe, not really."

"...the Pentagon raised the alert status to DEFCON 2," said the news anchor on the TV. *"...only seen a few times before, during the Cuban missile crisis and after the 9/11 attacks..."*

Ben looked at the TV again. The idiots. By the time Nomad arrived, humans might have already destroyed the world. Maybe this *was* the hand of God wiping the Earth clean.

The TV announcement was enough to pull Roger from his computer screen. He watched with Ben for a few seconds before asking, "So what do you think Nomad is, then?"

"I think Nomad is a black hole pair, formed during the creation of our universe."

"Still doesn't explain how it's moving so fast."

Roger wasn't thinking deep enough. "Ever hear of gravitational recoil?" Ben's laptop pinged. The data from LIGO. He opened the attached spreadsheet and looked at the data from the day before.

"Ah..." Roger squeezed his eyes shut so hard it looked like it hurt. "When two black holes merge?"

"Exactly. When they coalesce, their combined gravitational waves carry linear momentum, sometimes enough to eject the core from a galaxy. Theoretical limits are accelerations of thousands of kilometers a second."

"Okay, that's possible." Roger nodded. "Unlikely, but possible."

"Some people think the universe hasn't existed long enough for the massive black holes at the center of galaxies to form. That it would take longer than fifteen billion years for the million-plus solar mass monsters to exist just by stars falling into them."

Ben entered the LIGO data into his calculation spreadsheet.

"Primordial black holes might have formed during the creation of our universe," he continued. "Maybe the start of our universe was a giant game of billiards, with trillions of medium-sized black holes merging into the galactic cores, while some of them, like Nomad, shot free. If I'm right, I think Nomad is shrapnel left over from the Big Bang."

He frowned at his spreadsheet. That couldn't be right. A knot formed in his stomach, his cheeks flushing. He stared at the number on his screen. *That can't be right.*

"Can you check this for me?" Ben clicked *forward* on the LIGO data email, sending it to Roger. "See if you can come up with a relative velocity?" He glanced at the TV. The images of street protests changed to a room with a table of men in ill-fitting suits. Scientists.

"...latest reports indicate that there is no significant radiation detected in central Rome," said one of the men around the table, *"leading our experts to conclude that the bomb over Rome was not a nuclear device."*

"What was it then?" asked the news anchor.

A grainy image of a large air transport filled the screen. An object dropped from the back of it, a parachute opening above it. A second later, the screen went white. *"This is a security camera footage of what we believe to be the device detonated over the Vatican. It resembles a Russian MOAB, a ten-ton conventional munition similar to the BLU-82 used by American forces in the Vietnam War. It has a yield of about twenty tons of TNT, with a blast radius of..."*

So it wasn't a nuclear device. There was a chance. The TV switched to an aerial view of central Rome. While the Vatican, and buildings around it, were rubble, on the other side of the Tiber, the buildings stood intact. That's where Jess and Celeste were. They had to be alive.

"Jesus Christ."

Ben blinked and turned to Roger. "What number did you get?"

"This can't be right," Roger whispered.

Ben saw the shock on Roger's face. "What did you get?"

"Eight."

"At what combined mass?"

"About forty."

Ben swallowed hard. "Me too."

"What trajectory did you get?" Roger looked nervously at Ben.

"...the Pentagon is saying that Chechen rebels worked with a splinter group of the Pakistani army to steal a MOAB from the Russian army," said the news anchor in the background. *"...would never have been so bold to launch an attack, but were spurred by the announcement of Nomad which they view as a biblical event like the one described by Noah..."*

Calculating the three dimensional path of an invisible object was no easy thing. Ben checked his spreadsheets, clicking in the data from LIGO. Together with the new radial velocity searches and visual observations of Uranus, it narrowed down the list of solutions. He checked the numbers again. "Declination of one-eighty-one, inclination of one-point-five with closest solar approach of seventy four million kilometers, and forty solar masses, plus or minus."

"About what I got, too." Roger rubbed his shaking hands together. "I guess that explains it."

It all made sense.

They couldn't see anything because Nomad was a black hole, and not only that, but a binary pair of them. No visible microlensing, at least not the sort they were looking for. Two smaller black holes, rotating around each other at high speed, would create a flickering microlensing that might be impossible to detect, even at close range. It wasn't what the Gaia team was even looking for.

And the reason why it seemed to come from nowhere: eight thousand kilometers a second. Like Roger said, *nothing was supposed to move that fast.* Especially not something that massive.

But there was no arguing with the data.

Only in the last decade or two have humans had devices sensitive enough to perform radial velocity searches of distant stars. And in that time, scientists *had* measured Nomad's presence, but the data was subtracted as some unknown dark matter mass in the nearby spiral arm of the Milky Way. And they might have been right—this might actually be a chunk of the fabled *dark matter*.

Like a train on a straight track that stretched to the horizon, it seemed almost stationary as it approached, but take your eye off it for a second—and only in the last few hundred yards do you realize how fast the train is coming. In this case, the last few hundred yards was the last few hundred billion kilometers—the distance Nomad had traveled in the past year—just a fractional distance in cosmic terms.

Nomad was heading straight into the center of the solar system at eight thousand kilometers a second. A cosmic runaway freight train on a bullseye course.

And it wasn't twenty billion kilometers away.

It wasn't even ten.

Nomad—two tiny invisible objects spinning around each other, each barely ten kilometers across yet with a combined mass fifty times that of the entire solar system—was already inside the orbit of Uranus, halfway from there to Saturn. Less than three billion kilometers away, and Ben and Roger were the only people on the planet who knew.

But not for long.

Tomorrow morning, Uranus was going to look like a toy grabbed by a dog and thrown around the sky.

His mouth dry, Ben glanced at the TV. "*…the United States and NATO are preparing for a retaliatory nuclear strike…*"

In three days, Nomad would destroy the Earth.

If we didn't destroy it first.

SURVIVOR TESTIMONY

#AR84;

Event +112hrs
Survivor name: Ain Salah;
Reported location: Al-Jawf, Libya;

Rain, so much rain. Where are you again? Italy? (*coughs*) Yes, it is dark here now as well, days of darkness, but also rain. I've worked in oilfields deep in the Sahara for ten years. In all that time I've seen it rain here, one day of rain in ten years. There are mud brick buildings in the old town that have stood for a thousand years in the baking sun, and now they're gone. Washed away. It hasn't stopped raining in three days.

The temperature here? Usually forty degrees—a hundred and ten in your Fahrenheit—but now it's cool. Maybe fifteen degrees. But so much water, I've never seen so much water…it's as if God…rivers, lakes forming in the depressions…

Transmission ended in static. Freq. 7442 kHz/NSB.

Subject reacquired pgs 15, 24, 38…

DAY SIX

October 11th

22

Chianti, Italy

"LET ME OUT!" Jess screamed, her face pressed against the cold metal bars of the door. She had worried about ending up in jail, but could never have even imagined this. Her mind reeled, skidding off the tracks of reality. A bile of anger rose inside her, *how can he treat us like this?* What were they doing to her mother?

This couldn't be happening. But what *was* happening?

Through the metal bars of the stable door, she watched the crescent moon rise. She was left in the stable all night, freezing cold, in near pitch-blackness. It smelled of damp stone and hay. She didn't pace around. Balanced on her crutches, with just one foot swinging between them, she didn't want to slip and fall into a pile of horse manure. So when she got tired of yelling, she sat on a bench against the wall, in the dark, or stood, resting her armpits on her crutches, and looked out the window to stare at the stars. The sky was calm, serene, but every hour was another hour Nomad approached.

This was a complete clusterfuck.

"Giovanni!" she screamed, her voice hoarse from hours of pleading. She leaned against the stable door, her face against the metal bars, her thigh burning from supporting her body. "Why are you doing this?"

There were no lights on in the courtyard, no lights in the castle. And apart from the rustle of the oak trees, no movement or noise in the empty blackness for hours. On the horizon, the stars began to wash away in the pre-dawn twilight, only Venus remaining, its yellow disk burning bright.

"Wrong?" The words floated from the darkness, poison in them. Ghost-like, Giovanni's face appeared in the faint light, a few feet from

Jess. "Have you done something wrong? I think, perhaps, that is a matter between you and God."

He stared at her, his eyes piercing Jess's soul. What was he talking about? And then—did he know her secret? But how would he know? Did he talk to Celeste? Did she even know?

Gripping the metal bars, her knuckles white, Jess turned her fear inside out, transformed it into anger. "What the hell is wrong with you?" she spat. "If you hurt my mother, I'll *kill* you."

"That might be the first thing I believe from your mouth all night."

"What…? Have you been listening?" She'd been ranting for hours, alternating between threats and begging for help.

In the gathering twilight, the outlines of the courtyard became visible from the blackness, with old L'Olio, the ancient olive tree, the eldest Ruspoli, standing in the center—judging her—its gnarled roots digging into the hard earth. Giovanni dragged a wooden bench from beside the wall in front of the stable door and sat on it.

"Most of the night, yes." Giovanni adjusted himself on the bench, leaned over and lit a cigarette. He faced her, his face lit orange in the glow from the burning tip of the cigarette. He took a puff.

Jess ground her teeth together. Taking a deep breath, she released the metal bars, unclenching her fists. *Calm.* Ranting wasn't going to solve anything; wasn't going to get her any information. But first things first. "I don't know what's going on, Giovanni, but I need to call my father, tell him where we are. All of our possessions were stolen in Rome."

"Stolen? From you?" Giovanni scoffed. He puffed on the cigarette. "And I saw your father on television, saying Nomad might be nothing. Seems a different story than the one you told me. Who should I trust?"

Jess shook her head. "I think he's trying to calm people down." She took a deep breath, and her lungs filled with a pungent whiff of the cigarette smoke.

Her father used to smoke when she was little, in his study at the cottage in the Catskills. She loved the smell, even though she knew it was bad for you. The same odd way she loved the smell of gasoline. Someone said it was a sign of an addictive personality. She loved it just the same.

"I don't understand why you're acting like this," Jess added. "You're the one that texted me, asked me to come back here if we had problems."

Giovanni stared at her, took another puff and dropped the cigarette, coughing. Still sitting on the bench, he ground the cigarette out underfoot, crunching the gravel back and forth.

"After Nico dropped us at the airport, you and I exchanged text messages," Jess explained. "Don't you remember? I even told you where I was staying." She narrowed her eyes. Did Giovanni send Enzo? Why would he do that?

"And can you show me this…" Giovanni waved a hand in the air. "…text?"

"Like I said, everything we had was stolen in Rome."

Giovanni raised his eyebrows in mock surprise. "Convenient."

"You think this is convenient?" Jess growled, wrapping her fingers around the cold metal bars again, wishing she could wrap them around Giovanni's neck. "They stole my *leg*."

Clenching her jaw, she tried to fight it, but a tear spilled down her cheek. She wiped it away, turning her head to one side. When she looked back—just for an instant—Jess saw the tenderness she'd seen in Giovanni's eyes before, but it flashed away.

His brows came together in a scowl. "Something far more precious has been stolen from me."

Stolen? Jess exhaled and shook her head. Was he really so fixated on material possessions at a time like this? Staring at him, she waited for details about what was stolen, but he just stared back at her. She frowned. "Wait, are you saying you *didn't* text me?"

"The police were here again." Giovanni ignored her question. "Asking about *Rome*." He paused to take out another cigarette and lit it. Taking a drag, he let the smoke curl out slowly. It wreathed around his head. "Were you involved?"

Jess pressed her forehead against the metal bars, letting their damp chill seep into her head. Why would the police still care about her selling that car? Didn't they have bigger things to worry about? She shrugged aggressively. "Yes, I did it."

"So you admit it?" Giovanni shot to his feet, his hands flying wide.

"I didn't think you cared—"

"About destroying Rome?" Giovanni demanded incredulously.

"WHAT?" Jess let go of the metal bars, backing up into the recesses of the stable. "I sold a car, that's all I did. You think I had something to do with the bombing in Rome?"

Giovanni stared at her, his face stony. "That's what the police were here for, looking for you. A terrorist connection. Said they had a video."

The air sucked from Jess's lungs. She felt disembodied, the opening in the stable door floating away in the blackness. "That's insane." The words, barely more than a whisper, seemed to come from someone else's lips.

"On that we can agree." Giovanni took an aggressive pull from his cigarette, the tip glowing, bathing his face in an angry red. "You come here, prophesying about the end of the world, telling me to protect myself. So I bring in security, make preparations…then I see your father on TV, saying not to worry. And then Rome is destroyed."

Jess shook her head. "I just think he's—"

"And the police are back here looking for you, after I protected you, and then here you are again." Taking a deep drag from the cigarette, he erupted in a fit of coughing. Shaking his head, he dropped the smoke and stamped on it. Breathing deep, he returned to staring at Jess; angry creases brought the frown in his face into high relief, even in the dim light of dawn.

"I know this is crazy," Jess pleaded. She tried to think. "You did text me, though. Go and check your phone." She pressed her face against the metal bars, reached one hand through them. "And what was stolen from you? I had nothing to do with that."

The muscles in Giovanni's jaw rippled. "Hector."

"What about Hector? What did he do?"

"He did nothing," Giovanni said from between gritted teeth. "It is Hector who was stolen."

Jess blinked, pulled her hand back. "Hector was kidnapped?"

"He is gone, that is all I know." Giovanni slumped onto the bench. He put his face in his hands. "I called the police yesterday, before you arrived, but they have more on their hands right now." He looked up at Jess. "Perhaps I should call them again, tell them I have you. That might get them back here."

Jess let go of the metal bars again, retreated a step on her crutches. "No, don't do that."

Stuck in an Italian jail, interrogated for terrorism? As much as it didn't make sense, she believed what Giovanni was telling her. But if the police took her now, she'd never get out. She glanced at the brightening sky. How much time was left? She needed to get out of here.

"Why shouldn't I?" Giovanni demanded, getting to his feet. "Tell me everything. No more lies."

"Christ, Giovanni, I don't know what's going on." *Think, come on, think,* Jess urged in her head. "The people you brought here, for security—is anyone else gone? Who could have taken Hector?"

"Nobody else is gone." Giovanni took a step toward the door, toward Jess. "I sent Leone to follow Massarra, your new friend that drove you here…and Enzo, we sent him into Rome to collect some things, but we haven't—"

"Enzo?" His face flashed in Jess's mind. When their things were stolen. Half-glimpsed, she wasn't one hundred percent sure before. But now Giovanni was saying that Enzo was in Rome? *Sent* by Giovanni? "Did you send him? He's the one that stole our things."

Giovanni took two more steps to the door, his face inches from Jess's. "Why would he do that?"

Enzo had creeped Jess out the moment she met him. Something in his eyes. Still, a creepy feeling wasn't proof of anything. Then she remembered his eyes, staring at her in the staircase, when she came down from the observatory. Jess cursed. "He heard me, when I was talking to you, saying that Nomad was coming."

"In the observatory?"

"Yes." Jess nodded emphatically. "After we talked, I came down the stairs, and he was there."

She hadn't made much of it at the time, but the enormity of it now weighed on her. Revealing that death and destruction was coming, but keeping it a secret? "Did you talk with him about it later?" she asked

Giovanni.

"No." He shook his head. "You said not to tell anyone. I closed the castle, made preparations and asked Hector's mother and father to return, but I didn't tell any of the staff, not except for Nico." He pointed to his right. "He's the only one I trust."

Jess followed his hand and peered into a dark corner of the courtyard to see Nico sitting on another bench. She hadn't seen him before. She looked back at Giovanni. "You closed up the castle after I told you about Nomad? And you didn't tell Enzo why? Don't you think he might have…I mean…"

Nico stood. "I'm afraid Jess might be right."

Giovanni's head spun to look at him. "What? Why would Enzo attack Jessica?"

"He might not be stable." Nico walked toward them. The sun broke over a mountaintop on the horizon, spilling bright light into the valley. "Your father hired him as a favor to a friend. Enzo was in jail. A new start is what your father was trying to offer him."

"Why did you never tell me this?" Giovanni slammed the door with his fist.

"Your father asked me to keep it a secret, but I've been watching him. For the past three years, he's been perfectly faithful and reliable…but now Jess is saying he attacked her in Rome." Nico joined Giovanni at the door. "I believe her. And Enzo hasn't returned our calls since he left."

"Rome is a mess," Giovanni countered.

"Yes, but I did some digging on Enzo when we hired him. He doesn't come from where he said he did."

"And you never told me?" Giovanni's face reddened.

"Your father, he died, and I promised…"

Giovanni closed his eyes. "Hector is the last in an unbroken line of a thousand years of the Ruspoli family. We *need* to find him." He turned to Jess. "Excuse us, I need to talk to your mother, confirm something."

Giovanni put an arm on Nico's shoulder. "Could you get Jessica something warm?"

Nico nodded. "Of course."

Shaking his head, Giovanni walked away, past the twisted branches of L'Olio, and up the castle's exterior staircase.

"I am very sorry," Nico said as they watched Giovanni disappear into the main building. "This is just…"

Jess shivered. "Crazy, I know."

23

Chianti, Italy

A FLY BUZZED through the cool morning air, darting between the bars of the stable door to zigzag above Jess's head. Slumped against the stone wall, sitting on a cold wooden bench, she watched the fly climb toward a spider's web bejeweled with dew drops that dazzled in the slanting rays of sunrise.

One wrong zag, and the fly ensnared itself in the web, ejecting a spray of droplets. The spider appeared, darted forward and sank its fangs into its hapless prey. In a moment, the struggle was over, the spider wrapping its prize to eat later at its leisure. The fly never realized a predator lurked in its midst—not in such a beautiful, quiet space.

Metal scraped against metal. Ancient hinges groaned. The stable door opened and Giovanni's grimacing face appeared. "I am very sorry, I must apologize—"

"I told you never to apologize." Grabbing her crutches, Jess stood. "I would have done the same if I were you."

Even so, relief washed through her. And it was the truth. If she'd been him, she might have done worse—if someone stole her child in the middle of these strange coincidences piling up. How would she react? Violently, if she had to guess.

Giovanni tried to offer her a hand. "Yes, but…"

Jess ignored him and swung forward on her crutches, letting the brown woolen blanket Nico had given her an hour before fall to the hay-strewn floor. Exiting the dark and damp into bright sunshine, Jess shivered. What a relief to get out of the overpowering stench of horse manure. Two nights in these clothes. She stank, her hair a matted and tangled mess.

His head hung low, Giovanni backed away. He took off ahead of her and jogged up the stairs to the main building. "This way. Your mother is waiting."

"So you believe me now?" Jess followed and grabbed onto the stair's railing to hop up. "What about the text messages? You didn't send them to me?"

"No, I didn't." Giovanni stopped at the top of the stairs. "My phone was stolen. It must be Enzo."

"And that must be how he found me."

"How he found you?" Giovanni frowned.

"I texted you the address where I was staying," Jess explained.

A part of her could see how Enzo might be angry. Jess would be angry too, if someone hid a deadly danger and lied about it. She'd want to lash out. Maybe that's what this was. It made a certain sense. Jess hopped the last step onto the patio, straight into the arms of her waiting mother.

"Are you okay?" Celeste hugged her, pulling a woolen sweater around Jess's shoulders. "This has all been a terrible misunderstanding. Enzo must have taken Hector, and—"

"I know." Jess gently pushed her off, smelling strong soap and perfume. Her mother hadn't quite gotten the same treatment she did. She smelled like she just got out of a shower, and that was just what Jess needed.

Behind Celeste, under an oak tree on the stone patio, was a picnic table laid out with a red-checked tablecloth, its surface filled with breads and cheeses. Her mouth watered. She hadn't realized how hungry she was. Food before shower.

Giovanni followed her eyes. "Do you want to eat first? I'll run you a hot bath in one of the guest rooms, and after that I have a little surprise."

Jess swung forward three paces on her crutches, leaned onto the table and sat heavily. She stuffed a lump of cheese into her mouth. "Not sure I want any more surprises from you."

She chewed. The cheese was incredible, a pungent burst spreading across her tongue. She stuffed another wad into her mouth and sighed. Glancing over the table, the valley below glowing green, the sky painfully blue, the lines and angles sharp and detailed. Everything felt sped up, all her senses amplified and sharpened. Every breath became more precious now that every breath was numbered.

Celeste came up behind Jess, put her hands on her daughter's head. "Oh, I think you'll like the surprise Giovanni has for you."

"What kind of car is this again?" Jess asked.

"Maserati." Giovanni coasted to a stop on the gravel road beneath the spreading branches of a thicket of juniper trees, their trunks knotted like muscles. Downshifting into neutral, the high performance engine whined high.

"Why don't you show me what it can do?" She loved cars, and despite the ordeal of the night before, she'd struggled to contain her excitement when Giovanni turned on the lights in the downstairs garage and illuminated two rows of glittering machines. Even with the convertible's top down, the interior oozed the scent of polished leather.

A dusty cloud enveloped the car as they crunched over the gravel to a stop at the intersection. Giovanni revved the engine, glancing left and right on the main road. "What do you want to see?"

The sun was hot on Jess's skin. She couldn't see Giovanni's eyes through his dark sunglasses. "Fast, show me fast."

Giovanni revved again, glanced left up the road and nodded. "Okay."

Stomping on the accelerator, the car lurched out of the intersection, tearing up gravel, then rocketed off in a blue haze as it hit the pavement. Squeezed against her seat, Jess smiled, the wind ripping at her hair. A tiny thrill was just what she needed.

Giovanni still hadn't revealed where they were going.

A surprise.

Where did he want to take her? Jess had resisted, but her mother gently insisted. With Hector missing, Jess couldn't imagine what could be so important that he needed to show her, right now. Despite cleaning up, she was exhausted after barely sleeping in two nights.

Perhaps he wanted to illustrate why he'd been so harsh?

He didn't need to do that, not with Hector kidnapped. She understood. They'd called the police again, left an offer of a huge reward. After talking to Hector's father in Africa—they couldn't get flights back—Giovanni even contacted the local mafia. Old family connections, Giovanni had explained.

After eating, Jess soaked in a hot tub of water in an ornate bathtub, washed her hair twice, luxuriated in drying herself with thick white towels. On the bed in her room she found a collection of summer blouses and slacks. From Giovanni's mother, Celeste had explained. Jess had never even asked about his mother. She didn't like to pry, and he hadn't ever spoken of her. She was sure her mother knew the whole story, but that could wait. The clothes fit perfectly.

Celeste tried calling Jess's father, Ben, to tell them where they were. Frustratingly, his phone was off again. They left voice messages, and then email messages telling him they were back at the castle and safe. They tried calling the ESOC at Darmstadt directly, even using the emergency number Ben gave them, and Giovanni managed to find a contact that got them through to the overloaded main desk. But the receptionist only said that yes, Dr. Rollins was at the facility and she would try to get him to contact them.

The car hugged the road, Giovanni saying nothing as he expertly piloted it through olive groves and lines of vines sagging under loads of purple grapes, workers hunched over in the rows between them. They crested a ridge, moving from the shade of the junipers into bright sunshine. Emerald pastures dotted with the dark green spikes of cypress trees and spiky stubble of vineyards stretched to the horizon.

Jess felt like they soared across the countryside, the frustration and tension of the last two nights ripped away by the air streaming through her hair. They'd find Hector. Jess figured Enzo just wanted money, and Giovanni had enough of that. Everything would be fine. She leaned forward to turn up the satellite radio tuned to BBC World News.

"...new reports indicate that Uranus is shifting dramatically in its orbit. NASA and the European Space Agency still have not been able to see Nomad, but scientists are saying it's already affecting Earth's orbit, and will enter the solar

system in a matter of weeks..."

"Goddamn it, I wish we could talk to my dad," Jess muttered under her breath.

"...breaking news..."

It was hard to hear over the rushing wind. Jess increased the volume.

"...unrest in the Middle East taking a rapid turn for the worse...Egyptian and Iranian forces amass troops on the border after Israeli airstrikes into Lebanon yesterday. Israel is saying that no options are off the table, including a nuclear response...this just after a similar threat by Pakistan this morning with renewed fighting in Kashmir as NATO threatens tactical strikes within its territory..."

Giovanni grimaced. "Turn it down."

Leaning forward, Jess switched the radio off. She wanted to hear what was going on, but evidently he didn't. Reaching the bottom of the valley, they wound their way back up the other side. The feeling of elation had passed, and Giovanni sensed it, reducing their speed. Bales of hay dotted a pasture to their right. They passed a farmer getting onto his tractor, another already out tilling his fields.

Jess watched them in disbelief. "What are they doing?" The workers in the fields, the farmers planting crops—it seemed so futile. Didn't they have something better to do with their last days?

Giovanni glanced at her. He looked back at the road and downshifted as the hill grew steeper. "The reconverted farmhouse you stayed in, across the valley. Do you remember it?"

The night before Jess and Celeste had arrived at *Castello Ruspoli* the first time, they had stayed in a guesthouse in another part of Chianti. Giovanni must have done his research and checked their story. Jess nodded. "The one run by the English couple."

They crested the hill and Giovanni upshifted and nodded. "That's right. They bought that farmhouse from two old brothers who have lived in the valley since they were born. The old men are twins, almost seventy years old. For the past fifty years, they've earned a hand-to-mouth living by gathering olives and squeezing them for oil, harvesting and selling grapes for others to sell wine."

Up ahead, they twisted through crumbling stone fences to a town nestled atop a hill. Jess shielded her eyes from the midday sun, squinting to make out the ancient walls ringing the town. She shrugged. "They must have made a bundle selling the place." She remembered the property had fifty acres of olive groves, and stunning views onto the *Valle D'Orsace.*

"Over two million Euros, that's what it sold for." Giovanni downshifted. They approached a gate through the city wall. "Do you know the only question the brothers asked the English couple who bought their place?"

Jess had no idea. "Advice on where to go to the beach?"

The road narrowed to a single lane, and they passed through a portico gate, a heavy wrought-iron door with savage teeth hanging above their heads. Giovanni laughed. "No, they asked if you had to lie flat in an airplane when you flew from England."

Jess frowned at Giovanni. "Are you kidding?"

"Not at all." Giovanni let the Maserati glide up a narrow cobbled street, the air turning cool in the shadows. He pulled onto the side and stopped, turned the engine off, and turned to face Jess. "Those two brothers lived in their valley for seventy years, but they never even traveled to Rome, not even to Florence—just thirty miles away. After getting their two million Euros, guess what they did?"

The smell of warm bread filled the air, and Jess glanced at the shop next to them. A bakery. Her mouth watered. Even with her stomach full, she had to resist an urge to jump up and walk into the shop.

She turned to Giovanni. "I'd bet the brothers traveled the world, no?" It seemed like a logical thing after asking about airplanes.

"No. They moved here." Giovanni held out one hand to the town around them. "They didn't want to be anywhere else. The only reason they sold their farm was because they were getting too old to gather the olives by hand. Now they live in that apartment." He pointed at an open window, blue curtains billowing out. An old man sat there, looking out, and waved at Giovanni. He waved back. "They are happy here, there is nowhere else they would be."

"So what's your point?"

"That the end of the world is coming for all of us, one way or the other, our own personal apocalypse will find each and every one of us. But, if you are happy, being where you want, with the people you want, and are at peace—then why go somewhere else when the end comes? That is why the farmers are still tilling their fields."

Jess smiled and waved at the old brother in the window. "Is that why you brought me all the way out here?" It was a good point, but she was tired.

Giovanni shook his head. "No." He opened his car door and came around to Jess's side, opening her door to offer a hand. "We came to visit here."

Jess looked up at the shop they had parked in front of. A painted-black door with two bay windows in lead glass to each side. A small sign, *Protesi e Stampelle*, hung in front of frayed white curtains in one of the windows. "It looks closed." She took Giovanni's hand, felt the warmth of his grip, and got up from the low sports car to balance on her crutches.

"I talked to the owner earlier," Giovanni assured her. "He is waiting for us."

The curtains parted and a man's face appeared. A moment later the door swung open. "*Ah, Barone Ruspoli, buon giorno.*" A slender man in a brown suit and bow tie smiled at Jess and Giovanni, strands of hair combed across his balding pate.

Giovanni embraced the little man, kissing him on both cheeks. "*Signore* Hamel, thank you for making time for us. This is Jessica Rollins, my friend I told you about. Jessica, this is *Signore* Hamel."

"Ah, *si.*" The small man's mouth twitched, and he looked down at Jessica's crutches and leg. "*Un piacere.* Please, call me Ernesto." He backed away into his shop, opening the door wide for them to follow him.

Giovanni held a hand out, offering to let Jess go ahead of him. She still had no idea what they were doing, not until she swung through the doorway. Inside, one wall was lined with shoes and boots on display, but on the other side of the shop were prosthetic half-legs, all standing at attention in white and brown shoes. Creepy.

"You've got to be kidding me..." Jess muttered, coming to a standstill.

Ernesto indicated a chair in the middle of the room. "Please, sit, yes?" He disappeared through curtains into the back of his shop.

Jess felt her cheeks burn in embarrassment. "Look, I'm not going to attach some wooden peg-leg."

"Trust me." Giovanni rested his hands on Jess's shoulders. "Sit."

Shaking her head, Jess sat. Anything would be better than these crutches, but having Giovanni see her like this, exposing her disability—it felt like an invasion of privacy. She closed her eyes. Upon opening them, Ernesto appeared, holding a surprisingly modern-looking prosthetic.

"Barone Ruspoli called ahead, gave me your size," Ernesto explained. "Do you want to try?" He handed it to her and backed away.

Giovanni pulled up a chair by the wall.

Jess inspected the leg. Not the same as the one stolen from her, and not custom-fitted, but still, it was decent. Leaning forward, she unclipped the safety pin on her slacks below her stump and hiked the fabric up, but winced in pain. In the fight at the apartment, she must have bruised a rib. Spending the night in a stable and walking around on crutches had made it worse.

She leaned back, grunting.

"You want some help?" Ernesto hovered over Jess.

"No, please." Jess shooed him away.

Ernesto glanced at Giovanni. Jess tried to lean forward again, but groaned in pain and slumped back in the chair, squeezing her eyes shut.

"Here, let me help." Giovanni appeared in front of her, taking the prosthetic from her hands.

"No, don't—" Jess protested, but it was too late.

He gently took hold of her left leg and gripped her exposed, scarred stump with his right hand. She flinched, but had no energy to lash out. He eased the leg onto her stump, pushing it firmly in place. "How's that?"

Jess inched forward, took hold of the straps and pulled. This one didn't have a suction valve to attach it. "Not bad, actually."

His warm hands were still on her leg. She never let anyone touch her there, not even in the most intimate moments. Her face flushed again.

"You can attach it?" Giovanni asked.

Jess nodded. She could lean forward far enough to clip the straps. "Thank you."

The drive back was quiet. After thanking Ernesto, they got in the car, pulled around the one-way street system of the hilltop medieval village, and drove down the valley. Halfway back, Jess asked for Giovanni's cell phone.

"Can I try Darmstadt?" she asked after trying her father's number again with no success.

"Dial the number for Paul Collins," Giovanni told her. It was a man in the press corps at Darmstadt, a friend of a friend of Giovanni's. He was the one who had connected Jess to the receptionist at Darmstadt when they called before.

She dialed the number, spoke briefly to Collins, and was passed to the receptionist again.

This time, instead of being ignored, the person at reception blurted into the phone, "Ms. Rollins? This is *Ms. Rollins*?"

"Yes, I'm looking for my father, Dr. Benjamin Rollins, he's supposed to be there," Jess yelled into the phone, trying to make sure she was heard over the rushing wind in the convertible.

Giovanni put the brakes on and pulled the car to a stop under an olive tree on the side of the road.

"Please stay on the line," said the receptionist.

Jess glanced at Giovanni. "They're connecting me."

"Ms. Rollins," came a man's voice over the telephone.

"Yes?"

"This is Dr. Müller of the Jet Propulsion Lab."

Jess frowned. "Okay…"

"Have you been in contact with your father?" Dr. Müller asked.

"That's why I'm calling you. Isn't he there?"

Mumbling and yelling on the other end. "Ms. Rollins, where is your father?"

24

Basel, Switzerland

"WHERE ARE WE?" Roger asked. He'd been staring into his laptop screen for the last half hour.

Ben pointed to the right side of the rental car's windshield, at the wall of a ten-story parking structure stenciled with huge red block letters: BASEL. "That bridge back there? We just crossed the Rhine and entered Switzerland."

They hadn't turned on their cell phones yet for worry of being tracked, and Ben had stripped out their batteries despite Roger's protesting it wasn't necessary. Ben needed to be far enough away from ESOC that they couldn't be turned back. He leaned forward to look up at the green traffic sign hanging over the three-lane highway: *Basel-Sud, Luzerne, Zurich.*

Directly in front of him, a huge multi-carriage tractor-trailer ground to a halt in the traffic. He checked the time on the car's clock. Half-past seven in the morning. Rush hour.

Patience. Patience.

Ben tapped his finger against the steering wheel, glanced around the truck along the two-story high aluminum noise walls lining the road, a yellow stripe hugging the concrete pylons securing them to the ground. Looking past the truck, the green foothills of the Alps rose in the distance.

As soon as they passed Zurich, they could turn on the phones. That was his plan. To get out of Germany, be far enough from Darmstadt that Dr. Müller wouldn't be able to use the local authorities to stop him.

Soon, the news about how close Nomad was would be

announced. Ben had left the LIGO data on Dr. Müller's desk in the middle of the night, detailing their suspicions about the gravity waves confirming Nomad was a binary black hole. By now, Müller had to know, and soon, the whole world would, too.

But Ben had an edge of a few hours, a head start to get south as quick as possible to find Jess and Celeste. He hadn't heard from them, not since news of the bombing in Rome. A hundred thousand feared dead, but the detonation was only a massive conventional bomb, not a nuclear weapon. It was the only good news Ben had heard in the past week. He hadn't heard from them, but somehow, Ben knew Jess and Celeste were alive.

And he had to find them.

Twelve hours to Rome, that was the driving time from Darmstadt.

There was still time.

Time—a funny thing for a physicist. It didn't even exist, not in the deep recesses of quantum physics where Ben's mind often wandered. Time had no strict direction in physics, but in the real world, in the here and now, every second ticking by felt wasted. A moment that could never be regained. Every moment was precious.

Hundreds of thousands dead in Rome, but this was just the first raindrop of the coming storm. The world was already in convulsions, and when the update about Nomad hit the news, Ben was sure chaos would follow. He made his decision to leave the moment they deciphered the LIGO data, and discovered that Nomad would be here in three days.

Not even three days now.

He was obsessed with the digital clock on the car's dashboard. He looked again and did a mental calculation: seventy hours and thirty minutes till their best guess at Nomad's closest approach. Armageddon now had a date and time: six a.m. on October 14th.

Plus or minus an hour.

And plus or minus tens of millions of kilometers.

Neither NASA nor ESOC had managed to get a visual fix on the damn thing yet. An invisible ghost. If they hadn't had deep space probes out there, they might not have even noticed it coming yet. Even surrounded by all our technology, Nomad might have dropped from the sky on an unaware world.

And maybe it would have been better that way. Maybe it was better just to die in an instant, to not to know what's coming. The whole thing still felt unreal, but there was a sense of finality to it. Like entering a doctor's office and being told you have days to live, with some terminal disease named. In the back of your mind, your whole life, you always knew it would end, and now—as terrible as it was—at least you knew how.

Realizing there was no running away, no escaping, Ben's thoughts turned to his loved ones, to Jess and Celeste. Why had he kept them away? Why hadn't he spent more time with them? Ben had gone through the stages of shock and depression as he sat alone in a bathroom stall the night before, numb and crying. Thinking of Jess, of Celeste, guilt overcame him. Guilt of not being a better husband. Of not being a better father. Of abandoning Jess.

If there was no escaping Nomad, he at least had to escape Darmstadt.

At 3 a.m., with only a skeleton staff on hand in the ESOC building, Ben had snuck into the press lounge and stole an ID from a CNN reporter. He stole the reporter's car keys as well. Ben had never stolen a thing in his life, not even a pack of gum, and he'd never imagined that he would one day steal a car. What might he be forced into doing tomorrow?

Ben revved the engine of the reporter's rental car and stared at the back of the tractor-trailer in front of them. Both of their cell phones were still turned off. They had the car's satellite radio tuned to BBC World, but the announcer was only rehashing stories from the previous day.

Roger's laptop was plugged into ESOC's satellite data network and downloading regular updates from Gaia and LIGO. His connection was anonymized into the Internet, but even so, Ben had only allowed him to turn it on once they passed into Switzerland.

Inching the car forward, Ben glanced at Roger. "Anything yet?"

Roger shook his head and nodded at the same time, his head circling. "Some amateur astronomers in Australia just posted a report about Neptune and Uranus shifting more than predicted…"

Ben nodded grimly. It wouldn't be long until the world figured it out, one way or the other. Moving forward another few feet before stopping, he cursed and jammed the ball of his hand into the car's horn. "Come on, damn it!" Seventy hours till Armageddon, and they were stuck in traffic.

"Did you find out what Ufuk Erdogmus wanted?" Roger asked.

"No, I didn't talk to him again."

"Pushy guy." Roger buried his face in the laptop screen. "Guess that's how you get to be a billionaire."

"Yeah," Ben said. "I guess." He replayed the short conversation with Ufuk Erdogmus in his head. Had the billionaire been offering some kind of safe house? He said something about sanctuary. He should have talked to him.

And was it his imagination, or had Roger seemed to *not* want him to talk to Erdogmus?

Ben looked at Roger. He was surprised when Roger had scurried out of the ESOC building in the dead of night to join him. Roger still had his booking on a flight back to New York that morning. It was probably the last opportunity for him to get back to the States, but Roger had insisted he come with Ben, mumbling something about it being safer with him. Ben hadn't argued and was happy to have him along. Stealing a car in the middle of the night scared him enough that his hands shook as he had tried to get the key in the door.

Their escape was uneventful. The half-asleep guard at the entrance hadn't cared who exited the compound. He only had strict instructions on who could enter, Ben had guessed. Minutes later Roger and Ben were on the *Autobahn*, speeding south with dawn coloring the horizon. They didn't need maps or GPS. They just had to follow the Rhine south till the border with Switzerland—not more than three hours—then cross past Zurich, climb through the Alps and drive down into Italy on the other side.

A piece of cake.

The first few hours were peaceful, the rolling pastures of the lower Rhine Valley steadily giving way to electrical towers and tram lines near the Swiss border. They sped along a clear road, under a rising sun and blue sky.

Ben held his face to the sun when he could, marveled at it, amazed at how much he took sunrise for granted. How much he might miss it. He might be witnessing one of the world's last sunrises. As the sun climbed higher, Ben felt like he could sense Nomad rising up behind it—like a deep vibration in the flawless sky, the growl of the monster that would swallow the world.

"Ben!" Roger said. "I just got an email from Jess. They're okay!"

Ben gripped the steering wheel, his knuckles white, his eyes tearing up. His face contorted into something halfway between a smile and grimace. "I knew it."

"They've gone back to that castle, the one in Chianti," Roger continued.

"They're not hurt?" Ben gritted his teeth.

Roger scanned the email. "No, they're fine. Nobody's injured."

Not that Jess would say anything, even if she were hurt. "Good. And that's two hours closer to us."

"...this just in..." said the news anchor on the car's radio. *"New fighting reported this morning in Kashmir, with India and Pakistan threatening nuclear strikes if the other doesn't back down..."*

The truck ahead of them jolted forward. Ben shifted the car into gear. They moved a hundred feet, out from under the shadow of a fly-over bridge, before grinding to a halt again. "Damn it!" Ben grunted, slamming the steering wheel.

Glancing left, past the bridge, he could see that the highway wound all the way into the hills in the distance. The snow-capped peaks of the Alps shimmered beyond that. Reflections from windows of cars and trucks glittered all the way along the road. This wasn't just a traffic jam, Ben realized. It was something more than that.

People might not realize how close Nomad really was, but they knew something was happening. People were heading for the hills, for the seclusion and safety of the mountains and countryside. Ben didn't want to get *into* the Alps, however, he wanted to get *through* them, to the other side.

"That castle in Chianti might be the best place to ride this out," Roger said, echoing Ben's own thoughts.

"Being in the Alps might not be a good idea when Nomad passes," Ben agreed. "Those jagged peaks could tumble like dominos."

"And my best guess still is a closest approach to Earth of about eighty million kilometers." Roger sucked air in through his teeth. "Plus or minus eighty."

Ben grimaced. "If it passes under ten million kilometers, it'll pop the Earth like a water balloon hitting a wall. Under thirty million, tidal effects will be enough to repave the entire surface of the Earth in magma. Nothing would survive."

"But sixty, seventy million?" Roger glanced at Ben. "That might be survivable, at least for a few days until the Earth's atmosphere freezes after we're flung away from the sun."

Ben stared straight ahead. A few extra days. That was the calculus of life now. Would the extra days be worth living? Of course they would. Nobody wanted to die.

"Eighty million kilometers will trigger massive earthquakes and eruptions, but a bigger problem is going to be water." Ben pressed his face into his hands. "The Earth's oceans are going to slosh around like a toddler having a fit in a bathtub. But it won't start until Nomad is almost on us, not until the last few hours."

Roger nodded and looked up, performing some mental calculation. "Ten hours away, at three hundred million kilometers, the tidal forces are going to start overcoming the moon's. On the coast it'll just seem like an unusual tide."

"Five hours later, at a hundred and fifty million kilometers," Ben said, thinking out loud, "tidal forces will be fifteen times that. Open ocean tides measure about two feet, but tides at the coasts are governed by geography of the ocean bed—New York has six-foot tides where London's are eighteen. Some places will be worse hit than others."

"And the surface of the Earth is rotating on its axis at a speed of a thousand miles per hour." Roger circled his hand in the air and then pointed upward. "With Nomad coming from behind the Sun, it's going to pull a wall of water toward it, and that wall is going to race across the surface at thousands of miles an hour, obliterating anything in its path."

"We're lucky the Mediterranean has some of the lowest tides in the world." Ben had looked it up. Near Rome they were less than two feet. "And that wall of water approaching from the Pacific and Indian oceans is going to have to squeeze through the Red Sea and Suez Canal before spilling into the Med. This mountaintop *Castello Ruspoli* is as good a place to ride it out as anywhere."

"One thing we haven't thought of." Roger tapped on his keyboard, then turned the screen to Ben.

"What?" Ben shifted into gear and advanced another twenty feet.

"I'm getting new data from FLARECAST, that new early warning system for solar flares."

Ben nodded. A combination of orbiting and ground-based observatories paired with high performance computing installations.

"They're predicting *massive* coronal ejections if Nomad gets as close as we're thinking," Roger said. "Like orders of magnitude bigger than anything before."

"Of course..." Ben realized Nomad would drag the sun along behind it like a puppy on a leash, but he hadn't thought through the implications.

"A few hours before Nomad gets here, it'll trigger huge solar storms," continued Roger. "Bathing the Earth in a flood of high energy particles."

"That'll raise ground voltage—"

"And fry power stations and electronics." Roger breathed deep and stared at the laptop screen. "Should be pretty, though. Light up the sky like a Christmas tree." He rubbed his eyes and closed the laptop. "I can't read any more of this."

Ben put the car into neutral and stepped on the brake. He looked carefully at Roger. "Why did you come with me? Isn't there someone at home you want to be with?"

In the stress of the moment when they escaped Darmstadt, Ben hadn't given it much thought. Now, when all he could think about were his own loved ones, Ben realized how little he knew about Roger.

About his personal life.

Looking down, Roger exhaled through pursed lips. "My mom, she died a long time ago, and my dad…well, we haven't talked in years. Maybe I'll give him a call."

Ben let the moment linger for a few seconds. "But you didn't want to go back? Isn't there someone else?"

Roger's face twitched. He laughed nervously. "I guess this isn't the time for secrets, huh?"

Ben put the car into gear and pulled forward another few feet before stepping on the brakes again. "What do you mean?" He turned to study Roger's face, watched him wrestle with something inside.

"Remember two years ago when I started at your lab?" Roger said after a pause. "We had lunch with Jess at the Mexican place around the corner?"

Advancing the car another ten feet, Ben grunted, "Uh huh."

"Well…" Roger rubbed the back of his neck with one hand. "Ah, we sort of hit it off."

Ben frowned. "Who hit it off?"

"Me and Jess."

Ben jammed on the brakes and turned to look at Roger, creases furrowing his brow. "What? You never told me that."

"You were my boss, and Jess didn't want to say anything. She's kind of private, you know?"

Shaking his head, Ben looked back at the road. "Oh, I know." The revelation surprised him, but now that it was out, it also didn't surprise him. It was just like Jess.

"She was practically living at my place, last year," Roger added. "Things were great, and then suddenly, she took off to Europe."

The truck in front of them accelerated, and Ben pulled forward, the traffic finally moving. "She can be like that."

"So, well, if the world's ending…the only person I really want to see is Jess."

Ben gritted his teeth, but not in anger. He held back tears. His little girl. Roger loved his little girl. "Well, let's get us there, then." He'd had enough of this. Pulling onto the shoulder, Ben passed the truck.

"One thing…"

Ben glanced at Roger. "What?"

"What happened to her? I mean, not her leg, I know that story, but when she was a kid?"

Ben pushed his foot down on the accelerator, and in the rear view saw other cars pulling into the shoulder lane behind him. He wasn't the only one who'd lost his patience. He glanced at Roger. "You know, I'm not sure I really know…"

25

Chianti, Italy

JESS STARED AT an ancient suit of armor set against the stone wall. She inspected the intricate detail of its hinges and interlocking plates. A hard shell to protect a fragile interior, designed to fight off an unforgiving world. She understood. "So Dad is on his way here?"

She'd just returned from the drive with Giovanni. Bursting through the doors into the entrance hallway of the *castello*, she announced that she'd spoken to people at Darmstadt. Her father wasn't there.

To which her mother replied, yes, she knew.

"I saw the email on your account just after you left," Celeste added. Standing beside Jess, she tried to put a hand on her shoulder. "Ben said he was driving here. He's already in Switzerland. He'll be here tonight."

Giovanni sat on the edge of a copper-studded red leather chair near the entrance, the keys to the Maserati still in his hand. Nico had just told him about a ransom note he found an hour before.

"And you didn't call me?" Jess turned from inspecting the suit of armor and paced the length of the hallway.

She tested her new leg. It felt looser than her old one, but it wasn't bad. Better than some she'd had. At the far end, away from the entrance, was a massive stone fireplace, big enough to stand inside. She stopped in front of it, looked up at the collection of stuffed wild boar heads on the mantle, at the pointed arches of windows above that, the midday sun streaming in. The ceiling was a geometric patchwork of interlocking beams in dark wood.

"I tried, but the mobile networks are still jammed," Nico answered. He stood to one side, leaning against a long mahogany table littered with family photographs in frames. "Sometimes it works, sometimes not."

"I need to tell you something," Celeste said. "Maybe you should sit down."

Jess turned on her new foot. She hated that expression. Why would people want to be sitting down when bad news came? She preferred to be mobile. She needed movement. Sitting still made her feel trapped. Just the same, her heart rate kicked up a notch. "What happened to Dad?" she blurted out.

"Nothing like that." Celeste's lip's trembled, her hands mashing a cream silk scarf. She wore some of Giovanni's mother's clothes as well. "Ben, he knows what Nomad is…"

"And?" Jess took four quick steps to Celeste, who looked on the verge of tears. A rock, that was how Jess imagined her mother—she'd never seen her like this. She put her hands on her mother's shoulders. "What is it?"

Everyone stared at Celeste.

"Nomad will be inside Earth's orbit in three days. It's a black hole, or two of them. A binary pair, he said."

Nobody said anything. The seconds ticked by.

"*Merda Madonna!*" Giovanni picked up a porcelain lamp and heaved it against the stone wall next to him. It exploded, scattering fragments that clattered across the floor. "*Merda! Merda! Merda!*"

His face apoplectic red, he turned away, hanging his head low. Turning back to Nico, he rubbed his face with one hand, his jaw muscles rippling. "And this ransom note, what does it say?"

"Monday, we are to deliver five million Euros in gold bars. Leave them in a truck in front of this address in Saline." Nico held the handwritten note up. He found it nailed to the front door of the exterior entrance just after Giovanni left. "If we want Hector alive, it says."

"This is not the time for this." Giovanni pulled at his hair, snarled with gritted teeth.

Not the time for this? Jess frowned. When was there *ever* a time for this? Something didn't make sense. It was like he expected the ransom, as if it was some kind of game.

"And how do we contact, these"—the tendons in Giovanni's neck flared, both hands balled into white-knuckled fists—"kidnappers?"

Nico read the note again, but shook his head. "No instructions, no way to contact them."

"Monday will be too *late*!" Giovanni screamed the last word. He put one fist to his mouth and bit on it. "Today is Friday. We can try calling Florence, see about getting money, but gold? And by Monday it will be too late, if what you're saying is true." He turned away, put both hands against the wall and hung his head between them.

"*Signor*, if I may?" Nico almost whispered.

Giovanni let out a guttural roar. "What?"

"As I said before, I did a background search on Enzo…"

"And…?"

"And I found his family home, his relatives all live in Vaca."

Giovanni spun around. "Vaca?" His brows came together in a scowl.

"Yes, and I'm sure he doesn't know that I know. He's not very—" Nico paused to choose his word. "Smart."

"Vaca," Giovanni muttered, pacing back and forth in tight circles.

"What's going on?" Jess asked. Something was happening between the lines.

"And you have an address?" Giovanni asked Nico.

"Yes," Nico replied. "We can be there in an hour and see if I'm right." He added something in rushed Italian.

Giovanni continued to pace. "No, I will go alone."

"Where's Vaca?" Jess prickled in annoyance. "Giovanni, what's happening?"

"It's a village on the coast, not far." He stopped pacing and faced Jess, bringing his hands together. "Nico thinks this is where Enzo may have taken Hector. It will only take a few hours to check." He turned to Nico again. "You stay here, close all the gates, call our bankers in Florence and start loading gold and silver from the museum into the Land Rovers. We will give them what we can. We need to get Hector back."

"At least take the two guards with you." Nico held his hands wide. "For protection."

He meant the security guards Jess had seen earlier. They stood on the entrance walls, watching for anyone else that might approach the *castello.*

Giovanni nodded, the crimson red in his face washing away. "Good."

Jess glanced at her mother, then looked Giovanni square in the eyes. "I'm coming."

"This is too dangerous." He turned on his heel and walked through a doorway leading out of the hall.

"Dangerous?" Jess followed. "The whole world is about to be incinerated, and you're worried about *dangerous*?"

"Stay with your mother. It is a gift that you have her, that you are together at this moment." Giovanni didn't turn as he stalked down the hallway. He stopped at a metal door and fumbled with his keys. "Your father will be here soon. Do you know what I'd give to have my father here now?" He opened the door and flicked on the light switch inside. A brick-lined staircase wound down.

"This is my fault." Jess followed him down the stairs, limping, not used to the new prosthetic. "If I'd been more careful, not opened my mouth in public like that."

And it *was* her fault. She hadn't realized the enormity of the words coming out of her mouth when she spoke to Giovanni at the observatory. A death sentence to the world. And she hid it, purposely, from people nearby. Jess thought she understood Enzo's anger, if not the bizarre way he seemed to be acting it out.

But then, Jess had anger of her own. Steal *her* leg?

She wanted to help Giovanni, that was true. But she also wanted to satisfy her own anger, right the wrong done to her, the burning humiliation of being turned into a cripple and stranded in the street. She wanted to look Enzo in the eye. After that, she wasn't sure. But she wanted to be there.

Reaching the bottom of the stairwell, Giovanni fumbled with the keys again before opening a reinforced metal door. It swung inward heavily. He clicked the inside light switch. "Those security men, they're professionals. Ex-military, Interpol, they'll be able to find Enzo if he's in Vaca. This is no place for…" He stopped and winced, sensing his misstep.

"What?" Jess pushed her way into the room behind him. "No

place for a woman?"

She looked around. It had to be the castle armory. Two pairs of assault rifles, which she recognized as AK-47s, hung on one wall, with a row of handguns on shelves on the other.

Jess whistled, impressed. "Is this legal?"

Giovanni snorted. "As if *legal* matters to you." He leaned over to pull out a cardboard box, ripped open the cover and pulled out an ammunition magazine, then grabbed one of the AKs from the wall. He looked at the magazine, turned it around. "And no, Jessica, this is not going to be any place for a woman."

It was Jess's turn to snort. He obviously had no idea how to load an AK-47. Shoving her way in front of him, she grabbed the rifle and magazine, and in one quick motion snapped them together. She stood in front of him defiantly. "Let me ask you a question."

Taking a step back, Giovanni frowned at this woman, in front of him, holding a loaded assault rifle. "What?"

"How do you think I lost this leg?" She swung the rifle's barrel down and tapped her new prosthetic.

"I don't know. A climbing accident?"

"Relax, Giovanni. The safety is still on." Jess flipped down the safety lever and pulled back and released the charging handle. She smiled. "*Now* it's loaded. And now answer the question."

Giovanni's face reddened. "I don't know. Why don't you tell me?"

"Afghanistan. An IED explosion hit our Humvee on a reconnaissance mission. I was in the Marines for two years." She clipped the safety back into place. "I'm coming with you."

SURVIVOR TESTIMONY

#GR3;

Event +52hrs;
Survivor name: Heidi Hilfker;
Reported location: Zermatt, Switzerland;

Please stay on this frequency. We haven't been able to contact anyone else yet. You need to send help. The road's out, there is no way…

We knew it was coming, so we hid in the mountains. We knew it was coming, but nothing prepared us for the earth opening up. When the lights came in the sky, I watched, terrified, and the tremors started so I ran outside into the flat ground. All the buildings collapsed, so many dead…the roads torn apart. I watched the Matterhorn crumble like chalk. Send help. Please. The ash and snow, waist deep…not many of us left.

Transmission ended in sign-off. Freq. 4644 kHz/NSB.

DAY SEVEN

October 12th

26

Vaca, Italy

MOORED SAILBOATS BOBBED on gentle swells inside stone breakwaters just off the gravel-and-seashell beach. Jess watched them, her mind exhausted. How nice it would be to stretch out on the deck of one of those boats, feel the sun on her skin, drop off to sleep.

Giovanni sat next to her on the *pizzeria* terrace, his face impassive behind dark sunglasses and a baseball cap pulled low. Jess's wide-brimmed hat fluttered in the breeze, and she glanced around the cobblestone *piazza* in front of them. A decorative anchor was set in poured concrete at the center. Wind-swept juniper trees faced the ocean to the west, and European Union and Italian flags snapped in the breeze to each side of a plaque proudly emblazoned with the town's name: VACA.

Scooters parked shoulder to shoulder, just off the terrace, bordered a long line of people waiting to get inside the restaurant. It was one of the few still open. When Jess and Giovanni, with the two security men, drove in at dawn, it had the feeling of a ghost town, but the hot sun drew what few people remained from their homes, to herd together and eat.

"Anything?" Jess asked Giovanni, flicking her chin at the walkie-talkie on the table between them.

"Nothing yet."

Mounting a manhunt wasn't like stepping outside for a walk. Once they committed to the idea, they had to plan it out. They started by bringing in the security guards Nico had hired, explained the situation to them. Giovanni told them that Nomad might be arriving sooner than expected, but the sum he offered both men sealed the deal—gold, and lots of it. Giovanni had a safe filled with bars of it in the basement of the castle.

Giovanni turned up the volume on a battery-powered satellite radio he brought with them. *"...riots continue in America, with a bomb this morning in a Washington mall and an explosion reported at government buildings in Sacramento, claimed responsibility by a cult saying Nomad is Nibiru returning..."* They had it tuned to the BBC. *"...global stock markets and currency exchanges have crashed, sending gold prices skyrocketing..."*

After a series of terrorist attacks in Tel Aviv, Israel took control of the Gaza strip, prompting a wave of attacks by the PLO from neighboring Lebanon. Continued fighting in Kashmir had pushed the United States to send armed air support to Indian troops. In America, a renewed explosion of riots from LA to Detroit, at least from what they could tell from the radio. The situation in Europe seemed calmer, more resigned.

The night before, Giovanni arranged for delivery trucks to bring supplies to the castle. On the ramparts, Jess had improvised human-sized wooden dolls, their heads covered with large hats. Good enough to fool someone watching the castle from a distance, at least for a few hours.

In the small hours of the morning, under cover of night, Jess and Giovanni and the two security guards had smuggled themselves out in one of the delivery trucks, just in case someone *was* watching. Nico seemed to try to dissuade Giovanni from bringing Jess, a heated argument behind a closed door, but in the end they left Nico and Celeste to arrange collecting as much gold as they could in case they needed to produce the ransom.

The yeasty warmth of fresh bread wafted out of the door next to Jess, mixing with the salty freshness of the sea air and ever-present hint of coconut oil that seemed to permeate every seaside vacation town Jess had ever visited. She glanced inside, at an old couple happily serving customers. They looked like they were doing what they wanted to do—like the brothers from Giovanni's story—and were where they wanted to be. She watched the old man take a twenty Euro bill as payment. Twenty Euros. It wasn't even worth the paper it was printed on. If death came today, Jess sensed the man would be freed by angels, not torn by demons.

What she would give to be him.

A woman in short shorts and flip-flops, with a pink bikini top, stopped in the doorway. "*Veni,*" she urged, waving her hand.

Glancing inside, Jess saw a small boy, with a Sponge Bob-printed beach towel around his neck, standing and staring at the *gelati* freezer. He wanted ice cream. The mother urged him forward again, but he stamped his foot and pouted. The mother glanced at Jess, shaking her head, but shrugged and went back in.

What do you do when the world is ending? Come to the beach.

The futility of it annoyed Jess. Go and do something useful, she wanted to shout at the people in line. But then life was futile. What was the point? Why do anything? Sitting by the ocean under a blue sky, her sense of detachment had shifted into a deep melancholy of hopeless dread. She stroked her finger along the trigger of the handgun in her purse. Just lift it up, put it in her mouth and pull the trigger—it would be over.

The waiting. The tension. The futility. All of it over. And the *guilt,* that would be over too.

She glanced inside at the young boy, not more than five. He got his ice cream.

The image of a black hole ringed in white danced through Jess's mind, and she looked down and away from the boy. She dragged the black duffel bag at her feet, filled with assault rifles, grenades and ammunition, back under the table.

Many of the people lining up to get into the pizzeria had backpacks. How many had guns or knives in them, how many of these innocent-looking people had dark thoughts like Jess did, even as she smiled back at them?

Looking out at the sprawl of houses that stretched up into the hill, she knew people had to be barricading themselves in, protecting themselves and their families. Soon they would be crawling over each other to survive, even this peaceful place literally a hell on Earth.

Jess checked her watch again. Seventeen minutes past eleven. One minute past the last time she checked her watch. Giovanni glanced at his wrist as well. Checking the time had become obsessive, impulsive.

Forty-three hours to Nomad.

Or, forty-three hours until when her father said Nomad would be here. Conflicting stories and scientific reports flooded the Internet and news channels. It was impossible to decipher one from the other, to trust one source more than another. In the past twelve hours, amateur astronomers cataloged a dramatic shift in the outer gas giants' orbits, but some said it meant Nomad was headed away. Earth's orbit had already shifted, but there wasn't one straight story.

NASA's official stance: Still weeks away.

But it wasn't weeks, but hours. Jess felt it in her bones. She leaned back, squinted up at the midday sun. Nomad was still behind it, but soon it would be exposed. Be upon them. The hand of God.

"*Zio*," crackled the walkie-talkie.

Zio—the code word they had chosen for Giovanni. He picked it up. "*Sì?*"

A stream of Italian flowed from the walkie-talkie. "What's going on?" Jess asked.

Giovanni exchanged a few more words. "They're coming."

"The security guards?"

"Yes."

They had sent them out to look at the address Nico had given them. Better them than Jess and Giovanni. Enzo didn't know the security guards, wouldn't recognize them even if he ran into them. And they were surveillance professionals.

"Did they find him?"

Giovanni shook his head. "I don't know." He put the walkie-talkie down. "They're on their way here."

An elderly couple walked past them toward the beach. They held hands, and the man looked at the woman and kissed her. She kissed him back, long and hard. Public displays of affection turned Jess off, but she stared, fascinated. The way the man looked at his wife, the love. The tenderness. She glanced back at the people in line. Most of them were elderly.

Two weeks ago, if you asked Jess about getting old, she would have laughed. *I doubt I'll ever get old*, she liked to joke. Except it wasn't just a joke. Her recklessness, a death wish her mother called it, was one of the reasons her mother had difficulty spending time with her. Celeste often said that part of her was waiting for the call. About an accident.

And part of Jess was waiting for it as well. The same drive that pushed her to quit school, quit her degree in astronomy, and join the Marines.

But now, faced with the real prospect of imminent death, perhaps days away, she didn't want to die. She watched the elderly couple walk onto the beach, hand in hand, the old man stealing glances at his wife. Jess didn't want to die. She wanted someone to look at her like that.

Leaning forward, Jess took Giovanni's hand in hers. "We'll find Hector, I promise."

Taking a deep breath, Giovanni nodded, his jaw muscles flexing. "Thank you. And thank you for coming."

"Of course." Jess squeezed his hand. "I'm so sorry. All this is my fault."

"I thought you said you never apologized?" Giovanni managed a wry smile.

Jess smiled back. "You've been very good to us, very nice to *me*." She leaned closer. "You don't deserve this, not at the…"

"At the end?" Giovanni squeezed her hand back. "We don't know what the future holds, Jess. And this isn't your fault. It's Enzo; *he* is the one causing this."

The mother, in her flip flops and bikini top, dragged the little boy, ice cream cup in hand, out the door past Jess.

"*…breaking news…*" Jess glanced at Giovanni and turned up the radio's volume. "*…Islamic Caliphate forces from Iraq have taken the Golan Heights after flooding through Syria, and have now invaded Israel with fierce fighting in the West Bank. Egypt is amassing forces in the Sinai, saying that the Israeli occupation of Gaza…*"

"*Scusi, signora,*" said a gruff voice.

The two security guards, in matching black suits and aviator sunglasses, stepped around the mother and her boy. Giovanni stood and fired off an excited question in Italian.

"*…the Israelis are now fighting a war on three fronts as the United States has withdrawn its representatives from last-minute peace negotiations. Israel is threatening use of nuclear…*"

"What's happening?" Jess got up.

"They found him."

One of the security guards held up his phone. On the screen was an image of someone opening a door, trash bags in hand. Pork pie hat, mole on his left cheek. It was Enzo. "*Si, all'indirizzo.*"

"He's at the address Nico gave us," confirmed Giovanni. "They've rented an apartment across the street we can do surveillance from."

"...Dr. Menzinger of the Swiss astronomical society is now saying that Nomad is not months away, but may be entering the inner solar system in under a week. NASA has refused to comment..."

Giovanni reached down to turn the radio off.

"Let's go." Jess stooped to grab the duffel bag, but one of the security men held up a hand and took it for her.

She shrugged and followed them through the lengthening line of people outside the *pizzeria*. She checked her cell phone. Still no messages.

By now her father should be at the castle.

27

Southern Alps, Switzerland

PAST THE FORMED-metal guardrail, the hulking shoulders of snow-capped Alps stretched into the distance under a brilliant sky. The highway coiled down the slope behind them like a snake, clinging to the cliffs, sliding through the trees into the bottom of the valley where a lake glistened. Cool wind blew through Ben's hair as he hung his head out of the passenger side window of the car, breathing deep the mountain air.

It was a beautiful view.

Or would be if they weren't inching along.

When he planned this, the route seemed simple: down the Rhine into Switzerland, cross the Alps, then down into Italy. Simple because there was only one road through central Switzerland and into Italy—through the Gotthard Pass.

Simple.

Unless the Gotthard Pass was jammed.

Actually, there were two routes that paralleled each other. There was a surface road through the Gotthard Pass itself, but at nearly two miles in altitude, it was often impassible from snowfall. To create a year-round route from Zurich to Milan, the Swiss had constructed the Gotthard tunnel, the third longest in the world at over ten miles in length.

Problem was, a vehicle fire closed the tunnel, at least that was what Roger found out when they stopped at a service station. It was what caused the massive traffic jams. Instead of waiting for the tunnel—a modern highway that cut through and under the heart of the Alps—to be cleared, they opted instead to take the surface road high into the mountains.

That might have been a mistake.

This small mountain road was never designed to handle this kind of traffic. If the tunnel were open, it wouldn't have been a problem. Busy, but not a problem. With this volume of people trying to get into the mountains at once, it was like a hundred-mile-long parking lot.

"What's our distance from Basel now?"

Roger exhaled loudly. "One hundred and eighty-two klicks."

A hundred and eighty two kilometers in twenty-seven hours. That was how long they'd been stuck in traffic. Ben did a quick mental calculation. Just over four miles per hour. A fast walk. They could have walked here.

Twenty-seven hours.

When the angel Gabriel, at the Pearly Gates, asked Ben what he did with the last hours of his life, he might be answering: I was stuck in traffic. He checked the clock again.

Forty-four hours to Nomad.

He looked into the sky. Serene. So blue it seemed to go on forever.

Ben leaned forward to get his laptop out of his bag by his right foot. Something he didn't recognize was in there, so he pulled it out.

"Hey, that's my cellphone," Roger said, grabbing it from Ben. "I have two of them," he explained, "that's my international."

Ben glanced down. He'd looked in the wrong bag. His was by his left foot.

"Sorry. Want me to put it back in?" Not that a cellphone was doing them any good. Ben looked at the device now in Roger's hand. It didn't look like any cellphone he'd ever seen. It was fat, at least two inches thick. He tried to take it from Roger, but Roger leaned over to put it back himself.

Ben caught a flash of an image on the cover of the cellphone as it disappeared back into Roger's bag. A yin-yang symbol inside a white octagon. Where had he seen that before?

"What's with the yin-yang?" Ben asked.

Roger sat upright and rubbed the back of his neck. "Where?"

"On that cellphone thing. A white symbol inside an octagon."

Roger snorted. "Nothing. Just trying to be cool. You know, Chinese symbols."

Ben frowned but let it go. "How's the gas situation?" he asked.

"Holding steady at a third."

The truck ahead of them advanced a few feet and stopped. Roger inched the car forward, then clicked the engine off. They had to conserve fuel.

Right after leaving Darmstadt, Ben had stopped to fill up their stolen BMW 3-series diesel. Roger checked online: this car had a range of 1200 kilometers on a full 60-liter tank. Ben constantly had to do the math in his head—3.8 liters to a gallon, 1.6 kilometers to a mile—even as a scientist working in metric when measuring the cosmos, he wasn't used to using it for day-to-day things like driving. Rome was less than 1100 kilometers drive; the castle less than 900. Easily within the range of this car with a full tank of gas.

If it wasn't idling for hours on end.

But, it seemed to use less than a half a liter of diesel for every hour of idling, as best as they could calculate. And they had hours to calculate and analyze. As they progressed up into the mountains, the shoulder became littered with less efficient cars that ran out of fuel. Stranded motorists begged for rides. The service stations they passed had lines that stretched back for miles. Good thing the drivers were Swiss and German, and not American. Good thing people here didn't have guns in their cars.

Roger flicked his chin ahead, at the staircase of winding pavement that zigzagged up the mountainside. "We just need to get over that next ridge, and we'll be on our way down."

"Finally," Ben grumbled. He'd had to resist the urge to get out of the car and walk more than once.

"...best estimate of Nomad's position is ten billion kilometers, and already affecting Earth's orbit..." They had the radio tuned to the only English news station they could find, BBC Europe. *"Scientists are predicting a sharp drop in global temperatures after Nomad passes..."*

"It's been a day already," said Roger. "Dr. Müller has the data we gave him. They have to know Nomad is less than two days away. Why haven't they announced anything?"

Ben stared at the mountains. "Why do you think?" Thinking of Dr. Müller sparked an image in his mind. The yin-yang symbol. Dr.

Müller's signet ring had exactly the same image on it, Ben was sure of it.

"...last minute negotiations to avert full-scale war in the Middle East, the Americans have asked both sides to come back to negotiations..."

The truck pulled forward another few feet. "I just don't see how it was possible that we missed seeing Nomad until now," Roger muttered.

"Ever heard of Trajan's column?" Ben took a long look at Roger.

Roger inched the car forward. "No."

"It's a monument in the middle of Rome. It's been on display for everyone to see for the past two thousand years, maybe one of the most analyzed artifacts in the history of mankind. For hundreds of years, scholars have been studying it and writing papers about it. On its surface is a visual history of the Roman legions."

Roger pulled them forward another ten feet, put on the parking brake and frowned at Ben. "What does that have to do with Nomad?"

"Because, last year, for the first time, they noticed that there were women engraved on Trajan's column. For hundreds of years, scholars had said that only men appeared on the column, because Roman legionaries weren't allowed to be married."

Roger shook his head. "Still don't see where you're going..."

"People only see what they want to see, that's my point." He nodded toward the back seat, at his backpack. "Or someone wanted it to be invisible."

"A conspiracy? Hiding something this big?" Roger stared at Ben.

Ben's head snapped forward, his laptop slamming into the dashboard, the crunching roar of grinding metal filling the air. Dazed, he looked up. The truck in front had slid backward into them, impacting their car and rolling up the metal of the hood. Cursing, Roger slammed the car into park.

Ben threw off his seatbelt and jumped out of the passenger side, dropping his laptop into the seat. "What the hell is wrong with you?" he yelled at the truck.

No reply.

He was about to walk around the front of the truck when he heard on the radio: *"...breaking news..."*

"Roger, can you turn that up?"

Roger nodded and leaned forward, twisting the dial on the radio. The car's engine whined.

"Dr. Menzinger of the Swiss astronomical society is now saying that Nomad is not months away, but is already inside the solar system and will be passing the Earth in two days. NASA and the European Space Agency have refused to comment…"

"Jesus Christ." Ben raked one hand through his hair. For the past day, he'd been holding his breath, waiting for this news to drop. Now it was out. He had hoped to be at the castle in Italy now. They had to get moving, *now*. He took a step forward, slapping the truck's siding, leaning to look into the truck's cabin. "Hey, can you move forward?"

Ben and Roger weren't the only ones that heard the news. All around them, horns started beeping, engines revving.

"Hey!" Ben yelled, taking another step. "Can you move the goddamn—"

The truck slid back another two feet, crushing the hood of the car. Another car had jammed into the side of it and was trying to push through between them.

Roger was still sitting in the driver's seat, his seatbelt strapped on.

Ben slammed on the side of the truck again. "HEY!" he screamed.

The car trying to squeeze past the truck gunned its engine and rammed forward, and at this impact, the truck slid back again, but this time not just two feet. It released completely, slamming into their car, pushing it sideways into the metal guardrail behind them. Ben glanced back just in time to see Roger's terrified eyes as the car plummeted over the edge.

28

Vaca, Italy

"THAT'S HIM," JESS whispered.

The setting sun cast long shadows down the street, but the man opening the gate across the street was definitely Enzo. Looking left and right, he walked thirty feet to the street corner and dropped a black plastic bag. Scanning the street again, he wiped his hand and returned to the gate to go back inside the house. It was a single-story bungalow, with terracotta roof tiles and white stucco walls, surrounded by a well-maintained six-foot hedge that made it impossible to look into the yard from street level.

Jess and Giovanni watched from a second-story perch across the street. They lay on a bed mattress dragged out onto the concrete balcony of the small apartment, lying flat, spying through the two-inch-high drain-gap in the bottom of the balcony wall.

After locating Enzo, Giovanni's security guards had somehow rented the apartment across the street. It was empty except for a couch and coffee table and the stripped-down bed they dragged onto the balcony. The mattress was surprisingly clean, looked and smelled new.

Jess was impressed.

Giovanni's security guys were definitely professionals, in just a few hours establishing a complete surveillance operation. Driving the ten blocks from the waterfront to the back of this apartment, the men had dropped off Jess and Giovanni, then took up their positions on the ground floor and rear of Enzo's house.

"*Brutto figlio di puttana bastardo,*" Giovanni swore under his breath, staring at Enzo going back in the house.

Jess grabbed Giovanni's shoulder, restrained him from getting up. "We need to find out if Hector is inside," she whispered. "And we need to find out who else is in there."

Still holding Giovanni's shoulder, she glanced back at the house through the drain gap. A garden surrounded the bungalow on three sides, with just the front and side doors as entrances and exits. Beige covering obscured all the windows, something like drapes or sashes but more solid and blacked out. Light still bled out from the edges of the windows. Jess counted the four windows on this side, and from scouting the house knew there were two more in the back. There were maybe two bedrooms, a bathroom, a kitchen and a living room. Lying with her face flat to the floor, the scent of a flowering chamomile bush in the gardens below managed to overpower the smell of damp concrete and sunbaked skin.

"How do we find out?" Giovanni growled. "We don't have time."

Jess pushed Giovanni back to the mattress more firmly. "We don't even know if Enzo *has* Hector. Maybe he just came home to see his family."

Her stomach lurched. She should be with *her* family. She hoped her father was at the castle by now. They'd called Nico to say they'd located Enzo, but as of two hours ago, Jess's father still hadn't shown up.

The castle was just an hour away, Jess told herself. Just around the corner. She could leave at any time and get back there. And having something to do—a purpose, a mission—felt good, like she was doing something useful, something important.

"Maybe we should just go and knock on the door." Giovanni held up his Beretta handgun. "We ask nicely."

It was a good thing she had come along. Jess shook her head. "No, your guys are right. We've found Enzo, now we need to gather more information and form a plan. Patience."

The walkie-talkie crackled softly. "*Hai visto?*"

"*Si, si,*" Giovanni answered.

"Tell them to hold their positions, only contact us if someone leaves the house." Jess adjusted herself on the mattress to get a better look. Across the street, the side door of the house opened, spilling light into the garden. She nudged Giovanni's shoulder. "Look..."

Enzo came out of the door, holding something in his hands. Another man followed him, a rifle slung over his shoulder. The sun was down now, twilight softening into darkness. A third man came out of the door, hunched over, talking to someone. He straightened up. And there *he* was, walking beside the third man.

Hector.

"*Che palle,*" Giovanni muttered, his knuckles going white as he balled his hands into fists, but he didn't get up.

Enzo dropped what he had in his hands. A soccer ball. He kicked it to Hector, who ran forward and kicked it back. The other two men, their rifles slung across their backs, joined in the game.

"At least they're treating him well," Jess said softly.

She was almost shocked when Hector appeared through the doorway. A part of her didn't really believe that Enzo had kidnapped Hector, or that it was even Enzo in Rome who attacked her. It seemed too far-fetched, too much of a coincidence. She squinted, tried to make out the faces of the other men. Were they the ones from Rome? She didn't recognize them.

Giovanni gripped his Beretta. "I say we just go now."

"No, we wait." Jess watched soccer game across the street. "Those aren't the guys that attacked me, so maybe they're inside. We wait to see who else comes out, goes in. We wait for the light to go out, and then we go in."

"We wait?" Giovanni growled. "Time is one thing we don't have a lot of."

Jess checked her watch. "We've got time."

Across the street, Enzo knelt and picked up the soccer ball. He said something to Hector, then to the two men. They nodded, and one of them collected the soccer ball. They all walked back inside. A few seconds later a light clicked on in the room all the way to the right. It clicked off a minute later.

"I'd bet that's the room they're keeping Hector in," Jess observed.

Giovanni nodded. "How long do we wait?"

"Let's wait until after midnight. We can watch until then, see who goes in or out. We're only an hour from the castle. Let's get this done right, and we can be back home and safe."

"And how long do we have?"

He meant until her father's estimate of when Nomad would arrive.

"Thirty hours until things start to get weird."

"Thirty hours? That's what your father said?"

Jess nodded.

NASA and ESOC still maintained Nomad was more than a week away, but conflicting estimates flooded the news channels. Dr. Menzinger and several amateur astronomers predicted Nomad was just two days away, as her father had said. There was still some room for uncertainty, and maybe this explained NASA's position, but Jess suspected worse. There wasn't enough time to do anything, not enough time to evacuate cities. No way to evacuate an entire planet.

And Jess trusted her father. "My dad's best guess is that Nomad will pass eighty million kilometers from Earth."

"Best guess?" Giovanni raised his eyebrows.

Jess nodded slowly. "That's as good a guess as we're going to get. Might be closer. If it gets as close as twenty million kilometers, the gravity of Nomad will overcome the pull of Earth's own gravity for anything on the surface, literally levitating anything not tied down, dragging it into space. At that distance, it'll pop the Earth's crust and turn the surface into a sea of molten rock."

Giovanni's face contorted as if he bit into lemon. "And at eighty million?"

Jess rubbed a hand across her face, calculating in her head. Tricks for performing quick mental arithmetic had been a game her father played with her as a teenager. "We'll experience a brief tug upward a tenth of Earth's gravity. It'll generate tidal forces almost two hundred times the moon's, with coastal tsunamis hundreds or even thousands of feet high."

"And the Earth's crust? What about earthquakes, volcanos?"

"Very difficult to predict. My dad did say we'll probably get huge solar flares on its closest approach to the sun—about five hours before reaching the Earth. It'll bathe the Earth in a shower of high-energy particles in the middle of the night. Light up the sky like a neon tube."

If her father was right, these auroras would be the warning.

"In thirty hours the sky should light up. Then we'll know for sure." Jess glanced into the darkening sky. No shimmering light, not yet.

"That should give us a four or five hour warning, more than enough time to get to the castle."

Giovanni looked up and took a deep breath. "Thirty hours until the end."

Jess felt him relax.

She stared at the house across the street, imagining how she would get in—her and Giovanni in the front, the two security men from the back, then quickly cover the side entrance. It would be over in a few seconds.

A couple walked slowly by in the street in front of the house, hand in hand.

Jess watched them pass in silence. She took a deep breath and exhaled long and slow. "People seem so calm." The seaside town was mostly deserted, people having headed inland or into the mountains, but some had remained.

Jess turned to Giovanni. "In some places they're burning down cities before Nomad even gets here."

Giovanni nodded, his eyes fixed on the house across the street. "To exist is literally amazing—but that same wonder is also burdened with a finite end. There is a self-deception in denying the dark underside of existence, that the question, 'Why am I here?' is answered with resounding emptiness."

Jess would usually roll her eyes at something like this, but now she nodded.

"In most of the world," Giovanni continued, "even talking about death is unseemly; they only view the value of something based on its ability to enhance happiness or enjoyment. Just discussing death is viewed in bad taste, as if we're immortal. So when the end comes suddenly, it's no surprise that some people are running around tearing their hair out. But death is the only thing certain in life."

Jess frowned. "That's morbid."

"See what I mean?" The edges of Giovanni's mouth curled in the saddest of smiles. "Most of the time this is a philosophical question, but now…"

"I see what you mean," Jess admitted.

"Just weeks ago," Giovanni added, "many people wouldn't believe scientists who said we were destroying the Earth with global warming. Now they believe these same scientists who say that the Earth is about to be destroyed by some invisible object, some speck in space that they can't even see yet—and they scream in panic because it is *their* lives that may be ending, not the lives of their children."

"And what do you believe?"

"I believe in the primacy of action." Giovanni thumped his chest, taking his eyes off the house. "I am here! I believe in living in the moment, in living life to its fullest, even to the end." He looked her in the eye.

In the twilight darkness, Jess stared into Giovanni's eyes. She held his gaze, felt his warmth beside her on the mattress. This might be the last time she ever saw a man look at her like that. A sense of urgency rushed through her; all the fear she'd been holding in rippled up her back, tingling her scalp. I am here, she repeated in her head. I am alive.

She reached around Giovanni and pulled him to her, kissed him hard on the mouth. She slid on top of him, kissing his eyes, his forehead, his neck while she unbuttoned his shirt.

Above them, the first stars of the last night glittered.

29

Vaca, Italy

LEANING AGAINST THE cool concrete of the balcony enclosure, Jess pulled her jeans back on and stared up at the stars. No shimmering light, nothing unusual. Just the sliver of a crescent moon rising.

The pain of living, the fear of dying—their lovemaking was desperate, almost violent, but also quiet. Tendons and muscles strained in near silence. They both listened for any crackle of the walkie-talkie that might signal something happening at the house. Now that it was over, Jess retreated and pulled her limbs into herself, curling into a ball.

Giovanni was still undressed, lying naked on the mattress, his chin flat to the ground, straining to see through the drain gap. He pulled a pack of cigarettes from the pocket of his slacks, rumpled on the floor beside him, and lit one with a gold lighter he produced from the same pocket. The concrete enclosure of the balcony provided shielding so that nobody across the street would see it.

Jess smiled at him. She'd seen him smoking before, at the castle. "You didn't strike me as the type that smoked."

Giovanni returned her smile. "You think these might kill me?" Leaning down, he glanced through the drain gap again. "I quit, years ago, but..."

"Give me one."

Shrugging, Giovanni handed her his cigarette and reached to take another from the pack.

Jess took the cigarette and lifted it to her lips, taking a deep drag. The smoke burned her throat, her lungs, and she coughed. She hadn't smoked since she was a teenager, and even then only to rebel.

Coughing again, she frowned at the cigarette, then stubbed it out against the concrete wall. "That's gross."

Giovanni looked at the cigarette he just took from the pack and nodded. "You're right."

"Zio," the walkie-talkie crackled.

Dropping the cigarette, Giovanni grabbed the walkie-talkie. *"Si."*

"Alla ingressa."

They both flopped onto the mattress and looked through the drain gap. The front door to the house opened, illuminating the gravel walkway. Two men stepped out, followed by Enzo. They stopped, exchanged a few words, and Enzo retreated and closed the door behind them.

"It's them," Jess hissed. "The men that attacked me in Rome." It was unmistakable. The tall man had his arm in a sling, the same arm Jess had twisted. She hoped it was broken.

Walking through the front gate and down the sidewalk to a car, the men drove off.

"This is it," Jess whispered. "This is our chance."

She stood and limped to the couch inside the apartment. They kept the lights off. Grabbing a headlamp from the coffee table, she clicked it on and scribbled on a notepad.

Giovanni grabbed his clothes, and, hunched over, walked to the couch while he pulled his slacks and shirt on. "Now? We go now? I thought you said we should wait until after midnight?"

"This changes everything. Two of them just left, and I doubt he has more than two other men in there with him." She pointed at her drawing on the notepad. "Your security guys say there is one large living room in the back, right?"

Giovanni nodded.

"And I bet there is a kitchen off that." She scribbled again. "A bathroom somewhere in the middle, and two bedrooms off to one side. That right side room, the light hasn't gone on since we saw them go in with Hector?"

Giovanni spoke into the walkie-talkie softly, asking a question. It crackled a response. "No, it hasn't," he confirmed.

"So I bet that's where Hector is. Right now is our best chance.

You and I go in through the front door, your two security men in through the rear. We get Hector while they surprise Enzo and his guys in the back."

Nodding, Giovanni smoothed his pant legs. "Good, good, so we go?"

"We need a way to coordinate going in." Jess looked at Giovanni. "Synchronize our watches or something?"

"Why don't I just give them a signal on the walkie-talkie?"

Jess stared at him for a second. Yeah, that was a better idea. "Perfect."

"So we go now?"

"The sooner, the better, while those guys are gone. Can you explain to your men?"

Nodding, Giovanni walked to the back of the apartment, next to the door. While he explained the plan over the walkie-talkie, Jess grabbed a bullet proof vest—a benefit of the Ruspoli armory—from the couch and secured it around her torso, gripping and pulling the Velcro tabs tight. Nomad might be coming tomorrow night, but this night she intended to live through. Giovanni walked back from the door, stooping to pick up his own vest.

"So we're all set?" Jess grabbed the AK assault rifle.

"The guards are going around the back right now. When I give the signal, '*Ora*,' they'll crash the rear entrance." He looked at Jess inspecting the AK as he secured the straps on his vest, then he picked up his Beretta from the table.

"*Ora*?" Jess grabbed another Beretta from the table and secured it in the small of her back. "What does that mean?"

Giovanni smiled at her. "*Now*, it means now."

Jess followed him to the apartment's door. They made their way down the interior stairs, and then out the back of the complex onto a street that faced a park. Palm trees, dimly lit by the crescent moon, swayed in the ocean breeze. A thick carpet of stars hung overhead. No shimmering lights. Jess smelled the oil of her rifle and the new plastic of the ballistic vest tight around her chest.

Tapping her shoulder, Giovanni nodded and they walked to the corner. She hid the rifle behind her back with one hand.

Holding hands, they walked across the street slowly like a couple on a stroll, until they reached the cover of the shrubs on the other side. They hugged the bushes and stopped at the gate of the house. Jess wanted to go first, but Giovanni had insisted that he lead.

She could have insisted that she go in first, but the truth was, she was scared.

Jess might have been in the Marines, but for all her bravado, while she'd technically been in 'combat', she'd never been in a firefight. For the first month of her rotation in Afghanistan, she was consigned inside the wire of Camp Rhino in Registan Desert, the first base that US troops established. It was on her very first mission, a low risk pickup of field reporters, that her Humvee had hit an IED. The blast destroyed the entire left side of the truck, and taken her left leg with it. She was sent home in pieces. In a life filled with half-finished business, she never even managed to finish a tour of duty with the Marines.

Her heart in her throat, Jess waited as Giovanni leaned forward to slide the gate open. They jogged to the front door, keeping low. Giovanni glanced at her, his hand holding the Beretta shaking.

"Take a deep breath," Jess whispered as much to him as herself. "We go in, straight to the right. You get Hector, I'll cover you."

Crickets chirped in the silence. Nodding, Giovanni took a step back and held the walkie-talkie to his mouth. "*ORA*!" he said loudly, standing up straight.

He lifted one leg and crashed it into the door.

It barely budged.

The smashing of glass echoed from the other side of the building, the quick pops of gunfire erupting amid yelling.

Swearing, Giovanni kicked the door again, then heaved himself forward to slam into it with his shoulder. It gave way, splintering, and Giovanni fell inward, tripping over his feet to ram his head into the hallway wall. Jess jumped in behind him, bringing her weapon up, and stepped over Giovanni. She glanced down the hallway to the right. More screaming from the other side of the house, the crack of gunfire. Striding three big paces down the hallway, Jess tried the door handle. It swung open.

And there was Hector, sitting up in bed in Spider-Man pajamas, his eyes wide.

Jess smiled and took a step back into the corridor, swinging her weapon around. "Get him," she said to Giovanni, who was back on his feet.

He stepped past her and scooped Hector into his arms.

"*Li abbiano*!" yelled a voice down the corridor.

Giovanni looked at Jess. "That's Vlad, one of my guys. He says they have them." He held Hector tight, his little face mashed into Giovanni's chest.

"Wait here." Jess inched down the corridor, her back to the wall.

Stopping at the end, she crouched, then stole a quick look around the corner. She saw Enzo and the two men she'd seen outside on their knees, Giovanni's two security men standing over them. She looked back at Giovanni. "It's good."

Giovanni stared at her, gripping Hector with both arms, the Beretta in one hand. He nodded at the front door. "Let's just go, get out of here."

Jess shook her head. "No, let's make sure. We don't want to be followed."

His chest heaving in and out with each breath, Giovanni brought a shaking hand up to wipe the sweat from his forehead. He stared hard at Jess, then called out, "*E sicuro*?"

"*Si*," replied the same voice, Vlad.

The truth was, they *could* have just left, and Jess knew it. Giovanni's security men could have tied up Enzo, made sure they couldn't leave. Their car was just on the next block. In less than an hour they would be secure inside the castle. Safe. Or at least, safe until Nomad tore the world apart.

But Jess wanted to see Enzo's face, wanted to see him squirm when he looked at her. She wanted recognition of what he did to her. Thoughts flashed through her mind. Maybe she could tie him up outside, leave him a front row seat to watch the heavens.

Coming around the corner, she glared at Enzo. "So you thought you could get away with it?"

Enzo smiled, his hands behind his head, kneeling before the two security agents. "I see you have a new leg."

Jess took two quick paces to him. "So it *was* you."

Giovanni came up behind Jess, shielding Hector. "Come on, let's go. They can handle this."

But Jess couldn't resist. She slapped Enzo across the face, knocking his pork pie hat off his head, almost knocking him over. "You should be more careful who you pick on."

Enzo steadied himself with one hand, his eyes closed, a red welt rising on his cheek. He opened his eyes and righted himself, staring up at Jess. "No, actually, I think it is you who should be more careful."

Laughing, she pointed her AK at his head. "Oh yeah, and why is that?"

Something cold pressed into Jess's neck. She turned to see what it was when someone tried to grab the rifle from her hand. She held on, turning her head. "Hey, what the hell?"

Vlad, Giovanni's security guard, smiled a menacing grin at Jess. The cold in her neck was the muzzle of Vlad's AK. Glancing left, she saw the other security guard pointing his weapon at Giovanni.

"You should choose who you work with more carefully," Enzo said as he stood, pulling a rifle from behind his back with one hand.

"Hey—" was all Jess could say before something crunched into the side of her face.

SURVIVOR TESTIMONY
#AR34;

Event +92hrs;
Survivor name: Andrei Zasekin;
Reported location: Gobi Desert;

We knew they lied to us when the skies lit up. I am Corporal Zasekin of the Russian Border Patrol, my English is good, yes? I lived in Canada for three years, in Montreal, when I studied abroad before returning to the army. So. We were stationed near Irkutsk, near the border of Mongolia. Nikolai was just coming back from a night of drinking when he saw the lights eating the skies. About seven in the morning. I woke everyone and told them to pack their gear. The day was overcast, but even through the clouds we saw the fingers of fire burning around the sun. At noon the first tremors shook the ground, tearing the streets, and it seemed God pulled a plug from the bottom of Lake Baikal. The water just disappeared. A few minutes later eruptions started. Clouds of steam shooting into the sky. I loaded my men into our Czilim hovercraft as the streets of Irkutsk flooded with blistering water. The northern end of Baikal opened up, a tremendous explosion throwing blackness into the sky. For hours we drove south, blind, seeing not more than twenty feet in front of the hovercraft as we skidded across snow and ash. Finally we descended into the Gobi, but the skies are now black, ash falling endlessly while Baikal roars behind us in the darkness. We have stopped to clean the hovercraft manifold and intakes. GPS is down, all computers not functional, but we are sure we are just north of Ulan Bator…

Transmission ended ionization static. Freq. 5144 kHz/USB.

Subject reacquired pgs 34, 109.

DAY EIGHT

October 13th

30

Vaca, Italy

JESS HATED BEING confined, hated any sense of something tying her down, but she'd never literally been tied up. She twisted and tore at the ropes until her wrists bled; until they kicked her into submission. The coarse black sack pulled over her head smelled like a horse's ass, and little bits of straw sucked up her nose on every breath. She gagged and coughed, cursed at them to take it off, told them that they didn't know the danger they were in.

All she got in return were cruel laughs.

She'd been dumped in the back of what felt like the bed of a pickup truck. Hitting a bump in the road, Jess tossed to one side, slamming her head into metal. She squirmed to stay upright, her hands bound painfully behind her back.

Stupid.

The word circled around and around in her head, beyond the pain and fear.

She could have been at the castle with her mother and father. So many things she had to say to them. In twenty-four hours it would be too late. Why did she volunteer for this? Just another stupid decision in a life-long list of stupid decisions. Most of them had been to spite her parents, in one way or the other, to prove to them…

To prove what?

To prove she wasn't worth it. She joined the Marines because she loved her country and wanted to serve, but that was only half the story. She also knew it would shock her mother and disappoint her father when she quit college and was shipped off around the world to kill people. She *wanted* to disappoint them. Not that she didn't love them, quite the opposite. She wanted to disappoint them to punish *herself.*

Groaning, Jess pushed her back against the metal wheel well.

But at least this time, her misadventure was for something good, to right a wrong. To help someone. That was good, wasn't it? But really, in her heart, she knew it was driven by a thirst for revenge. If she hadn't had an opportunity to capture Enzo, to gloat over him and teach him a lesson, would she have come? Maybe. Probably.

But maybe not.

The truck roared over another bump in the road, sending her flying. She landed on her left shoulder, her prosthetic leg twisting painfully on her stump, nearly coming off. Jess pushed herself upright again.

After Giovanni's men turned on them, they'd bound and gagged Jess, then tied Giovanni to a chair and used him as a punching bag. She pleaded with them, apologized to Enzo for not telling him about Nomad. She said that they had gold and money at the castle, explained that Nomad was coming in a day, that they'd all be killed. Enzo laughed, took a break from pummeling Giovanni, and replied that the castle would be theirs anyway.

They didn't believe her story about Nomad. They figured it was a scare tactic.

And it *was* a scare tactic.

Just a true one.

In the small hours of the morning, under cover of night, they'd pulled the bag over her head and dragged her outside into the back of the truck. She heard Hector crying, begging them, but she couldn't understand what he said. Something else was dumped into the back of the truck. She shimmied around, felt for what it was: the inert body of Giovanni.

The truck drove down the road, and Jess felt it take a sharp right onto what she assumed was the main coastal road. It continued on for about fifteen minutes before taking a curving left onto a rough gravel road where she was bumped up and down and thrown around.

The truck skidded to a stop, the cabin doors opened and slammed closed. The black hood was pulled from Jess's head and she gulped in a mouthful of air and blinked. Night was over, the sky already blue-gray, the new day beginning. Green hills stretched up on all sides. They were in a small fishing village nestled into the folds of a valley that fell into the sea. As she looked up at the hills, the sun broke over them, bathing Jess in golden light.

Perhaps the last sunrise she'd ever see.

"Where are we going?" Jess croaked.

Enzo stood on the other side of the truck, inspecting Giovanni, whose swollen eyes were open just enough to know he was conscious, his face battered and bloody. Enzo laughed, said, "He knows where we're going," and pointed out across the water. "*Isola del Gigli.*"

Jess's eyes followed his hand. Past the breakwaters of the fishing village, a rocky crag of an island, less than a mile offshore, stood out of the still waters of the Mediterranean. Dark green trees sprouted at the base of the island, a small jetty just visible. The walls of a structure rose up from the stony cliffs, lights twinkling in the upper rooms.

Someone grabbed Jess's arms, almost pulling them out of their sockets. She cried out. It was Vlad, one of Giovanni's men who had turned on them, and he dragged Jess out of the back of the pickup.

"You don't need her," Giovanni whispered from between cracked lips. The other traitor guard pulled him to his feet.

"Oh, but we do." Enzo walked ahead of them, to a wooden dock the pickup was parked next to. A green and red fishing boat, paint peeling from its sides, sat at the end of the dock.

"Not for this," croaked Giovanni, stumbling forward.

"Exactly for this." Enzo smiled as he jumped into the back of the boat.

Vlad pulled on Jess's arms, pain lancing through her shoulders. "Come on," he commanded.

Jess ambled forward, her prosthetic loose. How humiliating if it came free and she sprawled spinning into the dirt. She kept her head low, watched the seaweed-covered rocks at the edge of the dock. The seaweed covered only a foot or two of the rocks coming out of the water. A foot or two. It had to be low tide.

The boat was filled with a tangled mess of white netting and orange floats, and stank of rotten fish. Jess realized it would be futile to try and resist, so she did her best to step carefully into the boat. Giovanni wasn't as accommodating. Vlad shoved him from the dock and Giovanni fell into the bottom with a sickening thud.

The large man who had attacked Jess in the apartment in Rome came behind them, holding tiny Hector, who squirmed in his arms. Once they were all aboard, they threw off the lines and the boat's engine roared to life, belching blue fumes out behind it. The boat left the dock and growled into the bay.

Pinned in the big man's arms, terrified Hector stared at Jess, his eyes wide.

"Don't worry," Jess whispered, "it'll be okay."

But she didn't know if it would be.

Giovanni's body hadn't moved since he landed in the bottom of the boat.

Seagulls squawked, wheeling in the sky over the boat, expecting a meal. Jess looked up, squinted into the sun. She felt its heat and warmth, but more than that, she sensed malevolence. Nomad was coming from behind the sun. In a few hours it would pass the sun, and might be visible to Earth-based observatories for the first time. This close, they might be able to see it.

She looked into the blue sky. Would it arrive earlier than her father predicted? Would she be able to see the auroras in the sky, even during the day? She didn't see anything. Her dad said it would knock out the electricity grids. Glancing left, she saw lights on in the fishing village. So she still had time.

Gritting her teeth, she pulled on the ropes. *Goddamn it.*

The boat churned across the water.

Jess performed a calculation in her head. Twenty-four hours until Nomad made its closest approach. If her father was right, it was closing the distance at thirty million kilometers an hour. It had already passed Jupiter's orbit on its way in, and was halfway to Mars by now. That meant it was in the Asteroid Belt. If it collided with something there, they ought to see a flash, a momentary accretion disk. At least they'd be able to see it.

But probably not. Not at that speed; it would have to be a perfect hit. And the Asteroid Belt, for its name, was mostly empty.

An idea flashed into Jess's mind. *Tidal forces.*

She leaned over the side, kept her eyes looking down. It flashed blue, then beige. A sandy bottom, not more than twenty or thirty feet.

She glanced at the island. Maybe a bit more than a half mile from shore. She looked over the side again, kept her eyes on the bottom. Not deep blue, still light blue. Maybe fifty feet.

The two men in front of her laughed and Jess looked up. They looked at something on a phone's screen, then glanced back at her with sick grins. She squinted to see what they looked at. Two bodies, writhing together. Were they watching porn? Her skin crawled as she realized it was a video of her and Giovanni. They'd recorded them last night, in that apartment.

One of the men looked at her, realizing she knew what it was. He said something in Italian, laughing with a mouthful of broken teeth.

Enzo came out of the boat's cabin and glanced at what the men were looking at. "Would like to get her legs wrapped around my head, too," he laughed, but seeing Jess watching him, his face hardened. He smacked the man holding the phone. "*Spegnerlo!*" Enzo spat. "Show a little respect." He took the phone away, turned it off.

Jess hadn't expected that reaction. What was that about?

On the floor of the boat, Giovanni groaned and rolled to one side. He squirmed to sit upright and looked at Jess, then glanced at Hector and Enzo.

Enzo grinned at him. "We're going back to where this all started, Baron Ruspoli."

This whole time, Jess had a feeling she'd been missing something. "Where what started?" She looked at Enzo, then at Giovanni.

Giovanni avoided her eyes and looked down grimly.

Enzo laughed. "You didn't tell her, did you?"

Jess looked back and forth, at Giovanni staring down, at Enzo smiling at the both of them. "Tell me what?" she demanded.

31

Chianti, Italy

CELESTE SAT AT her favorite spot in the western gardens of the castle, at a stone table set under the huge oak trees with a view down the valley to the village of Saline. Sparrows darted overhead in an endless sky, songbirds sang in the boughs of the oaks. The gravel paths crisscrossing the lawns were now littered with fallen leaves. Old Leone, the groundskeeper, still hadn't returned.

In fact, nobody had returned.

Since the flurry of emails from Ben the day before—detailing everything he knew, saying he was crossing into Italy and just hours away—nothing. Just silence, the sound of the wind through the leaves, the crickets chirping peacefully through the long night. The evening before, Jess and Giovanni had left a message with Nico saying they found Enzo and Hector, and expected to be back by morning.

Yet here Celeste was, having breakfast alone.

Actually, not alone.

"More coffee, Madame Tosetti?" Nico asked. He deposited a tray of fruit and cheeses and cured meat on her table.

Celeste admired Nico's gentle eyes. "You've been so kind to me. A real gentleman." She took his hand. "And I mean a gentle man."

Nico bowed and kissed her hand. "It has been an honor to serve you, Madame Tosetti."

Celeste felt a tenderness from Nico, a closeness, as if he were family. Perhaps because she ached for hers. Her mother and father were long dead, and she was an only child. So her only family was Jess. And Ben. And if Ben was right, this was the final day before Nomad. What television stations remained broadcasting were filled with hysterical rants or endless, depressing snapshots of riots and burning cities, scenes impossible to reconcile with this beautiful, peaceful mountaintop.

"Would you sit with me for a moment?" Celeste asked Nico.

"Of course."

Nico sat opposite her, but instead of facing Celeste, he turned to admire the view, letting her enjoy the moment, sensing that she just didn't want to be alone. In the morning she'd tried to convince him to drive with her to Vaca, to try and find Jess, but he'd gently pointed out that they might miss them, or might not be here when Ben came.

They had to stay here, he'd argued.

Nico had locked the place down tight. It was a castle, after all. Designed to be defended.

"Don't you have people you want to go to?" Celeste asked Nico. "Family, loved ones…?"

Taking a deep breath, Nico turned to her. "I am where I want to be." He turned back to the view.

She turned up the volume on the digital satellite radio on the edge of the table. The news was frenzied, but she couldn't disconnect. She needed to know what was going on.

"…NASA saying that Nomad has entered the inner solar system, past Jupiter's orbit, confirming reports from independent observers and amateur astronomers that it will pass Earth in the next twenty-four to thirty-six hours. New fighting in Kashmir…"

So Ben was right.

Celeste glanced at Nico, but he didn't react, didn't look at the radio.

Had the governments been purposely evasive? Or was it just bureaucratic ineptness? In any case, it didn't matter. Riots had destroyed whole cities; the world plunged into pre-death spasms with wars erupting in the Middle East, Congo, Indonesia and the Indian sub-Continent. She turned the volume down. She could only take it in small doses.

Pressing her lips together, Celeste turned to stare at Nico. He was sweet, but it was odd. He didn't react to any of the news, not to anything they heard.

Something beeped, and Nico looked at his phone. "Excuse me," he said, getting up. "I need to talk to someone."

"Of course." Celeste smiled as he walked away. She was glad he had someone. She stared back at the beautiful view, dappled sunshine falling through the oaks onto her. It was peaceful.

She just wished Jess was here with her.

But then that was her daughter. Always running away. She knew her daughter's pain, and now, she wished she'd done more. An image of a long-ago snowy day filled Celeste's mind, of two children running in the yard, of her sitting at her desk. The day she lost her family, the day she lost Jess.

"...this just in. A reporter from NewsCorp alleges that Dr. Ben Rollins..."

Celeste put one hand to her mouth hearing her husband's name. What happened?

"...the celebrity astronomer who spoke to media when Nomad was announced, had evidence of Nomad over thirty years ago. The revelation has sparked a massive backlash. Why did he hide his research paper, and why did he lie to the media? With more, we go to..."

Jess had told Celeste about Ben's research paper, but he hadn't hid it. It was never published. She hoped Ben wasn't listening to this. They made it seem like he was to blame. Hateful vitriol oozed from the radio. Celeste turned it down.

And where was Ben?

Celeste always thought she'd be scared when the end came, but she didn't feel fear. She should have been a better wife. A better mother.

Guilt.

Guilt filled her.

Was she afraid? A little perhaps, but knowing there was nothing to do, all her thoughts came back to her family. Why hadn't she done more to keep them together? Why hadn't she spent more time with them?

Now there was no more time.

Tears fell into Celeste's coffee as she sobbed, bringing one hand to her mouth.

All she could hope for was to see Jess and Ben again, to be able to say goodbye, to say all the things that had remained unspoken.

"...breaking news..."

Sighing, she leaned forward to turn the radio up.

The announcer coughed and let out a long sigh. *"We...there...are reports of nuclear detonations in the Middle East, over Beirut, Mosul, Damascus and Tehran...Israel is claiming responsibility, invoking its right to existence after attacks on three fronts by Arab nations..."*

Seconds ticked by in silence and Celeste was about to check the radio to see if it had turned off.

"...we all want to exist," continued the anchor. *"I think, in this final hour, perhaps this is the only thing that humanity can agree on: that we all want to exist."* Another pause. *"This is as good a moment as any to announce that* BBC World News *is signing off. Our skeleton staff is no longer able to maintain the broadcast, and I know we all want to go home."* He took a deep breath. *"To everyone listening out there, good luck, and may God be with you."*

The radio beeped once, twice, followed by a long continuous tone. Celeste cycled through the other preset channels on the satellite radio. All of them were blank. She turned it off.

Giovanni had shown Celeste all the trekking gear he used on expeditions, stored in the basements, including the communications gear. Celeste had retrieved a shortwave the day before and shown Jess how to use it. It was time to revert to older technology. There had to be chatter from amateur broadcasters on shortwave frequencies, from all over the world. She'd go and find it in a minute. Right now she needed to digest everything.

On the stone table in front of her, she had a world map from Giovanni's office spread out. She spent the morning scribbling on it, red dashed lines for major faults lines, hash marks at geologic hot spots. There were over a thousand potentially active volcanoes spread across the Earth. As a geologist, she dredged as much as she could from memory, never having suspected she might need to use her knowledge like this.

Nuclear war in the Middle East.

In another time, the news would have shocked her, but she was already numb. Just another nail in a coffin already going into the ground. It surprised her how easily her mind seemed to absorb news of the death of millions. It had to be millions. The announcer hadn't said, hadn't even hazarded a guess, because it didn't matter anymore.

Even a nuclear war was a sideshow to the coming main event. These wars were one last chance to enact revenge, one last chance to show God was on their side.

Celeste grew up Catholic, her mother and father devout followers of the Pope. She'd gone to church on Sundays, read the Bible, but it had faded as she got into college, more so after she met Ben. Passing the Vatican four days ago, hearing that the Pope was going to speak, she had to admit she felt a thrill, wanted to join the crowds.

The destruction of the Vatican had an effect on her she hadn't expected. Terrified, of course, horrified at the carnage she'd witnessed. Now she found herself praying, to a God she'd abandoned, to a God humans seemed determined to destroy.

But she'd lived a good life, hadn't she?

She just wished she'd spent more of it with Jess. And Ben.

Celeste took a red marker and drew hash marks from Lebanon to Iran to Egypt, her guess at areas already destroyed.

When Nomad passed, major fault lines were sure to slip. She circled the Pacific Northwest of America, drew a thick line down the San Andreas and across the New Madrid fault running through the Midwest. Staring at America, with her thick red marker she circled the supervolcano under Yellowstone.

She looked at Europe, then stared at the view in front of her. Italy had its own recently active volcanoes. In the distance, a flat-topped mountain—Monterufoli—was ten miles away, maybe fifteen? A volcano almost next door.

A wind rustled the leaves above her, and she could have sworn it whistled her name. She listened hard, but heard nothing more. Sitting back she refilled her coffee and dried her tears. It was a beautiful day for the end of the world.

Ben leaned his head out of the farming truck's open window, looked up through the olive trees at a beautiful blue sky. The truck bounced along a gravel road, climbing up the side of the mountain. The farmer had picked them up in the morning, after they'd spent last night walking five miles off the main A1 highway that ran from Milan to Rome. Roger sat beside Ben in the back seat, on a long bench of torn green plastic in the back of the old Chevy. Wedged between them was Ben's backpack, the one with the tape spools and CDs of old data. Roger had a bandage taped over his right eye, and a bloody cloth tied around his left arm.

They'd managed to salvage Ben's laptop from the wreck when their car slid over the railing. Roger was still upset about Ben trying to rescue the backpack before saving him. They walked the last five miles, over the top of Gotthard Pass out of Switzerland, and then managed to hitchhike their way down the other side where the highways started into Italy.

They had their cell phones, but there was no service, not since Switzerland. Ben sensed it was more than just overloaded circuits. While half the world burned from riots and war, the other half had gone home to loved ones. Communication networks still needed humans to maintain them, and the humans were gone. Not there today.

And probably not tomorrow or ever again.

A clearing opened in the olive trees. Stone walls rose into the sky. "*Castello Ruspoli*?" he asked the driver.

"*Si*," the old farmer replied, his face tanned and creased old leather. He held out a shaking hand. "Ruspoli." He stopped the truck.

Ben could hardly believe they made it. Still twenty-two hours to Nomad. Time enough to talk to Celeste, to talk to Jess, to get ready. Could they survive it? Maybe for a few days. That was all he could hope for right now.

"Can you walk?" Ben asked Roger.

Roger nodded. "Yeah, I'm fine."

Ben knew he wasn't fine, but nodded and got out of the truck, grabbing his backpack with his laptop and the data spools. Roger jumped out behind him, wincing as he hit the ground, shouldering his own bag. The farmer waved and put the truck into gear to crunch off across the gravel. Ben started walking up the roadway to the castle walls, a closed entrance not more than a hundred yards away.

"What's so important about that old data?" Roger asked. "Christ, I almost died back there."

"You almost killed yourself getting your own bag. I could ask you the same thing."

Roger dusted himself off and shrugged. "Just reflex, I guess. But you practically crawled over me to get to your pack."

Ben kicked a pebble from the packed earth underfoot. He looked into Roger's eyes, studied him for a moment. "When we were in Darmstadt, I said not all the data was in that paper I published thirty years ago, the one you read..." He looked down and kicked another rock. "I made a mistake."

"A mistake?"

"I was just a grad student, still learning the ropes. I didn't transform the coordinates of the location of the flashes properly in the paper I submitted. I realized it after I sent it in, but when it wasn't accepted for publication..."

"You didn't make a correction."

"I didn't see the point at the time."

"And so the data in that backpack," Roger continued Ben's thoughts for him, "might contain the only record of the location of Nomad thirty years ago. Which might be the only way to calculate its trajectory accurately."

Even with Gaia and Earth-based observatories, they would only be able to get an approximate location of Nomad as it got closer. Once it reached the Sun, radiation from solar eruptions would cripple any observatories and satellites. Scientists might be able to pinpoint a location of Nomad, but to get its exact trajectory, they'd need a long axis point.

Ben turned to Roger and smiled. "Exactly." He turned to the castle wall, banged on the wooden door, and searched for a buzzer or button. Nothing. He slapped the wooden door again. "Celeste! Celeste, are you there?"

Looking around, he found a staircase that led down. Jumping down the stairs, he saw that it led into a half-basement of poured concrete with no doors. Maybe he'd have to climb the walls. He dropped his backpack into a dark corner of the cellar for safe-keeping and jogged back up the stairs. The place looked abandoned. A sinking feeling settled into Ben's gut. They'd better be here.

"Hello?"

Ben spun around. A man stood beside Roger, smiling. Roger shrugged.

"Ah, this is Castello Ruspoli, yes?" Ben asked.

"Yes, it is," the man replied in very good English.

"I'm looking for Celestina Tosetti and Jessica Rollins," Ben added.

The man nodded, still smiling. "And you are…?"

"I'm Jessica's father, Ben Rollins…I'm Celeste's husband." Ben wagged his head. "Or, well, we're separated…and this is Roger, my student."

"A pleasure," the man replied.

Ben frowned. "Are they here?"

The man paused, squinted. "Yes, yes, of course."

32

Isola Gigli, Italy

BARE ROCK WALLS supported rough-hewn beams, the room empty except for a metal-framed cot covered with a gray blanket. Jess paced around the room, not more than ten foot square, stopping to hammer on the wooden door again. "Let me OUT!" she screamed, her fist raw and red.

Still no response.

A prisoner in a castle for a second time this week. Italy was getting on her nerves.

She circled the room, limping on the awkward prosthetic. Goddamn thing, it scraped her stump on every step. A single window mercifully let in some fresh air. The window was open with no bars or restraints, about two feet wide and three high. It didn't need bars. She stopped to look out—she could easily squirm through, but a fifty-foot sheer cliff of stone and brick sloped away beneath it. Below that, a guard stood watch, almost directly below her window.

Peering left and right, she estimated the island was half a mile long, a craggy rock rising up from a base of stone and sand. The whine of an engine. Looking down, she saw a man with a rifle slung over his shoulder pull up on a dirt bike. He chatted with the guard stationed below her. Doing the rounds. The engine whined again, and the man wound his way down a zigzag trail, through the trees near the water and out onto the dock. He parked the bike and got onto the fishing boat.

Jess watched the boat pull away from the dock, water churning behind it. On the way in, she watched for any other boats. There was just the one dock. The rest of the island was jagged rocks into the water. She looked at the boat pulling across the water, watched the sandy bottom refract through the waves.

She craned her neck further out of the window. The sun was low on the horizon. Past seven o'clock. She looked back at the dock. It should be high tide. Squinting, she could just make out the rocks, seaweed hanging off their tops. At least two or three feet below the high tide line.

So her father's timing was right.

A knock on the door.

Jess pulled her head inside.

The door opened and Enzo walked in, a grin spread from ear to ear. "Ms. Jessica, I must apologize for the accommodations, and for our—"

"What the hell is wrong with you?" Jess sputtered. "Look, I'm sorry about not telling you about Nomad, about hiding it—"

"This has nothing to with that." Enzo raised both hands and wiped his eyebrows, adjusted his pork pie hat. "As I was trying to say, I never meant for Anthony to hurt you or steal your leg in Rome. And I apologize for the room here. We had to remove everything, after hearing how…violent you can be."

Jess stared at Enzo, her emotions unbalanced, unsure of how to react.

Why was he apologizing? Enzo never struck her as very intelligent. This wasn't making any sense. Was this just a kidnapping scheme gone sideways?

"Is this about money? Giovanni has gold, in the castle." She pointed out the window. "I know you don't believe me, but something terrible is about to happen, destruction you can't imagine will kill us all in a few hours."

Enzo took a step toward her. "You are right, a terrible thing has happened, and I am fixing it."

"Fixing it?" Jess's bewilderment rose with her eyebrows. "Why did you follow me? Attack me in Rome?"

"It wasn't my intention to *attack* you," Enzo replied. "We just needed to keep you here."

Keep her here? Jess's mind raced. "So it was you that texted me from Giovanni's phone?"

Enzo frowned. "Text?"

"Yes, the messages to my phone. You texted me from Giovanni's phone? Told me to come back to the castle."

His face brightened. "Ah yes, I was text to you."

Did he just not understand English very well? She didn't bother to correct him. "Why?"

"Why?" Enzo took a step toward Jess, their faces not more than two feet apart. "So he never told you? The *Baron* never told you?"

Jess was beyond tired of this. "Told me *what*?"

Enzo leaned toward her, waved a hand between them. "There has been a fight between our families for hundreds of years. The Ruspoli wiped us out, and it was here on Gigli that they signed the papers that took our villa a hundred years ago."

Jess grimaced. "So what, this is that feud? Some kind of vendetta?"

"A vendetta! Yes." Enzo's face lit up. "*Our* family was forced into disgrace, forced out of the Saline valley six generations ago."

A light bulb went off in Jess's mind. "So that villa across from Castello Ruspoli, the one connected by a cable car across the valley, that's your family's villa?" Giovanni said it was a new addition, just added to the family a hundred years ago.

"Yes, yes!" Enzo's face lit up.

His face was right in Jess's. She smelled garlic and the sour stink of alcohol. Taking a step back, she demanded, "What does this have to do with me? And why do you keep saying *'our'*?"

"*Our* family, the Tosetti." Enzo punched his chest. "*We* are family. You and I."

Jess took another step back and slumped against the stone wall by the window. Seagulls squawked. A tingling dread crept up her spine. "What?"

"Your mother is one of the last in the direct blood line of the Tosetti." Enzo stepped toward her again, trapped her against the wall. "We have been planning this for a long time, to avenge the cruelty inflicted on our family by the Ruspolis." His eyes glittered, sweat beading on his forehead. "But now, we were forced to act."

Jess remembered her mother saying her family moved out of the

Saline valley, to America over a hundred years ago, part of the immigration wave into New York. But this, this was crazy. "There's no way I'm related to you in any—"

"Oh no?" He put one arm on the wall beside her head, raised a finger to an inch from her nose. "Tell me that vengeance doesn't flow in your veins? I've seen it in your eyes."

Jess tried to squirm away, but there was nowhere to go. The room spun, Jess's vision swam. "But now, you choose this moment, with Nomad coming…?" She stole a look out of the window at the setting sun. "This is insane!"

Enzo slammed the wall by her head with his fist. "This is the divine hand of GOD! It proves the Tosetti are the favored ones. That He smiles on us. It is a sign, no? There will be no more Ruspoli."

"And no more Tosetti," Jess whispered. She pushed along the wall away from him. Taking deep breaths, she steadied herself and looked down at the floor. "So that was you?" She looked at Enzo. "That was you who sent my mother the Facebook message?"

The whole reason they came to stay at the Ruspoli Castle, back to the Saline Valley, was the Facebook message her mother received, from a long lost relative. But the person hadn't responded after they arrived in Italy.

Enzo nodded. "Yes. I Faced her."

Somehow Jess doubted Enzo even knew how to send an email, but he kept nodding his head. Jess watched his eyes carefully. "And this is all a coincidence, Nomad—?"

"I told you, not a coincidence. This is divine. This is GOD!" The tendons in Enzo's neck flared out, his face burning crimson.

"Okay, okay," Jess held her hands out, appeasing him. He looked psychotic. "It's God."

She glanced out the window at the setting sun. Less than twelve hours. "What about Hector? He doesn't know about all this. Why don't you let him go?"

Enzo laughed. "There is a plan for him."

Jess closed her eyes, the vision of the little boy's face, ringed in white, swallowed by the black hole. She opened them, took a step toward Enzo. "What if *we*"—she pointed at him, then at her chest—

"took him, raised him as our own?"

"We?" For the first time, Enzo looked unsure.

"Yes, you and I." She took Enzo's hand. "We're family. That would be sweet revenge, no? To take the final Ruspoli heir, turn him into a Tosetti?"

A scowl passed across Enzo's face, slowly replaced by a menacing grin. He laughed. "You see, I told you that you were a Tosetti."

Jess forced a smile, squeezed his hand. "We have to hurry." She pointed out the window. "We need to get away from the coast. This place will be destroyed tomorrow."

Enzo shrugged. "Perhaps, perhaps not. Today is a beautiful day, the most beautiful of my life." He kissed Jess's hand. "We will talk tomorrow morning." He dropped her hand, took three paces to the door and rapped on it. Metal scraped against metal and the door opened.

Jess pulled the cot into the middle of the room so she could stare out the window. Steely pinpoints of stars pierced the inky sky, a silver moon rising over the fishing village nestled in the hills by the shore. Lights twinkled in the houses, almost a mile away across the water. Jess checked the dock every half an hour, as best as she could estimate, and watched the water sink lower. It was at least four feet below the high tide line on the wooden dock supports.

Far below any tide this place had ever seen. Looking out the window, a ghostly green flickered across the sky, like God shining a flashlight over the roof of the world.

It had begun.

How was this possible? How could her and her mother have been dragged into Italy, into the middle of this ancient blood feud, just at the same moment as the Nomad disaster was announced? And her father being tied up in the middle of discovering it? It defied all explanation, seemed to exceed all possibilities of odds or coincidence. Was it chance? If not chance, then what?

But it didn't matter anymore. Not how she got here. That was the past. Jess wrung her hands together and paced around the room. She didn't bang on the door. She didn't beg for release anymore. She had to think.

All her life, she'd never really committed. Not really. She'd always run away. Like to the Marines. Just another half-baked escape. She always thought she was running *away*, but alone in this room, she realized she was only running from herself. She'd never even allowed herself to love anyone. It wasn't that she didn't want love. She did. If she was honest, she wanted it desperately. But she didn't deserve it.

And in a few hours, she would die here, alone.

She always scorned the idea of a family, yet now, at the end, all she wanted was to be near hers. All the pain she put her mother and father through, all the things she did to them, she regretted now. The great secret she'd been carrying all these years.

The pain and guilt gnawed at Jess's soul.

She was the nomad. *She* was the terrible thing hurtling through peoples' lives, tearing them apart.

A half-finished degree; a half-finished tour of duty; the endless road kill of half-finished relationships in a half-finished life. Was this how it was going to end? She even only got halfway out on the ice that day…

Right now, she could run.

If there was ever a time to run, it was now. Save herself. Get back to the castle, find her mother and father. Burrow into their embrace.

But she'd be running again.

Or would she stay?

And save the boy from the black hole.

OF THE DAY NOMAD

October 14th

33

Isola Gigli, Italy

BOATS IN THE fishing village harbor tilted left and right as their keels came to rest on the sands, the water at least fifteen feet below high tide now. Jess estimated it was 2 a.m. The ocean wasn't disappearing, though; it was being sucked away to the other side of the planet by Nomad. Jess imagined the Indian Ocean swelling upward, pulled by tidal forces already ten times the moon's—and this was just the beginning, the gentlest of caresses from Nomad before it pummeled the planet.

Jess closed her eyes, tried to visualize the Earth in her mind, spinning like a top.

A growing wall of water, now fifty or even a hundred feet high at the coasts, was being pulled around the surface of the Earth at more than a thousand miles an hour. And that wall would grow exponentially higher in the next few hours. Now Nomad drained the Mediterranean, but soon, as the Earth turned and Italy spun from darkness toward the sun—toward the onrushing black holes—a wall of water, hundreds or even thousands of feet high, would crash through the Red Sea, roll across Greece and into Italy.

Time had run out.

Opening her eyes, Jess walked to the door of her room and banged on it. "I need to talk to Enzo, please. It's very urgent."

"*Che cosa*?" came an answering reply.

"Enzo!" Jess yelled. "I need to speak to him."

"*Uno minuti*."

Walking back to the window, she checked the dock one last time. No guards, and the dirt bike was still there. Sticking her head out the window, she looked down. The guard down there seemed asleep. She paced back and forth, and was about to bang on the door again when the heavy bolt squealed and the door swung open.

"What is—" Enzo started to ask.

Jess threw herself at him, wrapping her arms around his neck, forcing herself not to recoil from a cocktail stench of booze, cigarettes and sweat. "You were right, nothing is more important than family." She kissed him on the neck, forcing back bile in the pit of her throat, and kissed him again.

With Jess's weight on him, Enzo took a few steps back to balance, moving back into the middle of the landing.

The guard who opened the door stepped away, raising his eyebrows and smiling.

Jess glanced at him and smiled back, taking a moment to size him up: slender, not more than a hundred and thirty pounds. Just a boy, really; he wore beige linen slacks with a white shirt stuffed in at the waist, a brown beret on his head cocked at an angle, his rifle slung carelessly over his right shoulder with the safety still on.

Enzo hesitated when Jess first threw herself at him, seeming to half-expect a punch in the face, but he put his arms around Jess. "Ah, so you are not angry?"

Jess stepped back, still keeping hold of his hand. Two hallways led off the landing; one extended to her left, with three doorways. She'd heard Hector whimpering over there. To the right an exterior door led to the terrace she saw from her room. "No, I'm not angry. You just took me by surprise. I didn't know that was you in Rome."

She glanced down the stairs. It led to a main hall where five men played cards on a table littered with empty wine bottles and overflowing ashtrays. This wasn't a *castello*, it was more of a *villa*, a large house. Like the one across the valley from Castello Ruspoli.

"We talked about all this, in my Facebook emails, about the Ruspolis?" Jess continued. "Don't you remember?"

A gamble.

Enzo's brows came together in a frown. "Facebook?" The frown vanished, replaced by a smile. "Yes, the Facebook, of course. But why didn't you say something before?"

"I was trying to do the same as you." Jess squeezed his hand. "Seduce the Baron, get inside the *castello*, you understand." She beamed her best high-wattage smile.

The frown returned to Enzo's face. "You were?"

Jess leaned in to whisper in his ear. "But now, that's all over. Come inside"—she nodded to the open door of her room—"and let me show you."

"Show me?"

Jess nuzzled his neck, whispered into his ear. "Privately."

Narrowing his eyes, he took a long look at Jess. "Private?" He looked at the young guard. "You took everything out of that room, yes?"

Enzo wasn't the sharpest tool in the shed, but he wasn't that stupid. He said it in English so Jess understood he didn't trust her.

The guard nodded. "Yes, everything. Just the cot and blanket."

"Okay." Enzo nudged Jess forward. "Show me then." He smiled at the young guard and winked as he followed Jess into the room, closing the door behind them.

Walking into the middle of the room, Jess sat on the cot and pulled the blanket over herself, patting the spot next to her and inviting Enzo to sit.

"So what did you want to show me?" Enzo asked as he sat down, reaching under the cover to hold Jess's thigh with his left hand. He kept his right on the gun holstered on his hip.

Jess didn't flinch, but overcame her revulsion and inched closer to him, putting her arm around him. "I wanted to show you that." She pointed out the window.

Following Jess's finger, Enzo squinted. "What, the window?"

"No, look at the sky."

White fingers of light danced across the starry night sky, visible even from the bright interior of the room.

"What is it?" Enzo's eyebrows came together as he squinted harder.

"Look closer," Jess urged. "Auroras from a massive solar flare triggered by Nomad. We need to get out of here, Enzo. And look down at the water."

Enzo stood and walked to the window to stare up. "So it's true." He leaned out and looked down. "*Madre di Dio*, where did the water go?"

While Enzo stared out the window, Jess was busy. Keeping her eye on him, she unstrapped her prosthetic leg under the covers. Quietly, she stood, balancing on one foot, holding the bottom metal rod of her leg with both hands, wielding it like a baseball bat. She swung her arms back, coiled her midsection around like a spring. "I heard what you said on the boat."

Enzo still had his head out of the window. "What?"

"That you'd like to get my legs wrapped around your head."

He pulled back from the window and turned. "You must have—"

Jess swung as hard as she could, cracking Enzo in the side of the head. He staggered and dropped to his knees, his head flopping as if it wasn't connected to his shoulders. Taking a hop forward, Jess raised her club-leg and gritted her teeth. As he slumped forward, she savagely cracked his head again.

Panting, Jess wobbled on her good leg and sat back heavily on the bed.

With a shaking hand, she wiped a smear of blood off the top of her prosthetic, watching Enzo's inert body, blood streaming from his nose, as she strapped her leg back into place. "Didn't anyone ever tell you to be careful what you wish for?" she muttered under her breath.

34

Isola Gigli, Italy

"OH, ENZO, DON'T stop." Jess moaned loud enough for the guard outside to hear as she shoved the cot across the floor to the window. She stooped to grab Enzo's sagging body under the shoulders, "Oh." This time she grunted for real, straining to heft his torso onto the cot. "Yeah."

Gasping for air, she put a finger to Enzo's neck. A weak pulse.

She grabbed his legs and pulled them onto the cot, stopping to mop some of his blood from the floor with the blanket, which she then threw onto Enzo. Before she attacked him, she'd already ripped several lengths of the blanket into strips, using a sharp edge of the metal cot. She gagged and hog-tied Enzo with the strips. Bouncing up and down on the cot, hard enough to generate loud squeaks from the rusty bedsprings, she moaned theatrically the whole time.

That should give her a little time before anyone came in.

She stopped again to feel his neck.

Nothing this time. She waited, leaned her face to his mouth. He wasn't breathing.

Her hand trembling, she pulled her fingers from his neck. Her scalp tingled. She had never killed anyone before. *But maybe that wasn't true.* Images of snow-covered hills flashed through her mind.

Staring at Enzo's slack face, his lips already tinged blue, she saw herself in her mind's eye, raising her club the second time, smashing it into his skull. The first blow was probably enough; he was probably already unconscious. Then again, rubbing her shaking hands together, it made things simpler. In her mind, she was halfway to stuffing the blanket into his mouth, pressing it over his nose, to suffocate him.

Too much risk if he woke up. And anyway, he deserved it, didn't he?

Jess reached under the blanket and unholstered his gun, checked the chamber and loaded a round into it, stuffing the gun into the front pocket of her jeans. She rummaged in his pockets, found a knife and put that into her back pocket. Tightening the straps on her prosthetic, she took a deep breath and stood up on the cot to lean out the window.

Fifty feet below, it looked like the guard was still asleep. Looking up, the ghostly fingers of light danced ever brighter across the carpet of stars. Taking another deep breath, Jess grabbed her left leg and hefted it up onto the window ledge, then, with a grunt, grabbed onto the frame and swung her other leg up. Rolling onto her belly, she felt the cold metal of the gun pressing into her hip.

Carefully, carefully, she inched her way over the edge into open space, her right foot searching for the tiny ledge she'd spotted about three feet down. *There.* She rotated her foot sideways, trying to get the best grip.

Sneakers weren't the best rock climbing footwear.

Gripping the window ledge, she put her weight onto her right foot and angled her body out of the window, scanning the wall to her right. It was a sheer stone wall, but there were cracks. She'd inspected the wall earlier, leaning out of the window, and already had a route planned. Just forty feet sideways along the vertical wall, the holes and cracks and handholds obvious, easy even. Something she could have done in her sleep when climbing with friends, but this time she had no safety.

No ropes.

No second chances.

She glanced down. A fifty-foot drop onto jagged rocks and cement.

Calming her breathing, Jess focused, zeroed her attention into the inches just ahead of her. A familiar sensation, one that she loved, the reason why she participated in extreme sports. No past. No future. Just the moment.

Gripping the window with her left hand, she leaned to her right, her face against the cold stone, her fingers searching. There, a crack. Looking down, she shakily managed to position her prosthetic foot onto the tiny ledge while she reached with her right to find a metal post sticking out of the wall. Letting go of the window, she pulled herself right, now a spider trapped against the wall.

Another crack, another hole, another tiny ledge—she silently edged across the wall. Ten feet from the terrace, reaching as far as she could with her right hand, she found a hole between the stones and she slid her fingers in as deep as she could, then twisted, jamming them in solidly.

Her foothold slipped.

Jess dropped a foot and a half, her legs dangling in space, her full weight wrenched onto the two fingers jammed in the rock and a tiny outcropping her left hand fingers barely held onto. Pain shot through her arm, her fingers on fire, cracking, straining.

Just let go, a voice said in her head. It's what you always wanted, isn't it? Why do you put yourself in danger so often?

Because you want it taken away.

Your life.

Just let go, and it will all be over.

Jess dangled in space, pain ripping through her fingers, her arm burning, her eyes tearing. Looking up, she glimpsed the crescent moon over the edge of the wall, its outer circle just visible. Through her watery eyes she saw a boy's face, disappearing into the moon, into the black hole ringed in white.

No.

Tears streaming down her face, Jess strained, scrabbled her legs against the wall. She pulled with all her might. Up an inch, then two. Her right foot found a flake, and she pushed on it. Gulping lungfuls of air, she pressed herself against the wall and used her left hand to find another crack. Another few feet and she swung her right foot out to the terrace's railing, then pulled herself onto it.

She collapsed onto the cold stone floor, her chest heaving to pull in oxygen.

Giving herself a minute to recover, she wiped the sweat from her brow with her left hand and grabbed on to the railing to get to her feet. She flexed her right hand, tested her fingers—nothing dislocated or broken, despite the intense pain. Leaning forward, she stole a look inside through the terrace door window.

The young guard sat in a chair by the door of her room, his eyes closed. She glanced to her right. Stairs led off the terrace, down past the rocks. From there she could walk through the trees to the dock.

Run away.

No.

Jess straightened up and exhaled, took a moment to tousle her hair and roll her shoulders back. She unbuttoned her shirt all the way down, exposing her bra and torso, and unbuttoned the top of her jeans. Taking a deep breath, she opened the terrace door and crept inside. She walked up to the guard.

"Aberto," Jess whispered.

The guard opened his eyes with a start, looking back and forth before seeing Jess standing in front of him.

"Aberto," Jess repeated. "Enzo wants to speak with you." She flicked her chin toward the open terrace door.

Frowning, Aberto's puzzled eyes were unable to keep from wandering to Jess's open shirt.

"Out there," Jess whispered, pointing out the door.

Hooking his right thumb under the strap of his rifle, Aberto stood, glanced at Jess's breasts again, then peered onto the balcony. Jess took a step past him. Aberto craned his neck to look out the door, and Jess slipped behind him, brought her right arm around his neck and jammed it locked with her left.

He barely outweighed her, and was no match for her wiry strength. The rear naked chokehold, one of the most basic martial maneuvers to swiftly disable an opponent. The goal wasn't to deprive the victim of air—it was to stop the flow of blood into the brain. Done just right, it closed off both carotid arteries and the jugular in one motion, induced cerebral hypoxia and unconsciousness in as little as three seconds.

Jess pulled Aberto back into the chair, wrapping her right leg around his waist. Confused, he clawed at her, trying to yell through his closed windpipe. Nothing came out, not even a wheeze. His body jerked back and forth, the chair rocking beneath them.

Jess held on. It was a move they practiced over and over in her martial arts courses in the Marines. They even choked out each other, just to experience it. Jess's instructor had done it to her. Just a momentary panic before sleep descended. She felt Aberto's body stiffen. Five seconds. Six. His body relaxed. Eight seconds. Nine.

If she let go now, in ten seconds or so he'd regain consciousness. Hold on for a few more seconds, and it might take a minute for him to come back, and another minute or two for him to regain his senses from what felt like a deep sleep. Jess knew how it worked. Fifteen seconds, she counted. Sixteen.

But never—she heard her martial arts instructor's words in her head—never hold more than thirty seconds, never past when you feel the body start to twitch.

From that point is brain damage.

Death.

He was just a boy, really. Maybe nineteen. A teenager. Jess had no argument with him, not really. He was probably dragged into this, offered a job; he might have had no idea what was going on. He had a sweet face. He was somebody's little boy.

Tears came to Jess's eyes. "I'm sorry," she whispered into Aberto's ear as she felt his body twitch and shudder. "I'm sorry, Aberto."

Thirty seconds. Forty. At a minute, Jess released her hold on his neck, slid out from under him, took his keys from his pocket, and arranged him on the chair. He looked peaceful. Asleep. But he wasn't. He was dead. She brushed his hair back from his eyes and kissed his forehead, tears in her eyes.

She had killed two people in the space of ten minutes. When she was in boot camp, she'd heard that you never knew if you'd be able to do it—kill someone—if the time came. Some people just couldn't kill.

Apparently Jess could.

A fit of laughing erupted downstairs and Jess stiffened, adrenaline pumping, bolting upright and stepping into the shadows of the hallway. She glanced around the corner, down into the main hall. Four men at the card table now, more empty bottles littered around them than before. Where was the fifth?

Enzo came up maybe fifteen minutes ago? She needed to hurry. So far they hadn't seemed to notice the light show going on in the sky. If they had a TV or radio on, there had to be announcements of the destruction that was already happening on the other side of the world.

The scientists knew it was coming, but there were too many conflicting estimates. Jess wasn't even sure her father's time estimate was right until she saw the water draining from the bay. The speed of the water disappearing gave her a frightening estimate of how close Nomad might already be.

But these guys, drunk and playing cards, were isolated on this island. They had no idea. Jess needed to keep it that way as long as possible.

Creeping down the hallway, she pressed her ear against the first door. Silence. At the second door she heard shuffling, then the sound of muffled crying. She tried a few of Aberto's keys before the lock clicked over. Ever so slowly, she opened the door.

There, inside, Hector was on a cot, his knees pulled up into his chest, his eyes wide. Jess held a finger to her mouth—*quiet, be quiet*—and motioned for him to come. He uncoiled his legs, his small chest heaving in and out with quick breaths, and slid off the cot to take a step toward her.

"Come on, it's okay," Jess whispered. "We need to go."

He stopped two feet from her, his lips trembling. Jess held out her hand. He stared at her, then lifted his hand and pressed his cold little fingers into hers. Jess scooped him into her arms.

"Giovanni?" Hector whispered.

Jess closed her eyes, gripping Hector tight.

Giovanni.

He almost got her killed. He hid things from her, even as she risked her life. Why didn't he tell the truth? An ugly surge of spite rose up in her ancient brain-stem.

But then again…

Truth was a slippery thing. Sometimes, our lies became our lives. Jess knew that more than anyone.

"Which room?" she whispered to Hector.

He pointed at the second door down the hallway, near the end.

Jess listened to the voices downstairs while she crept along the hall, fumbled with the keys until she found the right one.

The door swung open.

On a bare metal cot, Giovanni was tied up with rough yellow nylon cord. His face purple and swollen from the beatings, he opened one puffy eye, barely even registering surprise at Jess standing in front of him with Hector in her arms.

"Go," Giovanni whispered from cracked lips, "go without me."

"You're coming with us," Jess whispered back, putting Hector down and pulling the knife from her back pocket.

She raised her eyebrows at Hector, nodding at the door. *Keep watch*, her eyes said. Hector nodded and tiptoed to the door, peering out. Jess cut the ropes binding Giovanni, and he winced as he sat upright, rubbing his wrists.

"Can you walk?" Jess whispered urgently.

"I think so."

"Then let's go."

35

Isola Gigli, Italy

GIVING GIOVANNI THE knife, Jess pulled Enzo's handgun from her front pocket and led them out the door, sneaking across the landing. Giovanni pointed at the slumped body of Aberto, thinking him asleep, but Jess shook her head, don't worry, keep going, she mouthed silently.

As they passed Aberto, Jess fixed her eyes on the staircase down, listening to the voices. Giovanni stared at the inert body of Aberto, glancing back at Jess, then back at the dead body.

Hector crept along between them.

Out onto the terrace and down the exterior stairs, Jess led the way. She limped on her unfamiliar prosthetic, while Giovanni stumbled behind her, wincing in pain on every step. He stared up at the glimmering light show in the sky but said nothing.

"What are we going to do?" Giovanni whispered as they reached the cover of the trees. "Is there a boat?"

"I don't think so." Jess pressed forward, the hair on her neck prickling in anticipation of shouting behind them. Just a few hundred feet to the dock from here.

"Then we swim?" Giovanni tripped on a root and tumbled into the ground, cursing. He got onto his knees, his bloody face contorted in agony. "It's a kilometer to the shore. I can't swim that, not now." He waved his hand at Jess. "Give me the gun. I'll hold them off while you take Hector."

Jess hauled him to his feet. "We're not going to swim."

Giovanni doubled over, panting. "Then what?"

"We walk."

"What?"

Jess grabbed Hector and marched forward to the edge of the trees.

"Have you lost your mind?" Giovanni hissed, staggering behind her. "How do you expect to…"

Jess pointed at the water. Or what was left of it. Wet mud glistened in reflected pink and greens from the lights in the sky, rocky outcroppings covered in seaweed dotting the almost empty bay.

Almost empty.

A thick band of deep water still stretched in a channel between the island and shore, but the water was still draining out—churning whitewater visible over the rocks even from this distance.

"We walk," Jess repeated, grabbing Hector's hand. "And we need to hurry. Nomad will be here in four or five hours."

"Four or five HOURS?"

"How is this a surprise? It's almost exactly as my dad predicted."

They reached the edge of the tree cover, and she put a hand out, telling Hector to stay. She looked cautiously from left to right before stepping out of the shadows and onto the dock.

"When the water comes back, it's not going to be gentle. Not like the way it left."

"What are you doing?" Giovanni hung back in the shadow of the trees by the side of the dock.

Jess hurried to a small wooden shack near the end, the tire of the dirt bike still sticking out from behind it. The keys were in the ignition. Finally, some luck. She wheeled the bike out and down the dock, scanning the villa up on the rocks for any sign someone saw them. Still nothing.

"Come on, let's keep moving," Jess urged as she passed Giovanni and Hector, pushing the bike off the dock, down across seaweed covered rocks and onto the sandy mud.

In her mind, Jess visualized the Earth, their location spinning toward Nomad as it raced at them from behind the sun. What time was it? Past three a.m.? The tidal forces still emptied the bay, but soon it would reverse as they rotated toward Nomad. "We don't have much time."

She glanced up at the light show, pulsing and glowing, building in intensity, then at the village across the bay, lights twinkling in some houses. Nobody was outside looking up. The town looked deserted. Even here they must have heard what was coming. The men in the villa, though, they were disconnected. Unaware.

Too bad for them.

"Thank you for rescuing me," Giovanni said as they plodded forward.

Jess didn't reply. She kept her head down and pushed the bike, keeping an eye on Hector. She didn't want to start the bike, not yet. The whine of its engine would alert the men. Still too close. The sandy bottom near the shore gave way to thickening mud less than a hundred feet from shore. On each step, Jess had to pull her feet from the muck, and she felt her prosthetic almost coming away more than once.

"Thank you, Jessica," Giovanni repeated.

They trudged past a mound of seaweed covered rocks, crabs scuttling away from them. The moon had already set. It would have been pitch black save for the ghostly light show above their heads. Coming over the ridge of a sand bar, a large fish flopped back and forth, its mouth opening and closing.

Giovanni grunted and took three quick steps toward Jess. "What's wrong? Are you mad at me?"

Gritting her teeth, Jess shoved the bike forward, but Giovanni put a hand on her shoulder.

"Jessica?"

She turned to him. "When were you thinking of telling me?"

Giovanni stared at her, pressing his swollen lips together, grimacing but saying nothing.

"That our families are mortal enemies?" Jess snorted and turned away, pushing the bike up across a sand bank and sliding down the other side into a mess of mud and seaweed. "Didn't you think that might have been an important detail?"

It all made sense now. Why Giovanni acted strange when her mother first said her maiden name, and why he locked her and Jess up when Hector was kidnapped. Why didn't he just say something?

"I'm sorry." Giovanni hurried behind Jess.

"Sorry? You're *sorry*?" She waved a hand at the luminescent sky. "It's a little late for sorry, no?"

"This thing, it consumed my father. I think it was how my mother was killed, when I was a child." Giovanni did his best to run forward, to get in front of Jess. "But I wanted no part of it. It's why I was always away, why I wasn't here when my father died."

"Is this some kind of game to you?" Jess pushed past him, climbed onto the top of another sandbank. "Were you and I some kind of twisted part of it?"

"No, no. I had no idea this feud was still going on, didn't suspect until Hector was kidnapped. But even then, I wasn't sure. I didn't want to spoil—"

A brilliant green ribbon of light flared through the sky, interrupting him, bathing them in radiance. As they watched, the ribbon wobbled and split into orange and blue, fluorescing the heavens with neon tendrils. Beside them, in a dark pool, fish tried to splash away. The twinkling lights in the houses of the village winked out. Jess glanced behind them, at the villa. The lights went out there as well.

And someone yelled.

Men stood on the terrace of the villa, three hundred yards away. One of them pointed at Jess and Giovanni, the others staring into the sky. Another man came out, holding what looked like a broom handle. He pointed it their way.

A chunk of rock exploded next to them, followed by a sharp crack.

Not a broom handle.

The man reloaded his rifle.

Turning, Jess raised the gun still in her right hand. She fired four, five times. The men scattered. Jess swung her right leg over the bike, jammed the muzzle of the gun into her pocket and reached to turn on the ignition.

"Get on!" Jess kicked the starter down. The engine sputtered.

Another bullet thudded into the sand at her feet. She kicked the starter down again as Giovanni deposited Hector on the seat behind her. He jumped on himself, grabbing tight to Jess's waist, cradling Hector between them. The engine roared to life and Jess clicked it into gear, spraying up sand. Glancing back, she saw men sprinting onto the dock, not more than two hundred yards away. They jumped off the dock into the mud, running at them.

Jess coasted across the sand, lit in orange and greens from the glowing skies, and looked for a way through the channel of water still separating them from the shore. The waters weren't receding anymore; the churn of whitewater out of the bay had stopped. She gripped the throttle, pulled it all the way back, her fear of the men behind her eclipsed by the fear of what she felt was coming.

Scanning the thick band of dark water, Jess saw no way through.

She raced along the edge of it weaving past rocks, crab traps and piles of discarded fishing nets, and there, in the distance, by the breakwater of the fishing village, a path of dry ground. She'd need to backtrack a half mile, but there wasn't any other way. Crouching low, feeling Giovanni's fingers digging into her stomach, she gunned the throttle for everything it had.

Behind them, the running men reached the channel of water. They saw what Jess was doing, realized they could cut her off by wading and swimming through the channel to run up the bank to the other side.

Pulling up to the jetty beside the breakwater, Jess slowed to pick her way through the rocks, trying to keep her balance. More than once, Giovanni kept them upright, bouncing his legs beside the bike.

They reached dry pavement as a deep reverberation shook the ground. Seagulls squawked, birds filling the dark skies above them. The roar came from the ocean, but Jess didn't look back. She clicked the bike into its highest gear, held the throttle all the way back, and kept her head low.

Speeding past the pickup truck that she'd been dragged here in, Jess glanced left, at the men from the villa scrambling up the rocks from the bay. They weren't more than fifty feet away, but they didn't stop to shoot at Jess and Giovanni.

Jess saw the terror in their eyes, and she allowed herself to look behind them. An explosion of glowing foam, hundreds of feet high, burst around the villa, still nearly a mile away. A wall of black water surged behind it, towering above them.

She reached the first turn in the road that zigzagged up the valley. Leaning into the turn, she gunned the throttle again. Racing up the hill, she watched one of the men jump into the pickup truck, squealing its tires as he reversed, the other men throwing themselves into the back. A rushing sheet of water slammed into the truck, picking it up, turning it end over end before disappearing in the roaring foam.

Jess stopped looking. Keeping her eyes on the dark pavement rushing toward her, she ignored the rumbling behind her and raced over the hilltop.

36

Tuscany, Italy

LOW HILLS AND farmland glowed under the walls of shimmering light towering high into the skies. Jess knew they were sheets of high energy particles, thrown off the sun in vast coronal ejections triggered by Nomad. Funneled by the Earth's magnetic field, the high energy particles concentrated in sheets that impacted atoms high in the ionosphere, kicking off electrons and photons—exactly the same way that neon tubes glowed bright, except that these were shifting neon walls stretching a hundred miles into space.

They sped through towns and villages. Here and there, a few people stood in the streets, some staring up, some packing cars, but it was mostly deserted. Jess hoped her father, Ben, was secure in the castle with her mother by now.

Everything was dark. And not just lights out. No power.

The high energy particles streamed all the way into the ground, raising the ground voltage, frying power grids. And at these intensities, it wasn't just frying power grids, but even exposed electronics and bombarding the DNA of living cells of plants and animals.

They had to get underground, as soon as possible.

If the streaming lights in the night sky were frightening, even more frightening was the horizon they raced toward. Gaining color. Sunrise. Or rather, they rotated toward the sun. Toward Nomad rushing toward them. Every fiber in Jess's body wanted to turn around, to run. But run where? Back into the raging waters? She knew they needed to head east, toward the glowing horizon and the safety of the castle.

But they also raced toward Nomad.

Giovanni tapped Jess's arm from time to time, yelling to turn left or right as they wound through the roads. After escaping the bay, the huge wave that crashed in had receded. It was just the first. Jess was sure more were on the way.

Every turn, she thought they'd finally reached Saline valley and could climb up and escape into the hills. Each time Giovanni pointed her forward, told her to keep going. Jess tried not to allow herself to think, forced her mind into the now, on the next stretch of pavement, and the next after that. No time for fear, not now.

Her arms burned, her back ached.

And always, she felt the small package of Hector, sandwiched between her and Giovanni.

"This is it!" Giovanni yelled. He pointed up a gravel road.

To Jess it looked like any of a hundred others they passed, but she veered off the road, started to climb, eager to get some altitude. Up through olive groves, Jess recognized a wooden shed. Two more switchbacks and they cleared the trees, the walls of Ruspoli Castle appearing over lines of vines. She skidded to a stop by the wooden door next to the main portico gate. Everything looked locked down with gates barred and windows shuttered, no lights on anywhere.

Giovanni picked Hector up from between them, and Jess felt them getting off the back. Panting, she dropped the bike to one side. Her hands shook. Then her legs. Was it the effect of gripping the bike for so long? Jess's vision seemed to wobble, the world shook around her. She turned to Giovanni. Was she having an attack of some kind?

"Get down!" Giovanni yelled, pulling at her, crouching. "Earthquake!"

Her legs buckled and Jess tumbled to a ground that seemed to slide from side to side, hammering up and down. She'd never experienced an earthquake before, and she dug her fingers into the rattling earth and gritted her teeth. Debris and rocks scattered from the ancient walls of the castle, showering them in dust, and she put an arm around Giovanni, coming together with him to shield Hector between them.

The shaking subsided.

But Jess didn't stop shaking. It felt like the Earth wanted to swallow them, eat them whole. The fear she'd been pushing away broke through and she curled into a ball in the dirt, trembling.

Giovanni got to one knee, then forced himself to stand, his battered face covered in dirt and dust. "Come on, it's okay. It stopped." He offered her a hand, and she took it and stood unsteadily.

Squeezing her hand, Giovanni let go and hobbled to the wall of the castle, kneeling in the semi-darkness. Jess dusted herself off, rubbed her shaking hands together and looked at the horizon. Streaming lines of fire danced from the dark skies behind her to the brightening spot where the sun would rise, just over the horizon. Nomad had to be halfway from the Sun to the Earth, tearing off the Sun's corona, a stellar-mass rag doll being shredded before her eyes.

She forced herself to look up from the horizon. Nomad should be right there, but she saw nothing.

"Jess!" Giovanni yelled. He opened the wooden side door in the castle wall, Hector at his side. "Inside! Now!"

Nodding, she tore her eyes from the horizon and limped to the door. They stepped inside and slammed it shut. Panting, they closed the latch. Together they turned around.

Nico stood in the middle of the gravel courtyard, pointing a gun at them.

Jess's mother appeared from a doorway behind Nico. "Oh, my God," she cried, running across the courtyard to scoop Jess into her arms.

Staggering back, Jess put her arms around her mother.

Celeste squeezed Jess, then let go, stepping back to inspect her. "Are you—"

"I'm okay. We're okay."

"We've been listening to the short wave radio," Celeste said breathlessly. "India and China have been devastated by tsunamis, a massive earthquake destroyed Japan, and Yellowstone is erupting, it's…" She glanced at Giovanni, at his beaten face, one eye almost swollen shut. She looked down, at Hector. "Oh, thank God."

"Yes, thank God," echoed Nico from behind Celeste. He slowly lowered his gun. "What happened with Enzo?"

"He's right behind us," Jess lied, keeping an eye on Nico.

Nico's arm relaxed, the gun swinging down to his side. Jess took a step forward, opening her arms to hug him. Nico glanced at Celeste, now wrapping her arms around Hector, and opened his arms to Jess.

But she didn't hug him.

She grabbed the hand that held the gun and tried to wrestle it from him, but he reacted too quickly. He pushed her back and raised the gun again, and Jess pulled hers from her front pocket.

"Giovanni!" Jess yelled. "Get Hector away."

"Jess, what are you doing?" Celeste shrieked.

"And get my mother out of here, too." Jess kept her eyes on Nico.

They stood feet apart, pointing their guns at each other's heads. Scrambling on the gravel behind her, she saw Nico's eyes dart to her right.

"No, no, no," Jess growled, shoving her gun closer to Nico's head. "Eyes on me."

Bewildered, Nico took two steps back, alarm opening his eyes and mouth.

"Get out," Jess commanded. "Enzo isn't coming. I killed him, and his men." She took three steps toward Nico. "And I'll kill you too."

The ground shook, a low rumble shaking the walls of the castle, a cascade of dust and pebbles showering onto the courtyard around them.

The look on Nico's face shifted, a storm of anger and frustration bringing his brows together. "You don't know what you're doing. His family, the Ruspolis, they killed *our* family," he growled, his voice low and menacing. He shoved his gun at Jess. "*Your* family."

"One more word, and I'll put a bullet in your head," Jess said in a flat voice, advancing toward him. "What's one more dead in all this?"

He snarled, but scrambled back, toward the door in the wall. "You don't know what you're doing," he repeated.

Jess stood her ground, her arm steady, her gun pointed at Nico's head. "I know what I'm doing."

Nico turned, unlatched the lock and opened the door.

"No," he said, pausing to look Jess in the eye. "No, you do not." He stepped through the door.

Jumping forward, Jess slammed her shoulder into the door and twisted the latch closed.

"Giovanni!" she yelled. "Go and check the other entrances. Make sure we're locked down." Her hand with the gun shook, the adrenaline flooding her bloodstream finally getting the better of her.

Giovanni nodded and scrambled off, limping, toward the stairs that led into the main building. Celeste held Hector, both of them crouching beside a large terracotta urn flowering with azaleas.

"It was Nico," Jess explained, seeing the look of utter confusion on her mother's face. "It was always Nico. I talked to Enzo. He said he was the one that emailed you on Facebook, but he lied when I said we exchanged mail. He barely understood what Facebook was. And Leone, when we arrived, said Nico and I looked like brother and sister, don't you remember? And the security guards? Nico told us to take them. *He* hired them. He was behind it all."

Celeste looked wide-eyed at Jess, still not understanding.

"There's some kind of blood feud between Giovanni's and Nico's families." Jess pointed at her own chest. "*Our* family. Nico is our family. The Tosettis. That's why he emailed you on Facebook. He wanted to get us here."

The ground rumbled again, a distant thunder echoing beyond the walls.

"I'll explain more later." Jess looked up. A black cloud billowed high, obscuring the bending and patterning tendrils of light in the brightening sky. "We need to get underground." She took a deep breath, gulping in air. "Where's Dad? Did he get here?"

Celeste shook her head. "He never arrived."

Jess sobbed, bringing one hand to her mouth. What happened to him? She had so much she wanted to say, but it was too late now. She held back her tears.

"JESSICA!"

It was Nico's voice, yelling over the top of the walls.

She ignored it. "Come on, let's get into the caves."

"JESSICA!" screamed Nico again. "Your *father* wants to speak with you."

Halfway across the courtyard, Jess froze, her face tingling. She turned to Celeste. "You never saw Dad?"

Celeste shook her head. "No."

"You take Hector into the basement. I need to check." Jess turned, sprinted to a stone staircase leading to the top of the portico gates, hopped up them as quickly as she could.

Reaching the top, the rising sun momentarily blinded her. She shielded her eyes. White tendrils snaked out of the sun, fiery spider legs spreading into the sky, enveloping the Earth.

A thudding detonation startled her and she glanced to her right. Red flame gorged from the top of Monterufoli volcano. Lightning crackled through thick black clouds billowing from its cauldron. The ground rumbled. Past Monterufoli, the plains stretched into the distance—to the Mediterranean—but in the brightening twilight, the water wasn't on the horizon as it usually was. An undulating sheet of liquid had swallowed the entire plain and was churning into the foothills below.

"Quite the family reunion, no?" Nico stood in the gravel driveway, standing behind her father with his arm around Ben's neck, a gun pointed at his head.

Jess squinted to see in the dim light.

"I'm sorry," Ben croaked, his voice hoarse. "This is my fault—"

"Shhhh," Nico hissed, tightening his grip around Ben's neck, choking off his words. "We can have touching words later. A trade. The Baron for your father, and I will leave."

Jess closed her eyes. "This is insane." She gripped the gun. A tremor shook the castle walls, the sky blistering in yellows and reds.

"Throw the gun down," Nico commanded. "And get the Baron out here. Then you can have your father."

"I'll go," said a voice behind Jess. Giovanni put an arm around her.

She hadn't heard him coming up the stairs behind her.

"I'll go," he repeated, his voice barely more than a whisper. "You risked your life and saved me, saved us. You can take care of Hector."

"No, this isn't the same as *risking* your life. He'll kill you." Jess took one look at the gun in her hand and threw it over the wall.

"Why did you do that?" Giovanni stared at the gun hitting the gravel below.

"It wasn't loaded. No more bullets." Jess forced a small smile. She'd bluffed Nico out of the castle.

Giovanni stared at her in amazement.

"This is very touching," Nico yelled from below. He pointed his gun at the clouds ballooning from Monterufoli. "But we might not have much time. And Giovanni..."

Giovanni turned to face him. "What?"

"If you haven't guessed yet, your father, *Baron* Ruspoli. He did not die naturally. Aconite from the Monkshood flowers, all through the vineyards—I used his own earth to poison him."

It took a few seconds for Giovanni to process. His face went white. "You bastard, he trusted you like his own son."

"Maybe his own son should have been here, no?" Nico's lips trembled. "Come down now! Or I will kill Dr. Rollins." He snarled a wolfish grin. "And just to show you I'm serious, we'll kill someone else first." He whistled.

From behind a low stone wall, a hundred feet away, a muscular man dragged a smaller one across the gravel. Jess squinted. She knew that face. "Roger?"

"Jesus Christ, Jess, do whatever they're asking. They're going to kill me," Roger screamed as he was dragged across the dirt.

"Who's Roger?" Giovanni asked quietly.

Jess gritted her teeth. "My boyfriend."

Giovanni's brows came together. "Your..."

"He *was* my boyfriend." Jess winced. "Before I…never mind."

"Don't do it," Jess's father wheezed, his hands behind his head. "Nomad will be here in an hour, get underground—" He gagged as Nico tightened the pressure around his neck.

"NOW!" barked Nico. "I want to see Baron Ruspoli coming out of that gate right now."

The muscular man dragged Roger next to Nico, forced Roger onto his knees with a gun pointed at the back of his head.

"Jess, please," Roger cried, cringing.

A hot wind blew in from Jess's right, a roar rising, blowing the leaves back on the trees. Rain fell.

"There's no other way," Giovanni said, turning to Jess. "I'll go out. We have no weapons, no way to fight back."

Jess shielded her face from the rain. It pelted down painfully.

Looking down, she realized it wasn't rain. Tiny white pebbles bounced off the stones. The scorching wind intensified, roaring over them, bringing with it a shower of hot rocks from the sky.

"I'm coming!" Giovanni roared, trying to shield Jess from the volcano's ejecta with one arm, pulling her down the stairs.

Jess cowered with Giovanni under the cover of a stone awning. "We have weapons," Jess yelled into his ear over the roar of pellets clattering into the gravel courtyard and off the stone walls, the noise almost deafening.

"You just threw our only gun over the wall." Giovanni shook his head. "I checked the armory. Nico took everything. We have no weapons."

Jess winced and grinned at the same time. "He didn't take *everything*."

The shower of rocks thinned, the hot blast of air passed.

"I just checked, there's nothing in—"

"Not in the armory." Jess turned and pointed at the two-story building just past the old olive tree. "In there."

"In the museum…?" Giovanni frowned in confusion.

"There's a thousand years of Ruspoli family weapons in there, isn't that what they say on the tour?"

37

Chianti, Italy

"I'M COMING OUT!" Giovanni yelled, his voice carrying over the walls.

From her second-story perch inside the portico gate wall, looking out through a narrow slit in the wall, Jess could just see the wooden door crack open, Giovanni's head coming out, both his hands over his head.

"I'm only coming closer if you let them go." Giovanni edged out of the door.

Overhead, a northerly wind sprang up, dragging dark storm clouds from the north into the billowing black ash clouds from Monterufoli. They swirled together, churning up the sky under dancing tendrils of green and orange flame snaking from the rising sun. The ground shuddered.

Nico tightened his grip on Ben's neck, wrenching him back. "No deals." He glanced at the large man gripping Roger's hair, the gun pointed at the back of his head. "Five more seconds till Roger dies."

"Let them go," Giovanni insisted, edging forward. "This is between us, not them."

A crashing roar echoed through the valley.

Jess shifted, tried to get a better view on Nico. Flakes of ash fell like snow. The gap in the wall was a narrow slit, three feet high but not more than four inches wide, the opening swept back at a high angle from the outside to inside of the wall. She'd seen openings like this in castle walls a hundred times before on tours and imagined medieval archers angling their arrows out of them in some ancient battle.

But she never imagined that she'd be pointing a crossbow out of one.

Pumice raining from the sky, she and Giovanni had sprinted across the courtyard, ran up the steps into the museum containing the ancient swords, pikes, and crossbows. They smashed the glass cases, Giovanni retrieving crossbows refurbished by local artisans—new gut strings and oiled mechanisms—and grabbed as many bolts as they could carry.

Jess grabbed the Medici dagger on the way out. A small but lethal close combat weapon.

She spied through the gap in the wall, feeling the weight of the gold dagger in her back pocket. Shifting on her knee, she kept her eye low on the crossbow bolt, aiming down it at Nico. "Come on, come on," she muttered, waiting to get a clear shot.

Nico scanned the tops of the walls. "Where's our Jessica?"

"Down in the caves, with her mother," Giovanni growled. The ground trembled.

"Just let him go," Jess whispered, her bolt trained on Nico's head. Sweat dribbled down her forehead, stinging her eyes. The light of the rising sun was fast being extinguished by the swirling black clouds overhead, even dimming the crackling aurora.

"Let her father go, and you can have me." Giovanni took a step into the open, toward Nico, his hands up. "That's what you want, isn't it?"

Nico scanned the walls again. He glanced at the man next to him and shrugged. "Yes, that's what I want." He let go of Ben, shoving him forward, and pointed his gun instead at Giovanni, not twenty feet away.

It was all Jess needed. Saying a small prayer, she squeezed the trigger on the ancient crossbow, aiming dead center on Nico's chest. *Thwack*, the bolt loosed, the crossbow kicking back into Jess's shoulder, knocking her off balance.

Overhead, the clouds closed together, sealing off the last of the sun's rays and casting the courtyard into darkness. Regaining her footing, Jess peered through the slit as she put down the crossbow and picked up another one, preloaded with a bolt cocked back. In the sudden gloom, Jess wiped her eyes, squinted to see. Had she hit him?

Yes.

Nico staggered back, the crossbow bolt buried deep in his right chest, his right hand holding the gun dangling uselessly at his side. He looked down at his chest at the bolt sticking out of it, and wiped his mouth with his left hand. It came away dark red.

Giovanni roared, reaching behind his head to pull out a sword. He raised it above his head and charged at Nico.

One thing about crossbows—they were almost silent.

The big man next to Nico stared at him, still not sure what was happening. He was quick, though. He raised his gun from Roger's head and aimed it at Giovanni as he ran at Nico, ready to bring the sword down and cleave Nico's head from his body.

Swearing, Jess aimed the new crossbow bolt at the big man. Just as she pulled the trigger, Roger jerked to his feet to sprint away. The bolt caught him in the left shoulder, spinning him around into the big man who fired his gun in the same instant.

Jess watched in horror as blood sprayed into the air from Giovanni's chest, the bullet's impact knocking him sideways. Throwing her second crossbow down, she grabbed the third one, brought it up to the slit. Giovanni fell to his knees, the sword dropping from his hand. Roger fell back into the big man, who shoved him aside and brought his gun up again.

This time Jess didn't miss.

The crossbow bolt snicked through the air straight into the big man's neck. He dropped the gun and clawed at his neck, blood spurting across the gravel. Holding his shoulder, Roger staggered to his feet and ran to the wall, while Giovanni slumped to the dirt, blood pooling around him.

Nico had figured out where the attack was coming from. He snarled at the wall where Jess hid, but paused to smile at Giovanni in the dirt before turning to run, his right arm holding the gun dangling at his side. Jess grabbed her fourth pre-loaded crossbow, brought it up, but Nico made it into the cover of olive trees to the left of the driveway.

Cursing, Jess jumped to her feet and hopped down the winding stone staircase to the courtyard. At the bottom, she bounded to the open entrance door.

Her father was at Giovanni's side, bent over, dragging him across the gravel to the entrance, leaving a trail of blood. Roger leaned against the doorframe, the bolt deep in his left shoulder. Painful, but not life threatening, was Jess's instant assessment. She ran past him to her father. Scanning to her left, through the olive grove, she looked for any sign of Nico. Nothing. The coward ran.

"How is he?" she blurted out, grabbing one of Giovanni's arms. She slung the crossbow over her back.

"Not good," Ben replied. He'd taken the gun from the big man, and offered it to Jess.

"You keep it," Jess told her father, crouching over Giovanni, his eyes half-open. She kissed him. "Hang on, just hang on."

Smiling weakly, he whispered, "We got your father." He coughed up mottled red blood and mucus.

The clouds in the sky thickened, the gloom deepening.

Jess glanced at Giovanni, his eyes closed, his body twitching. He wasn't going to make it. She grabbed an arm and helped her father pull Giovanni, glancing left into the olive groves again.

A hiss erupted between the trees. Whitewater churned through the valley below, a black sludge surging behind it. Looking up, lightning crackled through the angry black clouds, a peal of thunder rolling through the valley. The ground juddered, shaking rocks from the castle walls.

"We have to hurry," Ben urged, grunting, pulling Giovanni through the entrance into the courtyard. "We're almost at Nomad's closest approach. Tidal forces will increase cubically. They'll triple in the next hour. It's going to rip the crust apart."

"Down through the stables." Jess pointed to their left. "We can get into the caves below."

Roger stumbled in behind them.

Over the roaring wind and water, the crack of a gunshot, then another.

Screaming.

Her mother's screaming.

Jess let go of Giovanni's arm and turned, ran up the stairs to the house as her mother ran out.

"What is it?" Jess grabbed Celeste.

"Nico came in the side door, shot through the locks," Celeste cried. "He took Hector."

"Is he inside?"

"No, he dragged Hector out, into the olive groves on the north side."

Jess hung her head, closing her eyes and listening to the rush of the water. The entire valley to the north was submerging. No way he'd get out there. This mountain was fast becoming an island. Where would he go? He knew they had the gun from his partner, so he wouldn't risk coming in here. Would he just kill Hector?

No.

He'd want something more symbolic.

Jess looked at her mother, wiped swirling ash from her face. "I know where he's going."

38

Chianti, Italy

"*STA 'ZITTO*!" NICO yelled at Hector, who squirmed in his arms.

Putting the boy down, he swung his left hand back and slapped Hector hard across the face, knocking the child into the dirt.

Fat droplets of black rain hammered onto the tin roof of the cable car control shack, spattering onto Nico. His eyes burned. It stank of rotten eggs, of sulfur. Pain flared in his right side. He'd snapped off the crossbow bolt, but the point was lodged deep in his right shoulder. It burned, and he'd bled badly. He was lightheaded, but it was almost done.

The ground trembled under his feet, black water churning in the valley below while lightning crackled in dark skies above. Nico smiled grimly, shaking in fear. This would be the end of it. This would be the end of *everything*.

After securing his prize, the final Ruspoli heir, little Hector, Nico would have disappeared down into the valley if it hadn't been filled with churning water. Instead he was forced to escape up here, outside the north wall, up through the rocks to the highest point. The cable stretched over the valley floor, connected to Villa Tosetti on the other side.

Pulling the boy out of the dirt, he opened the control room door and peered down the slope. Surging black sludge flattened olive trees just hundreds of feet away, sucking along in it floating cars, the remains of shattered homes and a fishing boat. No, if he wanted to get across, this was the only way. Thick rolls of steam crawled over the sludge below. To his left, fingers of magma flowing from Monterufoli glowed dull red through the darkness. Tremors rattled the metal cage.

Hector crouched on the floor by his feet.

Nico growled. "*Andiamo!*"

God had extinguished the sun above. Leviathan had swallowed the sky, and darkness crawled over the valley. Only God could judge him now.

He reached down to grab the boy.

Hector shot sideways, turned and jumped at Nico, windmilling his arms. Nico tried to grab him, but an explosion of pain in his left side staggered him sideways. Hector scrabbled along the floor, a desperate animal trying to escape, but Nico overcame the flaring new pain and grabbed the boy by the neck.

The boy squealed.

Nico gritted his teeth and looked at his side. With the thickening clouds, light fell by the minute, his eyes still adjusting to the darkness. A jagged piece of metal stuck out of his ribs.

"*Bastardo*," Nico roared, throwing the child against the metal wall.

Hector thudded to the floor, mewled and curled into a ball.

Grunting, Nico swung open the door from the control room to the cable car itself. He leaned over to grab the boy, dragging him into the cable car and closing the door. Almost pitch black inside. This old machinery didn't need any power, though. It was gravity operated. From here, two hundred feet above Villa Tosetti on the other side, all he had to do was release the clutch mechanism, the handle protruding from the floor in the middle of the carriage.

Nico cursed at Hector, still curled into a ball at his feet.

Stepping sideways, Nico stood in front of the clutch switch. It was over. He glanced to his left, noticed the other side door of the cable car was open into the empty blackness beyond.

From the shadows at the back of the cable car, Jess watched Nico slam Hector into the wall.

Anger, pure hatred boiled through her veins as she watched him drag the boy into the carriage. She killed three people in the past day.

What was one more? Nico caused all this pain. Trapped her family here. Killed Giovanni. Tortured this child. She gripped the Medici dagger in her hand, felt the sharpness of its blade as a part of her.

Nico glanced left, at the open cable car door leading into empty space, a hundred foot drop onto the black rocks below.

Jess stepped forward, brought the blade around Nico's neck with her right hand, and gripped his body with her left. The booming thunder of Monterufoli erupting echoed off the rock walls of the canyon, the stinking black rain spattering off the metal walls of the cable car, burning her skin and eyes.

Nico's eyes darted down. "Ah, the Medici dagger."

He sounded calm.

Jess gritted her teeth and blinked. Tears ran from her burning eyes. She resisted the urge to pull the blade deep into Nico's neck and feel his hot blood splash across her face. "Why did you bring us here?"

"God brought you here," Nico replied. His lip twisted into something between a snarl and a smile.

"That Facebook message, convincing my mother to come." Jess needed to know. She expected him to fight, to try and twist away, but Nico remained loose in Jess's grip.

Nico snorted. "That wasn't me. That was God."

Jess felt the rage rising inside her. She didn't believe him. If it wasn't him, then who? It had to be him. "Is this a game to you?" she grunted, forcing the words out between gritted teeth.

"No game. This is no game." He held one hand out to the churning darkness. "But my hand was forced by events beyond my control."

"Then what is it?"

"Revenge, you understand revenge, no?" He laughed, his voice hoarse. "I'm no monster, I wasn't going to kill the boy."

"Then why take him?"

"You want to know why?" Nico heaved labored breaths in and out. "I wanted nothing to do with this stupidity, but my uncle, Pietro Tosetti, was killed in a car bomb, ten years ago. He was a *padrone* in the Naples mafia." The veins in Nico's neck flared, his hands balling into white fists. "That bomb killed my wife and daughter. A bomb the

Baron Ruspoli planted there."

"You're saying Giovanni planted a bomb?"

"An eye for an eye, that is the Old Testament, no? The Old God of vengeance is upon us today, and I claim the child as my own, for the child taken from me."

"I can't let you do that," Jess said, his voice gravel in her throat.

"Then take your revenge. I know what you feel. Your blood is mine, your rage is mine."

"It's not the same." She pressed the blade to his neck.

"It's not?" Nico didn't resist her. "Does it matter that an offense happened many years ago? Does time diminish a crime?"

"Giovanni didn't kill anyone."

The squall of black rain pelted the cabin, a sulfurous choking in the air. The cabin rattled as the ground rolled from side to side. Before Jess's eyes, the other side of the valley slipped, fell into the churning black below in a roaring rush.

"Ask him why he was in Antarctica when his father died," Nico snarled. "Sons answer for the sins of their fathers."

There was no time for this. If she let him go, he'd kill her, take the boy. He'd never stop. Jess gritted her teeth.

Nico laughed, his body going limp. "The only thing that burns in hell is the part of you that won't let go. Hell is no punishment, but a freeing of the soul. I'm not scared of dying, Jessica. If you're frightened of dying, you'll see devils tearing your life away at death, but if you've made peace—"

"Then you'll see angels freeing you," Jess whispered, completing his sentence. Where had she heard that before? Jess's grip slackened.

"Yes, you see?" Nico lifted one hand and tried to pull the dagger into his throat. "I've paid my demons, now release me."

Jess pushed back, now using every ounce of her strength to keep the blade from his neck. Looking down, little Hector stood in front of them, staring, the whites of his eyes almost glowing. The little boy's face disappeared into the blackness.

Vengeance had filled Jess's life. The desire to get even. The need to punish for past sins.

Enough.

Jess wrenched the dagger away, but held Nico close. "I forgive you," she whispered into his ear and put the dagger in her right pocket.

Stepping around him, she took Hector's hand, and backed away to the cable car door on the left, the one open to a hundred feet of empty blackness to the sharp rocks below.

"I'm sorry, Billy," Jess whispered. She picked up Hector and held him close. Standing at the edge of the open door, she leaned forward and hit the clutch mechanism.

The cable car shuddered and released. It started sliding down across the valley.

Jess stepped back toward the open door, crossed her arms around Hector and fell backward into blackness.

39

Chianti, Italy

WEIGHTLESS, JESS FELL backward through empty space, clutching Hector in her arms. The cable car disappeared upward and away against a maelstrom of black and crimson clouds. Nico's face stared at her as it receded into the distance.

She hoped she got this just right. Clenching her teeth, she gripped Hector with every ounce of her strength.

The cord bit into her waist and armpits, savagely ripping at her body. She'd wrapped a length of the cord around Hector, and she cradled him, did her best to shield him as she felt the cord stretch behind her, the wind whistling as they swung in a downward arc. Her right foot slammed into the ground, dragged through the grass for an instant before they swung up and away.

Two seconds later they reached the top of the arc, and began to swing back. When she ran up here, through the castle, she arrived before Nico and grabbed the improvised rope swing she'd set up a few days before.

Spinning, holding Hector with her left arm, she pulled the dagger from her right pocket. Lifting it above her head against the cord, she pressed the blade into it, forcing it back with all her might as she felt her leg graze the ground again. The blade cut through and they tumbled through space, landing hard in a tangled heap on the grass. She kept the blade high, felt pain lancing through her shoulder as they crunched into the earth.

Jess spat out a mouthful of dirt and grass and rolled to one side. "Hector," she groaned, "are you okay?"

It was dark, and Jess struggled to look at Hector. Tangled underneath her, he didn't move. Panic flooded her veins. "Hector!?"

Coughing, he pulled himself from under her. Trembling, he smiled at Jess. "*Che figata!*"

Jess laughed, squeezing him into her. "You liked that?"

His eyes darted up, and Jess followed them, craning her neck around. The cable car was still visible, halfway across the valley, illuminated by the glow of Monterufoli. Nico's pale face was a dot of white against black. Booming thunder. The ground trembled again, a thick cloud of ash swirling over the top of the cliffs.

As Jess watched, the cables swung up and down, vibrating with the ground. A cable jumped its guide, and in slow motion, the cable car hopped up and then down, spinning, tumbling from the sky. It fell hundreds of feet into the surging sludge below.

The cloud of ash enveloped them.

"Hector, which way?" Jess coughed.

She knew there was a doorway from the ledge, a tunnel leading into the caves. They used it when Giovanni showed her around, when they first came out there. Sitting upright, she cut away the improvised harness she'd tied around herself.

Wiping dirt and ash from his eyes, Hector stood, looked to his left, then right. He pointed.

"Good boy." Jess pulled the last of the rope from her body and staggered to her feet.

A blast of hot wind brought with it a soup of ash, fine particles and thick flakes. Jess pulled Hector's torn t-shirt up around his mouth, doing the same for herself. Holding his hand, she followed him into the swirling black soup, scrambling over rocks. They reached the vertical cliff face, but she could only see for a few feet. Her eyes stung, watered, and she tried to wipe them but that only made it worse.

Hector stood bolt upright, shaking. He wiped his eyes, smearing them black, tears streaming down his face. Cracking thunder boomed, the ground shuddered. Pebbles showered onto them from the cliffs above.

"It's okay." Jess held him to her, holding up one hand to shelter them. "Come on."

She grabbed his hand, pulled him to the left, wiping her eyes. They picked their way through the jumbled rocks, searching for an opening, but they reached a yawning edge of blackness.

Jess swore under her breath. They must have missed it. She didn't remember this edge. The ground was disappearing from beneath their feet, the cliffs shearing off into the valley. Another blast of hot air enveloped them, the soup of ash swirled thick and acrid. Cradling Hector, she crouched in the rocks by the wall. "We'll stop for a minute and let this pass."

But she didn't know if it would.

The ground pitched sideways in an ear-splitting roar.

"It'll be okay." Jess held Hector's face to her neck, his arms around her, his body stiff with fear. "It'll be okay."

She pressed her stinging eyes closed.

Something grabbed her shirt. Opening her eyes, a face loomed out of the darkness, fly-away white hair streaming from a slick scalp.

"Come," growled Leone, the old groundskeeper.

He wrapped his calloused hands around Jess's waist and lifted her and Hector up, cradled them in his arms. He ran forward, stepping through the rocks. A sharp left, then downward.

The air cleared and Jess took in a deep lungful of clear air, coughing and spitting. She leaned against the jagged rock wall of a tunnel, illuminated by an emergency light stuck to the ceiling. Leone pulled the heavy door shut behind them, forcing it shut.

With a thud, the door closed.

Panting, Jess looked at the door. She wiped ash from her face. The tunnel rattled in a violent thunder.

Leone shoved past her, still with Hector in his arms. He turned to Jess. "Nico?"

"Dead." Jess doubled over and gagged. A wheezing cough strained from her chest.

Leone nodded, and without saying another word, he led the way down. Jess took one last look at the door, feeling the oppressive weight of the mountain around her, and followed him into the labyrinth.

The ancient tunnel wound its way through the rock. After fifty yards it opened into the wine cavern that Giovanni had showed her around. Except now it wasn't filled with ten-foot high barrels standing shoulder to shoulder. The crates had been disassembled, their ribs collected against the rough-hewn rock walls. They were replaced by piled wooden crates, cardboard boxes and plastic bags that stretched the length of the thirty foot cave. Fifteen feet overhead, the harsh white of six emergency lights beamed down.

Two young men knelt at the side of the cavern, busy putting together a table. Jess recognized them. Lucca and Raffael, the teenage brothers who worked for Leone. She'd watched them play soccer with Hector in the gardens. Their faces lit up when they saw Jess, and they dropped their tools when they saw Hector in Leone's arms. They jumped up to greet them, gesturing wildly and whooping with excitement.

But Jess hardly saw them. Her eyes locked onto something almost unbelievable. Beside Lucca and Raffael, in the center of it all, stood Jess's mother and father. Kissing. Their arms were wrapped around each other.

Jess hadn't seen them kiss in years, hadn't seen them hold each other, not since she was a child. She brought a hand to her mouth, tears coming again to her still-stinging eyes. Her scalp tingled. She didn't want to move, didn't want to breath, for fear of breaking the spell.

From the corner of her eye, Celeste saw Jess and pushed away from Ben. "Jess! Oh my God!"

Pushing past the knot of Leone wrapped up with Raffael and Lucca, with Hector sandwiched between them, Celeste ran straight at Jess. Her arms spread wide, she almost knocked Jess over, gripped her so tight Jess felt the air squeeze from her lungs. Ben wrapped his arms around the two of them, his body wracked with convulsing sobs.

"We sent Leone to find you." Celeste wept, tears flowing, crushed between Ben and Jess. "Ben was running around the walls, looking everywhere. You didn't tell us where you were going."

Jess laughed through her tears. "I'm sorry."

The ground swayed and almost knocked them from their feet. Rocks crashed from the ceiling onto the packing crates. An emergency light tumbled from the ceiling and smashed against the rock floor. Jess gripped her mother and father. Even here, there might not be much time. The mountain itself was coming apart. Deafening booms echoed through the caves from the bombardment overhead.

Jess gritted her teeth and pressed her eyes closed, and saw, for the millionth time, the image of the small face disappearing into the black hole. "I'm sorry," she moaned. "I'm so sorry."

"Baby, what are you sorry for?" Celeste kissed her daughter's forehead, her eyes, her cheeks. "We're all together, there's nothing to be sorry about."

"No." Hot tears streamed down Jess's face.

She stared at her mother. She'd never told anyone before, had kept this terrible secret for twenty years. It was the demon that tore at her soul. Jess needed to be free.

"I'm sorry about Billy. It was my fault." Jess gasped in a lungful of air before blurting, "I told him to go out on the ice."

Time stopped for an instant, the booming above receded. Hurt blossomed in her mother's eyes. The dam inside burst, twenty years of pressure releasing. Jess crumbled. Her knees buckled, her body wracked by heaving sobs.

Celeste and Ben grabbed Jess together, held her limp body up while tears streamed down her face.

"That wasn't your fault." Celeste's voice was a ragged whisper.

"It *was*." Jess heaved air in and sobbed, her head turned away. "I was mad at you."

The dam broken, memories of that long ago day flooded Jess's mind: When she was six, and her little brother Billy just four, back at the cottage in the Catskills mountains. Her mother had just scolded her for taking the big blocks from Billy; but they were *hers*, Jess had squealed. Go outside and play, her mother had said, and take Billy.

But make sure he doesn't go on the ice.

Jess wouldn't have folded so easily, wouldn't have let her mother win, but she decided to teach her a lesson. So she went outside, walked down through the snow to the creek, and told Billy it was okay to go on the ice. She hadn't meant to hurt him; she didn't even know it was dangerous, not really. She thought he might fall in, get wet, scream and cry until their mother came out. That would teach her mother a lesson.

And her father took her and Billy across the ice all the time, to sled on the opposite bank.

She just didn't know, at six, that it was a warm week.

That the ice was thin.

She had heard the crack. She saw Billy slip and squeal, his terrified eyes locked onto hers. As if pulled by an invisible hand, he slid under, and Jess had stood transfixed. Terrified. She'd watched her little brother's face disappear into the black hole, ringed in white, his eyes on her.

Afterward, Jess ran back into the house, screaming, crying, saying that Billy was gone.

But she'd never admitted that she told him to go on the ice.

In revenge. She killed him. She killed her little brother. All these years, she'd kept the secret and been punishing herself for it. Her family was never the same. She never saw her mother and father embrace again. Not until now.

"I'm so sorry," Jess cried, her body trembling for air, her eyes shut tight, her fingers gripping her mother and father. "Everything was my fault."

The ground tilted to one side, vibrated, and then tilted back. They stumbled sideways as a unit and crashed into the cave wall.

Celeste took Jess's chin and pulled her head up. Jess opened her eyes, gathered the courage to look at her mother again, but the shock and hurt in Celeste's eyes had been replaced with gentle warmth.

"It's not your fault," Ben said softly, laying a hand on his daughter's head to stroke her hair. "You were a child. You didn't know. It was my fault. I should never have taken the two of you across the ice to play. It was irresponsible. It was *my* fault."

Another massive tremor rocked the cave. The lights flickered. A stack of crates crashed from the wall onto the floor behind them.

"No, no, it was my fault." Celeste wiped her tears with the back of one hand. "I was trying to write my research grant paper. I was annoyed. I told you to go outside, but I didn't watch. I should have been watching."

Sobbing, Celeste gripped Jess's neck, and all three of them came together again. It felt like little Billy was standing in the middle of them. Jess had never admitted it before, never told anyone the truth. The demon eating at her soul disappeared into the cracks in the cave walls.

"*Dove è Giovanni*?" said a small voice.

Jess looked down into Hector's blackened face, his eyes wide. Leone stood behind him protectively. Hector reached for Jess's hand. Leaning down, she scooped him into her arms, felt his tiny body against hers. "Oh, sweetheart." How to tell him that Giovanni was dead? "I'm sorry, but—"

"He's alive." Ben pointed to an opening at the end of the cave. "In the next room."

"Go, go," Celeste urged, letting go of Jess. She sobbed, new tears streaming down her face. "Take Hector. Go and see him. We can talk again in a minute."

Ben nodded and let go as well.

Glancing at both of them, Jess gripped Hector and hobbled through the fallen crates. The lights flickered again. Around the corner, another smaller cave. The struts of the disassembled barrels were laid out on the floor as an improvised bed, and there, in the middle, swaddled in blankets, was Giovanni, his head propped up on a cardboard box.

Jess ran. "Giovanni! I have Hector!"

The ground rumbled and she almost fell into him. Giovanni lifted himself up on one elbow. Kneeling on the wooden floor, she pulled back the blanket, revealing his chest covered in bandages soaked in blood.

"It looks worse than it is," Giovanni croaked, his face still swollen and battered. "The bullet grazed my side, straight through, mostly soft—"

Jess kissed him, deep and hard.

Giovanni kissed her back, but flinched and sucked in air.

"Sorry, sorry, did I hurt you?" Jess retreated.

Giovanni managed to chuckle. "A little, but then that's to be expected with you, no?"

Jess pointed at the crates and boxes. "When did you do all this?"

"When you told me disaster was coming. I didn't entirely believe you, but what is that expression? Better safe than sorry? I had workmen clear out the caves and brought in supplies. Why not? More useful than wine."

Hector rushed in to hug his uncle, and Giovanni did his best to wrap one arm and hold him tight. Tears rolling down his cheeks. Jess didn't think she had any crying left in her, but more spilled out.

Only then did she notice Roger, propped up on his right arm in a cot on the opposite wall. He stared at her. His left shoulder was a mass of bloody bandages from where she shot him with the arrow. He said nothing, but his eyes said it all.

How could someone be jealous at a time like this? "Roger, my God, I didn't see you there. I'm sorry, I didn't know—"

"I'm glad you're safe." Roger grunted, swung his feet off the cot and got up. "I'm going to help Lucca and Raffa."

Jess sat back on her haunches. "Roger, wait." She held up one hand. "Why did you come here, what happened?"

Roger balanced himself as another tremor jolted the ground. "I came for you, Jess." He glanced at Giovanni, back at Jess, then turned and stalked away.

40

Chianti, Italy

BEN LEANED DOWN to pick up the edge of a fallen crate. He strained to lift it back into place. Celeste jammed her body beside his. Together, they pushed the crate back against the rock wall.

They slumped into each other and sat against it.

"See, we can do anything together," Ben laughed, putting his arm around his wife.

He'd been a fool, pushing her away, hiding his own pain. His own guilt.

"Well, we made Jess, didn't we?" Celeste laughed and kissed her husband.

The ceiling rumbled, detonations spraying them in a mist of falling pebbles and dust.

"I'm so happy." Ben kissed Celeste back. A happiness he hadn't felt in years. Here, at the end of times, buried alive, his love burned bright.

Jess came around the corner from the other room. The cavern walls shook.

"Come sit with us." Celeste held one hand out to her daughter.

Standing and stopping for a moment to admire her parents sitting together, Jess took her mother's offered hand and squeezed in between them.

Ben kissed his daughter's head. "I thought I'd never see you again. My God, you're crazy, you know that? You should have just left me."

"I couldn't do that." Jess craned her head sideway and kissed her father's cheek. "Neither could Giovanni." She felt her mother putting both of her arms around her, squeezing her tight.

Closing his eyes, Ben shook his head. "He's a good man, Giovanni." He put his hand on Jess's chin and pulled her face to look him in the eye. "He's a *good* man. We're lucky to have him." He chewed his lip. "And Leone, Lucca, Raffael…these are good people." He looked away, his voice trailing off.

"I can believe it took this to get us together." Ben's face creased up, his eyebrows high. "How on Earth did you convince Celeste to come to Italy?"

Jess hadn't ever mentioned it to him. "It was a Facebook message sent to Mom, from a someone who said they were family and wanted to meet us."

"And did you talk to them?"

Jess shook her head. "No, they never responded after we got here. It must have been Nico, trying to drag us into the middle of this insane blood feud."

"How did he…" Ben didn't finish his sentence, but looked at the ceiling. "But thank God."

"Nico denied it," Jess said. "Even when it made no difference, he still denied he sent any messages. *He* said it was God."

"The man was deluded," Celeste said.

Jess took a deep breath. "Yeah, I guess so." But she understood Nico. His wife and daughter—he had something precious beyond comprehension stolen from him. In the final moment, she understood. She forgave him. But why would he lie about sending the Facebook message? At the end, she saw rage and pain in his eyes, but no deception.

Ben took off his eyeglasses and wiped his face with one hand. "Speaking of Nico, he's really gone?" He put his glasses back on and looked Jess in the eye. "Did you kill him?"

"I didn't kill him," Jess said, her voice quiet and flat. "I almost did, but I let him go. He tried to escape on a cable car that connects to the other hilltop. He fell into the valley. Into the…" She wasn't even sure how to describe what was out there.

"Good," Ben whispered. "Good." He looked at his hands and clasped them together.

Jess wasn't sure if he meant that Nico was dead, or that she wasn't the one that killed him.

"What's happening, the world will be changed forever," Ben said after a pause. "I need you to promise me something." He looked at Jess again.

"What?" Jess took his hands in hers. "Anything. What do you need?"

"I want you to promise me that you'll never give up, that you'll always struggle to survive, no matter what."

An ear-splitting detonation shook the cavern. The lights flickered, dust spilling onto them from the cavern walls. Jess held her breath. The shaking subsided. "Why are you saying it like that?" she asked her father. "Of course, we'll be together."

"I need you to live, to *want* to live. For us. For Billy. For Giovanni and Hector." Ben took Jess's and Celeste's hands in his and squeezed hard. He looked her in the eye. "Promise me."

Jess stared into his eyes. "I promise."

His grip eased, but just a little. "And don't lose your humanity. Never give up, but not at the expenses of sacrificing your humanity."

Jess stared deep into his eyes. She hadn't told me about the Aberto, the boy she killed at the villa, or Enzo. One thing at a time, and now definitely wasn't the time. "I promise."

Ben smiled. "Good."

He let go of her hands, and put then down to push away from Jess and Celeste. He sat cross-legged in front of them. "What they said about me. That research paper, the one they said I hid—"

"I know you didn't," Jess said. "Why would you?"

"But somebody leaked that," Ben said grimly. It was a short list of suspects. But why? "As soon as this is over, we need to try and get in touch with a man called Ufuk Erdogmus. Use the shortwave, try and track him down."

Jess frowned. "You mean the famous entrepreneur? The Mars First mission guy? You knew him?"

"Not really. I mean, a little. He was at the hotel in Rome when Dr. Muller discussed Nomad. And he was in ESOC, at Darmstadt. He said he needed to talk with me, no matter what, but I left to come here."

"What did he want?"

"He said something about sanctuary. Maybe he has a bunker? If anyone could survive this, he'd be the one to do it."

"We'll do it together," Jess pointed out.

"Yes." Ben pressed his hands against the rock floor. "But just in case, remember that name."

It wasn't a difficult name to remember. Erdogmus was famous. "Okay."

Ben looked left and right. "I have a question."

"What?"

"When you were with Roger, back in New York…"

Jess looked away and exhaled. "I was going to tell you about that."

"No, no, that doesn't matter." Ben inched closer to his daughter. "Was Roger…ah, how do I put this…was he religious? I mean, not Catholic, but Taoist? Did he have yin-yang symbols on stuff, maybe tattoos?"

The question took Jess completely off guard. "Huh?"

"Like a special cellphone, I saw a yin-yang symbol on it. Not a sticker, but engraved. Ring any bells?"

Shaking her head, Jess shrugged. "No. I mean, no, he wasn't the least bit spiritual."

Ben held her gaze for a long moment. "Okay."

"What's this about?" Jess asked.

"I'm not sure…" Ben looked up, over her shoulder. "Speak of the devil."

Jess swiveled her head around. Roger walked toward them, coming from the other cavern. He glanced at them, but avoided looking at Jess.

"Roger," Ben called out, "why don't you come and sit with us?" He pushed down with both hands and got to his feet.

"I think I'm going to check on Giovanni." Jess got to her feet as well. She flashed a tight-lipped smile at Roger and walked past him.

Ben watched his daughter walk away while Roger tried not to watch her go. Even entombed in the heart of a mountain, the world around them disintegrating, jealousy and pride reared their ugly heads.

"Lucca and Raffael finished assembling the table," Ben said to Roger. He strode over and clicked on a butane kettle he'd filled a few minutes earlier. "How about a cup of tea?"

Nodding grimly, Roger picked his way through the bags and boxes. "Tea? Like we're in a London tube station during the Blitz."

On cue, the ceiling trembled again, a distant roar echoing.

Ben nodded. "And we're lucky to be here. This place is a goddamn fortress, dug into the granite heart of a mountain a thousand feet above sea level. Could withstand a nuclear strike."

"I think it just about is."

The walls shook, glasses inside the crates rattling.

Ben, Celeste, and Roger sat together at the table. To Ben, it felt like they were kids, hiding in a fort, the fear and terror subdued by the joy of being together with Jess and Celeste. Only hours ago, all had seemed lost—he never thought they'd survive this long, never imagined he'd be reunited with his family. Now there was a chance, one he hadn't allowed himself to even consider. Despite the eruptions, the massive earthquakes, and the flooding oceans, the Earth hadn't opened up and swallowed them. Not yet.

The kettle pinged and turned itself off.

"This is the worst of it." Ben poured hot water from the kettle to plastic cups, then dropped tea bags into them. He looked at his watch. "We're past Nomad's closest approach." He put the kettle down and looked at Roger. "Do you feel lighter?"

"What?" Roger's face contorted in a scowl.

"Lighter. Do you feel lighter?"

"How do mean, lighter?"

The edges of Ben's mouth quivered into the barest of smiles. "Judging by the way the oceans flooded, from what Celeste heard on the short wave radio, and the last data I saw from NASA on my laptop on the drive here—I'd put Nomad at seventy million kilometers away. Should be exerting..." Ben paused, closed his eyes and tapped the table top. "...about a tenth of Earth's gravity, straight up. If we had a scale, you'd be ten percent lighter right now. Incredible, isn't it?"

Roger exhaled and rolled his eyes. "Trust you to be fascinated by this." He picked up his cup of tea and tested it.

"A piece of creation is flying over our heads right now, a left over fragment of the primordial universe." Ben looked up, his jaw flexing. "It's hard not to be awed."

Celeste took a sip of her tea. "I wish it would go away."

Ben took her hand and squeezed. "And it will. That's the amazing part. As fast as Nomad arrived, is just as quick as it will leave. In a few hours, it'll stop bending the Earth's crust and will release our oceans." He stared into Celeste's eyes. "We're going to survive."

Roger snorted and slammed the plastic tea cup down. "For what? A few days until we freeze to death? I think the lucky ones are the ones already dead." He hung his head, winced and held his bloody left shoulder. "Nomad is going to toss the Earth into deep space like a child's toy. Two days from now it will be as cold as the arctic here, and a few days after that, colder than Mars."

Roger took a sip from the tea cup. "Global warming? All that carbon dioxide we've been worrying about?" He lifted his head and laughed. "It'll be the first to liquefy at minus fifty-seven Celsius, and at minus eighty you'll see carbon dioxide frost cover the ground. A few weeks from now the atmosphere itself will start to solidify, first oxygen at minus one-eighty, then nitrogen at minus two hundred. We'll be a frozen chunk of ice, wandering through interstellar space. How long do you think burning those barrels will keep you alive?"

Ben stared at Roger in stony silence. The ceiling shuddered, sending down a shower of dust. "You're probably right. Nomad is dragging us along behind it like a dog on a leash, but it's also dragging the sun. Did you see the last of the simulations?"

He meant gravity simulations of the solar system. Ben and Roger ran them continuously on their laptops on the long journey in the car over the Alps.

"Of course I saw. I was the one running them." Roger put his tea down, mashing his lips together as if he tasted something disgusting. "By now, Mercury and Venus have been ejected away from the sun by gravitational slingshot, and Saturn pulled into a retrograde orbit, and the Earth, well…"

"Exactly, it was right on the cusp. We don't know the exact trajectory of Nomad. It all depends on the geometry."

Roger shook his head. "And right now, we *could* be headed straight into the Sun."

"At least we wouldn't freeze." Ben grimaced. A bad time for jokes. "But that's not possible. We know the trajectory of Nomad down to one degree of resolution, and none of the solutions near that throw the Earth into the sun."

This didn't have the effect of cheering anyone up.

Ben took another sip of his tea and put the cup down. He squeezed Celeste's hand, stared into her eyes, then looked back at Roger. "We need to go outside. Right now."

Roger looked Ben in the eye. "I was thinking the same thing."

"What?" Celeste pulled her hand out of Ben's. "Why?"

"To get my backpack. I left it in that half-basement, outside the walls, when Nico kidnapped us."

Celeste pulled Ben to face her. "What on Earth could be so important?"

"The long axis coordinates of Nomad appearing thirty years ago. That bag has my old data, maybe the only data that still exists that could pinpoint the exact trajectory."

"What about all the satellites? The government agencies?"

"When Nomad finally appeared from behind the sun, we were bombarded by a massive solar flares. Hopefully my laptop was deep enough in that basement not to get fried by the radiation, but there's no way any satellites survived that. They had an hour or two *at most* to get a direct view of Nomad when it came from behind the sun, and even then, it'd still be invisible. And who the hell would be sitting at a desk to monitor all this during Armageddon?"

"He's right." Roger balled both of his hands into fists. "Even if they did pinpoint it in space, that would be only one point. They'd need a long axis to determine the trajectory."

Celeste looked back and forth at Ben and Roger. "And why would that be important, for God's sake? It'll be gone in a few hours. That's what you said."

"Because," Ben said slowly, "if we know the exact trajectory, we can use modeling software to predict where the thousands of large and small asteroids and debris will be kicked out."

"And if they might hit Earth." Roger added.

"Exactly."

"Assuming the planet doesn't fall into the sun or freeze solid." Roger took a deep breath. "I'll go." He glanced at the opening in the cave wall, to where Jess was. He sighed. "There's nothing for me here, anyway."

"I'll go with you." Ben squeezed Celeste's hand. "You don't know exactly where I put it. And two of us will be safer than one."

Roger stared at Ben. "There's something I need to tell you."

Ben returned his gaze. "Tell me on the way. The longer we wait, the more chance that it'll get destroyed."

"Can't it wait?" Celeste begged, holding his hand tight.

Ben shook his head. "This is important. We've got to get it."

Roger got up from the table. "Let's go."

Celeste stared into Ben's eyes for a long moment. "Be careful."

"I will." Ben stood, then leaned down to kiss his wife. "I'll be back in a minute." He stared at her. "Promise me you'll stay here."

Celeste nodded.

"Don't tell Jess," Ben added. "She'll try to stop us."

The tiniest of smiles tugged at the corners of Celeste's mouth. "She'd just go herself."

"Yes," Ben laughed. "Yes, she would."

Clapping Roger on the shoulder, Ben strode through the boxes, taking a turn into the left-hand tunnel, the one leading up into the main castle. Roger followed.

Celeste watched them go. Crunching thuds shook the ceiling and walls. Her hands shaking, Celeste took another sip of her tea and put the cup down. She stood, turning to grab a thin coat, and ran down the length of the cave, following Ben.

Leone came into the cave just in time to see her disappear up the stone staircase.

"Where are my parents?" Jess asked, walking in behind Leone.

"Out." Leone pointed at the tunnel with the staircase leading up. "*Sono andati lassù*"

"They went out?" Jess pointed at the stairs, raising her eyebrows. "Why?"

"*Non lo so.*" Leone's soot-streaked face creased up, his wisps of white hair matted against his glistening scalp. "I do not know"

Why would they go upstairs? Adrenaline flooded Jess's bloodstream, the hair prickling on her exposed arms. She grabbed Leone. "We've got to go—"

A massive concussion rocked the ground, knocking Jess from her feet. She crashed into a wooden crate that split open onto her. The rumbling continued, burying Jess under a mountain of medical supplies spilling. She strained and scrabbled to get out. A wiry hand gripped and pulled her free.

Gasping for air, she pushed her way out of the pile, dragged by Leone. She rubbed her eyes. "Leone, help me, we need to…" She didn't finish her sentence, but stood in dumb silence.

Half of the cave had collapsed, rocks and boulders crushing the crates on the other side of the room, the tunnel to the staircase gone.

"Mom!" Jess screamed. "Dad! Where are you?"

Ben struggled to his feet, dusting himself off and trying to quell the fear rising inside him. "Are you okay?"

"I'm fine." Roger groaned and pulled himself from a pile of rubble. Part of a wooden wall fell onto him. "Maybe we should go back, come later."

Ben shook his head. "No, we need to do this."

Hot wind blasted smoke and ash through the stable past the open door. Clicking on his headlamp, Ben stumbled forward. He coughed, almost gagged. The air was noxious, stank of rotten eggs and burnt wood. He pulled a cloth around his mouth, his lungs burning, his eyes watering. His headlamp cut a conical pool of light twenty feet in front of him before being swallowed by the gray-black soot swirling in the air. Pushing forward, he reached the door. "That was no quake."

Outside was a hurricane of dark ash.

A boulder the size of a school bus had impacted the main structure of the castle, coming to rest between the main staircase and the two-story museum. In the dim light, it glowed faintly red. L'Olio, the three-thousand-year-old olive tree, remained, just in front of the smoking boulder-projectile. Its leaves were stripped off, but it still stood, naked and defiant.

"Let's get this over with," Ben wheezed as loud as he could.

The tops of the walls surrounding the courtyard had crumbled, spilling a jumble of boulders and cement across the ground, but the main portico gate and wooden entrance was still intact. Jogging across the courtyard, Ben pulled open the wooden entrance door. His bag should be just to the right, not more than twenty feet away. Stepping through the door, he stopped in his tracks. "My God…"

The valley of Saline, to his right, glowed red—a carpet of magma stretching from Monterufoli, further than he could see in the dust and dirt. Dark vortexes churned the sky, lightning crackling sideways through clouds that billowed almost to the ground, all lit in a pulsing dull red. A blast of hot wind rose up from the valley, covering Ben and Roger in flaming ashes.

Dusting off his arms, Ben forced himself to focus and began searching along the wall. "Over there," he yelled to Roger. He pointed at an arch in the half-destroyed wall, just visible in the beam of his headlamp. Roger nodded, but instead of coming toward Ben, he walked the opposite direction, away from the wall.

"Where are you going? It's here!" Ben yelled. Monterufoli boomed in the distance, the concussion waves echoing off the hills. The wind howled. "Roger!" Ben screamed. "Come back. It's just here."

Roger had disappeared into the swirling maelstrom.

Ben swore. What the hell? He hesitated, almost ran to fetch Roger, but stopped. The bag. He needed his bag. He ran under the arch, down the steps below it into the wall, and there, in the light of his headlamp, just where he left it in the corner of the half-basement, was Ben's backpack. He crossed over and picked it up, then jogged back up the stairs. Easy.

"Roger!" Ben screamed again. "I've got it."

Something caught Ben's eye. Someone coming through the entrance door through the wall. But it wasn't Roger. "Celeste? What are you doing?"

She stared down the valley, her eyes wide, her scarf wrapped around her mouth.

"Honey, I've got it." He ran to her. "Let's get back—"

A crunching concussion knocked Ben off his feet, throwing him sideways. His ears rang. He shook his head and propped himself up, using his left hand to take off his glasses so he could wipe his stinging eyes with the back his hand holding the backpack. The ground around him was littered with boulders. Glancing behind him, the wall section he'd just been into was completely gone. Blasted to the ground.

Celeste pulled him to his feet. "Are you hurt?" she screamed over the wind, dragging him toward the opening in the wall.

Ben shook his head. "I'm fine."

"Where's Roger?""

Ben pointed into the churning darkness. "He went that way." He turned to his wife. "Why did you come up here?" he yelled through his cloth.

"I'm not leaving you alone again." Celeste reached up to wipe dirt off her husband's glasses. She stroked his cheek. "Whatever we do, we do it together from now on. Okay?"

The ground juddered, sending a shower of pebbles onto them from the wall. "Okay. Together. No matter what." It was too dangerous to keep her up here. If Roger didn't come back in ten minutes, he'd come back with Leone to search for him.

Ben reached for the door, but had the sensation of something horribly wrong. Looking up, a dark shape rushed toward him. He grabbed Celeste, cradled her underneath him as a three-story wall of stone collapsed onto them. Straining, he did his best to hold it back, but the crushing weight fractured his arms and his legs. The mountain of rock cracked and crushed his chest, squeezing out every drop of air. As blackness descended, an image flickered in his mind, of Jess as a child, holding Billy in her arms.

Please, no…

41

Chianti, Italy

JESS SHIVERED AND tried to find a comfortable angle to lean on Giovanni, her thigh resting on the wooden floor of the wine cave with her head nestled on Giovanni's stomach. She knew he was doing his best to accommodate her. He had a gunshot wound through the flesh on the right of his chest, and was beaten mercilessly the night before. Still, Jess needed someone, perhaps for the first time in her life, to hold her close and tell her everything would be all right.

She hated feeling trapped, and the walls of the caves seemed to close in around her. The air felt fetid, and a fine dust covered everything. Buried alive. That's how she felt.

"I'm sure they're fine," Giovanni murmured. He stroked Jess's hair.

Jess nodded, but she wasn't so sure. Hector was curled between them, a blanket covering the three of them together. Hector coughed and grimaced.

The air was rancid. It literally stank like hell. Brimstone. Jess knew it was hydrogen sulfide from the volcano. It was one of the last things her mother had explained to her. She wondered what other gases they were breathing in. A headache banged inside her skull. Giovanni had one too. They all did.

Beside them, the shortwave radio hissed. It was attached to an outside antenna, a cable snaking through the wreckage into the outside. Two days ago, her mother had shown her how to use it. They'd been able to raise dozens of channels, but now, everything had fallen silent. Giovanni cycled through the frequencies, but found nothing. Nobody else out there.

For the past ten hours, she'd been digging through the rubble, trying to move the rocks blocking the tunnel to the staircase. Her fingers bled, her shoulders and back burned, but she ripped and tore into the pile. Lucca and Raffael and Leone tried the other tunnel, the one leading to the ledge under the cable car, but that side of the cliff had sheared away. She'd stared into the roaring blackness; thought of trying to scale the sheer wall, but it was madness. So she returned to the tunnel, tore her fingers to shreds until they forced her away.

Forced her to sit down.

The crunching bombardment died down in the first hour as she pulled the stones away, and in the hours since, the world above had gone eerily silent. Hours ago, the hot wind pressing through the rock had turned cool, but the sulfurous stench of rotten eggs remained. The only sound now was the steady thump and groan of Lucca and Raffael, working steadily on the rocks, slowly working their way through the rocks blocking the tunnel.

Jess wrapped her arm around Hector tighter, not for him, but for her. Her body and mind were utterly exhausted. She couldn't remember the last time she slept.

For ten hours she'd been digging.

Ten hours.

By now, Nomad was three hundred million kilometers away after its closest approach to Earth. A staggering number. Three hundred million kilometers in ten hours. Jess turned the number over and over in her head. Three hundred million kilometers was halfway to Jupiter, but Jupiter wasn't where it used to be. She had a sense of vertigo, like a roller coaster out of control. Nomad was gone, but where was the Earth? Was the sun already receding, disappearing? When they got topside, would they see the sun as just another star in a black sky?

After surviving all this, were they doomed to a frozen death in a matter of days?

The oceans were already slipping back across the land, settling into their basins; the crust relaxing, the surface of the Earth, cracked and damaged, now sinking back. But the damage was done. The tidal effects of Nomad, at this distance, were almost back to what the Earth felt from the moon.

Jess laughed. *The moon.* If *that* was even still there.

"What are you laughing about?" Giovanni asked softly.

"Nothing very funny. Did I tell you that I killed my brother Billy?" She said it matter-of-factly, like she just knocked over a glass of water.

She thought Giovanni would stiffen. She half-expected some outcry, something...but he continued to stroke her hair.

"What happened?" he asked.

"He fell through the ice at our cottage, when we were kids."

"Doesn't sound like you *killed* him."

"I told him to go out on the ice." Jess pulled her legs inward. She wasn't used to her secret being out. Her entire adult life was a lie, a cover up, but no more. "I was mad at my mother."

"I'm sure you didn't mean to hurt him."

He was right. She meant to hurt her mother. Show her that she couldn't tell her what to do.

"And that was a long time ago, Jess," continued Giovanni, "you need to let go. You've paid for whatever mistake you might have made, and you were just a child. I'm sure if Billy was here, he wouldn't want you to suffer like this."

Even now, more than twenty years past, she could still see little Billy's eyes. Giovanni was right. She sighed. Billy wouldn't want her to suffer. She felt a weight lifting. "Maybe."

"And let me tell you something," Giovanni added.

Jess felt the oppressive weight of the mountain holding her down. She was happy to move on to something else. "What?"

"I abandoned my father." Giovanni let out a long sigh. "I told everyone I wanted to explore, be an adventurer, but the truth was I just wanted to be away from him. This whole blood feud with the Tosetti, it consumed him. I think he might have even had people killed. I wanted nothing to do with it. So I ran away, just like you."

"That doesn't sound so bad." In Nico's final words to Jess, he said to ask Giovanni why he was in Antarctica. Now she knew. She didn't need to ask.

"I might have been able to stop it. I didn't even try." Giovanni's chest shuddered. "I even...I even wished for him to be dead, sometimes, so I could return and be free here."

Jess didn't say anything.

"I wished my father dead, and Nico killed him. Maybe I could have stopped that, could have stopped all of this. This is all *my* fault."

Looking up, Jess saw tears in Giovanni's eyes. "No more secrets, then."

"No more secrets."

Jess settled her head into Giovanni's stomach, pulling Hector into her.

So tired.

She closed her eyes.

AFTER NOMAD

DAY ONE

October 15th

42

Chianti, Italy

IN THE CONICAL beam of light from her headlamp, Jess watched fat purple snowflakes fall in the grainy black soup enveloping her. Looking down, the beam glistened off rocks frozen together in a slurry of mottled black ice and ash. She brought her hands together, blowing on them. A plume of vapor dissipated into the chilled air with each labored breath. "Are you ready yet?" she called out, her voice muffled.

The air was putrid and thick, breathing and speaking difficult from behind the N-95 particulate masks Giovanni had scrounged from his supplies. He brought his scuba tanks up to top, to give everyone a blast of fresh air from time to time. A headache throbbed between Jess's temples, her senses scrambled, shapes shifting in the darkness. She was lightheaded from whatever they breathed in—hydrogen sulphide, carbon monoxide and dioxide. Slow poisoning, but they had no choice. They had to find her parents.

"One minute, just one second," Giovanni croaked, his voice disembodied in the darkness.

Jess pulled her mitts back on and sat on top of the generator. She inspected the yellow cords snaking out of it, umbilicals feeding some unseen monster. The purplish snow accumulated in hoary clumps on the rocks.

Eerily quiet.

They finally broke through the tunnel to topside about two hours ago. Jess slept the whole night before, if night was really a thing anymore in this suffocating underworld. For fourteen hours Giovanni let her sleep, said she needed it. She was furious when she awoke, her head splitting in pain, but she went straight back to tearing away the rocks in a panic. Lucca, Raffael, Leone and Giovanni did their best to help, wheezing and coughing. By five p.m., the five of them had opened a gap big enough for her to squeeze through.

And she scrambled out.

Up top.

Into this blackness.

Nothing seemed to be where she remembered. She stumbled around for ten minutes in the freezing darkness, gagging and gasping for air in a black tomb that used to be the world.

"Ben! Celeste!" she'd screamed, her voice hoarse. "Roger, are you out here?"

Giovanni found her, brought her a coat and mitts, brought the oxygen tanks up. For another hour she circled, trying to make sense of the piles of rock looming in the small pool of light from her headlamp. But nothing.

No answering calls.

Just silence. No crickets. No rustling of leaves. No sound at all.

It seemed nothing was left alive. Had the world fallen into the black hole? Her father always said that the rules of physics disappeared at the event horizon. While she slept, had they passed over, in the rumbling thunder, into a netherworld? The world above seemed to have collapsed into a dark shell, floating disconnected. Her mind barely felt connected to her body in the blackness.

"Okay, now." Giovanni's voice echoed.

Jess pulled one mitt off and stood. The cold bit into the stump of her left leg. It rubbed painfully against the ill-fitting prosthetic. She'd never get a new one now. One more in a long list of things that were no more. How long could they even survive in this?

Leaning over, she grabbed the red handle of the generator and pulled back as hard as she could. It sputtered, then roared to life.

She looked up. "My God…"

Six floodlights glowed to life. Through swirling ash and snow, they illuminated the castle and walls, or what was left of them. Most of it was gone, nothing more than a pile of rubble. The southern and western walls were flattened; the two-story museum crushed under a boulder the size of a semi-truck. Only the north-eastern tower remained, the observatory dome unscathed. In the middle of the devastation, L'Olio, the ancient olive tree, stood proud. Its leaves stripped and branches scorched, but still it stood.

"*Sparsi*!" Giovanni waved his hands at Leone and Lucca and Raffael. "See if you can find anything." He hobbled forward, intent on helping, even bandaged and battered.

Jess put her mitt back on. Over-sized, they were from Giovanni's arctic expedition boxes. He had crates of gear stored in the caves, none of it her size.

The air temperature dropped to near freezing already, down from almost eighty Fahrenheit less than forty hours before. But it fluctuated. On the side of the castle closest to Monterufoli, it was ten degrees warmer. The temperature depended on the direction of the wind.

Jess didn't let her mind dwell on any of it. Only one thing circled in her mind: she had to find her mother and father. They were out here somewhere. If they didn't find them soon, they'd freeze to death soon.

Shots like cannon echoed from the darkness.

It had to be Monterufoli volcano, invisible in the choking murk. The snow thickened, flakes sticking to her eyelashes.

"Over here!" Giovanni yelled. "Jessica, over here!"

Jess bolted upright and almost slipped off the frozen rock pile she was trying to get across. "Did you find them?" Her heart raced.

"We found something, not sure what." His voice a muffled echo in the darkness.

Doing her best to quick step through the boulders and rocks, Jess tried to triangulate Giovanni's voice. "Where are you?" she yelled, stopping still and closing her eyes.

"This way!"

His voice was louder to her right. Climbing over a boulder, she reversed course. She'd gone around the back wall, the floodlights a dim glow from where she was. Slipping and sliding across the ashen snow, Giovanni's outline finally emerged from the gloom. He was gathered with the workers and Leone by a pile of rubble next to the twisted remains of the iron portico gate. A strong northerly wind began blowing an hour ago, finally clearing away some of the putrid stench.

She arrived just as Leone heaved away a chunk of flat concrete. Lucca and Raffael stood back. Giovanni's lips pressed together. He grimaced and looked at Jess.

"What?" She skidded to a stop.

There, sticking from the pile of rock, a hand. Not just any hand. Jess recognized the gold wedding band. Her father's.

"Get him out," Jess shrieked, diving at the rocks.

Leone and Giovanni jumped in beside her, grunting to pull away a huge slab.

Ben's face appeared in the glare of their headlamps. Even in the dim, unnatural light, Jess saw the purple bruises, his skull crushed, his lips blue. She brought one hand to her mouth and sobbed. Giovanni wrapped his left arm around her, his right hanging in a sling under his winter coat.

Gently, Leone reached in and pulled away another wall fragment.

The blood drained from Jess's face, her knees buckling. Giovanni strained to hold her up. A keening, animal wail echoed off the rocks. Jess realized the sound was coming from her own lips.

Celeste's body was below Ben's, his arms around her, cradling her. Her face as blue and bruised as his.

Her mother and father.

Dead.

"Come on, let's go in," Giovanni wheezed. Jess knew he was in pain. "Nothing we can do for them now." He squeezed Jess.

She slipped free, dropped to her knees. Kneeling, she stroked her father's hair, kissed his cold cheek. She leaned deeper and kissed her mother's forehead, the skin freezing cold, hard.

"Have the Lucca and Raffa search around here, see if we can find Roger," Giovanni said to Leone.

"Should we bring them in?" Leone asked.

"No." Jess pushed herself up. They almost looked asleep, their arms around each other. "Leave them here, as they are."

What could have been so important that they came up here?

Jess squinted.

What was that under her father?

Leaning in, she grabbed a strap. Pulled. A backpack slithered out from between Ben and Celeste. She sat in the snow and looked inside to find his super-ruggedized laptop along with some notepads. A metal box was in there too, filled with old tape spool and CDs. Taking a deep breath, she rocked her head back. Is this what he came out for? His work? The north wind blew hard. Jess shivered and stared into the blackness above.

Blackness.

But not blackness. Tiny dots of light danced across it.

"Stars," Jess whispered, pointing up. "Stars!" she yelled.

Giovanni and Leone looked up, their mouths dropping open.

"What time is it?" Jess got to her feet, closing up and shouldering the backpack.

"Almost midnight," Giovanni replied.

"Come on, I need your help." She strode forward two steps, but stopped and turned. "And Leone, could you get us some paper and pens?"

Metal screeched across metal. The observatory roof looked undamaged from the ground, but it was battered, dented. Slowly the dome awning squealed open as Jess frantically cranked the mechanical winch by the stairs. She had no idea how long the opening in the clouds would last. Could the Earth have been knocked over? No, it spun like a top, a giant gyroscope. Even if it was sucked away from the sun, the northern hemisphere would still point the same way.

"Where are you, my friends?" she whispered, barely hoping to hope.

Staring up, the dots of stars appearing as the roof's mouth shuddered open. The tail of Ursa Minor rewarded her. And then Ursa Major. The simple pleasure of something so familiar tingled the back of her scalp. Something of her old world remained in this dark, alien place she'd been transported into.

"What are we looking for?" Giovanni asked, stamping his feet. On each breath, a white plume of vapor circled his head in the glow of his headlamp.

"Mercury, Mars, Jupiter, Saturn," explained Jess, "they're all visible to the naked eye, but I really want to find Venus. It's the third brightest thing in the sky, after the sun and moon. It's what you see at sunset, at twilight before sunrise, the yellow disk that people think is a star. But it's not. It's Venus." Even if they didn't use the telescope, the observatory tower was the best place to get a view.

Giovanni shivered. "Okay, a yellow disk."

Jess finished winding the roof back and walked to the telescope, inspected it. Not damaged at all. She wheeled the gimbals and it swung back and forth. Perfect.

Looking up and south, she found the Libra constellation, hanging just over the top of the dim black cloud bank. Libra. She squinted. At this time of year, Jupiter should be just in the middle of the four stars forming the base of Libra. She didn't see anything, but she wheeled the telescope around.

Nothing.

Jupiter was gone.

Not gone, it had to be somewhere else. But where?

She looked further south. Venus should be just there, but it wasn't. She scanned her head back and forth, looking for the shimmering red dot of Mars, the yellow disk of Venus. Nothing.

Giovanni tapped her shoulder. "I'm no astronomer, but..." He pointed behind her.

Jess turned. In the northeast, the sliver crescent of a waning moon rose over the black clouds. She smiled.

Old friend, you're still with us.

She looked harder. It seemed bright, but was it as bright as it usually was? Were they further from the sun? Did Nomad drag the sun away behind it? The moon reflected light from the sun, the Earth occluding the light falling on the moon. It was still about the same phase as she remembered it from three nights ago. That was something, right? The pieces fell together, a small part of her world still intact.

When she was a child, she remembered her father teaching her all about the constellations, the moon, the tides, the sun. A gift whose value he could have never imagined.

Giovanni tapped her shoulder again. "And is that your Venus?"

Jess turned. A yellow dot near the horizon. "That's Venus."

She's in Leo. The hair on Jess's arm prickled. What the hell are you doing there?

The excitement of seeing the moon faded into dread. If Venus was all the way over there, where was the Earth? She swung the telescope around and looked through the viewfinder, pulling out the pad of paper from her jacket pocket and scribbling notes and star positions.

Half an hour later, they found Mars just as the clouds rolled back in, the crescent moon skimming the tops like a silver surfer riding black fog. In the beam of Jess's headlamp, plump gray snowflakes drifted in a suspension of twinkling ice crystals.

Far to the east, the black sky lightened into blue, then pink. For an instant, the sun burst over the horizon. In the jumbled, broken courtyard, Leone and his workers stopped what they were doing and stared up. In the ray of sunlight, a single green leaf fluttered on top of L'Olio, the ancient olive tree.

The clouds closed up. Darkness descended.

Jess stood and stared at where the sun had been, an impenetrable haze enveloping them. It was the sun, but was it as bright as she remembered?

It seemed weaker.

Colder.

She blew on her hands, and returned to the stairs to winch the roof cover back.

AFTER NOMAD

DAY TWO

October 16th

43

Chianti, Italy

*SHHHH...SHHHHHHH...*RADIO static hissed.

Giovanni picked up the microphone and clicked it. "Say again, Jolly Roger?"

Jess sat across from Giovanni, her back to the rock wall of the cave, her leg stretched out for her foot to soak some warmth from the wood burning stove Leone had managed to kludge together in the main room, with a metal duct-work chimney snaking out the tunnel to the sheer cliff face. She fought the sensation of being buried alive. Even going topside, it felt oppressive, the darkness and ash and snow drowning out the world. Nothing lived out there. Nothing.

They hadn't found Roger. His body must have been swept away, or buried under the crush of rubble somewhere. The northerly wind continued to blow, mercifully bringing clearer air. A thick fog of particle and vapor still clogged the air, but it wasn't as thick or oppressive now the wind blew away from Monterufoli. Clearer air, but colder. Much colder.

Jess had her father's laptop on her knees, plugged into an extension cord connected to a generator running outside. The laptop's screen was filled with a 3D model of solar system simulations he'd been running on software called Universe Sandbox. It was a detailed physics simulation of the entire solar system—all the planets, their moons, their rings, even thousands of asteroids and smaller objects. She hit reset, and the dot representing Nomad streaked through the middle of the solar system, scattering the planets and dragging the sun behind it.

"Jolly Roger, are you there?" Giovanni tried again.

The radio crackled. "...yes, mate...my name's Leaming, engineer onboard the RNLB Jolly Roger out of Gravesend station, just south of London…"

Giovanni scribbled notes on a pad of paper: *Survivor testimony #GR14; Event +62hrs; Name: Aubrey Leaming; Reported location: England, undetermined.* He compiled a log of all the survivors he contacted.

This morning, at least morning on their clocks, there was a rush of excitement when Giovanni contacted their first other survivor group. Excitement and tears. They weren't the last people on Earth. All digital electronics aboveground had been fried in the solar storms, but some older electronic equipment seemed to have survived, things like shortwave radios.

Giovanni leaned his ear toward the speaker of the shortwave. He'd run another antennae up the way up the tunnel, patching together wiring he scavenged up top, all the way to the observatory tower.

"…your location?" the speaker asked.

Giovanni clicked the microphone. "Italy, we are Station Saline, again, repeat, Station Saline in northern Italy."

Jess paused her simulation. The Earth and planets stopped moving, frozen in space. She zoomed in, locked her viewpoint into the Earth, then panned to celestial north and looked for Venus. Her father's notes were scattered on a pile of barrel wood beside her, the backpack open, the tapes and spools spilling out of it.

She pushed reset on the simulation, adjusted Nomad's trajectory, and let it fly again, tearing through the middle of the solar system. Increasing the speed of the simulation, to one week for one second, she watched Mercury shoot away from the Sun as if it was fired from a cannon. Venus looped outward past Mars, while Saturn was dragged backward into a retrograde orbit, rotating around the sun in the opposite direction. The Earth, though, that was the key: in this simulation run it was dragged into a high elliptic orbit.

It didn't look like it would leave the Sun, not entirely.

Opening a climate simulation tool within the software, she watched the estimated average global temperature of the simulated Earth. Normally, this hovered at an almost-constant global 15 Celsius. As the Earth in Jess's simulation climbed in the elliptic, the global average temperature dropped rapidly, to below 8C, then started rising as the Earth dropped back toward the sun. 15C. 20C. 30C.

Too hot.

Everything on that planet was fried. She stopped the simulation and rubbed her eyes.

"Temperature here is…" Giovanni paused to convert from Celsius, relaying information to this new band of survivors he got in touch with. "…twenty-nine Fahrenheit and dropping. What is your temperature? Do you have cloud cover?"

He glanced at Jess. This morning, they'd even contacted someone in America. On a pad of paper beside him, Giovanni scribbled names, locations, frequencies of anyone or anything they contacted. Shortwave operated by bouncing radio waves off the ionosphere, skipping them inside the Earth's atmosphere, sometimes all the way around it. Atmospheric conditions were unpredictable. The ionosphere was probably still glowing. Communications were patchy and sporadic.

Still, Giovanni had spoken to pockets of survivors all over the world. Moscow, Paris, Madrid, Baghdad, Kampala, Nairobi, even Brasilia in South America. They hadn't spoken to anyone in coastal cities, except this one Coast Guard ship from England that had somehow survived. Africa seemed to have been the least affected.

They were starting to piece together a picture of the new Earth.

Whole areas of the Middle East, India and Pakistan were destroyed by nuclear strikes, becoming irradiated wastelands before Nomad even had a chance to tear them apart. The radioactive fallout must have carried up into the atmosphere, mixing with the vapor clouds and ash from hundreds of simultaneous volcanic eruptions.

Temperatures had plummeted around the globe, although the fastest and most dramatic was in Europe. Clouds covered the skies everywhere they talked to people, and were getting thicker and darker as freshly opened volcanic rifts spewed ash across the continents.

"Temperature here is five Celsius," the radio crackled, coming to life again. "Thick cloud cover, almost as dark as night during the day. How many people are you, Station Saline…?"

When Giovanni told Jess he found someone in America, she got excited, but this quickly turned to numb terror. A contact in the Pennsylvania mountains had detailed what he'd pieced together staying in touch with other radio operators when Nomad hit.

It started with a huge quake in the Pacific Northwest, destroying Seattle and Portland, sending towering tsunamis up the coast. The San Andreas fault had followed, laying waste to Los Angeles and the San Francisco Bay area, and then the New Madrid fault had devastated Indiana, Missouri, Arkansas, Kentucky, Tennessee.

This was only the beginning.

Power grids and electronics were fried in the massive solar flares just as the Yellowstone supervolcano had erupted. It had covered the entire Midwest, from Iowa and Montana out to Illinois and down to Texas, in two to four feet of thick ash, smothering everything. The final blow was a wall of water a thousand feet high that swept in from the North Atlantic, destroying New York, Boston, Philadelphia, Miami. Washington was gone.

America didn't exist anymore.

It was almost as bad everywhere else. Coastal cities and any low-lying countries seemed totally wiped from existence, and the Baikal Rift, another supervolcano at the edge of Russia and China, had erupted as well, blanketing wide swaths of Asia under a thick layer of ash. No electrical infrastructure had survived, and all satellite communications had ceased.

"We are six survivors," Giovanni said into the radio. "In mountains outside the Chianti region."

Six people: her and Giovanni and Hector, Leone and his teenage workers, Lucca and Raffael. Their family was in the south, past Rome. Of course they were desperate to try and get to them, but there was nothing to do right now. The lucky six.

Or maybe not so lucky.

She watched the Earth in her next simulation, spinning out past the orbit of Mars, slowly freezing.

Crackle. Hiss. Giovanni twiddled the dials on the radio but shook his head and sighed. "That's it, can't raise them anymore. Maybe we'll get them later."

Jess nodded, hitting reset on her simulation, adjusting the trajectory of Nomad once more. She slid her foot closer to the wood stove. Outside it was freezing, but deep in these mountain caves it stayed warmer. Still chilly, but not freezing, and the wood stove brought a cozy feeling.

Giovanni had stocked the place well.

They had water, food rations, and survival gear of all sorts. A comfortable nest in the heart of a mountain. The only problem was toilets. Even after just two days, and a musky permeated the caves despite their best efforts to use buckets and clean up. Six human animals made a lot of mess.

How long could they survive? Giovanni had stocked up bunker-style supplies of food: rice, chick peas, cans, survival bars, and he kept one of the massive, fourteen-foot-high wine barrels intact and filled it with almost forty thousand liters of water. They could live down here for three years or more, if it came to that.

Three years.

The walls closed in, crushing the air from Jess's lungs. She gasped involuntarily, trying to push the space back open in her mind.

Spinning the dials, the radio hissed. Then a voice—loud, clear: *"God's will has been done, as in the time of Noah and Abraham, as it is now. The great Devil of America has been wiped from the Earth, the scourge cleansed. The Caliphate will rise from these ashes and repopulate the Earth—"*

Giovanni clicked to a different frequency. "Enough of that," he muttered.

Propaganda broadcasts from an Islamic fundamentalist sect. Not that the airwaves weren't full of religious zealots, crying and screaming, asking why God left them behind. But there were also the extremists, both Christian and Islamic. To them, this was a new beginning, ordained by God, and the shortwave broadcasts were full of these rants as well.

On her simulation, Jess lobbed another Nomad through the solar system, then paused it on yesterday's date. She zoomed in to Earth point-of-view, spinning to look at the northern celestial hemisphere.

"Hello, hello, this is Station Saline, does anyone copy?" Giovanni said into the radio microphone.

Jess's eyes went wide. She sat bolt upright. "Giovanni, you've got to look at this."

"What?" He clicked the microphone with his left hand again, his right hanging in the sling. "Hello, hello—"

"GIOVANNI!" Jess yelled, pointing at her screen. "Look!"

Frowning, he put down the microphone and, wincing in pain, adjusted himself to slide sideways toward her.

Jess turned the screen to him. "Look at that."

All Giovanni saw was a screen full of stars and the arcs of planets, the Sun glowing bright in the middle. "What am I looking at?"

"Venus, it's right in the middle of Leo." She pulled out the diagrams she scribbled the night before. "Look, it matches exactly. And Mars." She pointed at the left side of the screen. "It's almost perfect."

Giovanni shook his head. "I don't understand."

"This simulation I just ran. It puts Venus and Mars in exactly the right places, as viewed from Earth last night."

"And…?"

Jess stared at him incredulously. "Don't you see? Those two points constrain the solution. This is it." She pointed at the line showing Nomad's trajectory. "This is the path it took, the right mass, the direction. It matches observation."

"And what does that do for us?"

Her hands shaking, Jess lifted one finger over a button. "If I push that, the simulation will run forward in time, show us where the Earth is headed." The climate modeling window was open in the right corner of the screen, the average global temperature at 14.8C with the simulation paused. "We'll see if we've been ejected into deep space, or will drop back into the sun, or if Mars will crash into us—"

"So hit the button," Giovanni urged. She had his attention now.

Her finger hovered, shaking. Giovanni gently took her hand in his and pressed down.

The Earth and planets set back into motion, at one second per week of simulated time. Mercury was catapulted outward, Venus dragged away from the Sun violently as well, with Mars being pulled toward it. The Sun itself was dragged along behind Nomad, until Nomad sped away into space and released it. Saturn was dragged backward, into a retrograde orbit, circling behind the Sun. Just like Jess's other simulation.

And the Earth…

Nomad pulled the Sun, but it also pulled Earth.

While the other planets were tossed around randomly, the Earth continued to orbit the Sun. Jess watched the climate simulation: the temperature dropped from 14.8 Celsius, to 14.4 and then 13.8…but then it climbed, back to 14.2. The Earth completed a full circuit around the Sun. Slightly elliptic, but well within the green-highlighted habitable zone. Jess stopped the simulation.

"Hey, what are you doing?" Giovanni was entranced.

"Running it again." She hit the reset button, watched Nomad tear through the solar system, the planets scattering. But not the Earth. It lazily circled the sun as if nothing had happened.

How was it possible?

A mass forty times the Sun, passing half the distance from the Sun to the Earth, and the Earth remained in an almost stable orbit? Jess traced her finger along the path of Nomad, stared at the Sun and Earth, her face erupting in a smile. She laughed, clapping her hands together. "Yes, yes!" she cried.

Giovanni stared at her as if she were mad, but her smile was infectious. He grinned. "What does it mean?"

"It's all in the geometry of the encounter," Jess explained, pointing at the laptop. "The center of mass of Nomad passed almost in the solar plane, and passed the Earth and Sun at almost exactly the same distance, like a speeding bullet." She took a deep breath. "Have you ever seen that video, where one of the Apollo astronauts, standing on the moon, drops a hammer and a feather side by side?"

Giovanni shook his head.

"The hammer and feather fall at exactly the same speed, they hit the ground at the same time. Same experiment that Galileo did from the leaning tower, dropping a pebble and a cannon ball. They both hit the ground at almost the same time. It doesn't matter what the mass of an object is—a grain of sand or an elephant—if they experience the same gravitational field, they'll accelerate exactly the same.

"That's what happened." Jess pointed at the screen. "All the other planets, Nomad passed at different distances than it passed the Sun, they all experienced a different gravitational acceleration from

Nomad."

"But the Sun and Earth experienced the same gravitational acceleration?" Giovanni asked, still not quite getting it but smiling all the same.

"Exactly!" Jess clapped her hand again. "All the other planets accelerated at different rates, so they were pushed in random directions. But not the Earth. The Sun and Earth were both pulled the same amount in the same direction, even though the sun is three hundred thousand times heavier. Pure luck of geometry. I mean, there's a lot more going on, but that's the big brush strokes."

"So…we're saved…?" Giovanni said tentatively.

"Look at the simulated global temperatures. Hovering right between 14 and 15 degrees."

Giovanni pondered this for a second before responding, "Then why is it so cold outside? It should be twenty Celsius at this time of year. It's at freezing and dropping."

Jess ran the simulation again, marveling at it. "That's the ash and dust thrown up into the atmosphere. Hundreds of volcanic eruptions have covered the Earth in a thick blanket. We're not getting much heat from the Sun."

"And the Gulf Stream. I'd bet that's why Europe is so much colder than anywhere else. Nomad churned up the oceans. Those researchers we talked to in Greenland? Might have pulled off enough of the ice cap to disrupt the Gulf Stream."

Giovanni tapped his teeth together. "And so?"

"At this rate, Tuscany is going to freeze colder than Antarctica in a few weeks."

Giovanni rubbed his face, nodding. "Then we need to get south. Most of Africa survived intact. It's even raining in the Sahara." He tapped his pile of scribbled notes. "And we have a branch of our family that lives in Tunisia. They have a villa in the Atlas Mountains on the edge of the desert."

"Have you contacted them?" Jess asked breathlessly. Sheer hopelessness had suddenly transformed into a bright, burning possibility.

"Not yet." Giovanni shook his head. "And Hector's parents were in Africa. If they go anywhere, I would guess they would try to reach our family in Tunisia."

Jess glanced at Hector.

"So we go south?" Giovanni asked.

Jess bit her lip. "That's our only hope. The Earth isn't stressed anymore, so the eruptions should calm down. And it might take years, but when that ash settles, it will cover the ice in a black coating—"

"That will absorb the Sun's heat, start to warm back up." Giovanni continued the thought for her. He balled his fists. "We have food, water. We have weapons and gold, and we have the Humvee and Range Rover in the garage I think we can salvage, maybe even the old Jeep."

"We need to move." Adrenaline spiked into Jess's veins. A plan. *Hope.* "The longer we wait, the more the snow and ash will make roads impassable. But how do we go south? Around the Mediterranean?" If they went around, they'd have to go through the Middle East. The nuclear wasteland.

"No." Giovanni shook his head. "We don't go around."

"There aren't icebreakers in the Med, and I'd bet it's already freezing over. We can't take a boat."

Giovanni pursed his lips and smiled. "We walk."

"We what?"

"We walk. If it's getting as cold as you say, then the Mediterranean will freeze over. I've done treks of hundreds of miles over ice in the Arctic. It's a hundred miles from Sicily to Tunisia. I have sleds and equipment in storage above."

Jess stared at him. That just might work. She looked at her computer screen and frowned. The simulation had stopped, nineteen months from now. But she hadn't pushed a key to halt it. What was going on?

Giovanni was already on his feet, looking at the crates stacked against the walls. "We pack everything up, we could be on the road tomorrow—"

"We might have another problem," Jess said quietly, pointing at her laptop screen. Giovanni squinted and followed her finger.

"In nineteen months, the Earth might collide with Saturn."

44

Chianti, Italy

IN THE DIM eternal twilight of this new Earth, Jess stared across the twisted remains of the Castello Ruspoli, blanketed in ash and dirty snow, then out across the destroyed landscape below—the blackened valley of Saline, knots of frozen magma climbing the hills in the distance, steam and vapor crawling across them. Menacing clouds blanketed the sky, almost close enough to touch. Behind her, Leone and his work crew stacked crates and boxes inside the Land Rovers they'd salvaged from the underground garages.

"So, we go south?" Giovanni stepped beside her, putting his left arm around her shoulder. They both wore thick arctic coats and gloves, all of it four sizes too big for Jess, but they'd managed to scrounge cold weather gear for their whole crew.

"As soon as possible," Jess agreed. Every day they waited, the ash and snow would get deeper and the temperatures colder.

"Once we get out of the hills, it should warm up a few degrees, and more as we go south."

"Not too much, we need the Mediterranean to freeze over."

Giovanni nodded. "We'll find a way."

"Did you contact them yet?" Jess asked. She meant his relatives in Tunisia.

"Not yet." Giovanni took a deep breath. "And the simulations? Did you get anywhere?"

She shook her head. In nineteen months, the Earth would pass very close to Saturn, that much was sure. Whether it would hit the gas giant, that was still up in the air.

Up in the air.

Jess smiled grimly.

The accuracy of her scribbled notes, the diagrams of Venus and

Mars she saw in the sky against the stars, translated into a large margin of error in figuring out the *exact* path of Nomad, and thus the exact path of the Earth and Saturn.

She looked up.

There was no way anyone was getting another look at the stars from anywhere on the surface of Earth. That night she saw the stars, right after the event, was a freak occurrence. Now the entire planet was covered in a thick blanket, that much they'd managed to gather from talking to survivors around the world. It might be years before they saw clear sky again. For the next few years, Earth, and everyone on it, would be flying blind.

Any satellites in orbit were fried by the massive solar storms, so nobody was getting any more views from space. But NASA, or another agency, must have had a chance to fix Nomad's exact position, speed and mass just after it appeared from behind the sun, before everything was destroyed. Someone out there had to have that data.

From the information her father had managed to infer, Saturn and the Earth would come close, but it might be ten million miles, still a hair in cosmic terms, or hundreds of thousands of miles. But even a miss of hundreds of thousands of miles with Saturn was perilous. Its rings stretched out that distance, and its collection of dozens of moons reached out a million miles. To know exactly might mean the ability to get out of the way, to hide on the opposite side of Earth from whatever might be coming.

But there was a way to find out.

"We need to decode my father's data." Jess patted the backpack, the one she found sandwiched between the dead bodies of her mother and father. "And we need to find someone from NASA who recorded the event."

Now she understood why her father had gone outside. Why he had risked it.

She'd read his notes. In those old tape spools and floppy disks were the exact coordinates of Nomad from thirty years ago. It would provide the long axis for Nomad's trajectory and provide the last few hundredths of a degree of accuracy—enough to see what asteroids could come close, what might hit the Earth.

They had detailed simulation data on her father's laptop. The first step would be to decode the disks and tapes, and to get even better resolution, to find someone who had data on Nomad from just before the event.

But how to do that, in this wrecked world?

Giving Giovanni a kiss on his cheek, she stepped through the boulders to the remains of the front walls. She stopped, clicked on a floodlight. It illuminated a placard atop a pile of rubble, a headstone: "Here lies Benjamin Rollins and Celeste Tosetti, husband and wife, loving parents."

It was all she could think of.

All that needed to be said.

And at least they came together, in the end, and now rested together. Forever.

Jess glanced over her shoulder, at Lucca and Raffael swinging Hector between them, running beside Giovanni. She'd always scoffed at the idea of having a family, but now she had one to protect.

And she would, to her last breath.

Looking south, Jess squinted into the darkness, ash and snow falling gently over the tortured earth. Her father's last words to her echoed in her mind—*survive, no matter what.*

It was time to go.

Thanks for reading!

In the next section is the first chapter of

SANCTUARY

Book Two of The New Earth Series

Now available on Amazon.

In the section following, I have a discussion on current research into *Nomad*-like events, and instructions on finding a video you can watch of me running a 3D physics simulation of the *Nomad* encounter. You can even run the *Nomad* simulation yourself.

AND PLEASE…

If you'd like more quality fiction at this low price, I'd really appreciate it if you could leave a review on Amazon. For self-published authors, the number of reviews a book accumulates on a daily basis has a direct impact—and I read each and every one.

AND FINALLY…

To stay in touch and get free advance reading copies of my books, come see me at

www.MatthewMather.com

SANCTUARY

Book Two of The New Earth Series

1

Bandita, Italy

A BULLET RICOCHETED off the open truck door.

"Get out!" Jessica Rollins screamed at Lucca and Raffael.

The faces of the teenaged brothers shone white in the dim light, their eyes wide. A second bullet punched a frosted hole through the windshield and lodged itself in the metal screen behind the seats. Jess crouched lower and stole a glance around the door. "*Andare!*" she yelled.

That did the trick. Keeping low, Raffa slithered over the driver seat, opened the opposite door of the Humvee and disappeared. Lucca climbed over Jess and gracelessly tumbled into the dirt and snow at her feet. Jess pointed at her own eyes, then at a pile of twisted metal and bricks ten feet away. *One, two*, she mouthed silently, and on *three* she swung around the truck's door and squeezed the trigger on her AK-47. *Pop. Pop.* Two controlled rounds. She felt Lucca move behind her and fired again, then rolled through the gray snow to scramble next to him. Raffa slithered on his stomach to join them.

A bullet whined overhead.

She had sensed something was wrong the moment they drove up to the bottleneck in the road. A jumble of car parts blocking the street seemed a little too neatly placed. She'd stopped short of the road's choke point, but there had been no easy way to back out.

"Giovanni," Jess whispered into her walkie-talkie, in as low a voice as she could manage. She sucked air in between her teeth and exhaled heavily, trying to ease the flood of adrenaline. Her hands shook. "Do you have Hector?"

The walkie-talkie crackled softly. "In the brick schoolhouse half a block behind you."

Jess turned the volume down. She peered behind her through the murk and saw an arm waving, a hundred feet back on the opposite side of the street, behind the Range Rover. *Schoolhouse.* Indistinguishable from other piles of snowdrift-covered rubble. "And

Leone?"

"He's with me. What can you see?"

What can I see? Jess almost laughed. In the dying light, dirty snowflakes fell through an indistinct soup. Daytime was an oozing sludge-brown twilight that clawed its way from the suffocating black of nights. The feeble rays of flashlights and headlamps drowned in the murky aerosolized soup they breathed. It stank of rotten eggs, the sulfurous-brimstone stench burrowing its way into the brain and filling their lungs with black phlegm, smothering everything in a pasty layer that scratched the eyeballs and coated tongues.

Removing her goggles, Jess rubbed her eyes and strained to see through the semidarkness. The temperature had dropped ten degrees in the past two hours. Another frigid night. The Humvee's headlights barely pierced the muck.

There. A head peered around the corner of what looked like the entrance to an open garage. No more than a hundred yards away. A second shape appeared behind the first, the body and head twitching, more like a cornered animal than predator. Jess pushed the *talk* button. "I see two, probably men. Do you see anything?"

"Nothing."

Jess brushed snow from her face and pulled her gloves back on. Three-story buildings lined the street, some with windows still strangely intact. It reminded her of bombed-out villages she'd seen on her tour of duty in Afghanistan; almost everything destroyed, buildings reduced to twisted piles of brick and steel. Yet every now and then a reminder of civilization endured, like the marble statue that stood untouched and defiant at this town's entrance as they drove in.

The two figures ran, doubled-over, behind the jumble of car parts blocking the middle. Had they seen Giovanni exit the rear car and run into the school? She had to act fast. This had been planned as an ambush, but the playing field was level now. Whoever had lain in wait for them had lost their advantage.

"Leave Leone with the shotgun to protect Hector," she instructed Giovanni over the walkie-talkie. "Then take Lucca and Raffa down the side street, south. Sending them to you now." She looked at Lucca, his rifle gripped in white-knuckled fists, and flicked her chin in Giovanni's direction. The teenager crouched and took off at a half-run with his brother trailing. "I'm going up to the roof. When we get into position, toss two grenades into the open garage door of the red building. That'll force them out. Open fire from one side; I'll pick them off from the other." Flank-and-flush.

Static hissed over the walkie-talkie. "Maybe we just turn the trucks?"

Two heads bobbed out from behind the burnt-out car in front of her, and one of the men jumped into the open to duck behind a pile of rubble twenty feet closer to Jess. Her hands tightened on the AK-47. "We need to scare them off."

Hissing silence. "Okay. I have the boys."

"Tell me when you get there."

"You're *sure* you want to do this?"

She closed her eyes and tried to take a deep lungful of air, but a wet cough erupted mid-breath. She pushed the *talk* button. "We have to."

A pause. "We're on our way."

Jess tried to steady her shaking hands by clenching them into fists. Her army consisted of two teenagers, the elderly groundskeeper Leone and the Baron Giovanni Ruspoli, who'd probably never shot at anything more threatening than a clay pigeon before. It was on her to keep them safe.

A third head appeared carelessly out from the doorway ahead. She hoped a few grenades and some well-placed sniper fire would be enough to scare them off, but people were desperate. Beyond desperate.

Jess slung her assault rifle over her back and tightened the strap snug. She shuffled behind the Humvee on her knees and kept going until she reached the cover of a fallen wall on the other side of the street. She stopped. Listened. Peered into the gloom. Sensing nothing, she got to her feet and jogged to the drainpipe going up the side of the three-story building. She removed her gloves, stuffing them into the pockets of her parka, then blew on her hands and gripped the frozen pipe to begin climbing. She pulled herself up onto the railing of the first floor balcony and slid over into a pile of snow, but landed awkwardly and her prosthetic leg wrenched loose.

She cursed and pulled it back into place, feeling it rub into the raw stump just below her left knee. Getting to her feet, she balanced against the wall and propped herself against the railing. She shimmied her way onto the second floor balcony and stopped there, straddling the railing so she could pull her gloves back on to warm her already frozen hands. Leaning out, she saw one of the scavengers emerge from the pile of car wreckage to take a potshot at their Humvee.

"In position," Giovanni's voice whispered over the walkie-talkie.

Jumping up to grab another drainpipe, Jess pulled herself up to the edge of the roof. She held herself there as she scanned the debris for signs of movement. Nothing. She hauled herself up and twisted through more ash-ridden snow onto her back.

She thumbed the *talk* button and whispered: "One second."

Rolling onto her knees, she pulled her rifle off her back and popped the cover of its telescopic sight. She hunkered low and moved to the edge of the rooftop, then dropped flat onto her stomach. The lead scavenger had almost reached the Humvee. "Okay, in position. Drop those grenades in."

She slowed her breathing, steadying herself as she zeroed the crosshairs in on her target. The man turned, almost to face her, and her breath caught. He was no more than a teenager. Just a boy.

From the corner of her eye, she saw the shadows of Giovanni and Raffa dart out from behind the building across the street. With the crosshairs on the boy's chest, Jess's felt the pressure of the trigger beneath her finger, but released. How many had she killed already? She shifted the sight down, leveling the crosshairs on the fleshy part of the boy's leg, and pulled the trigger as a blinding flash burst in the street below. The first grenade's heaving concussion was followed by another a second later.

Windows blinked and shattered.

Screams filled the air.

A man ran out of the building beneath her, both hands to his belly. Another sprinted out, a gun clutched in shaking hands that he pointed at Giovanni. Jess swung her rifle left, this time aiming mid-torso, and fired. A red mist puffed from the man's chest and he fell. She glanced to her right. The boy held his leg, hopping back toward the wall.

More screaming.

An engine roared, and a second later a vehicle skidded out of the garage entrance.

Jess squinted hard, trying to understand what she was seeing. The body of an old Volkswagen Beetle, but with the wheel wells torn away. Large, circular rollers with jagged spikes had been welded onto the back axle, replacing the tires. Rudimentary skis had been placed where the front wheels should have been.

Slipping to a stop, the boy staggered to get in the passenger door, while two more of the scavengers perched in the open front-trunk. They fired random shots in Giovanni's direction. Jess lifted her rifle, locked a round into the chamber, aimed and fired. Her bullet punched through the roof. The two men ducked and the strange vehicle accelerated, kicking up a spray of dirty snow. It veered up the street and disappeared into the gloom.

It had been enough, but it could so easily have been worse. The man she had shot lay motionless. A seeping pool of black spread around him in the light of the Humvee's headlamps.

"Help."

Was that the man in the snow? She held her breath. Listened.

"Help me."

Was Giovanni hurt? In the sudden silence, she strained to hear.

"Please, help me."

No. It was coming from *inside* the building. Below her. Not Italian either; a distinctly American accent.

Giovanni, accompanied by Raffa and Lucca, appeared from the darkness on the other side of the street. Jess heaved a shaky sigh of relief and gave them a quick wave. Stepping through the foot of snow and ash covering the roof, she found the stairway down. The door was locked. She chambered a round and fired into the lock. The door kicked open. Clicking on her headlamp, she inched her way down to the first landing, scanning the frozen gloom, leading with the rifle.

"Please, help me," came the muffled call again.

Her finger dropped onto the trigger.

She swept each room with the AK-47, barrel just under her line of vision. Stomach tight, constantly searching behind and up. Clearing doorframes first, then into each room. Eyes wide, sucking in every detail. Sweat gathering despite the cold. Something kicked in her gut. Even scavengers should have been more prepared, put up more of a fight. Had it been too easy?

She shoved the thought aside and focused. Clearing the last set of stairs, she entered the lobby and opened the door to the garage. In the light of their headlamps, Giovanni, Raffa and Lucca stood encircling three people, all of them tied by hands and feet to a radiator. Rough sack bags covered their heads.

"Please, whoever you are, please let me go," one of them moaned. A man whose voice she recognized.

She marched to the pleading man, pulled the bag off his head, and stared in open-mouthed disbelief. "Roger?"

"Jessica?" The man's eyes bulged. "Thank God."

Her knife already out, she knelt and brought the blade to his face. Her hand trembled.

"Jess…" Giovanni took a step forward.

In one quick motion, Jess grabbed Roger's arms and wrenched them to the side. She cut the cords binding him, then the ropes around his feet.

Roger pulled his arms free and rubbed his wrists. He winced and extended a hand to be helped up. Instead she seized him by the throat, pulled him to his feet and pushed him back against the wall, the knife still in her hand. "What the hell happened?"

"Jesus Christ, what are you—"

"My father?"

"I don't know," Roger gurgled. "Where is he?"

"He's dead. They're both dead."

Giovanni put an arm on her shoulder and tried to ease her back with gentle pressure. She released her grip on the man's neck.

Roger wheezed and doubled over.

"How did you get here?"

"I was knocked unconscious when I went out with your father."

Wind whistled outside.

"Jessica?" A woman's voice echoed from the darkness.

Giovanni and Lucca raised their rifles. Dropping her hands, Jess turned. Someone limped across the dirt-streaked marble floor, but even in the dim light she recognized the shining blue eyes.

"Massarra?"

Hope you enjoyed the first chapter of SANCTUARY.
Please visit Amazon to get the full copy and continue the adventure!

In the next section I discuss the science and research work behind *Nomad*, and recent findings of other star systems that have crossed into our solar system. In the final section are instructions for watching the video of me running the 3D simulation of the *Nomad* encounter, with instructions on how you can even do it yourself.

OTHER BOOKS BY MATTHEW MATHER

CyberStorm

Award-winning CyberStorm depicts, in realistic and sometimes terrifying detail, what a full scale cyberattack against present-day New York City might look like from the perspective of one family trying to survive it. Search for CyberStorm on Amazon.

Polar Vortex

A routine commercial flight disappears over the North Pole. Vanished into thin air. No distress calls. No wreckage. Weeks later, found on the ice, a chance discovery—the journal from passenger Mitch Matthews reveals the incredible truth...
Search for *Polar Vortex* on Amazon.

Darknet

A prophetic and frighteningly realistic novel set in present-day New York, Darknet is the story of one man's odyssey to overcome a global menace pushing the world toward oblivion, and his incredible gamble to risk everything to save his family. Search for Darknet on Amazon.

Atopia Chronicles (Series)

In the near future, to escape the crush and clutter of a packed and polluted Earth, the world's elite flock to Atopia, an enormous corporate-owned artificial island in the Pacific Ocean. It is there that Dr. Patricia Killiam rushes to perfect the ultimate in virtual reality: a program to save the ravaged Earth from mankind's insatiable appetite for natural resources. Search for Atopia on Amazon.

Discussion of Nomad in the Real World

I've always been fascinated by black holes. I think it began when I was ten years old and watched the eponymous Disney film *The Black Hole*. The movie fueled my curiosity, and as a teenager I tore through black hole-related science fiction, from *The Forever War* by Joe Haldeman, to *Hyperion* by Dan Simmons, to *Earth* by David Brin.

The topic was as fascinating to me as it was to many others, spurring an abundance of books and short stories. Surprise, surprise, then, when I did some research and discovered that not a single book or film had ever covered the topic of the Earth encountering a medium-sized black hole. So, I decided to write *Nomad*, to fill that gap, but with a determined focus on making it scientifically accurate.

Before writing *Nomad*, I spent months talking to astronomers and astrophysicists to build up the science behind the encounter I envisioned. At first, the physicists said the event would totally destroy the Earth, but slowly, I managed to piece together a physics-based scenario where it was possible life could survive on the surface—otherwise it wouldn't make for much of a story!

It might seem that the events unfolded extremely quickly when *Nomad* made its final approach, but I carefully modeled the tidal forces affecting the Earth accurately in time and magnitude. Tidal forces are inverse cubically proportional to distance, which is why the sun only exerts half of the tidal force on the Earth that the moon does, even though the sun is almost thirty million times its mass (and four hundred times further away—so 400 x 400 x 400 equals sixty four million, and thirty million divided by sixty-four million gives us the one-half tidal force of the sun versus the moon).

In the end, I managed to convince a team of post-graduate researchers build a full three-dimensional gravity simulation of the entire solar system to lob my *Nomad* black holes through the middle of. All of the elements of the story—all the forces involved and the paths of the planets afterward—are based on real-world physics. If you want to see me run this simulation, just check it out on YouTube here (or search for "YouTube Mather Nomad Simulation"): https://www.youtube.com/watch?v=zXDqlAzAMFs.

There have been many books and movies illustrating the idea that the Earth is part of the ecosystem of asteroids and comets, planets and even our Sun, and that from time to time, an object may hit the Earth, or the Sun may flare, triggering catastrophic events. But what hasn't been explored as much is the effect of an ecosystem on a much larger scale—the effect exerted on the Earth by objects in our interstellar and even intergalactic neighborhood.

It might sound far-fetched, but it isn't.

In fact, much of the events we'd attributed previously to chance, like the asteroid impact that wiped out the dinosaurs, might not be random at all, but the direct result of the interstellar interactions the Earth has with passing stars (still random, but on a much larger scale). In school, we're taught that the closest star, apart from the Sun, is Proxima Centuri, at just over four light years of distance. It may seem like the interstellar neighborhood is static.

But it's not.

In February of 2015, researchers were dumbfounded to discover that just 70,000 years ago, near enough in time that our direct ancestors would have seen it, Scholz's star, a red dwarf, passed about a half light year from us. This led to a flurry of data crunching, leading scientists to discover that, for instance, four million years ago, a giant star, more than twice the mass of the sun, passed less than a third of a light year from us, and in just over a million years from now, another star will pass at just over a hundredth (yes, a *hundredth*) of a light year from our sun, grazing the solar system itself and possibly affecting the orbits of the planets.

Now scientists are saying that Sedna, the 10th planetoid of the Sun, the one after Pluto, isn't even an original planet of our Sun. It was captured from a passing star over a billion years ago, when our solar system collided with an alien star's planetary system. Hundreds of objects in the Kuiper Belt, the collection of planetoids past Uranus, are believed to have been captured from passing stars. So we are continually mixing together with others stars and interstellar objects, and not on a time scale of billions of years, but on a regular basis every few million years—some scientists now even think that alien stars transit our solar system's Oort cloud as often as every few hundred thousand years (http://www.bbc.com/news/science-environment-31519875)

A change in Earth's orbit might have triggered one of the biggest global warming events in its history (http://www.dailymail.co.uk/sciencetech/article-2125533/Global-warming-55m-years-ago-triggered-changes-Earths-orbit.html).

And scientists now think that a massive ice age, started 35 million years ago, might have been also been caused by another shift in Earth's orbit, and that this same event disturbed the asteroid belt enough to precipitate several large asteroid impacts, one of which formed the Chesapeake Bay. Some now believe these sorts of events might have been caused by the gravitational effect of a passing star.

Asteroids and comets transiting the inner solar system will of course hit the Earth from time to time, but there is an added element of the influence of passing stars that churn these objects into new and dangerous orbits, and even pulling the Earth itself into a slightly different orbit around the Sun. Which leads to speculation about the root cause of some large comet/asteroid impacts, such as the one that wiped out the dinosaurs. The point is that there are a lot of things in our universe, happening right around us, that we have no idea about.

And we haven't even talked about the 95% of "stuff" floating around us, dark matter, that we can't see or detect, other than knowing it's there from its gravitational signature. With upgraded sensors and increased power in the Large Hadron Collider (LHC) in 2015, the world's most powerful particle accelerator, many scientists had hoped to see evidence of dark matter.

But they've found nothing. Despite all of our technology and hundreds of years of peering into the cosmos, we still have no idea what makes up the vast majority of our universe.

It was Stephen Hawking who first proposed that the missing dark matter may be in the form of invisible "primordial" black holes that were formed when our universe itself was created in the Big Bang (http://www.technologyreview.com/view/418126/why-black-holes-may-constitute-all-dark-matter/).

Primordial black holes might have formed when Big Bang created a super-dense soup of particles, with densities high enough to spontaneously form black holes. Recent research results using the Kepler satellite have restricted the size range of possible "black hole dark matter" candidates, but it is still a viable theory.

Some theorists think it's possible that these intermediate-sized primordial black holes coalesced into the super-giant black holes that form the cores of galaxies, with the left over matter of the universe cooling around these to form stars. If so, some of these primordial black holes might still be wandering the cosmos, ejected at high speeds from galactic cores during the process of merger by something called *gravitational recoil.*

Perhaps farfetched, but perhaps not—truth is often stranger than fiction—and this is the story of *Nomad.*

I hope you enjoyed it, and that you continue the adventure in *Sanctuary,* book two of the *Nomad* trilogy.

All my best, and thanks again for reading!

July 27th, 2015

ps. Feel free to email me with questions at author.matthew.mather@gmail.com

Nomad Video and Simulation

To see me running a 3D physics simulation of the Nomad encounter, just search for "Mather Nomad Simulation" on YouTube or click here: https://www.youtube.com/watch?v=zXDqlAzAMFs

If you want to run your own physics simulation of Nomad, that's easy too! The folks at Universe Sandbox have amazingly provided the tools to the general public. Just search for "Universe Sandbox" online and follow the instructions for loading their software (it is a full, 3D physics-based model of the solar system). The cost is $25. Once you have it loaded, click the top left of the screen to access the menu, then click "Open Existing Simulation, " select "Fiction," and click the "Nomad" tab to start the simulation. Or, just search for the "How to Run Nomad Simulation" video on my YouTube channel.

SPECIAL THANKS

I'd like to make a special thank you to Allan Tierney, Theresa Munanga and Pamela Deering who did whole edits of the book as beta readers.

AND THANK YOU to all my beta readers (sorry I don't have surnames for all of you) Cliff Shaffer, Ken Zufall, Tomas Classon, Chrissie Pintar, Katrina Archer, Erik Montcalm, Angela Cavanaugh, Amber Triplett, Wendy Matthews, Bryan Scullion, Philipp Francis, Sun Lee Curry, Monte Dunard, David Dai, Ernie Dempsey, Nick Burnette, James McCormick, Fern Burgett, and so many more!

And of course, I'd like to thank my mother and father, Julie and David Mather, and last but most definitely not least, Julie Ruthven, for putting up with all the late nights and missed walks with the dogs.

-- Matthew Mather

About Matthew Mather

Translated into over twenty languages, with 20th Century Fox now developing his second novel, CyberStorm, for a major film release, Matthew Mather is a worldwide name in science fiction. He began his career at the McGill Center for Intelligent Machines before starting high-tech ventures in everything from computational nanotechnology to electronic health records, weather prediction systems to genomics, and even designed an award-winning brain training video game. He now works as a full-time author of speculative fiction.

AUTHOR CONTACT
Matthew Mather:
author.matthew.mather@gmail.com

Made in the USA
Coppell, TX
23 May 2021

WOMEN IN TUNE

Other books by the author:

My Glimpse of Eternity

Prayers That Are Answered

Super Natural Living

Angels Watching Over Me

Heaven, A Bright And Glorious Place
Help, I'm A Pastor's Wife !
Making Your Husband Feel Loved
Touching The Unseen World
Morning Jam Sessions (daily devotional)